BARBARA ERSKINE

ENCOUNTERS

HarperCollinsPublishers

HarperCollins*Publishers*
77–85 Fulham Palace Road,
Hammersmith, London W6 8JB

This paperback edition 1995
3 5 7 9 8 6

Previously published in paperback by Fontana 1991

First published in Great Britain by
Michael Joseph Ltd 1990

This collection © Barbara Erskine 1990
and as follows:

'Cabbage a la Carte' (*Woman's Weekly*) 1976; 'Feline Express' (*New Love* as 'Cupid Was
A Kitten') 1978; 'The Consolation Prize' (*Woman's World* as 'A Loving Invitation') 1984;
'There was a time when I was almost happy...' (*Woman's World*) 1979; 'Summer
Treachery' (*Rio*) 1981; 'Trade Reunions' (*Best*) 1988; 'The Bath: A Summer Ghost Story'
(*Living*) 1987; 'The Green Leaves of Summer' (*Woman's Own Summer Stories*) 1979;
'Encounters' (*Woman's World*) 1977; 'The Touch of Gold' (*The Writer*) 1976; 'The
Helpless Heart' (*Woman's World* as 'Give Me Back My Dreams') 1978; 'The Indian
Summer of Mary McQueen' (*Secrets*) 1980; 'The Magic of Make Believe' (*Woman's
World*) 1984; 'A Summer Full of Poppies' (*Secret Story*, Robinson) 1989; 'A Face in the
Crowd' (*Woman's World* as 'Forsaking All Others') 1983; 'Flowers Shouldn't Make You
Cry' (*Woman's World*) 1979; 'Someone to Dream About' (*Woman's World*) 1986;
'Milestones' (*New Idea*) 1980; 'Marcus Nicholls' (*Red Star Weekly* as 'Windows on the
Past') 1980; 'A Quest For Identity' (*Woman's World*) 1977; 'The Heart Will Understand'
(*Woman's World*) 1980; 'A Stranger With No Name' (*Woman's World*) 1980; 'Just An
Old-Fashioned Girl' (*Woman's World* as 'Love Never Changes') 1981; 'All This Childish
Nonsense' (*Woman's World* as 'A Promise is Forever') 1977; 'A Love Story' (*My Story*)
1976; 'A Promise of Love' (*Woman's World* as 'Don't Tread On My Dreams') 1978.

ISBN 0 00 647068 8

Phototypeset by Input Typesetting Ltd, London
Printed and bound by Caledonian International Book Manufacturer, Glasgow

Contents

Preface

I have always loved reading short stories and, like many authors, tested my literary wings experimenting with them. At first glance anyway, the short story seems an easy route for the beginner, largely because it is, axiomatically, short; one is not aiming for some distant horizon two or three hundred thousand words away. Short stories are self contained, feisty, fun; they are tricky, challenging – compact crystallizations, each of which must have as much substance in its own way as its big brother, the novel.

Having started to write them, hooked by the lure of so many plots, so many characters, so many scenes and the technical challenge of construction, I have found that I cannot resist the form, and this selection is taken from the hundreds I have written over the past fifteen years.

I did not plan to be a short story writer. I wanted to be a novelist – specifically a historical novelist – and it was years ago while a student at university in Scotland that I decided to write my first novel, the story of Robert the Bruce and the woman who set the crown of Scotland on his head. Consumed with excitement as I worked on the outline, spending much more time on it than I did on my studies, I visited the sites of the story and, absorbing the atmosphere, walked alone along mist-shrouded rivers and around the remains of countless castles. I wrote several thousand words, then I stopped. I realized I couldn't go on. I hadn't the experience of writing or of life to cope with the huge task I had set myself. Quietly and sadly I put my manuscript away. I knew I would write it one day – but not yet. (That book eventually became *Kingdom of Shadows* and, secretly, I incorporated those few thousand words unchanged into it – a debt to that student writer who had felt Robert and Isobel's suffering but had not then been able to put it down on paper.)

My confidence was shaken. I had wanted to be a writer since I was three years old and yet I had fallen at the first major fence. It was a case of wanting to run before I could walk. Obviously I had an apprenticeship to serve and so came the idea of trying to write short stories. I studied the markets and began to write articles and stories to fit those markets. Miraculously the first story I wrote was accepted and published by the *London Evening News*. I was much encouraged!

It was when we went to live in the Welsh Borders that again the longing to write historical fiction grew too strong to resist and I recognized consciously for the first time that I was one of those writers for whom the spirit of place is all important. The land around me, the hills, the forests, the seas, evoke echoes I cannot ignore. I have to write about them. I have to try and make my readers see and hear and even smell the landscape and its history as I see and hear and feel it.

Once more I began to plan a novel and this time I felt I had the experience and the confidence to do it. Not the story of Robert and Isobel – I still wasn't ready for that – but a novel of history and passion and mystery which was born of the mysterious, ancient landscape around me.

While I read and researched and visited the sites which were to become the background for *Lady of Hay* I went on writing short stories and, eventually, half a dozen short historical romances as well, perhaps to complete my apprenticeship before at last I could start writing the big novel.

But by now I enjoyed writing short stories too much to stop. Heavily involved in a book full of passion and hatred and fear it is nice to come up for air from time to time to write a humorous story, or an unashamedly sentimental one; a modern thriller or a plain old-fashioned love story, and I have chosen some of each of these for this collection. There are also, of course, ghost stories and a couple of stories where the past and the present slide together and the curtain which separates us from the past is temporarily drawn aside. Most of the stories are about places as much as about the people who find themselves within them, and most of them are, in one way or another, about encounters. I hope you enjoy them.

Barbara Erskine
Great Tey, 1989

A Step Out of Time

The house at the end of the long, winding drive was elegant Georgian. The windows, all perfectly proportioned, looked out across sweeping lawns – not quite as smooth as they might have been, but nevertheless beautiful – towards the Black Mountains, brooding in the heat haze of the August afternoon.

Looking through the windscreen Victoria tried to suppress the quick catch of excitement which she felt in her throat. They had already seen so many houses which looked idyllic. Before there had always been a snag. This house, she felt suddenly, would be right; it was as if, in some secret part of herself, she knew it already. She glanced at Robert and saw that he felt it too: the hope, the anticipation, the agitation. When they found the right house it was going to be very special. Their home. The first since he had come out of the army. The place where they could start their new life.

The young man from the house agent was waiting for them, standing beneath the porticoed entrance proprietorially jangling the keys as they drew to a halt. Robert glanced at Victoria and winked as he set about climbing stiffly out of the car. She fumbled with the door handle, not wanting to watch, knowing better than to help. Each time it was easier. Each time it hurt him less. Each time the excitement that this might be The House helped.

They shook hands and the agent, introducing himself as William Turner, inserted the key in the lock and pushed open the heavy door. Beyond it a cavernous hall opened up, elegantly if sparsely furnished, with at the far end of it a graceful staircase winding up to a galleried landing. There was a faint smell of dogs.

'Lady Penelope is away this weekend.' William's voice was reverently hushed. 'So we can go all over the house as we like.'

They followed him soberly from drawing room to dining room to sitting room to morning room – a room for every hour of the day – and on through to the large north-facing kitchen.

'Not modernized, I'm afraid.' William looked round in barely disguised disgust at the unmatched cupboards, the painted deal table and the small electric cooker. The water, Victoria noted with amusement, ran from an old wall-mounted water heater into a deep stone sink.

William was watching her. He gave a broad smile. 'Grim, isn't it?'

'It is rather.' Victoria liked the young man. He had not mentioned exotic fitted kitchens; he did not pretend it had been left like this for the convenience of the buyer. Besides, after the initial shock, she loved it. The kitchen had a quaint, old-fashioned charm.

'What's through there?' Robert nodded towards one of the internal doors. Beneath the grubby roller towel he had seen a key and three bolts. Three bolts seemed excessive for a door into a larder.

'Ah.' William gave his most charming professional smile, followed by a deprecatory shrug of the shoulders. 'Well, every house has a few drawbacks.'

'Oh?' Robert glanced at Victoria. His heart, like hers, had sunk. He flipped through the glossy brochure in his hand. 'No mention of any drawbacks here.'

2

'Perhaps you'd like to see the upstairs first? The principal bedrooms have glorious views across into Wales,' William said hopefully. He had seen how they felt about the house; he had seen her growing secretly more and more excited. He should have told them from the first. He glanced at them sympathetically. Robert Holland was tall, distinguished, in his late forties perhaps, his upright military bearing marred by an awkward limp. His wife was much younger, attractive, dark haired; slightly reserved, he guessed. The kind he thought of as deep and therefore probably interesting. He prided himself on his character analyses of potential clients. These people were understated, but that did not mean they weren't wealthy. He had learned that one very early in his career. Money, particularly old money, did not always show. It was new money that liked to flaunt it. They could afford the house; he knew already that they would not buy it.

'I think we should see the drawbacks first, don't you?' Victoria put in firmly.

'You're sure?' His humorous smile was putting them all on the same side – allies against whatever eccentricity was the other side of the door. It also helped to hide his fear.

The key was stiff and the bolts unyielding. He had opened the door some half a dozen times now, but it never grew any easier and he could never overcome his reluctance to go through it. When at last he managed to push it open they peered into a long dark passage. 'This,' he said dramatically, 'is the west wing. Lady Penelope seals it off more or less completely. I think she prefers to forget it's there. To be honest, the best plan would be to demolish it.'

They could all feel the cold striking up from the dirty stone floor. The rest of the house was hot and airless in the humid summer heat but here it was abnormally cold.

Victoria felt her mouth go dry. Suddenly her optimism

3

and her excitement had gone. 'I don't suppose there is any reason to see it if it's that bad . . .' she said uncertainly. A tangible feeling of dread seemed to surround her, pressing in on her from the cold walls.

'Nonsense.' Robert stepped into the passage. 'What's wrong with it? Dry rot? Again?' The again was for William's benefit. It might help to knock a thousand or so off the asking price.

'No, not dry rot.' William glanced at Victoria. He gave a tight protective smile as he saw that she had grown pale. About half of his clients seemed to feel it. The other half walked through without any comment, but even they hurried. He motioned her through ahead of him and reluctantly followed her.

With a quick, doubtful look at him she stepped into the passage after Robert. He had pushed open the first door on the left. Sunlight flooded across the empty room and into the corridor showing up the dust and scattered newspapers on the floor. 'It's a good sized room.' Robert walked across to the window, his shoes sounding strangely loud on the bare boards. He peered out. 'That must have been a formal garden once.'

'It still could be.' William was standing near the door. 'It only needs tidying up. There are seven acres here. The grounds are one of the best features of the house.'

'Why is there no mention of this room here?' Robert had turned back to his brochure. The inconsistency irritated him. He wanted room dimensions and particulars at his finger tips.

'There is.' Almost reluctantly William went over to him. He riffled through the pages and stabbed at one with an index finger. 'There. "Behind the kitchen quarters there is an unconverted wing with the potential for fourteen extra rooms".'

4

'Fourteen!' Victoria exclaimed in dismay. 'But that would make the house enormous. Much too big.'

'It does seem a lot, doesn't it?' Once more the disarming charm. 'The wing was added about a hundred years ago. As I said, I don't believe anyone ever uses it.' He glanced over his shoulder uncomfortably. The feeling was worse today; it was beating against his head like the threat of a migraine – fear and pain and nausea, gripping him out of nowhere. He swallowed hard, trying to stop himself retching. 'Look, Mr and Mrs Holland, would you mind if I left you to wander round for a few minutes. I have to make a phone call from the car . . .' He didn't wait for their reply. Already he was edging out of the room and back along the passage towards the kitchen.

Robert ignored him, but Victoria watched him disappear, fighting the urge to follow him. 'He doesn't like it through here, does he?' she said softly.

'It does have a bit of an atmosphere.' Robert squared his shoulders. 'You want to see it, though, don't you? I suggest we hurry round this bit, see the upstairs, then we can drive off somewhere and have tea. I'm frozen.'

'So am I.' Victoria shivered. 'And it's about 80° out there.'

'It must be damp in this bit of the house.' Robert walked back into the passage and peered through the next doorway. 'Another good sized room. And another. Good God, look!'

Victoria stared over his shoulder nervously. In the corner of the room was an enormous heap of old tin hats. Opposite them, near the window, a dozen long poles were stacked in the corner.

'Those hats must have been here since the war.' Robert picked one up.

'Don't touch them!' Victoria was suddenly frightened. 'Please don't touch them. Let's go. I don't like it here

5

either.' She could feel the unhappiness, the desperation. It seemed to pervade the room.

'Don't be silly. We must see it all now we're here. Look, the stairs are along here.'

'No, Robert. Please.' She felt panic clutching at her throat. 'Don't go upstairs. Don't . . .'

'Victoria!' He stared at her in astonishment. 'OK. You go back. Go and look at the garden with young Mr Turner. I'll have a quick shufty up here and then I'll come and find you, OK?'

'Robert . . .' She raised her hand as if to stop him but already he had set off up the steep stairs, awkwardly pulling himself up by the handrail.

She took a deep breath. At the foot of the stairs a door led out onto the old terrace. She rattled the handle, not expecting it to open, but to her surprise it turned easily. It had not been locked.

The heat in the garden hit her like a physical blow. After the unnatural cold in the house it was wonderful. She threw her head back and raised her arms towards the sun with relief, then abruptly she dropped them to her sides. There was a young man standing on the terrace. Dressed in shabby corduroy trousers and an open-necked shirt, he had his arm in a sling. He turned and grinned at her.

'Hello.'

Victoria smiled back. 'I'm sorry. I didn't know there was anyone else here.' She was embarrassed, and at the same time relieved to see him. After the silence and the oppressive atmosphere of the west wing it was wonderful to see another human being. 'Are you looking round too?' she asked. She paused and found herself staring at him again. She knew him. Confused, she fumbled for a name, but none came. She couldn't place him.

'Looking round?' He looked puzzled. 'No. I live here. For the moment.'

'Oh, I'm sorry.' She was still desperately trying to think where she had met him before. 'We understood the place was empty.'

'Empty!' He seemed to find the word ironic. 'Well, I suppose it is in a way. I hate it in there. It's so cold, did you notice? However hot it is out here. As cold as the tomb.' He shuddered. 'Why were you staring at me?'

She hastily looked away. 'I'm sorry, but we've met before somewhere, haven't we?'

He was the most attractive man she had ever seen. Shocked at her own reaction, she was trying to cope with the sheer physical impact he had on her. It confused and frightened her.

He didn't seem to have heard her question. He was concentrating on the flower bed near them. And he obviously hadn't seen the admiration in her eyes, for when he glanced back at her he scowled. 'Not a pretty sight, am I?' He half raised his injured arm. 'Don't look at me. Wouldn't you like to see the garden?'

'Yes. Please.' Desperately she tried to get a grip on herself. Middle aged – well, nearly – women did not go round the country ogling handsome young men and feeling their breath snatched away by waves of physical longing for complete strangers. She concentrated hard on the flowers, as he seemed to be doing, hoping he had not noticed her confusion. 'The garden is very beautiful.' She hoped that her voice sounded normal. 'Mr Turner told us it had gone wild, but it seems very neat to me.' A crescent of rose beds curved around the neatly mown lawn, brilliant with flowers; beyond them a herbaceous border stretched towards the cedar tree, a riot of lupins and gladioli and hollyhocks.

The young man glanced at her and smiled. 'A few of the chaps work on it when they've got the strength. I'm not much good. I can't keep my balance without this damn

7

thing.' As he turned to step off the terrace onto the soft mossy lawn she saw he was using a stick.

'You look as though you've really been in the wars,' she said gently.

He frowned. 'Who hasn't? But I'm lucky, I suppose. I made it back. Look. Look at the roses. God, they're lovely.' He stopped and stared at them with a strange intensity.

There was a long silence. Victoria felt uncomfortable, as though she were in the way. He had withdrawn from her into some unfathomable pain. Glancing nervously back at the house, she remembered Robert suddenly and wondered where he was. She wished he would come. He had been there: through the fear and resentment; he knew how to cope with pain.

The house on this side was smartly painted. She frowned. Several windows stood open and from somewhere she could hear the sound of music – a band playing on a scratchy record. Staring up at the windows, hoping to see Robert, she glimpsed a shimmer of white at a window. Her exclamation of surprise brought the young man's attention back to her.

'What's wrong?'

'I thought I saw someone up there. Someone in white.'

He gave a strained smile. 'Probably one of the nurses.'

'One of the nurses?' She stared at him. 'Do you have nurses to look after you?' Her eyes were wide with sympathy.

'Of course.' His eyes were clear grey, his face handsome, tanned. He glanced down at his arm ruefully. 'They're threatening to take this off.' Just for a moment she could hear the fear in his voice.

She didn't know what to say.

Visibly pulling himself together he stared at her. 'You were right. We do know each other, don't we?'

'I thought so.' She forced herself to smile.

8

'Yes.' He paused. 'Yes,' he repeated with conviction.

She frowned. Her emotions were sending her conflicting signals. There was something achingly familiar about his eyes, his mouth, his hands; something so familiar that, she realised suddenly, she knew what it was like to have been held in his arms and yet he was a stranger. She turned away abruptly. 'Perhaps we met when we were children or something.'

'Perhaps.' He smiled enigmatically. 'Who did you come to visit? It obviously wasn't me.' There was a trace of wistfulness in his tone.

'We came to look at the house.'

'Oh?' He stopped, gazing down at the grass. 'Interested in history, are you? It must have been lovely here, before they moved us in.'

Victoria smiled. 'Your family have lived here for a long time, have they?'

'My family?' He looked at her in amusement. 'No, my family don't come from here.' He stepped down onto the soft soil of the flower bed and picked a scarlet rose bud. 'Here. For you. It goes with your dress.' He held it out to her. As she took it their fingers touched and the electricity which passed between them left them both for a moment confused. She slipped it behind the pin of the brooch she was wearing.

'Thank you.'

He was frowning. 'You're wearing a wedding ring.'

She looked down at her hand, startled. 'Yes.' She bit her lip. 'My husband is here. He was looking round upstairs. I ought to go and join him, really.' She hesitated. She couldn't bear the anguish in his eyes. 'He was injured too – in the Falklands. He's out of the army now.' There was another long silence. 'I can't remember your name,' she said at last.

9

'It's Stephen.' He said it almost absent-mindedly, 'Stephen Cheney.'

The name meant nothing to her. Nothing.

'May I go and bring Robert to meet you?' she asked after a moment.

He was staring at her again, leaning heavily on his stick, his eyes intense. The silence between them was tangible. It stretched out agonizingly. Then at last he spoke. 'You and I were lovers once,' he whispered, 'in a land, long ago.'

She went cold.

For a moment they were both silent, stunned by what he had said, then he laughed. 'I'm sorry. I don't know why I said that. It's a quotation. At least, I think it is. If not it ought to be. Perhaps I'll write it myself. Yes, go and fetch your husband. I'd like to meet him.'

Victoria turned and walked slowly back across the grass towards the door into the house. She stopped as she put her hand on the handle and turned to look back over her shoulder. He was standing watching her. Jauntily he raised his stick in salute.

She let herself into the cold corridor with a shiver and ran to the stairs. 'Robert? Are you up there?'

'Here. Come and see this.' His voice was distant. 'This place is really weird,' he went on as she found him in the end room. 'Look at these –' He broke off. 'Victoria, darling, what is it?'

For a fraction of a second she hesitated, then she threw herself into his arms. 'Oh, Robert!' She buried her face in his shirt, clinging to him. 'Robert. Where have you been?'

'Only up here.' He steadied himself with difficulty and pushed her gently away from him. 'Victoria, what's the matter?'

'Nothing.' She took a deep breath. 'I'm sorry. I don't know what's the matter with me. I was suddenly so afraid

I was going to lose you.' She could feel it again; the terror; the pain; the dread. It spun around them in the air.

He laughed. 'No such luck, Mrs Holland. You're stuck with me. How was the garden?'

'It's beautiful.' She had to be outside again. She couldn't bear to be inside another minute. 'You must come down and see it. I met one of Lady Penelope's guests. He said he'd like to meet you.' She knew she was gabbling.

'I thought what's-his-name said the house was empty.'

'He obviously didn't realize. It doesn't matter.' She glanced round again, at the long empty corridor and the silent rooms leading off it and she closed her eyes, trying to stave off the overpowering feeling of unhappiness which swept around her. 'I saw Stephen's nurse up here from the garden. Did you meet her?' The air was stuffy; no windows were open. There was no music. The upper floor echoed with emptiness.

'A nurse?' He looked puzzled. 'No, there's been no one up here. No one at all.'

They both glanced over their shoulders.

'That's strange.' She bit her lip, trying to keep her voice steady. 'When I was out there, I could hear music. The windows were open . . .'

'No.' He shook his head. 'You must have been looking at another part of the house. Come on, I've seen enough.'

'We're not going to buy it, are we?' Suddenly she minded terribly. Irrationally, she wanted the house. She wanted it as she had never wanted anything before.

He shook his head. 'It needs too much money spending on it, I'm afraid and it is far too large for us, you must see that. Sad, though. It's a lovely place.'

She bit her lip. 'I want to live here, Robert. I must live here.'

He stared at her and something in her eyes alarmed him. He was swamped by a sudden sense of foreboding;

he could feel the cold coming at him from the walls, threatening to overpower him. Somehow he forced himself to smile; somehow he kept his voice calm. 'Well, let's see the rest of the place, then we can talk about it some more.'

At the foot of the stairs she put her hand on the door handle. 'Come and see the gardens. They're so lovely.' Her fear had subsided as quickly as it had come. It had been an irrational, silly moment. She pushed at the door and frowned, rattling the handle. It seemed to have locked itself.

'Here. Let me.' Robert shook it hard. 'You are sure it was unlocked?'

'Of course I'm sure. It must have latched.' He could hear the rising panic in her voice again.

'Never mind, Victoria darling, it doesn't matter.' He put his arm round her, pulling her to him. 'We can walk round the outside before we go.'

Victoria moved away sharply from his strangely alien embrace and with a little sob she turned and ran down the passage.

Robert stared after her in astonishment and fear, then slowly he followed her.

William was waiting for them in the main entrance hall. 'Ready to go upstairs?' He glanced at them surreptitiously. They both looked agitated; uneasy.

'Why not?' Robert followed him towards the staircase.

'What did you think of the west wing?'

'Not a lot,' Robert smiled tightly. 'What on earth happened to it?'

'The house was used as a nursing home during the first war and they used that wing for the operating theatre and wards for the worst injured men.' William glanced at Victoria who had gone white. 'When the family moved back in about 1920 they left it as it was. Just closed the door and pretended it wasn't there until they forgot about it. And I think each successive generation has done the same since. Did you see the stretcher poles? They always give me the creeps.'

'So that's what they were.' Robert shuddered. 'Something I know a bit about.'

'It's an unhappy place,' Victoria put in quietly.

William nodded. 'I suspect a lot of young men died here. Luckily the rest of the house seems unaffected. I wouldn't let it worry you.' He didn't give them time to react. Turning, he led the way up the broad unlit sweep of stairs. Halfway up he stopped. 'Mrs Holland?'

Victoria was standing where they had left her. Her face was drained of colour.

'The nurse. Stephen's nurse. She was wearing some sort of big white head dress . . .'

'No, Victoria.' Robert limped back down the stairs towards her. 'I know what you're thinking. Just stop it. What you saw was a real nurse. A modern nurse. She probably saw me in the distance and decided to go back downstairs.'

William was frowning at them from the staircase. He felt a shiver touch his spine. What had she seen? One of his colleagues from the firm had seen something when she had stayed to lock up after showing some people around a few days before. That was why she had refused to come this morning. 'You can deal with that place,' she had said. 'I'm not going there again!'

He glanced at Victoria. 'What happened?' he asked cautiously.

'I met someone in the garden, that's all.' Victoria said. 'A house guest of Lady Penelope's. He's been in some sort of accident and he has a nurse to look after him. I thought I saw her in the window upstairs, that's all.'

'Lady Penelope said the house would be empty.' William swallowed hard.

'Well obviously it isn't.' Suddenly Robert was impatient. 'Let's look round upstairs, quickly, then I think we should go.'

Hastily they trailed through the main bedrooms of the house, through the bathrooms and the guest rooms. The only one showing any sign of occupation was Lady Penelope's own. There there were piles of books by the bed, a bottle of aspirins and some spare reading glasses. The other rooms were all neat and impersonal and unused. There was no room obviously allocated to Stephen. Or his nurse. Victoria felt a pang of disappointment. His face, his voice were still with her. It was as if for a few short moments he had been a part of her.

'So. That just leaves the gardens.' William had escorted them finally back to the kitchen via the second staircase. Checking the door into the west wing, he noted that the bolts were all firmly closed. 'As you probably noticed when you came in they were once very beautiful. With some care and attention they could bloom again.'

He led them back to the front door and down the steps. The sun was high, beating on the gravel with the white reflective heat more commonly associated with a Mediterranean afternoon than with an English countryside, even in August.

They walked slowly round the south side of the house and wandered across rough uncut lawns, through untrimmed hedges, an overgrown vegetable garden and between rampant woody herbs. The garden was very silent. It was too hot for birds. The only sound came from the bees.

Beneath the cedar tree on the western side of the house they stopped. Victoria looked round expectantly. Then she frowned. 'I don't understand. I thought it was here I saw Stephen. It was near this tree. There were rose beds full of flowers and the house was painted on that side, and the windows were open. There must be another tree like this . . .'

'No.' William shook his head firmly. 'There is only one cedar.'

'But we were standing there, by the door . . .'

They all stared at the door into the west wing. It was boarded up.

'No.' She shook her head. 'I've got confused. It must have been another door. There were rose beds, and a bank of hollyhocks and a garden seat, and the grass was short. There were daisies everywhere. And music. Music coming from the open windows. He picked a rose for me.' She hadn't realized that her voice was rising.

William swallowed. He shivered again.

She had the rose in her hand. It was a deep damask red. Several small thorns still adhered to the stem and as she held it out to Robert one pricked her. A fleck of blood appeared on her thumb. 'It didn't mean anything. He just gave it to me. It was a silly gesture.' She could feel her eyes filling with tears. 'I . . . I'll go and look. There must be another part of the garden we didn't see. The other side perhaps. Somewhere . . .'

Before either of the men could say anything she began to run, ducking through the thick laurel bushes which edged the grass onto the gravel of the drive.

William looked at Robert, embarrassed. 'We have been all the way round the house, Mr Holland. There are no other gardens. There are no rose beds. Not now.'

Robert laughed uncomfortably. 'Perhaps she fell asleep and dreamed it all. In this heat anything is possible.'

Slowly they walked after her. Both men were thinking of the rose.

'There isn't anyone else staying here, Mr Holland,' William said after a moment. 'Lady Penelope rang us this morning to say she'll be away another week. She wanted

15

to check we were locking up properly. She said the house was empty.'

'Victoria, this is crazy. You can't go back there. I've told the agents we're not interested. And that's that.' Robert threw down the paper. Pushing his hands into his pockets he went to stand in front of the open window, trying to hide his despair.

Since the previous weekend she had not let him touch her. She had been tense, edgy and tearful and obsessed by the house.

'I can and I'm going to. I've already rung Lady Penelope. And I'm going on my own, Robert.'

He stared at her. 'You're mad.'

'It will only take me a couple of hours to drive over there and back. She's asked me to have a cup of tea with her.'

'But why? Why go? I've told you. We can't afford it. That house is going to go for more than we could pay. Be reasonable, Victoria.' He turned to face her desperately. 'I don't understand you, darling. What's happened to you?' She was a stranger.

She shrugged unhappily. 'I don't know. It was meeting Stephen. I have to find out who he is; where I knew him before. I can't get him out of my mind . . .'

You and I were lovers once, in a land, long ago.

She closed her eyes and shook her head, trying to rid herself of the echo of his voice, the image of his clear, grey eyes.

'OK. Go then.' Robert threw himself down onto a chair. 'Who was he? A boyfriend? You fancied him, did you? He was younger than me, I suppose; not crippled? Are you in love with him?'

'How could I be? I only saw him for a few minutes.'

16

She realized suddenly what he had said and for the first time she saw what she was doing to him. 'Robert!' She ran to him and put her arms around his neck. 'It's not like that. Perhaps he didn't even exist! Perhaps he was a dream! I don't know. That's why I've got to find out, don't you see? And he was crippled, as you call it, too. I told you. Look,' she hesitated. 'Come back with me. Come and meet him yourself. Please.'

He shook his head and tried to smile. 'No. You go. Whatever it is you have to prove, Victoria, you have to do it alone.'

Lady Penelope opened the door herself. She was a slim, elegant woman in her early eighties, with bright intelligent eyes. Once she had poured the tea she sat quite still behind the tea tray listening with complete attention as Victoria told her story.

When Victoria finished there was a long silence. 'Stephen Cheney,' she repeated at last.

'He and I knew each other once,' Victoria said softly. She looked down at her hands, covertly twisting her wedding ring around her finger.

You and I were lovers once, in a land, long ago.

'You do know him?'

'Oh yes, I know him.' Lady Penelope frowned. 'After tea, I'll take you to him.'

'He looked so ill.'

'Yes, poor boy, I expect he did.' Lady Penelope glanced up at Victoria. 'What made you and your husband come to look around this house?'

'The agents sent it. My husband has just been invalided out of the army and it seemed the sort of place we would like to live. We inherited Robert's father's house in London and neither of us wanted to live in town, so we sold it. But

17

I'm afraid this is going to be too expensive.' She smiled anxiously. 'Mr Turner from the agents said you'd already had offers above the asking price.'

'Even if I hadn't I wouldn't sell it to you, Mrs Holland.' Lady Penelope's smile belied the harshness of the words. 'This is not the house for you, my dear. You'll see why presently.' She stood up. 'Now. If you've finished your tea, I'll take you to see Stephen.'

The heat wave had broken at last and the air was cool and damp after a night of rain as they walked slowly round the side of the house, through the laurels and across the lawn beneath the cedar tree. The west wing was still tightly closed up. No music rang across the grass. Victoria stopped and stared at it. The whole place gave off a sense of deep sadness. Lady Penelope watched her, but she said nothing and after a moment she moved on. Victoria stayed where she was. He had been here. On the grass. Near the flowers. She closed her eyes. She knew already where they were going.

Her hostess moved with deceptive rapidity in spite of her eighty years and Victoria found herself almost running to keep up with her as they cut through the shrubbery and found themselves on another unkempt lawn. Beyond it a high yew hedge separated them from the church.

Opening a gate in the hedge Lady Penelope glanced at Victoria. 'I hope you're strong, I think you are.'

She set off up a path between huddled gravestones, overgrown with nettles, some of them lost beneath moss and lichen. One of them had been recently cleared. They stopped in front of it.

Stephen John Cheney
Born 20 June 1894. Died 24 August 1918
in God I trust

18

'I remembered the name when you mentioned it on the phone.' Lady Penelope poked at the grave with her walking stick. 'I came up yesterday to see if I was right, and cleared the stone. Then I went back to the records. We still have the nursing home ledgers in the house. My son found them years ago. I suppose they got overlooked with all the other stuff at the end of the war. Stephen died two days after they amputated his arm.'

'No.' Victoria stared down at the grave. 'No. You don't understand. I saw him. I spoke to him.'

'There is no Stephen Cheney now, my dear.' The old lady's voice was gentle.

You and I were lovers once, in a land, long ago.

'It's not possible.' It was a whisper. 'He gave me a rose.'

'Everything is possible.'

'Perhaps it was his son – or his grandson,' Victoria said uncertainly.

The old lady shrugged. They both stood, staring down at the mossy tombstone. Both knew somehow that Stephen had had no son.

'I learned the names on all these stones, walking to church every Sunday over the years,' Lady Penelope said slowly. 'My family have lived in this house for more than a century. We had to move out during the last war, just as we did during the first one. But they didn't use the place as a hospital again. The last time round it was the home guard. I brought my husband here in 1940, but we never lived here. He was killed in 1941, before our son was born.' She paused for a moment. 'The house is too much for me now. And my son doesn't want it. So, sadly, it must go.' She smiled. 'Are you all right? Do you want to sit down?'

Victoria was fighting back her tears.

'I'm sorry. It's such a shock.'

'There was no gentle way to tell you.'

'You must think I'm mad.'

'Oh no, my dear. I don't think you're mad. Far from it. On the contrary. I've heard their music from the old gramophone. I've smelt the Lysol in those wards. But I've never seen any of the boys. You are lucky.'

'Am I?' Victoria tried to smile through her tears.'Why did I know him? Why did he know me?'

He had touched her; given her a rose. She could hear his voice . . . see his eyes. She stared down at the grey stone, seeing it swimming through her tears. 'How?' she whispered. 'How?'

There was a long silence. Lady Penelope was staring across the churchyard into the distance where, through the trees, they could see the hazy mountains bathed in the afternoon sun. 'Maybe you knew one another in a previous life,' she said at last. 'Maybe you should have known each other in that life – his life – but he died too soon and you missed one another on the great wheel of destiny. Who knows? If it is still meant to be, you'll have another chance. You both stepped out of time for a few short minutes and one day you'll find each other again.' She put her arm around Victoria's shoulder. 'When you reach my age you know these things. Life goes round and round like the records those boys used to play endlessly on those hot summer afternoons. Once in a while the needle slips; it jumps a groove. That's what happened when you walked out through that door onto the terrace. You and Stephen heard the same tune for a while – then the needle jumped back. If it is meant to be, you will see him again one day.'

'You really believe that?'

'Oh yes.'

'But it won't be in this life, will it?'

'You have a lover in this life, Victoria,' Lady Penelope pointed out gently.

'You mean Robert?'

'If he is your lover as well as your husband.'

'Yes, he is my lover as well as my husband.' How could anyone doubt it? How could Robert have doubted it? She had left him alone, his face a tight mask of misery. But he had made no further attempt to stop her coming.

'Then don't hurt him.' It was as if the old lady knew what had happened. 'Stephen has had his life; now you must live yours.'

'How does it work? How could I see him? Was he a ghost?'

Her companion shrugged. 'It doesn't matter what he was. He was real. For you. And for me.'

They were both looking down at the grave.

'He told me he was afraid they would take off his arm,' Victoria said sadly.'He was so frightened. I wish I'd said something to reassure him.'

'Your being there reassured him.'

'Did it?' Victoria bit her lip. 'Do you mind living in a haunted house?' she asked after another long silence.

Lady Penelope smiled. 'Every old house has its ghosts, my dear. You grow used to them. I'm fond of mine. But that poor boy from the agents hates it here. He doesn't understand.'

'Why did you say we couldn't buy the house?'

Lady Penelope smiled. 'If you hadn't seen Stephen, it wouldn't have mattered. But you have and you recognized him. You cannot live in a house with two lovers, Victoria. It wouldn't be fair to your Robert, or yourself. Or to Stephen for that matter.'

'But fate must have brought me here.'

Lady Penelope smiled. 'There are times, my dear, when we have to turn our backs on fate. For the sake of our sanity. Always remember that.' She glanced towards the house. 'I'll go on back, my dear. You catch me up when you're ready.'

Victoria stood looking down at the grave for several

minutes after the old lady had gone. She made no attempt to reach him. Her mind was a blank. The churchyard around her was empty. There were no ghosts there now. Wandering on down the path she passed a wild climbing rose, scrambling over some dead elder bushes. Picking one perfect bud she took it back and laid it on his grave. Then she turned away.

As she walked back across the lawn she glanced up at the windows of the west wing as they reflected the late afternoon sunlight in a glow of gold. One or two of them were open now, she saw, without surprise. And, faintly, she could hear the sound of music. But the gardens were empty.

Visitors

'You know, I'm not sure that I do want to see you again after all, Joe.' I leaned back, beginning to enjoy myself, and shifted the receiver to the other hand. 'How long did you say it was?'

'Oh, come on, Pen. Don't be like that.' His voice was starting to sound the tiniest bit tetchy.

I hoped the smile on my face didn't come over in my voice. 'OK, then. As it's Christmas. You can come for the night. Spare room.'

'Spare room?'

'Spare room.'

I put down the receiver and stood up. Twenty minutes, he had said. Twenty minutes to tidy up, fix my hair and nails, slip into something infinitely casual and arrange to be very, very busy when he arrived. I glanced out of the window. The village street glistened beneath the dusting, melting snow. Rather as it had been when he walked out on me three years before. I had sworn I would never see the swine again.

Well, three years and a couple of morale-boosting affairs can do a lot for resolutions like that one. Anyway, I was curious. What had happened to my Joe in the last three years? I put a couple of logs on the fire and poured myself a drink.

*

I stayed where I was at my writing desk when I heard the car drive up outside. I counted to ten when the bell rang and then, slowly, walked to the door.

Damn. The sight of him could still make my pulses race. I stretched out a hand. 'It's good to see you again, Joe.' There were tiny unmelted snowflakes caught in the crisp curl of his hair. But his eyes were the same. Mocking; insolent; irresistible . . . 'Come and have a drink.' I put my hand on the door behind him to push it closed, but his foot was in the way.

'Pen, I'm not alone . . .'

As his voice tailed away I felt my nerves begin to throb warningly. 'Don't tell me you've brought a woman, Joe.' My voice was melodious, but I could see it made him uneasy.

'Of course not, I told you. It's all over. There's no one. But . . .'

Never in all the time I've known him have I seen Joe look shifty before. His eyes skidded away from mine and fixed, concentrating, on the battered coal scuttle on the hearth. I was taut with suspicion.

'I'm all alone, Pen,' he had said, on the phone. The liar. 'All alone, and it is Christmas Eve. Couldn't I come?'

I had been trying to forget it was Christmas Eve, in spite of the cards around the room, in spite of the coloured lights around the church and the village pub. Christmas is for families, not for the orphaned unmarried like me, however sociable we might be the rest of the year. But the crackle of sentiment in his voice had got to me.

'Come on in, Joe,' I said now, wearily. 'The house is getting cold. You'd better ask her in. One drink and you can go to the pub. Both.'

I turned my back on the door and stood, folding my arms defensively around me, in front of the fire. What did I care how many women he brought. No doubt he'd come for my approval before popping the question to someone who had finally been fool enough to say yes. It was the sort of crazy tactless thing Joe might do. I kicked a log and watched the shower of sparks. Whoever she was, she was a bitch.

There was a click as Joe quietly pushed the front door shut behind him with his foot. One. Two. Three. Four. Five. Six. Seven. Eight. Nine. Ten . . .

Slowly I turned.

Nobody. He was standing there with a basket in each hand, and he was looking sheepish again. What the hell was he up to?

'OK, Joe. Have a drink.' I sighed and went for the bottle as he set down the two baskets and came forward.

He took the glass from my hand. 'You're a real brick, Pen. Did I ever tell you that?'

Of course, I could have stepped back in time to avoid that kiss; as it was I stepped back just a little too late. As an experiment it was a success.

'I like your hair long. You look fabulous; really good.' He took a deep drink from his glass. I waited smugly for his eyes to water as he swallowed, but they didn't. I was impressed. It was neat and he had taken a big gulp. Perhaps he had been practising.

'Happy Christmas, fella,' I whispered. 'Now, stop flannelling and show me this friend.'

'His name is Paul.' He set down the glass.

'Paul?'

I watched as he went to the shopping. One of the baskets was stuffed with blankets and – I felt my eyes growing enormous – a small baby.

I stood there, for the first time in my life speechless, as Joe tenderly scooped it up and brought it to the fire. It had delicate, tiny features and warm pink cheeks. It was asleep.

'Isn't he beautiful?' Joe's voice was very gentle.

'Whose is it?' I don't think my voice was as harsh as it should have been. It really was, now he came to mention it, rather beautiful.

'This is my son.' There was no mistaking this time the pride in his voice.

And there was no mistaking the jealousy and disappointment that swept through me as he said it; silly fool that I was, still caring for a man like him.

'Do you want to hold him?' He spoke with the voice of one about to bestow a rare and lovely treat. I stepped back and firmly picked up my glass again.

'I'm not used to babies,' I said. 'I'd drop him.'

'I expect you want to know where he came from?' The shifty look had gone and the old mischievous grin was back, teasing me.

I raised an eyebrow. 'I've no doubt you have as many gooseberry bushes in town as we do here.'

'His mother doesn't like children. We had a conference when we split up and she said I could take him. So I did.' He was grinning all over his face.

'So you did.' I was stunned. 'Do you *know* anything about babies, Joe?'

He shook his head. 'She gave me a manual. It's quite straightforward, really. I've got all the gear. It's in the car, actually.'

'But, Joe, what'll you do when term starts? Who will look after it then?'

Joe, like me, teaches.

He shrugged. 'I'll find someone to keep an eye on him.'

Gently he laid the child down on the sofa and unwrapped a layer of shawl. I was torn between indignation and curiosity.

'Hadn't you better tell me who his mother was? Is?'

26

'Was. It has all been made legal. A lovely lady, Pen. You would like her . . .'

Like hell, I thought.

'. . . She's tall and dark and quiet, but absolutely set on being a top dancer. And she'll do it. She's good. And she's definitely not the maternal type. She nearly killed me when she got pregnant. Lovely girl.'

He positively licked his lips.

'You are a swine, Joe.' I thought it was time I said it out loud.

He laughed. 'You know, none of them have ever been like you, Pen. None of them.'

It was my turn to look modest. 'And how many of them have there been, if I might enquire?'

He shrugged. 'Trade secret, love. Who's counting? It's you I've come back to.'

'You and who else,' I said.

When he went to unpack the car I had a look at the baby. It was very like him, I had to admit.

I pulled back the shawl to have a better look and the infant Nureyev opened its eyes – and then its mouth. I leaped back as though it had bitten me. The squalling was deafening.

Joe was beside me in an instant. 'Did Penny frighten you, den?'

I put my hands over my face. 'Joe! I don't believe it. Not you. Not baby talk. Surely your son is an intellectual?'

'Of course he is.' Joe drew himself up. 'Who is an intellectual, den? Daddy's boy.' He laughed. 'You should see your face, Pen.' He put his arm around me and gave me a squeeze. 'Come on. Are you going to feed him? It's time he was asleep.'

'Me?' I hit an unseemly falsetto. 'I couldn't feed him.'

'Why not? Women do these things by instinct.'

'Evidently his mother doesn't. And neither do I,' I said firmly. 'It's all up to you, Joe.'

I watched fascinated as he bent and, rummaging in a paper bag, produced a feeding bottle.

'It's only got to be warmed up.'

'Can't we give it brandy, or something, just this once?' I quavered. Babies, it seemed, unnerved me completely.

He remembered where the kitchen was; and the kettle; and the mixing bowl. Damn him, he was completely at home!

I hovered ineffectually, listening with increasing unease to the baby's screams from next door.

'Pick him up, will you. Tell him it's coming.'

I had been afraid he would say that. Nervously I edged an arm under the convulsed little bundle and heaved it up. It was surprisingly heavy. To my amazement it stopped crying at once, and after a moment, beamed at me. I found myself beaming back. I felt ridiculously pleased.

'See, he likes you.' Joe appeared with a towel wrapped around his waist, the bottle in his hand.

I watched goggle-eyed as he stuffed the teat into the baby's mouth and tipped the stuff down and I almost asked if I could have a go myself.

'I knew you'd turn up trumps, Pen.' Joe took his refilled glass from me and raised it in salute. We had made the baby a bed in a drawer upstairs after he had changed its nappy – blessedly out of sight, to save my sensibilities – and it had gone off to sleep at once. Its mountain of belongings tidied away, my cottage began to look familiar again.

'You can't keep it, Joe. It's got to go back to its mother.' I looked at him earnestly.

'Rubbish. It's mother doesn't want it.' Joe grinned affably. 'When are we eating?'

Men!

He had to make do with an omelette; hardly Christmas fare, but he produced a bottle of wine from one of his paper bags, so I made the effort to go into the garden where the snow was beginning to settle a little and I cut some frosty thyme. One *fine herbe* at least. He sniffed over my shoulder as the eggs sizzled in the pan.

'None of my other women have been able to cook like you. You know, I sometimes used to lie and dream about the nosh I got in this cottage.' He licked his lips and I had to laugh.

'I should kick you for talking about all these other women all the time. Why on earth did you leave if I'm such a paragon?'

'You were a bitch as well.' He was warming the wine, like the feeding bottle, in a basin of hot water. 'And I wasn't mature enough to cope with you. Besides, you were becoming too set in your ways. I could see you getting bossy. My God! You've moved the glasses.' He straightened from the cupboard in the corner. 'Do you know, Pen, that is the first thing that's been different in this cottage. Three years and not a bloody thing has changed. That's what I mean about being set in your ways.'

'A lot has changed.' I could feel myself getting defensive. He had caught me on a sensitive spot. I knew I was in a rut without him spelling it out. 'The walls have changed colour for a start. There are new curtains in the sitting room. I've got new chairs and . . .'

'Stop!' he raised his hands in surrender. 'Stop. I didn't mean it. Forgive the old campaigner the gaps in his memory.' He grinned again. 'So, where are the glasses these days?'

'On a tray next door.' I flipped the omelettes onto two

warmed plates and piled some French bread and salad round them. At least he wouldn't starve.

We were half-way through supper when the carol singers came. It was the moment I had been dreading most before Joe arrived. The year before, I had put out all the lights as I heard them down the street, put my head under my pillow and wallowed in self pity as they missed my darkened porch, as I had intended they should.

This time we listened. Happy. The joyous sounds were slightly off key, but who cared.

I hadn't any change.

'My God, woman, you're still after my money!' Joe groped in his pocket and produced a pound coin.

'Joe, that's too much!' I murmured, but it was too late. And it was worth it.

Oh, it would be so easy to have Joe back. So very easy.

We whispered so as not to wake the baby as we made up a bed for Joe in the spare room. 'You're right about things not being the same round here,' he muttered ruefully as I pulled the blankets over.

'Dead right, they're not,' I hissed back. 'You promiscuous so-and-so. You keep your child company.'

I didn't lock my door, though, and I was quite disappointed when the dulcet tones of Joe's snores began gently to vibrate across the landing.

'Happy Christmas, darling.'

I was struggling up through layers of exhausted sleep, clutching at daylight. It was dark.

I could feel Joe's arms around me. 'What time is it?' I managed to ask before his mouth closed onto mine. After a moment – a lovely moment – he replied, 'About three, I should think, I've just fed Paul.'

I sat up abruptly, pushing him away. It wasn't going to be that easy for him. 'Three in the morning? You're mad. Go away!'

'But Penny . . .' his voice in the dark was hurt and pathetic.

'Get out, Joe. I told you.'

I was indignant. Three in the morning is not on, by anybody's standards. Not after three years. Not after all those other women who didn't know how to cook.

He went.

At breakfast he was looking innocent again. Dangerously so.

'Happy Christmas, darling.'

'You've said that once today already, if I remember.'

'Have I?' He smiled. 'I've got a present for you.'

In spite of myself I was excited. 'Really?' I should have been suspicious.

'Really.' He looked suddenly serious. He felt in his pocket and produced an envelope which he pushed across at me. Hesitating I took it. It had something small and hard in it. Without looking I knew what it was. The ring I had thrown at his head so long before. I pushed the envelope back.

'No, Joe, it wouldn't work.'

'It would. I'm more mature now.' He smiled wickedly and left the envelope on the table.

'It wouldn't.' I got up to make the toast. 'So, when are you leaving?' I bent down to light the grill pan. It meant my face was hidden and he couldn't read my expression.

'Ten years, or so?' He sounded hopeful.

I laughed. And in spite of myself my heart leaped. 'We'll try it until lunch,' I said.

Cabbage à la Carte

Kate pulled the mini thankfully into the parking space
and switched off. For a moment she rested her forehead against the cool rim of the steering wheel, breathing
deeply. Her hands were shaking. The first, the lesser, part
of the ordeal was over – driving the borrowed car through
the overcrowded streets on market day and finding a meter.
She leaned over to glance in the mirror and check her hair.
Her face was pink and shiny again, her lipstick had turned
too red.

She grabbed for her tapestry bag and applied a new
layer. It looked artificial and hard. She wasn't used to
bothering with make-up. She never usually dressed up.
She had never owned her own car. But today she was
endeavouring to be someone quite different. Kate Millrow,
painter, recently – very recently – of St Agnes's School of
Art, would never dare to try and sell her paintings to a
smart town gallery.

Miss Rowmill (she was especially pleased with the
name), artists' agent and talent spotter would be able to
do it every day. 'Think yourself into the part, Kate, think
yourself into the part,' she muttered desperately as she
climbed out of the car and groped for the money. The coin,
so carefully hoarded for this occasion, slipped from her
fingers and rolled away towards a gutter. Frantically she
leapt after it and caught it up before it disappeared down

the grille. Even putting the money in the parking meter once she had recaptured it was something of an ordeal. She studied the thing intently, reading the instructions. The slot seemed to be the wrong way round. She couldn't get the money in. Then at last the needle buzzed across and she found herself with two whole hours in which to carry out her mission. She pulled out the portfolio, locked the car and made her way slowly towards the gallery. She knew it didn't open until ten so she made her way slowly towards a coffee shop, clutching the cardboard folder awkwardly. Its sharp edges at the top cut into her armpit, at the bottom they sliced into her fingers.

Sitting down thankfully with an espresso she set down her burden. By rights she ought to be at college now, settling into her final year. What had possessed her to think she could make it on her own? The offer of the cottage in the country? Somewhere where she could really paint? 'There's nothing much else to do there, Kate. It'll keep you at it. Then we'll see what you're really made of,' John had said as he handed her the key before setting off on his trek to Katmandu. For a year at least she had the place, rent free, to herself. It was a dream come true. Only John hadn't mentioned the fact that the rain came through the roof, there was no electricity and the nearest neighbour was half a mile away.

She had been shocked, afraid and then angry in that order when she first saw the cottage. Was it for this that she had thrown up college and antagonized her family? Then eventually she had begun to see the funny side. Perhaps fate had presented her with a challenge. Anyway it was too late to go back. There was nothing to do but weed cabbages ('You won't starve, love, help yourself from the kitchen garden'), eat cabbages and set up her easel.

And surprisingly she had painted. She had painted non-stop day after day, as long as there was light. But the moment had come when she realized that she could not live on cabbages for ever, and even if she could she had to pay for the calor gas to cook them, and oil for the lamps.

Nervously she had painted a board, 'Millrow Studios', and hammered it to the gate, thinking someone might come and buy at the cottage. She had waited heart-thumping for half an hour for a car to come down the lane and then she had run out and torn down the notice before anyone could see it.

Her only visitors had been her nearest neighbours from the farm up the lane. They had been kind and helpful and once brought her a chicken and often eggs, and now today she had borrowed their mini. They had looked at her pictures, made noises of polite incomprehension and suggested the gallery in town. They knew it opened at ten ('Lazy devils; don't know the meaning of the word work') and directed her to the coffee house. ('The pubs aren't open then, but if you need a stiffener, that'll be the next best thing.')

It was ten past ten. Her knees wobbling, she paid her bill and crossed the road.

The girl in the gallery had round moon glasses and an expression of disdain. Kate forgot she was Miss Rowmill, agent and became shy and diffident Kate Millrow, beneath the girl's supercilious gaze.

'Are you the owner of the gallery?' she asked in a strained falsetto, totally unlike her own voice.

To her surprise the girl gave her a friendly smile. 'No, but he'll be back any minute. Take a seat.'

Kate sat numbly, the portfolio balanced against her knees. The paintings on the walls of the gallery were to her eyes mannered and uncomfortable. But they were good and very professional. And, dear God, they were framed! Perhaps she should have tried to frame hers before she

34

brought them in? She started to shake again, wishing she hadn't come.

Then the door opened and the owner appeared. He was a young man, tall and arrogant-looking. His lips, she decided instantly, were mean beneath the thin moustache.

Her only concern now was to get out as soon as possible, with the least embarrassment for everybody, especially herself.

The other girl had her coat on as soon as the man appeared. 'Here's Mr Chambers now,' she announced and she was gone without a word to him.

'Ask her to watch the place for five minutes and she acts as if I'd told her to swim the channel, the silly bitch,' he muttered angrily at her retreating back. 'Now, what do you want, young lady?' He sounded irritated.

He didn't seem to realize that she was Miss Rowmill, artists' agent. Nettled, she told him.

He was not impressed. 'We're fully booked well into next year,' he said coolly. 'But let's see what you've got.'

He leafed through the paintings and sketches casually, taking hardly any time to study them. Occasionally he muttered 'humph, not bad,' or 'weak, weak,' or 'very derivative'. Kate was mortified.

'They're all by the same girl?' he asked, not raising his eyes.

'Yes.'

'Where did you find her, art school?'

She was furious. 'No. She's a local girl. I think she has great talent, a great . . .' She hesitated, trying to think of a word.

'Potential?' He glanced up at her, smiling suddenly.

'Exactly.' She felt she wasn't playing her part sufficiently convincingly. 'I like to watch out for up and coming new names, and so,' she added pointedly, 'do *most* of my clients.'

35

'Indeed.' She did not like the way he raised one eyebrow.

He reached the end of the pictures and began to shuffle through them again. 'Did she have any oils, this Kate Millrow?' he asked casually.

'Oh yes.' Did she sound too eager? 'I didn't bring any today, but I could arrange to collect some.'

'No, no.' He held up his hand. 'I've seen enough. I'm afraid, Miss . . .' he hesitated over the name. '*Rowmill* was it? I'm afraid these are not really suitable for this gallery. However,' he glared at her as he saw her about to speak, 'however, I do believe like yourself in giving an encouraging help to the young occasionally, so,' he pulled out a watercolour and looked at it closely, 'I will take a couple of these if you agree. I'll have them framed and hang them in my next show. I'll take framing expenses plus ten per cent, agreed?'

Kate was speechless with joy. It wasn't the praise, the one man exhibition she had dreamed of, but it was something. Excitedly she gave him the address of the cottage.

'And now *your* address, Miss Rowmill. I generally prefer to deal through an agent direct if there is one.' He looked at her closely and waited, his pen poised. It nearly stumped her. She thought fast and then gave him her sister's address in London. It seemed to impress him.

It was not until she was nearly home that she realized that in real terms she had achieved very little. The condescending acceptance of two pictures by a stuck up opinionated gallery owner, out of charity rather than anything else, and a lot of quite unjustified rude remarks. 'Horrible prig!' she muttered to herself as she turned up the lane. And what was worse she realized, she still hadn't actually earned any cash, and her desire for some rather more exotic food than eggs and cabbage was increasingly daily, if not hourly.

Reluctantly, nervously, she rehung the notice on the

gate before she changed and took the car back to the farm. If Miss Rowmill could hang the notice up, she hoped desperately that she could persuade Miss Millrow to leave it there.

Once more dressed in jeans and barefoot, she selected the paintings Mr Chambers had made the least derogatory noises over and put them prominently round the room.

Then she sat back to wait. No one came. She left the notice on the gate, refused to be discouraged, went to dig some potatoes and then at last settled down to paint again.

'Derivative indeed,' she snorted. 'The man was an ignorant fool.'

It was on the Saturday afternoon that a car drove by, slowed and backed to the gate. Two people got out and wandered up the path, exclaiming at the honeysuckle and roses, pointing up at the fields behind the cottage.

Kate felt sick.

They knocked and she let them in, wishing she wasn't quite so shabbily dressed and that her toes weren't quite so grubby from the garden.

But they obviously liked to see her like that. She saw suddenly through their eyes a glimmer of the so-called glamour of the artist in the garret, and glad that for once she had got rid of the smell of cabbage from the house, she was content to let them wander around the room she used for a studio.

She crossed her fingers, praying they would buy something, but they completed a round of the paintings without seeming to see anything in particular.

Then the man turned to her hesitantly. 'Is anything for sale, Miss Millrow?' he asked.

Anything! He must be joking.

She smiled politely. 'Well, some of my best work is away on exhibition,' – was that Miss Rowmill talking? – 'but most things here are for sale, yes.'

She desperately tried to think of prices. Too high and they would be scared off; too low and they would think her valueless.

'I'll give you ten pounds for this, I love it.'

She could not believe her ears. Ten pounds for a tiny painting of a posy of spring flowers. It wasn't even modern in style.

'That seems very fair.' She smiled as graciously as she could.

She sat for a long time after they had gone, gazing at the two fivers on the table. Could it be true that at last she was earning her living by painting?

Two hours later she was chopping vegetables in the kitchen when there was a knock at the door. She opened it to find Mr Chambers standing on the doorstep. Her heart sank with embarrassment but he held out his hand blandly with absolutely no sign of recognition on his face.

'You must be Miss Millrow. How do you do.'

Had her make up been so good then? She stammered a greeting in return and showed him at his request into the studio.

Reaching into his pocket he produced an envelope. 'I'm glad to say I've managed to sell one of your paintings, Miss Millrow.'

'Already?' her voice came out in a squeak.

'Already.' He grinned at her amicably. 'It was lying on my table after you, that is your agent,' he corrected himself quickly, 'had left it with me and I had a buyer almost at once. It seems my initial judgement may have been a little harsh.'

'I'll say it was,' she muttered under her breath, and then out loud she asked. 'How much did you get?' She took the envelope with shaking fingers.

'There's thirty-five pounds there. I've already taken my commission.' He grinned again. 'I imagined that under the circumstances you would rather pay your agent her commission yourself.'

Kate felt herself blushing crimson. 'You must think I'm an awful fool.'

'Not at all. You'd be surprised how many people come in with pictures they say a "friend" has painted. Mind you,' he looked her up and down pointedly. 'Not many of them go to the lengths you did for a disguise.'

She blushed again. 'I'm afraid I'm rather a mess at the moment. I was cooking.'

He nodded. 'Cabbage. I had guessed.'

She smiled ruefully. 'I'm afraid I live on it.'

'Why don't you go and continue while I poke around here for a bit and investigate your,' he paused and winked, 'your potential.'

She fled.

It took only a few minutes to throw the vegetables into a pan and scrub her hands and then she ran upstairs to comb her hair and change her skirt. When she came down he had piled several canvases on the table.

'I'll take these next,' he said without preamble. 'Sale or return of course, and I'll buy this one myself . . .'

Again it was flowers, she noticed amazed.

'. . . if it's not exorbitantly priced. Now,' he looked at her again. 'Could that concoction you were making wait do you think? If you were to transform yourself, not into that hard hitting woman Miss Rowmill, but perhaps into a slightly tidier version of yourself I could take you out to dinner to celebrate your sales.'

She looked at him amazed. She had got the firm impression he despised her and her kind, and she certainly disliked him. So why ask her out? And anyway he was insufferably rude. A slightly tidier version of herself indeed. She curbed the desire to stick out her tongue at him.

Instead she lowered her eyes meekly to the floor. 'That would be nice,' she said. 'Much better than cabbage.'

She had a Laura Ashley dress upstairs and pretty Venetian sandals. Her hair beneath its gay scarf was at least clean. Oh yes, Mr Chambers. She could be tidier when she tried.

She debated over lipstick for several minutes in her bedroom and then decided against it. Miss Rowmill might wear lipstick, but she did not. She clipped on the silver bangle her parents had given her for her eighteenth birthday and gazed at herself in the stained old mirror. The image, she had to admit, was rather attractive.

Mr Chambers evidently thought so too, for he stopped being rude, told her his name was Derek and ushered her out to his car with exaggerated care. He even helped her with the seat belt.

'I have a ten per cent interest in you, my dear Miss Millrow,' was his only comment when she protested.

They drove back into town and he took her to the most delightful French restaurant she had ever been to. He almost talked her into having something called *Dolmas Maigre*, but the suppressed glee in his expression led her to guess it might have something to do with cabbage and to his chagrin she checked with the waiter before she ordered. Once that hurdle was over the evening continued fairly well. She found herself telling him about art school and John's offer of the cottage and her parents' anger when she had 'dropped out', as they of course put it. To her surprise he threw his head back and laughed.

'Dropped out, a prim little miss like you? Nonsense. Besides, they ought to be proud of you. You have a great deal of talent. And not only for painting. If you ever get bored with that, you could go on the stage.'

She looked at him to see if he was taking the micky, but his expression was all innocence. He quickly topped up her wine glass. 'Yes, Miss Millrow, you have a great deal of talent.'

To her annoyance she found herself blushing although she was quite sure he was teasing. His fingers had strayed towards her own on the blue table-cloth and as they so very casually, almost by accident, made contact, she snatched her hand away. She was not going to be that easy to placate. She took a gulp of wine.

When they parted that evening, however, it was on the understanding that they would meet again the following Saturday and that, if she could face the bus ride into town, she would go to see him at the gallery even before then.

'Now,' he said, looking up at her mischievously from the driving seat as he started up the engine. 'About what you wear when you come. Shoes, yes. Lipstick, no. Jeans, yes if decent. Right?'

She grinned. 'And next weekend?'

'Next weekend, if you're cooking for me, a large plastic apron, which I will personally provide.'

'Nothing else?' Her eyes widened.

He laughed. 'That, my sweet Kate, is up to you. But I'll live in hope.'

She stood waving as he drove off down the lane and then slowly she made her way back into the shadowy cottage where he had lit the oil lamp for her and left it, flickering slightly on the table. She was unbelievably happy.

'Damn cheek,' she muttered to herself. 'Who does he think he is?'

Metamorphosis

S he couldn't remember how she came to be on the train.
She knew the station had been huge and echoing and
she had walked through it as through the rib cage of a
dinosaur, to find the tiny womb of the compartment where
she was to sleep. It was safe there; warm and dark and
alone. When the man knocked and called out the different
sittings of meals she hid her head beneath the blanket and
he went away and then she still lay listening, as the wheels
beat the rhythm of a foetal heart.

She who had been afraid to walk the streets of London,
afraid of unknown lurking terrors, afraid of men and dogs
and children and women like herself, somehow she had
managed to change trains and between them she had
bought herself a tea from an anonymous uncaring man who
slopped the liquid across ranks of cups and watched it
gurgle, stewed and wasteful through a grating. She dared
not ask for a spoon, but she was well pleased with herself
for the tea. It was hot and good to drink. The station
had been alive with people and pigeons. Brisk sunshine
streamed through dirt-encrusted glass. She realized that
she was already no longer so afraid as she climbed aboard
the second train and waited for it to travel north.

There was a taxi to find at the other end. She stood on
the esplanade looking across at the fishing boats and sniffed

the glorious sea. It gave her strength. She felt in her pocket for the key; a large cold key; the key to sanity.

Her driver had the soft-spoken gentle ways of the west. He made her welcome and gentled her as he would a doe come down from the hills in the snow. She had the great dark eyes of a doe, he thought. And the unnamed terror. Was it life she feared, or herself? She sat beside him, her fingers clutching the purse she needed to pay him and he knew she dreaded the moment she must pay, for the human contact it involved. He told her the names of the mountains and the lochs and he soothed her with softly-aspirated vowels.

Skies as wide as for ever opened now above her head and she felt light and free again. There were no more buildings. The taxi was bumping and swerving away from yesterday and carrying her inexorably with it. There would be no more hospitals now, no more drugs, no more fears. But memories; there were still memories.

'What you need now is a holiday, Miss Tansley,' the psychiatrist had said, briskly misunderstanding. 'Is there somewhere you could go, by the sea perhaps; someone you could go with?' and he had looked at his watch. She wanted to cling; to stay; to come again. But he had finished with her. Her case was closed.

The sun reflected on a silver loch dazzling her eyes with its beauty. 'There is Appin,' she had said. 'I can go to the cottage in Appin.'

'Fine, fine. Do that.' His mind had withdrawn from hers. He was already thinking of the next patient.

So she had done it. Slowly and methodically she had arranged it all. The cottage would be hers for a month with the seas and the lochs and the islands beyond the west where men go when they die and stay for ever young. All of it was hers.

But it had all been almost too difficult. The world was

still a menacing place; a place of greys and blacks and angry red. She had had to fight to keep the panic away. And she had thought silently in her bed, her eyes fixed on the cracked crazed ceiling which was no ceiling in the dark, but an infinite chasm, of the silver and the blues of the western shore where she had spent her long happy childhood holidays and she grasped towards the healing and the reality which the salt air must bring to her soul.

'Will you be all right, miss?' The taxi driver's face, beaten red by the wind and sun was crumpled with concern. He waved away the shaking hand which held a painfully calculated ten per cent and picked up her case to carry it to the door.

She proffered the key and he took it and opened it for her. The great stone hearth was unchanged. The rocking chair was still there. But the people were all gone.

She stretched her lips to smile at him and stood when he had gone, a shiver holding her in the centre of the floor. She could hear echoes. Echoes of her voice as a girl, pretty, carefree, happy as only the ignorant can be and of her brother, more raucous his and loud, but with the same intonation. And the Fairburn cousins, their two shouts indistinguishable twin from twin, and the gentle remonstrations of her mother; and her father putting his hands to his ears as he sorted out the lines for the sea trout. And the barks of Romany and Diddakoi, the two Battersea waifs, so long ago buried in the garden beneath the apple tree. She shivered again and felt the tears pricking her eyelids.

'Cry, my child. The day you can cry you will be on the way to being cured,' the psychiatrist's level voice echoed in her head. The tears were there all right, but still they would not fall. As they had not fallen since the car had spun out of reality and into nightmare taking mother, father, brother, lover all from her in one clap of thunder.

Slowly she walked into the bedroom which had once

been hers. It was the smallest and it overlooked the island, shimmering in the evening waters. She opened the window and looked out, breathing sweet thyme and lavender from the flower below. The stone was cold and hard to her elbows but she leaned there a long time watching for the luminous highland night which almost never came. Then at last she lay down on the bed, her coat still on, her shoes kicked wearily aside and she slept, not hearing the owls, the jumping fish and the hill noises of the night.

Instinct told her she had to walk each day. Exhaustion brought forgetfulness. It brought sleep and slowly appetite and a suspicion of colour to her sallow cheeks. She would take crumbs to the squirrels and sit for hours beyond the great rock gazing at the sky. She took a sketch book and slowly captured the growing beauty as it fought its way into her consciousness.

Once she saw a small boy looking at her from behind the rocks. When she looked again he had gone and she found herself half-smiling, sensing his peeking eyes. To her he was just another squirrel.

She watched the men with their boats, the tourists with their cameras, the children, shadows of her own past, as they crossed her path, but she stayed silent and withdrawn. In the village store they decided she was some kind of a natural, harmless, lonely, to be watched over with gentle unobtrusive care.

Then came the old man from over the hill. He knocked at the door and greeted her with a grin. 'How are you, lass? I heard you were here. Would you be the same little Josie Tansley who came in my boat with her dad?'

She looked at him frowning, remembering. Strangers' faces had gone; only the dead were with her. She grasped for a name: 'Ruaraidh . . . Macdonald?'

And he shook her hand the harder. 'You remember an

old man, lass. Tell me. How are your family? Is your father well?'

He alone in all the world did not know, had not heard the thunder clap. 'They're all dead, Mr Macdonald.' She felt her lips speak, as her mind receded from the truth. 'Killed.'

She turned away blindly, but the old man came on. His arm was round her, his faded blue eyes near hers. She saw his spontaneous tears and suddenly her own came flooding. At last the dam in her heart which had held back all things broke and she knelt, her head on the knee of an old highland man and wept.

He knew about broken hearts. He knew about the loss which is too great to bear. He sat all night, her head in his lap, his eyes fixed on the embers of the fire as they died one by one to white ash. The night came through the open windows almost as bright as day, scented, warm, moonlit. Only owls were abroad. His dog lay on the mat, its ear pricked to the night noises, its eye occasionally opening, watching its master and the girl in her grief.

Then the dawn came; rosy, gentle, feeling with hesitant fingers round the undrawn curtains and she slept at last. He picked her up, laid her on the bed and sat beside her, his lined face sad with the knowledge of generations of death and grief, pondering on the words of comfort he alone must give.

When she opened her eyes at last she lay purged and dreamlike, and she listened to his quiet voice telling the stories of the centuries which console and heal and she smiled at him at last and reached for his hand. The pain had dulled; the scar inside her mind had begun to heal of its own. Sadness there would always be, but he gave her resignation and a little hope that day.

When the squirrels came again she looked round for the little boy and seeing him called out. He came, nervous, chubby, a wicked cheerful child and she ran with him down to the water and watched him throw stones that skidded and bumped on the glittering surface and after a while she tried to do it too. And when her pebbles sank with a plop into the water she laughed.

In the store they noticed the change and were glad for her. People stopped to look at her sketches now and she found she could talk again. The world was no longer hostile, no longer viewed behind a wall of thick black glass, against which she beat with bloodied fists. It was sweet and young and she could breathe again.

Slowly she found she believed once more in the future. She went to the phone box and dialled a friend. Once he had been more. He understood; he bore no grudges; he came to be with her and gently took her hand. He would be the first bastion against loneliness. The first positive step. She accepted too a puppy from Ruaraidh Macdonald and together the four of them, the boy, the girl, her friend and the dog ran on the sands amongst the ribbons of emerald weed.

Each night she cried a little less, each day she laughed a little more. The agony was numbed. Her eyes were learning how to shine again; she was beginning to know hope.

The friend saw that she had fallen to the bottom of a muddy pool wide-eyed and gasping, flailing with arms towards the depths of darkness. Then slowly she had risen, inexorably and involuntarily, the will to survive triumphing over the will to die.

He slept in the bedroom that had been her brother's. Each day he saw her opening a little, like a flower. But he kept his distance, watchful, afraid lest he overstep some faint invisible line which would drive her once more from the sun. For him she was a sacred virgin, inviolable and goddesslike in her bereavement, with her delicate blue-veined pallor of the skin.

By the great rock he would sit, the width of the rock between them, idly throwing pebbles at the setting sun, while she dipped her brush in the carmine-stained waters of a rock pool and traced the scene on her page.

'Shall we take a boat to the Island?' he asked at last after many days, screwing his eyes to watch a cormorant flop from its perch on a weed-draped rock into clumsy flight.

She nodded absently. 'It could be fun.' Once her eyes might have sparkled. Now they looked at him with quiet detached amusement. She saw him as an overgrown schoolboy, as playful and as harmless as the puppy.

They hired a boat and he rowed her, pulling quietly with the tide towards the dusky island. Trails of light still crossed the rippled water. The cormorant was back on its perch, its wings outspread to dry.

'The evening is like golden velvet,' she whispered, her fingers trailing in the cool. She faced him across the oars, watching his corded muscles contracting and expanding beneath the dark plaid shirt. Beads of perspiration stood on his brow. His eyes were over her shoulder fixed on the distance, the pupils small with the glowing sunset.

'Are you watching where we're going?' He had felt her gaze and smiled without looking.

'You're doing fine.' Her voice still cracked when she spoke from a long silence; cracked and hesitated before it sounded true. 'Don't hurry; it's so beautiful.' Her toes were bare in the warm greasy water which slopped on the bottom boards of the boat. A strand from the fringe of her shawl trailed in the wet, floated and unravelled, scarlet, unnoticed in the oily black of it.

When the boat grounded on the shingle he let the oars go, dead wings in the heavy rowlocks.

'Shall we walk or sit and watch the sunset?' he asked, his voice slightly raised above the rustle of the water on the stones and she stood up for answer, her arms out to balance as the boat rocked and she jumped clumsily to the shore.

They watched the clouds of midges dancing on the dusky water and whirling in columns above the beach. He slapped his neck and arms but her cool skin stayed untouched and she watched him, faintly amused again. There was a broch to see. They looked for it in the gloaming, amongst long dew wet grasses and listened to the lonely wail of a night bird echoing across the water. She held his hand over the uneven ground and to climb a fence and together they untangled the damp fringe of her shawl from the rusty wire. Their fingers touched by accident and she glanced up at his face.

He smiled and she felt the night wind cold about her shoulders. 'One day I must go back to London,' she whispered. 'To the flat.'

'I'll be with you, Josie. You needn't go alone.'

They gazed at the stones which had once formed a great tower.

'Was this it?' she whispered. 'Is this all that's left?'

'Josie, please.' His hand tightened over hers.

She was gazing at the black stones, thinking of the ancient hands which had built it strong and resilient. They were dead too, those men. 'What's it all for?' She sighed and turned away, not seeking an answer and he followed her, his eyes on the ground.

Near the boat she spread her shawl on the short turf and patted it as she sat down. 'Come. Make love to me now. That's all there is left to do.' She smiled enigmatically, the evening star in both her eyes. He knelt and held her shoulders, puzzled. Seeking to understand.

'You mean it, Josie? That's what you want?'

49

Slowly she unbuttoned her blouse and his fingers, gently seeking her breast felt a prickle of gooseflesh as the cool night wind stroked the warm skin. Somewhere an oystercatcher whistled down the strand as the man bent his lips to the small hard nipples.

She cradled his head in her arms and watched the distant loom of a lighthouse in the limpid night. She could still see the outlines of the trees on the opposite shore, even without the help of the silver crescent moon, lying on its back above the hills.

Quietly she slipped down till her head was resting on the ground and the night was eclipsed by the eyes of the man. She was not afraid any more. She was one with the past and the future, the day and the night. The living and the dead both were within her embrace.

They rowed home at last in the cool of the dawn, watching the spreading ripples as fish rose to break the surface and seeing the trails of weed colouring the turning tide's edge. Already she looked on the world with calm maternal eyes, sure of the seed she had desired. Her cool grey eyes met those of the man at the oars and lingered and at last she smiled, knowing that for her now there was a future.

She did not let him travel on the train. She carried within her a new self sufficiency such as she had not known before and she treasured it with the memories of the silver Appin seas. He stood to wave on the platform, half-guessing what she already knew, that she carried his child and that for now she needed no more of him.

She sat in her sleeping compartment once more quiet and alone listening to the beat of the wheels on the rails, her hands folded on her lap.

In her head she still carried the image of the velvet night in the north and she used it as an amulet against the towns the trains passed through, dense black jungles glowing with lights in the dark. Then came the outskirts of London in the early hours of the morning.

Josie slipped the key into the lock and stepped into her dusty flat, looking round with quiet resolution. The photograph of her broken family still lay face down beside the phone, where she had dropped it, splinters of glass scattered on the carpet. She stooped without stopping to take off her coat and picked it up, piling the glass carefully on to the frame. Beside it was a vase of dead roses. She swept them out, their stems long and dry and threw them in the bin. Then she went to open the windows.

'Come on, junior,' she said out loud. 'Let's choose which room you're going to have and then we'll go out and buy some paint. We're going to begin again, just you and me, as soon as we've unpacked.'

She caught sight of herself in a mirror and smiled gently, staring into her own dark grey eyes. 'It's all right, Josie my love, you're not talking to yourself. That's not been one of your troubles. You're talking to a real person; or at least he soon will be.' She unbuttoned her coat bit by bit and slipped it off, letting it trail from her fingers to the floor. 'And after you my little one, I have a feeling there may be another little brother to keep you company. I'll discuss it with your father when he gets in touch.' She thought of the quiet face on the platform, the wistful hand waving goodbye, and smiled again. Next week would be soon enough to ring him. She didn't want to hurry things. She couldn't go any further. Not yet.

51

Feline Express

It was one of those smouldering London nights when the air smells strangely bitter-sweet and exciting; a night for dancing on lawns or lying back in a punt and drifting beneath shadowy drooping willows. Those things were just dreams for me though. I was, as usual, at home; and in bed.

I sat up and groped for my clock. It was just after two. I must have been asleep, for the last time I had looked it had been midnight exactly. Cinderella's hour. I sighed uncomfortably, trying to find a cooler corner on the hot pillow for my aching head. Then suddenly I sat bolt upright, my heart thumping with fear. There was someone moving round in the kitchen next to my room. That must have been what woke me. I strained my ears. Silence. Then, quite distinctly I heard a scraping noise as though something were being pushed along the table.

I looked round desperately for a weapon of some kind to defend myself with. I didn't have a poker of course; the best I could do was a high heeled shoe. I crept out of bed and reached for my dressing gown, then, with the heel of the shoe held out menacingly before me in a shaking hand, I crept to my door and listened again. The whole flat was silent. Beyond my door lay the tiny hall off which led the kitchen door, next to mine, and opposite them the bathroom and the other room. Sally my flat mate had been sent to Brussels by her firm for six weeks, so I was alone. The telephone was in the kitchen. I quietly turned the handle of the door and opened it a crack. I looked out. The kitchen door was ajar.

Suddenly there was the most tremendous crash, followed by a terrified mewing and a scrabble of paws. I laughed out loud with relief.

Pushing open the door I clicked on the light. The kitchen, like my room, was at the front of the house. It had a small dormer window leading onto a broad parapet which ran along the house tops the entire length of the street. I had left the window wide open because of the heat. My visitor must have crept along from another flat and, seeing the open window, come in. My beautiful flowering geranium lay in the midst of its shattered pot on the floor beneath the window. There was no sign of the cat. It must have heard me and fled the way it had come, knocking over the plant as it leaped for the window. I got a dustpan and brush and swept up the mess, then checking everything else was in order I stopped to get myself a cold drink from the fridge.

'Mee-ow.'

I jumped. The frightened squeal came from very near me. Then I saw it. Hiding in the dark crack between the fridge and the cupboard was a tiny kitten, with enormous frightened eyes.

'Hello, puss,' I said quietly. 'Was it really you making all that noise?' I held out my hand and twitched my fingers at it enticingly. The eyes immediately stopped looking frightened and looked instead very intelligent indeed. It put its head on one side and scampered out to me.

I picked it up. It was a stripy kitten, with a ridiculous stump of a tail and enormous green eyes; clearly not old enough to be walking lonely parapets under the sky by itself at two in the morning.

53

I gave it some milk and took it back to my room. After exploring thoroughly for a while it scrambled up onto my low divan bed, curled up and went to sleep. It appeared that for the time being at least I had acquired a cat.

I slept beside it, not waking till the sun crept in at the attic-window and fell full on my face. I grabbed the clock. It was after eight and I was going to be very late for work. The kitten had gone. I called it vainly as I made breakfast and dressed, but it must have climbed from my bed to the bookshelf and jumped to my windowsill. I prayed it had not slipped on the parapet and that it could find its way back to its real home.

In the busy office during the day I didn't give the little cat another thought but at night, at home in the flat alone, I wondered where it had come from. It would have been fun to have a kitten for company in lonely London. Sally's friends were kind and often asked me out with them, but since she had been away the phone had stayed depressingly silent. I had only been working in London for a couple of months after all. I could not expect to know many people yet and I was bound to meet people soon, but that didn't stop me wondering and wishing as beautiful moonlit night succeeded moonlit night.

That night she, I decided she must be a she, came to see me again, about eleven this time, her tiny enquiring face all eyes, peering in through the open casement as I lay on my bed reading.

'Hello, Tiger, have you come to keep me company again tonight?' Pleased, I laid down my book to watch her. She jumped to the bookcase and stalked along it, her stumpy tail erect, mewing at me. She came and licked my hand with a tongue like sandpaper and then, politely, showed me where the door was. She licked her lips.

For four nights running Tiger came and had her evening milk drink with me and afterwards curled up with me to sleep. Each morning when I awoke she had disappeared.

The fifth night it poured with rain; heavy thundery rain which cascaded and bounced on the parapet and splashed into the room. Reluctantly I shut the window. Surely she would not come on a night like this. Entirely self-centred and demanding and affectionate only when it pleased her, my five square inches of visitor had a big enough personality to make up in many ways for my lack of human company in the evenings and I found I was missing her very much.

I left my windows open the next night and the next, but she didn't come and sadly I told myself she probably wouldn't come again.

Then one Saturday as I was cleaning the flat, my hair tied in a scarlet cotton handkerchief, she suddenly appeared at the kitchen window. Even in the short time she had not been to see me, she had grown.

I gave her some milk and let her play boxing games with my duster for a while, watching as she danced in the sunbeams on the rug. Suddenly she stopped jumping about, cocked her little head to one side and listened. Then in a minute she had leaped to the bookcase and out onto the parapet and was gone.

I went to the window and leaned out, edging forward beyond the angle of the dormer onto my elbows. To the left and right the long sunlit parapet stretched away the length of the street. I watched her trotting purposefully along, much too near the edge for my liking, till she came to another open window where she disappeared. I looked down nervously at the road, three storeys below and then began to wriggle back. As I edged back I glanced again at the window where Tiger had vanished. There was a young man leaning out, as I was, watching me. I smiled and raised a hand in greeting.

I pottered around with the duster for a while longer, but without Tiger to play with housework had lost all its appeal. So I collected my basket and my purse and ran down to go to the shops.

A few doors down from me a young man was tinkering about with an old car, his head under the bonnet. He stood up as I passed and I had a glimpse of brilliant blue eyes in a tanned face before I went on. I had the feeling he was watching me, but I didn't turn back. It was the young man at Tiger's window.

That night she came to me earlier than usual. I played with her and cuddled her for a long time before at last we fell asleep. Somehow I could not get the image of those blue eyes – her master's blue eyes – out of my mind.

I saw him again next morning climbing into his car as I set off for the post office. I almost hoped he would stop and offer me a lift, but he didn't. He glanced in his mirror though, to see me again after he had driven slowly by. The street seemed a hundred times more lonely when I got back later. The battered car was still missing and glancing up at our windows in the eaves of the high roof tops I saw that although mine were open, his were shut. Tiger would not be coming to visit me today.

His car did not return until after ten that evening, and although my windows stayed open all night Tiger never appeared. I stayed awake a long time hoping to hear her imperious voice from the windowsill, but it never came.

As I sat in the office next day leaning disconsolately on my desk I saw with sad resignation that the skies were clouding over. The heat wave, the weather forecast had said, was over. By lunch the first cold drops of rain were beginning to fall and I thought sadly of the long lonely evenings till Sally came back, my windows shut against wind and rain, my little visitor probably snug in her own basket beside someone else's bed. His bed.

It was coming down in big heavy drops when eventually I reached home that evening after volunteering to stay at work to do some overtime. I threw open the window and leaned my elbows on the sill. The streets were smelling of wet soot and sweet earth from the garden square round the corner. It was lovely to feel the cool freshness on my face.

Tiger arrived while I was still eating my supper, her fur wet and spiky. Around her neck was a little leather collar and attached to it by a little piece of string was some paper. I couldn't believe my eyes. My hands shook as I tried to untie it to take the paper. It was a note: 'How about dinner on Wednesday?' it said. That was all.

I stared at the writing, unbelieving. Was it meant for me? Putting the puzzled little cat firmly down on the carpet I went to the window and wriggled out a little way. His window was closed. He had put her out into the rain knowing she would have to come to me if she didn't want to get wet. To me, or someone else? I didn't know how many windows Tiger visited on her nightly rambles, how many lonely ladies she played with to earn a saucer of milk. There were many windows opening out onto her private cat walk.

I puzzled what to do; I wanted so very much to say yes. For a long time I sat in front of my writing pad, pen in hand while Tiger slept on my bed. At last all I could think of to say was: 'But I don't even know your name . . .' I tied it to her collar and crept at last into bed beside her.

In the morning she was still there and there was a huge puddle on the carpet from the rain which had poured in all night. I was furious. Picking her up I put her outside by force and shut the window behind her in spite of her pitiful mewing. I was angry as much with myself for leaving the window open as with her for not going out in the rain. Probably she wouldn't come back at all now after such an outrage, but my carpet was ruined and in the cold light of day I hadn't much faith in a silly scribbled message which was probably a joke. For a moment I regretted not removing my note and tearing it up. Then I shrugged. It would probably have dissolved by the time the poor little cat got home. I glanced out of the window. The rain was still sheeting down and the clouds were black and threatening.

I was like a bear with a sore head at work that day, as I sat gazing out at the rain. I so much wanted the note to be real, and for me. And I knew that it just couldn't be. Things like that don't happen in real life.

By about four o'clock the sky had cleared a little and as I walked home from the bus the sun broke through the clouds and glistened dazzlingly on the wet pavements. My heart lifted a little as I set the key in the lock. I had bought myself a new paperback and a pizza on my home to cheer myself up a bit. I was sure Tiger wouldn't come again after the way I had treated her that morning and I did not let myself even think about the message on her collar. I knew I wanted too much for her to come again with another.

She arrived about half past eleven, standing as if uncertain of her welcome at the window. I could see at once, with thumping heart, that she had a new message tied to her collar. I was terrified she would turn and run before I could scoop her off the windowsill and carry her to the kitchen. While she drank her milk I read the letter:

9 Westport Terrace (top bell)

To whom it may concern . . .
May I, Mowgli, being of sound cat-mind, introduce Jonathon Lazenby, bachelor of this parish. He is a respectable gentleman and most desirous of escorting a certain young lady, she being in the habit of tying her hair in a provocative red scarf, to the Bistro

Italiano at 7.30 tomorrow evening. Should she be willing to accept perhaps she would intimate the same to Mowgli who will pass on her message.

by Feline Express, Tuesday

I read the letter again and again, half laughing, unable to believe it to be true. Then at last I wrote my reply.

15 Westport Terrace (top bell)

Miss Anna Winton being the lady with the red scarf, thanks Mowgli very much for her impeccable introduction and has much pleasure in accepting Mr Jonathon Lazenby's kind invitation. She looks forward to meeting him tomorrow night.

by Feline Express

'I'll buy you a tin of salmon tomorrow, Mowgli,' I whispered in her ear as I tied the note to her collar. But I didn't have to. I found Jonathon had already done it and as he said, one tin at a time was quite enough for such a small messenger.

The Consolation Prize

'Would you like some more wine?'
            Under the low ceiling with its criss-cross of darkened beams a curl of smoke levelled and drifted up from the log fire, from the cigarettes of the loudly talking guests, and from his pipe.

Annette stood watching, eyes half shut, her contact lenses not liking the atmosphere, as she clutched the empty wine glass in her hand. She was thinking about the church.

The baby had cried – a high wail, echoing up under the roof of the nave, the sound curling like the smoke around the rose window. A lonely sound which had made her drag her eyes back down to the font, which someone had decorated with threads of white daisies, as she blinked back sudden stupid tears.

Celia's child. Duncan's child. The child which might have been hers . . .

'Some more wine?'

She was beautiful; exquisite. Tiny hands waving indignantly over the pale lace. Natasha Anne. Her hair as golden as her father's; her eyes already the same blue. Or were all babies' eyes that colour?

'Wine?'

The pleasant face was smiling at her; the green eyes quirky and humorous as they watched her. 'If I could deliver it to your planet, I would.'

'Planet?' She turned her full attention to him at last, bewildered.

'You *are* on another planet?'

'Oh, I see!' Embarrassed, Annette looked back at Celia, still standing near the door, the child in the crook of her arm. Then she laughed. 'I'm sorry. I was thinking about the baby.'

'Very appropriate at a christening.' He smiled again. 'I'm Rick Jefferson; your colleague in the godparent stakes.' He captured her empty wine glass and filled it from the bottle in his hand, expertly fielding the slopping liquid as someone jostled him from behind.

Suddenly she felt more cheerful; she smiled. 'Of course. I'm sorry. I'm being very rude, I'm Annette.'

He grinned again. 'Can I fetch you something to eat? Say yes. Then I can put down this bottle and pick up a glass of my own when I go to the table.'

He wasn't very tall; not much taller than she. But his shoulders were broad and his frame solid. She found herself giggling at his pantomime of self starvation. 'I'd love something to eat. Thank you.'

'And you won't fly back to Mars or Venus or wherever?'

'Promise.'

She watched him thread his way across the room towards the long table. He paused near Celia and she saw him smile and touch the baby's hand – then he moved on. He collected a glass and two plates of food, and she saw him turning back in her direction.

'All alone?'

Suddenly Duncan was standing in front of her. She felt her throat contract a little as she looked up at his face. Could she have so soon forgotten how tall he was?

'Rick is fetching me something to eat. She's a lovely baby, Duncan.'

He was looking down at her intently. 'Annette. You

61

really didn't mind us asking you to be godmother? It was Celia's idea—'

'Of course not.' She forced herself to smile. 'I'm honoured.' And she turned to Rick, reaching with relief for the plate he offered her. For a moment the three of them stood there in silence. Then Duncan smiled and shrugged and walked away . . .

Later, as she and Rick let themselves out of the French window, there was a breath of summer in the garden and a soft evening shimmer in the air.

Annette shivered, her coat around her shoulders as they slipped out of the hot noisy room.

Rick grinned at her. 'Are you sure you want to go out?'

Nodding she sipped her wine and stepped onto the grass. 'I get claustrophobia at parties.'

'Me too.' He followed her, leaving his glass balanced carefully on the head of a lichen-covered statue at the edge of the steps. 'Are you going to tell me about it?'

'What?'

'You and Duncan. There was a "you and Duncan" wasn't there?'

She nodded, suddenly not minding his knowing. 'Oh yes. There was a me and Duncan.'

The scent of flowers was almost overwhelming. It had been summer then too. The first time she had come to this house . . .

Her office door was permanently open, so people walked through it. That was the idea, Annette's boss said with a laugh and Duncan was the third person to walk through it that morning. By mistake.

He was tall, lean and untidy, wearing a cotton sweatshirt and jeans and quite obviously not in the right place.

He leaned on her desk, towering over her, his hair tousled. He was grinning broadly.

'I'm on the wrong floor, right?'

She found herself smiling back, drawn irresistibly by the smile.

'Right. Wrong floor. You'll be wanting...' She hesitated, looking him up and down, her head on one side. 'The architect upstairs?'

He grinned. 'Try again.'

'The accountant?'

'No.'

'Then it must be the Inland Revenue.'

'As a humble supplicant and blood donor? No.'

'But that only leaves the dress designer.' She collapsed in sudden irreverent giggles.

'At last, you guessed my secret.' His solemn expression was belied by the laughing eyes. 'Don't I look like a potential customer for a dress designer?'

She shook her head, intrigued and disbelieving. But he did not explain. Not then. He did that over lunch.

'Black sheep?' She put down her knife and fork, her voice sliding up into a squeak.

'Five hundred of them.'

'And Kevin Spiggs uses your wool?'

'That's right. His dusky dream range!'

She was very late back to the office.

'Can you believe it, Meg? He breeds black sheep. And Kevin upstairs is going to take all his wool for a season to make sweaters and dresses and sell them for *hundreds* of pounds each!'

Meg raised her eyes to the concealed lighting of the low ceiling above the desk. 'Only you, Annette, could meet a sheep breeder here in St James's! And I suppose you are going to see him again?'

She was.

*

Two weeks later he took her to the farm. It was a long drive and she was tired but the countryside enchanted her. Soft rolling hills, stands of oak and birch, green and silver in the sunlight and then the sheep – not black so much as chocolate and mocha in the soft meadows.

'I can't get involved, Annette. I'm sorry.' The boyish grin, the rumpled hair as he strode at her side through the mud beneath the trees cushioned the words and made them light and easy to ignore. They laughed together so much, finished sentences for each other without even realizing it, liked the same music in the evening as they sat together on the sofa hearing the distant fluting of an owl above the soft notes of the woodwind.

His arm was around her shoulders, drawing her to him; he was solid and warm and reassuring and she was already half-way to being in love. Later, upstairs on the landing, he kissed her goodnight outside her bedroom door, then placed his finger against her lips as she tried to speak. 'No, Annette. I told you. Sleep well, my love.' And he was gone, leaving her lonely and disappointed as she let herself into the dark room and groped for the unaccustomed light switch.

They began to make it a pattern. Duncan would come up to Kevin's office on a Friday, fill in time until five o'clock then together they would climb into his car and wend the long agonizing route through the heavy traffic towards the west. Sometimes they bought chips on the way; sometimes she made sandwiches. Once in a while they listened to the car radio but more often they talked. They talked about everything. Life. Work. Holidays; and sheep. But never about love.

Yet she knew he loved her. It showed in his eyes; in his hesitant glances when he thought she wasn't looking. In the deep, lasting kisses when they lay together on the sofa, listening to the records they had brought with them

64

from town, and finally and ecstatically in his tender love-making when at last he followed her into the now familiar bedroom and took her in his arms . . .

Next morning when she woke he had gone from the bed. She stretched happily and lay gazing at the faint light behind the curtains, listening to the plaintive whistling of a blackbird.

Duncan had gone out to the sheep; later he would come back with the papers and some coffee and perhaps climb into bed, his hair damp from the shower as he laid his head on her breast. Lying in his arms then, clinging to him, her heart full of love, she knew something was still very wrong. But she no longer cared what it was. It was enough that he was there and that she was with him.

Then he went away. 'Only for a couple of weeks, Annette. On business to Switzerland. I wish you could come too, my love.'

She'd known instantly, by the way he lowered his eyes and mumbled, unable to look at her, that he had lied. But which was the lie? That he was going on business, or that he wanted her to come too?

She swallowed her misery and worked extra hours at the office, trying not to think of what he might be doing in Switzerland, of what business a sheep farmer could possibly have in Geneva or the high mountains beyond.

When he returned she knew she had lost him again. Oh, he was pleased to see her; and his warmth when he drew her to him was real, but something had changed. His reserve had returned and she knew that, if she asked, he would say again, 'We must not get involved, Annette,' and that for him it would be true.

She cried a lot that summer, unhappy in her love, seeking comfort in the arms which were the source of her unhappiness, but unable to tear herself away.

It was his mother who told her. His parents lived not

far away, watching their son's farming efforts with tolerant amusement – but they were less amused by Annette.

She was a little in awe of his mother. Janet was so capable and hearty, so unruffled by anything. So it was a shock one morning to come down into the kitchen wearing Duncan's bathrobe to find Janet standing there, her coat still on, staring out of the window at the garden. The woman turned and looked at Annette, her face full of compassion. The expression hit Annette like a hammer. Her veins iced over as she guessed instinctively something of what was to come.

'Annette dear, Duncan tells me that you and he are not involved. That yours is an open relationship, whatever that means.' Janet's face had become unusually pink and shiny. 'I don't believe him altogether. I think you are more involved than he realizes and I don't want you to get hurt.'

It was suddenly so cold in the room.

'I won't get hurt,' Annette said cheerfully. 'Duncan's quite right. It is an open relationship.'

'And so you know about Celia?'

There was a lump of something in her throat, pressing down on her windpipe, stopping her breathing properly.

'Celia?' She had to pretend. She had to say she didn't care.

'His fiancée, Annette.' Janet's voice was unusually gentle. 'She will be coming back you know.'

'Where is she?' Her voice sounded strange in her own ears, thin and high, like a bird screaming in a storm.

'She's still in Switzerland, at the clinic. But she will be completely cured. And Duncan swore he'd wait for her, my dear. He swore.'

'Of course he did.' She sounded light and carefree now as she pulled the belt of the robe more tightly round her slim waist. 'You don't have to worry, Janet. Really.'

Oh God, why hadn't he told her? How could he have

let her go on imagining that it would all have been all right in the end.

The words echoed round her brain as she dressed and pulled on her light jacket. Duncan was out with a sick ewe. His mother had left the house, spinning the wheels of the car in her agitation. The house was silent and deserted; the house she had secretly, in her heart, thought of already as home.

She walked across the bare garden, hands in pockets and looked out across the fields. There were no sheep there now; they were desolate, like her.

Then he was there beside her, his face glowing, his eyes laughing, his warmth and humour reaching out to her. 'What about breakfast? I'm starving.'

'How's the ewe?' The steady cheerfulness of her voice amazed her.

'She'll be OK. Crisis is over. Was that ma's car I saw?' Annette nodded. 'She couldn't wait. Just looked in to say hello.'

And goodbye. Because, of course, Annette could never come to the farm again. She didn't say anything in the end. What was the point of screaming and ranting at him? He had made no promises, held out no hope of the future. He had assumed they were still working from the first blueprint. 'No involvement, Annette my love. Just a good time while we're both at a loose end, OK?'

In the house, as she made the coffee with absolute concentration, Duncan said, 'Paula and Tony have asked us to dinner next weekend to see how their extension is progressing.' He did not look up. His face was buried in the newspaper.

'Oh what a shame. I'd love to have gone.' She was pouring the coffee, not looking at him, but she heard the rustle of the paper as he put it down.

'Why can't you?' Amazed. Even slightly hurt.

'I can't come down next weekend, Duncan, I'm sorry. In fact not for several weeks. I'm tied up.' She put the cup on the table without raising her eyes to his. 'It's nearly Christmas after all. I've so much to do. I'm ashamed I've allowed myself to come down here so much!' That was it. Bright and brittle. Don't ever show how much you are hurting inside.

She could feel him looking at her; imagine the thoughtful puzzlement with which he was watching. And she knew she would not be fooling him for an instant. She looked up at last and met his gaze, smiling. 'You'll have to do without me, Duncan. I think it's best.' She could not fight a sick enemy, one she had never seen. Another flesh and blood woman, yes, with nails bared and teeth set, but not this pale consumptive image, with her overtones of tragedy.

Duncan stood up and came round the table. 'Annette . . .'

'No, please. Don't say anything. Make my apologies to Paula. Perhaps I'll come back after . . .'

After what? Christmas? His marriage? His birthday? After it stopped hurting?

In the afternoon she packed slowly not waiting to read the Sunday papers with him by the fire, taking from the kitchen a couple of carrier bags to put all the extras in. The things which she had grown used to leaving behind week after week. Her records, her boots, a couple of books, the heavy Aran sweater she never wore in town. She piled them by the front door and took the old duffle coat off the hook. That, too, must go back. When she looked round he was standing in the doorway watching her.

'My mother did this.'

'No, Duncan. I always knew it wouldn't last. I just didn't know how long I'd got.'

He put his hands on her shoulders and drew her to him. 'Supposing I told you I'd change. I've grown so fond of you, Annette. I don't know that I can live without you. Not now.'

She felt her throat constrict. 'You must,' she whispered.

He took her to the train at last and found her a corner seat with her bags, then he jumped off as the train was already moving – no time for any goodbyes. But there was no one sitting opposite her to shame her into holding back her tears and she felt them run scalding down her cheeks as she turned her face to the window and saw the countryside gathering speed until it blurred and faded behind the dirty glass.

On Friday, in case he came, she rang the office and told them she had a migraine. The following week she went in as usual, thinking she felt more able to cope, but she did not have to. He did not appear.

She did not know whether he came up to see Kevin Spiggs again. She suspected he had never really needed to anyway, after that first time. He had come only to see her.

It was three months before she heard from him again. He phoned her at the office. 'How are you, Annette?'

Her heart, cured, distracted, no longer his, turned upside down at the sound of his voice.

'I'm fine. How are you?'

She thought she managed to sound casual. She fixed her mind determinedly on Robert, the new man in her life, who would be taking her out later that evening; Robert who had three times asked her to marry him.

'Can I take you out to lunch tomorrow?' Duncan sounded uncomfortable and quite suddenly she forgot her own unhappiness in a wave of sympathy for him.

'That would be nice. But it will have to be fairly brief I'm afraid. We're very busy at the office at the moment.'

'Fine. I'll pick you up around 12.30.'

She got up an hour early the next day to dress with special care and put on some make up, and one look at his face told her that there had been no point. His love for her, if that was what it had been, had gone. Rising from her desk she picked up her bag and followed him out into the street.

'I wanted to tell you myself that I'm getting married.' He said it at once, before they had even ordered.

'I'm glad for you.'

She realized as she said it that she meant it. For herself she was desolate, but the shining happiness she had seen on his face was so special she could not grudge him. Not that. That was what love did to a man, or a woman. 'To Celia, I take it?'

He nodded and grinned. 'So you did know. Afterwards I was so angry with myself. I thought perhaps I'd misled you. I couldn't have borne it if I'd hurt you, Annette.' His hand was on hers on the table. 'You're very special to me, you know. You always will be.'

'And you to me, Duncan.' She drew her hand away gently. Had he really never guessed how much she loved him? Had he really believed they were both just passing the time? She looked up at his face and then sadly she looked away.

They saw each other twice more after that. Once by accident in the foyer of the office building and once for coffee in the lunch hour two weeks before his wedding. He had a brown paper parcel under his arm.

'This is for you. From Celia and me. A wedding present for you.'

It was an exquisite sweater in soft chocolate-coloured wool.

She did not tell him she had given Robert back his ring. If you did not love someone with the all-consuming joy with which Duncan loved his Celia, there could be no future. She was sure of that.

She had not heard from Duncan again for two years.

Then had come the letter asking her to be godmother to his first child.

At first she was angry; then she cried. Then she laughed, and after writing two indignant letters of refusal tore them up and rang the farm. Duncan answered.

'Are you serious?' she asked.

'Perfectly. I want my daughter to grow up with humour and understanding. Who better to teach it to her than you?'

Was that really the way she had reacted?

'What happened to Robert?' he asked after a pause.

'No sense of humour and no understanding!'

'I'm sorry.'

'So am I.'

Behind the half drawn curtains the christening party was in full swing. But in the garden it was very quiet. Rick was watching her.

'You're telling the story against yourself,' he said gently. 'I think Duncan was a bastard.'

She shook her head. 'When you think about it, he displayed all the virtues. It just happens they were not directed at me.' She shivered suddenly. 'Shall we go back inside. I expect they're going to cut the cake or whatever they do at christenings. Did you go to their wedding?'

He shook his head, 'Did you?'

'I wasn't asked.'

Suddenly Rick laughed. 'Do you know who I am?'

'No. Should I?'

'I'm the man who asked Celia to marry him in Switzerland. And she nearly said yes. The only reason she didn't was this mysterious man she'd left in England who, she said, would wait for her no matter what. I told her she was mad.' He took Annette's hand and she found herself

71

enjoying his warm grasp. 'So we're in the same boat, you and I. Rejected lovers.'

He grinned, looking anything but sad about it and suddenly she found herself laughing with him. 'You mean if I'd stayed with Duncan and fought, you'd have married Celia? She wouldn't have been left alone to fade away after all?'

'That's right.'

Annette was speechless for a moment. 'But she does love Duncan?' she asked hesitantly, after a long pause.

'Oh yes, she loves him again now.'

'And are you still sorry you lost her?' She looked at him squarely. He was staring up the steps towards the house, his expression enigmatic, his eyes narrowed in the dusk.

Slowly he shook his head. 'Not in the least. They deserve each other. After all, theirs is the classic love story. The happy ending against all odds.' He was still holding her hand as he led the way back into the house.

'And we were the odds?'

'I'd say so, wouldn't you?' He turned and winked at her as they slipped into the crowded room. Surreptitiously she looked at Duncan. He had grown stouter in the last two years and his hair was already thinning slightly. Perhaps, after all, she had not been as much in love with him as she had thought. She glanced up at Rick and found he was watching her.

'Do you think being godparents was the consolation prize?' she asked solemnly.

'It is often the custom, I believe.' He took two glasses of champagne from a tray and handed her one. 'Let's drink to Natasha Anne who introduced us!'

The Valentine's Day Plot

Of course it had to be a bouquet of flowers for St Valentine's Day. I chose them carefully, one by one, in the florist. Not less than 50p a bloom. She had always liked pink so those were the ones I selected. 'Would you like them gift-wrapped, Sir?' the girl in the shop asked, simpering, but I shook my head. That aspect of things I would deal with myself.

When I had finished with them I must admit they looked good. I tied an enormous bow of red satin ribbon round the bottom and stood back to admire the finished article. There was no way of seeing the little glass bottle deep amongst the glossy leaves until the bouquet was unwrapped. The bottle said Dior. I tied it in with thread to make sure it was secure; I didn't want it breaking and spoiling my surprise.

I knew she wouldn't be able to resist opening it and smelling it to make sure. And that, I confidently expected, would be the last inquisitive thing the lady ever did. It had after all been her nosiness which led to her finding out about me and to her lucrative career, at my expense, in blackmail. It's strange how some women take to that particular hobby.

I knew delivering the flowers would be a problem and I still hadn't decided at breakfast exactly how to do it.

Obviously I couldn't do it myself. One sight of me and she would suspect something.

Carefully I loaded the flowers into my car, propping them on the seat beside me and drove to The Avenue, which was just two streets away from her place. Then, pulling in to the side of the road, I sat and thought.

It was so easy of course, in the end. Two little boys came down the road, neat in identical grey shorts and blazer.

'Hey fellas!' I wound down the window. They stopped and looked at me suspiciously. I winked. 'Want to earn yourselves a pound on the way to school?' They looked at each other and hesitated. 'Each,' I added; that's inflation for you! 'Listen; it's not difficult.' I beckoned them close and lowered my voice conspiratorially. 'It's St Valentine's Day, right?' One of them smirked, and the other raised an eyebrow with horribly adult cynicism. I ignored it. 'I want you to take these flowers round the corner and give them to a lady. That's all. No problem?'

No problem. They took the flowers, listened politely to my instructions and to my threats of what would happen if they dumped the flowers and ran, and exchanged giggling glances when I gave them the address. Then they pocketed their money.

I sat back and watched them round the corner. They were just about young enough, I reckoned, to do as I asked with no lip. When they were out of sight I drove as fast as I could go to the office.

It was a pretty ordinary sort of day really, considering. I wondered when I would hear what had happened. I doubted if it would be on the evening news. It depended when that stuffy husband of hers came home and found her. I caught myself smiling quietly. After what she had done to me, the blackmailing interfering beautiful bitch, she deserved everything she was going to get. I glanced at my watch. Perhaps it was already over.

There was a lot of work to get through that day, so I ordered a sandwich lunch. When the phone rang I had just reached for my can of beer.

The strange thing was I didn't recognize her voice at first. Then she said, 'Thank you for the flowers, David.' Then I knew. She went on, sarcastically I thought, 'It was such a touching thought. Really the last thing I expected from you. You obviously chose them with such care.'

'What flowers?' The sweat stood out on my forehead suddenly. I had nearly been caught out and said, 'I'm glad you like them', or something equally fatuous.

'Oh come now,' her voice purred slightly. 'You don't have to pretend with me, David. Only you would send such a perfect bouquet. Your taste was always impeccable.

I stuttered slightly before regaining my cool. 'I'm glad someone still sends you flowers, love. Not me though, I'm afraid. Didn't they send a note with them or something?'

'No; no note.' She paused. 'It was so sweet, too, to put a bottle of scent in, David. You shouldn't have. Really. And Dior as well. You know, that's been my favourite perfume since we first met all those years ago.'

My hand was shaking a little as it held the receiver. 'Have you sniffed it to make sure?' I tried to laugh. 'You can't always believe the label, you know.'

'Oh indeed you can't, David.' She chuckled, and I could feel the small hairs on the back of my neck standing up at the sound. 'I'm afraid I didn't get the chance to smell your little gift, my dear. You see I'm afraid I dropped it. By mistake of course; out of the kitchen window actually. You'd never believe how concentrated they make perfume nowadays, David. It must have cost you a fortune. Do you know, it burned a hole right through the concrete. Imagine what it might have done to my poor nose.'

'Imagine!' I agreed sourly. The cunning female had seen through everything.

'What made you think it was from me, my love?' I asked casually. 'You know I can't afford to spend that kind of money on you. Not any more. You've milked me dry.'

She laughed, a beautiful tinkling sound, as though she were really happy. 'You had a spot of bad luck there, David. You see one of the little boys you bribed was my son. He'd been spending the night with a friend in The Avenue. You never met him before, did you? It just happens that they're both very keen on cars. You see you're the only person we know, dear, with a Bentley Continental with your initials on the number plate. Really, you should have come by taxi!'

I reached for my beer and swallowed the lot down fast.

'I don't think I will admit to anything,' I muttered. 'It might spoil the whole romantic illusion.'

'It would rather, dear.' I could actually hear her smiling. 'The trouble is, David,' she went on. 'I felt I had to tell my husband that you've started sending me flowers and I'm afraid he's immensely angry. You see he's a very jealous man. And he thinks you're in love with me.'

'More fool him,' I couldn't resist saying, but she went on as if I hadn't spoken.

'He really took it very badly, David. In fact he's on his way over now. I thought, for old times' sake I'd warn you,' and she hung up on me without so much as saying goodbye.

I sat gazing at the empty beer can for a few minutes, wondering. She couldn't be serious. Could she?

I don't quite know how he got past my secretary, but he arrived quite unannounced. He stood in front of my desk for a long minute, then he smiled.

'No other man woos my wife with flowers,' he said very solemnly.

'Dead right,' I was about to say, 'they don't,' but he

forestalled me. He took a revolver out of his pocket and hooked his finger over the trigger. He never gave me any time to explain.

But I won in the end: now I haunt them both.

'There was a time when I was almost happy . . .'

There was a brittle splintering as her foot slipped on the ridges of the cart track and the ice shivered delicately across the ruts in a labyrinth of crystal slivers. She hadn't been concentrating; she had been gazing into the distance where on either side of her the fields stretched like dull brown hessian towards the hedges. In the summer, when she had been here before, they had been a ripe, rich gold; somehow she had not expected them to have changed so much.

With a little shiver Jacie dug her hands deeper into her pockets and walked doggedly on. She had to get there before the mist-shrouded sun disappeared behind the hills and left her in the cold darkness. She almost wished now that she hadn't come at all. Perhaps it was a mistake to come back – to try and recapture those memories which haunted her. She hesitated for the first time, but already in front of her she could see the dark outline of the ruined arches rising starkly from the earth amongst the bare winter trees and irresistibly she was drawn on.

She stood for a while in the shadows, feeling the wind teasing her hair from the scarf around her head, gazing down at the patch of rimed grass where her feet and Brian's had stood, so close together. It had been like another lifetime then, in the summer, that time when she was almost happy.

She shrugged suddenly, shaking the loosened hair out of her eyes and pulled her collar up closer. The cool sun had gone now and night was coming faster than she had expected, moaning softly in the wind amongst the crumbling stones, darkening the fields. Suddenly, irrationally, she was afraid. She glanced over her shoulder, pressing back against the green damp of the stones, smelling their dankness, listening as she had that last time to the story they seemed to cry out of sorrow and pain. Her heart was beating fast somewhere high in the back of her throat and she pressed herself into the corner of the walls which had once formed the nuns' chapter house. It was then, glancing sideways, forcing herself to be calm, that she saw the web.

The spider had thrown its net across the corner between the rough stones, a hexagonal of perfect diamanté, glittering with frost even in the near dark. Jacie raised her hand in wonder and then swallowing a sob of relief held back, remembering the summer. Was it the same determined little creature which had returned and made good the wreck of its web which her clumsy fingers had torn into ashy fragments that last day? The sticky silken threads had been caught up and retied. She gazed at it until the dusk faded into darkness and she could no longer see even the frosty outlines of the shape. Would it be the same for her? Could the wreck of her own happiness be made good too? Would he come back to her and rescue her from herself again? Pressing her hands deep in her pockets she gave the dark corner where the web hung one last look, then she turned and slipping and stumbling in the dark she began to run back down the track towards the farm.

*

Ever since her childhood Jacie had felt different from other people. Partly, she now accepted, it was the way she was; partly it had been her mother's fault for not understanding.

'Jacie Stacey

Her silly vest is lacy!'

the children at school had sung, dancing around her as they changed for gym and the teacher had sent a note home to her mother: 'If Jane could wear something a little less elaborate . . . broderie anglaise is not really suitable for school wear . . .'

Jacie had looked up fearfully as her mother tore open the envelope, waiting for the explosion she was sure would come; somehow feeling herself to blame for the unacceptability of the trimming on her liberty bodice. There was an explosion, but not of anger; it was of laughter. Her pretty unpredictable mother had hugged her. 'Oh darling, I must buy you woolly vests and make you a conformist,' she had gurgled delightedly and Jacie had breathed a sigh of relief. She wanted nothing more than to conform in a woolly vest. It embarrassed her when her mother tried to make her different; it embarrassed her when her mother laughed and talked with the other mothers at collecting time and pulled her pigtails, saying, 'this one is mine'. All she wanted was to disappear and be wholly invisible. The more her mother drew attention to her and made her pretty – and she was pretty, there was no getting away from that – the more she hated it. If a teacher looked at her she trembled.

Later it had been the same. As she grew up she had hidden away from the other girls her own age, taking refuge in drawing which she found was the only way to express her feelings. She would hide in her bedroom, ignoring her mother's pleas to come out, endlessly sketching the roof tops and the trees which she could see from her window and putting into the strokes of her pencil all the pent-up emotion which she felt but did not understand.

'You'll grow out of it, darling. It's a phase. I was shy at your age,' her mother reassured her time and again, but Jacie could see the puzzled hurt in her mother's eyes and knew in her heart that her mother had never felt the way she did. She had never known the agony of not belonging and, worse, of not wanting to belong in spite of the ache of rejection, as first schoolgirls and then college contemporaries formed close circles which seemed to exclude her.

'What's wrong with me?' she asked in anguish, talking in the end in desperation to the same apple tree in the garden which she had addressed so often as a child. She received no reply.

Once she began working it was perhaps a little better. She gained confidence because she was good at her job. She was a designer; sometimes freelance, sometimes working for long periods for one firm and always, when she moved on, they were sorry to lose her. She was deft, competent and quietly efficient and managed to blend mutely with the grey carpet and beige wall, only occasionally being subjected to agonizing blush-making notice. Once or twice she went out with the men she met in these offices, but her terror and the rigid formality of her shoulders held them at bay. They never asked her a second time although long ago she had realized, catching sight of herself unexpectedly in a mirror, that she had inherited her mother's beauty.

There was one man she had liked a little; the partner in charge of her department at the last job but one. He was a rugged solidly built man with strangely flecked Irish eyes and enough shy charm to lull her into allowing a lunch hour break to drift on into the early afternoon, and they had gone for a walk in the park. They had stood side by side at the edge of the lake, watching the grey froth which lapped at the tarmac path beneath their feet.

'I like it here; it's so quiet.' She glanced up at him shyly with the half smile he found so intriguing glimpsed over the rim of her drawing board. Then avoiding his eyes she looked back towards the ducks, glossy in the plumage of early spring.

'I like quiet places too.' His voice took on a deeper note than usual as he moved little by little until, almost imperceptibly their elbows brushed. He had sensed her isolation; he did not want to hurry her.

'You can still hear the roar of traffic though,' he went on almost in a whisper. 'I'd like to show you somewhere really quiet. Why don't we take a drive down to the country at the weekend? Perhaps have lunch at a pub somewhere?' He too had been staring hard at the ducks as he spoke but now he turned to look at her. He found she was looking straight at him, her eyes wide, the pupils pin points in the light of the sun. Her face had drained of colour.

'It's awfully nice of you, but I couldn't. I couldn't possibly.'

'Why not?'

She shook her head emphatically. 'You hardly know me. You'd be bored. I'm not . . .' She was floundering unhappily. 'I couldn't. I'm sorry. I'm going to see my mother.'

She had drawn away, every muscle tense suddenly, resenting and fearing the brush of his elbow, the intimacy of his glance.

'Hey, I didn't mean – ' he found to his embarrassment that he was blushing too, disconcerted by her reaction. But already she was walking back across the grass, her shoulders squared beneath her coat.

'We're late for work,' she called behind her with a tight

apologetic smile and she almost ran in the direction of the park gates.

Later in the week she half hoped, half feared that he might ask again, but although his smile was just as friendly and his good morning relaxed and warm, he saw to it that they never found themselves alone together again.

And so the years passed. Time brought in the end a kind of serenity. Her shyness crossed the invisible road which turns it to reserve and she ceased to mind when her rejection of people led inevitably to their rejection of her. Or if she minded, she buried the hurt so deep that even she no longer noticed. Only her mother reminded her, and so now she seldom saw her mother.

Sketching, still her only passion, gave her the excuse for long lonely holidays in lonely places. There was one farmhouse in particular on a moor among the hills where she found solace and quiet dour friendship from the farmer and his wife. Once or twice a year, sometimes for long periods when she had saved enough, she made her way there, laden with sketchbooks and easel, to sit in the wiry heather with the wind teasing her hair and no companions save the sudden bulge-eyed hare and the distant wheeling, wheedling buzzards. It was a contented, restful time, for while she was there she forgot her inadequacies and her loneliness and found refuge and total confidence in her art and with the quiet couple with whom she stayed.

She had been going there for three years before she found the abbey. So often her footsteps retraced automatically the same paths through the heather and close-cropped tangled bilberries, taking her to landmarks of her own invention, that she rarely explored more distant valleys and dips in the rolling moors. There the fields, bright with ripening corn, encroached on the wildness of the landscape, reaching out to tame it with the richness of the fertile farms and thick growing woodlands. The ruins were hidden in a wooded valley of ancient trees, guarded by nettles and fierce sprays of thorn and bramble at the end of a cart track through the fields, and there she first met Brian.

She stumbled on him, almost literally, not seeing him until it was too late to turn and flee as he lay sprawled behind a low wall, field glasses pressed to his eyes, focused on a high fir growing out of the very stones themselves, or so it seemed. He turned furiously on her, mouthing silent curses and pulled her unceremoniously down beside him before turning once more to his watching. He never looked at her.

She lay trembling, her face pressed into the sweet grass, not daring to move although a nettle brushed her bare leg. Only when the great golden and russet bird which he had been watching lazily raised its wings and flew unperturbed away through the wood did he sit up and smile at her, obviously suddenly conscious of the formalities.

'Sorry about that,' he said, his deep voice softened slightly by the gentle lilt of the hills. 'She's nearly hatching her eggs you see and it would be a terrible crime if she were to desert the nest now. I've been watching her since she first laid.' He had a gentle quiet about him that reassured the scaredness within Jacie and allowed her to pull herself up to her knees, straightening her jacket and pushing the hair and grass and bracken tips from her eyes. The movement angered the nettle and she flinched as it rasped her skin.

'Hey, you've been stung – and it's my fault, I'm sorry.' His gaze had missed nothing and she sat wondering as hardly seeming to search for it his hand reached instinctively for some dock and soothed it against her skin.

'Do you know about birds?' he went on, as gently he replaced his salve with a fresh leaf. 'That was a kite. They're pretty rare round here and very timid.'

Jacie found herself smiling at him, reassured. 'I don't

84

really know very much, but I sketch birds sometimes.' Her glance went to the sketchbook lying in the grass where it had fallen with tumbled pages. He reached for it and slowly turned them, pausing here and there to look longer and nod. He came to sketches of birds – buzzards cleaving the sky on their arched golden wings; curlews, a pheasant – and she saw his face soften into something which was almost a smile.

'You've a good eye,' he said quietly and she found herself smiling, ridiculously pleased by his admission.

She was almost disappointed when he said suddenly, 'You'd best go now, before the other bird comes to sit his turn on the eggs,' but obediently she had taken back her sketchbook and half wriggled, half crept away from the ruins. Preoccupied again with his glasses he had not even raised his hand to say goodbye.

But he had found her two days later on the moor. And he smiled for the first time properly, his eyes matching the wash of ultramarine sky she was laying on the heavy-grained paper and for the first time in her life she was completely unembarrassed and at her ease with a man. The faint golden blush which he detected on her skin was put there by the wind and the green moorland sun, not by her realization that he was looking no longer at her picture but at her face. He had seen at once the beautiful eyes she had inherited from her mother.

It was then that he calmly asked her her name and told her that his was Brian. He stopped and picked up a discarded sketchbook from the heather and flipped through the pages. Then he set it down without comment, sitting easily beside her on an outcrop of slaty rock, one knee updrawn, clasped by his strong sun-burned hands. He watched as she bent once more to her paints, unselfconsciously continuing to work on the landscape. Their silence was companionable, uncommitted and she took his attention and lack of comment as a quiet compliment on the competence of her work.

She saw him several times after that; sometimes in the distance when he would lift a hand and stride on, making no effort to come over to talk and sometimes they would meet and would smile and walk together, falling naturally in step and talking of plants and birds and painting and sometimes of farming, but never of themselves. She thought he must be a farmer of some kind, but she never asked and he never told her what he did.

Nor did she see at first the quiet contentment in his face when he glanced in her direction as they walked together down the mossy tracks. When, almost imperceptibly, their hands touched she didn't draw away.

Then, once, turning to him, her face full of laughter as they talked she glimpsed suddenly the warmth in his eyes and the smile that was especially for her. Her laughter died for a moment on her lips and then she found herself smiling again, at him.

'It's good to have someone to walk with, Jacie,' he said quietly. That was all. But she understood.

It puzzled Jacie that she was at ease with him. One night she sat down in the dim light of her bedroom and tilted the flower-painted plastic shade on her dressing table lamp to throw a clear unflattering light on her face and gazed earnestly at herself in the mirror. It was an old glass, black-speckled with the image distorted slightly on one side, making her temple and hair ripple and move oddly. She smiled involuntarily and was amazed at the vivacity which suddenly lit her face.

Why, she was asking herself, was she not shy and embarrassed with Brian? Why should this man be the only man with whom she had never felt afraid – save her father, who had gone away so long ago and left an aching void in her life? She leaned forward to look more closely in the mirror, remembering suddenly how he would swing her up in his arms so she could wind her legs into the small of his back and bury her face in the strength and security of his chest. Always he had been there and she had known that he always would, until the day she came home from school and found her mother crying bitterly, face down on the bed. She knew now that her father had no strength, no security to offer and that he had made her mother miserable till the day he left, but rational adult explanations could not dispel that secure safe feeling which he had engendered and which lingered in her longing.

Brian seemed to have that feeling about him too. She knew instinctively that his were the kind of hands in which a wild creature would lie without fear and so – if ever he should ask it – would she.

She shook her head wearily and picked up her hair brush. It wasn't as though he were that much older than she either. Ten years? Probably less; automatically she ran her fingers over the tiny web of lines beneath her eyes, gently easing them flat. Then slowly she began to brush her hair.

'I hear you were talking to Brian Dexter up on the moors yesterday,' Mrs Finch commented as she fed Jacie scrambled eggs next morning. Who had told? The rocks? The lonely gossiping buzzards? 'He's a nice man, he is; but that wife of his . . . no better than she ought to be that one – Ann, she's called – having an affair with young Jim Lloyd like that! Serve her right that he's divorcing her. Divorce is too good I reckon. And he still loves her, you know; they say he still loves her. Some say he nearly went out of his mind when he found out and now he spends all his time alone on that moor, brooding. It's a wicked, wicked shame. And he's worth a hundred Jim Lloyds any day of the week.'

'I didn't know.' Jacie was gazing fixedly at her eggs.

There was a pause and then she went on quietly, 'He never talks about himself.' Nor of course did she.

She stared at the coffee pot as Mrs Finch picked it up, conscious of a sudden weight of sadness. It threatened her, this new intimate detail of Brian's life. She wished she didn't know, although it explained perhaps the nature of the bond between them now. For he too must mistrust the world, he too find himself apart . . .

That day, consciously, Jacie looked for him on the moors, but she didn't find him there and she didn't dare go back to the abbey. It belonged to Brian and his pair of kites. He would take her there in his own time to see his birds if he wanted and she must wait. For the first time since she had begun sketching the moors she found them lonely and a little melancholy as the warm summer wind rippled the heather and the green bracken and stirred the thorn bushes clinging to the scattered outcrops of rock.

He found her when he chose, which became more and more often as the weeks wore on. She never mentioned what she knew. She put the knowledge behind her as being part of his life which must never come between them, never spoil their careful impersonality. They talked though, all the time, and went for long walks across the countryside, climbing the hills and sitting on the edge of the river watching for kingfishers and laughing at the antics of the dipper as it plunged from its rock to walk beneath the water on the bed of the stream. And stealthily they went to visit the eyrie in its tall tree within the ruined walls of the abbey and Jacie saw the three ridiculous bald-fluffy heads of the young craning for their food as the parents swept down out of the sky.

They would picnic together, she and Brian, sharing her packed lunches which, though nothing was said at the farm, had mysteriously doubled in size and it seemed to Jacie that for the first time in her life she was almost happy.

'You must sketch the birds for me when they're flying,' he murmured as they crouched side by side behind the abbey wall watching the nest.

She nodded, her fingers gripping the cold crumbling stones which sheltered them. 'How long will it be now?' To her, the gaping beaks and the long necks visible in the nest seemed enormous already.

'Not long. Look! The hen bird.' His whisper made her look automatically up, but all she noticed was the firmness of the hand he had laid upon hers on the stones of the wall.

For a moment they forgot the birds and looked at one another and she saw the unspoken emotion in his eyes. Then he had turned away and abruptly releasing her fingers he raised his field glasses once more to the tree.

It was Brian who taught her, after he had teased her for huddling habitually under a scarf, to walk fearlessly in the rain, throwing back her head to feel the cold freshness of it on her skin as he made her shake out her hair to the damp and the fresh soft-scenting drizzle. And it was in the rain that he first kissed her gently, holding her against him and kissing her again as the cool drops ran down her upturned face, before he turned sadly away.

Summer grew heavy and languid and fearfully she began to count the days which remained of her holiday, willing time to slow down. In the abbey the young tested their wings and jumped up and down on the edge of their untidy nest high in the tree. They were ready to fly – and Jacie knew she was in love. But it was a humble, sad, compassionate, half fearful love that could not declare itself and dared not hint at its existence before the pain of the man at her side who still loved his Ann with such despair.

When at last the nest was empty they went more often to the abbey, walking up the cart track through the waist high ripening corn; they explored the woody valley in which it lay and the dark stone walls which so easily evoked an echo of pure voices sadly intoning the plainsong down the centuries. Jacie loved it there in spite of – perhaps because of – its sadness. It was Brian's place more than any other.

And there it was that she broke the spell of the summer. 'I have to go home soon, Brian. I hate to leave, but I must. I have to go back to work.' They were standing in the long seeding grasses in the chapter house of the nuns.

Silently he took her hand and squeezed it. 'I'll miss you, Jacie.'

Her eyes filled with tears. 'Brian, I shall come back. Next year.' And then it had happened. Her love and anguish had betrayed her and she had rushed on: 'By then the divorce will be over and you'll be free . . . I know you'll be free. You'll forget her one day.'

He didn't question how she knew. He said nothing, but his face tautened with pain and she saw misery and memories where only a moment before had been clear happy laughter.

In silent despair she walked away from him then, and there in the corner of the lichen-powdered wall she saw the neat intricacies of the spider's web looped across from stone to stone. She gazed at it for a moment and then bitterly swept her hand up through the threads, watching them snap and coalesce and cling fragmentarily to her fingers. That easy it was to break something fragile and beautiful. She could feel the childish tears welling under her eyelids. Then Brian was beside her. He said nothing, but she saw him looking at the ruin of the web and she felt desperately guilty and ashamed. She wanted to help him, to stand by him, to give him strength. But she did not know how. She wanted to be with him, but she didn't dare remain. Instead she walked away.

That was the last time she saw him. Two days later she

packed and went home, her shell once more tightly and protectively around her.

Mrs Finch sent her the notice of the divorce from the local paper. There was no editorial comment, just the bland headlines *'Well-known local farmer divorces wife'* and a few lines giving the names and addresses of the three people involved. So few words to cover so much that had happened.

She started to write to him then. But what do you say to a man in his position, when you ache with love and dare not say it? She tore up the half-written letter slowly and regretfully and let it fall, piece by piece, into the waste paper basket.

It was Brian who wrote in the end. A short note: 'Any chance of you getting up here in the New Year? You'd enjoy sketching the hills in the snow. The kites are still here.' That was all.

And so she went, and walked in the early dusk down the cart track to the abbey and found the frosted web which meant so much to her. She didn't find Brian that evening, but she didn't worry. She knew he would be there somewhere, and perhaps tomorrow, perhaps the next day, as she sketched in the snow on the moors he would come and find her, as he always had before.

Summer Treachery

The bedroom was high ceilinged and cool, lavishly furnished with a wealth of eau-de-nil silk.

'Well?' My sister was watching me closely as I threw my bag down on the double bed and looked round.

'Davina, it's lovely. Quite the most beautiful room I've ever seen.'

She looked pleased and for the first time since she and I had been alone together we exchanged a real smile.

I wasn't exaggerating. It was all quite fabulous: the room, the villa, the gardens which I had glimpsed as Tim and I left the car and walked up the broad flight of shallow stone steps to the porticoed front door. Everything.

I crossed to the windows and pushed back the shutters. Outside the Florentine sky was a blinding blue over the hazy valley. The shimmering afternoon heat hit into the room and I realized why every shutter on that side of the house had been closed. The view was breathtaking. If Tim and I could cement our love and happiness again anywhere it would be here.

Our marriage had not been happy. Perhaps I had been too young. Perhaps I had not realized what living with a brilliant but temperamental man would mean, especially when he was a man whose career as a sculptor brought him into intimate contact with so many beautiful women – and this while I had to keep on teaching to provide us with a steady income. Whatever the reasons, life had been hard for us. But now Tim was beginning to find recognition; I had given up my job and we had begun again.

Davina joined me on the balcony and we stood for a moment in silence. She was looking down the valley and I studied her surreptitiously. It was a year since we had met. That had been at her wedding to Simon Delacourt when I, her junior by five years, had already been married for eighteen months. Simon was rich, charming, clever; exactly what Davina had wanted. And who could blame her, with his country house in Sussex, his yacht, his executive jet and this fabulous villa in Tuscany?

We had always been close, but in her relationship with Simon she had been secretive; I had felt excluded, and wrapped up by then in my own unhappiness I had not paid my sister much attention, assuming that she had everything she wanted.

So why did she look so strained now? I studied her profile. There were lines at the corners of her eyes and between nose and mouth I did not remember.

She turned suddenly, groping in the pocket of her loose jacket and produced a pack of cigarettes and a small elegant lighter. 'Want one?'

'You know I don't. And you never used to, Davina.'

Her eyes met mine and she smiled again. This time it was brittle and automatic. 'You have to do something to occupy yourself.' She inhaled deeply on the cigarette and turned abruptly back into the room. 'How are things between you and Tim? Are you still supporting him while he lays every female in sight?'

I caught my breath. She hadn't used to be a bitch either.

I followed her back into the shadowy room, carefully pulling the shutters closed behind me. 'Actually he's becoming quite well known, so I don't have to support him any more,' I said. My voice was shaking slightly and I steadied it grimly. 'And we're happy now. Very happy.' We were also very hard up and praying that Simon might commission some work.

'Good.' She was studying her face in the lovely Florentine mirror over the dressing table and for an instant our eyes met in the glass. 'Let's go down and get a drink shall we?' she said tautly. 'I want to meet our other guests and we'll see where Simon and Tim have got to.'

Almost as soon as we had arrived Simon had whisked my husband away leaving us girls, as he put it, to get to know each other again. I could see why he thought we needed the time alone. Davina was a different woman.

The drawing room was rich and elegant, furnished in pale green and gold and it looked out across the formal gardens at the back of the villa. The line of tall windows shaded by ivory silk stood open. On the terrace outside I could see three figures reclining in the shade while beyond them in the sunlight the spray from an ornamental fountain hung like a rainbow in the still air. The two men stood up as we stepped out to join them. Both were casually dressed and wore dark glasses.

'Jocelyn and Maggie Farquer,' Davina introduced us offhandedly, 'and Nigel Godson – my sister Celia Armitage.'

Nigel Godson reached out a hand. 'Ah at last. The wife of the famous sculptor. I've heard so much about you both from Davina.' His grin robbed the words of some of their irony but nevertheless I felt a small flicker of warning. I had to be nice to these attractive rich strangers who came from a different world, for Tim's future success depended on the patronage of people like them.

Maggie Farquer patted the seat beneath the fringed

awning near her. 'Come over here, darling and have a drink. You must be parched.' She was a woman of about fifty, tanned, coiffured, jewelled, in Dior slacks and a crimson silk shirt. I smiled at her uncertainly as I accepted the tall frosted glass from Davina and felt myself grow suddenly shy.

My sister did not join us. She began instead to pace slowly up and down the terrace and I watched her as I answered Maggie's lazy questions about our trip through France in the car. I saw her stub out her half smoked cigarette in an urn full of tumbling pink geraniums and reach for another, then as I watched I saw her stiffen and return the cigarette to the pack. She was staring down the garden. I followed the direction of her gaze and saw Tim and Simon approaching slowly across the parched grass.

When the introductions had been made and Tim given his glass he sat down beside me on the seat. 'There's a cottage in the grounds I can use as a studio, Celia,' he murmured. 'I'll show you later.' He reached across and touched the back of my hand gently with his finger tip. It was a very private sign and I leant back against his shoulder sipping from my glass, happy and relaxed for the first time since I had sat down.

Davina was standing about three yards from us and I noticed suddenly that she had crushed the cigarette carton in her fist. Her eyes were fixed on the seat between Tim and myself where our hands touched on the cushion.

Tim was smiling later when he came back into our bedroom from the shower naked but for the towel knotted around his waist.

'What do you think of this set up?' he said softly. He put his arms around me and pulled me close. His hair was damp and he smelled of cologne.

95

'I love the villa.' I looked up at him.

'Not the people?'

'Not the people. Even Davina has changed.'

'We have to be nice to them, Celia.' He frowned. 'I hate to say it, but we need them.'

'Even men like Nigel Godson? I thought you said dealers were parasites and we could do without them.'

He laughed softly. His lips were in my hair. 'We can do without them only if we get the commissions direct.'

'And you think Simon will commission something?'

'Could be.' He sounded excited. 'He's had this cottage cleared of furniture so I can use it as a studio and work in peace while you're sunning yourself by the pool.' He grinned. 'He took me to see that too. You wait till you see it. Do you think I should suggest I do a head of Davina?'

'Do you want to?' My arms were around his neck and I could feel the towel slipping.

'Could do worse. She's very beautiful. I could tell the truth without offending.' He grinned again, reaching up for the zip at the back of my dress, beginning to slide it down. Reluctantly I wriggled away from him and went to sit out of his reach at the dressing table. I picked up my hairbrush.

'She is different, have you noticed?'

'A year older and wiser. So are we.'

'No, it's more than that. She's grown hard and neurotic.' I put down the brush and turned to face him. 'I think she's unhappy.'

He laughed. 'With all this?'

It did seem hard to believe, but as I watched her at dinner I became more and more certain I was right.

We sat at a long elegant table lit with candles in silver candelabra, waited on by the villa servants. Beside me Nigel Godson was attentive. Without his glasses he was also very attractive for his eyes were a warm hazel and they were without doubt fixed exclusively on me.

At the other end of the table my sister was dressed in white which against her tan looked quite stunning and she in her turn had eyes for no one but my husband.

He was studying her. I knew that look; I had seen it often and in the beginning I had resented it bitterly as beauty after beauty disappeared into his studio; I still found it hard to believe he was studying his subjects dispassionately and that he treated men to the same intense scrutiny. Davina had sensed his interest at once and was responding with an arch awareness which bordered on flirtation, looking up at him under her eyelashes as her fingers toyed with her wine glass. I felt a quick surge of hurt anger at her as I watched.

I dragged my attention away from the cameo at the end of the table to find that Nigel Godson was speaking to me again. 'Perhaps if your husband is going to work while he's here you would allow me to drive you down to the city to explore a little?' He smiled and I saw Maggie Farquer watching us through the candlelight from across bowls of stracciatella. On my left, sitting at the head of the table was Simon, a large florid man in his early forties. He was busy eating and did not appear to be listening. Nor had he noticed his wife flirting with my husband.

Maggie caught my eye and smiled. 'That's a splendid idea,' she murmured. 'I shall beg a lift down with you, Nigel. No – ' she made a deprecatory gesture with her hands. 'Don't worry, I'm not going to play gooseberry. I want you to drop me off somewhere on your way. A dear friend of mine has rented a house there for the summer and I've been dying for the opportunity to look her up. More than a friend actually, my erstwhile partner in crime.' Her smile had not faltered but I sensed she was no longer speaking to Nigel and myself any more; she was watching Simon. I glanced at him as well. He had laid down his soup spoon and was sipping from his glass. 'I believe you know her, Simon sweetie.' She was speaking to him directly now. 'It's Sarah. Sarah Cummins.'

Later we took our coffee and liqueurs out onto the terrace. An enormous orange moon hung above the cypress trees and the darkness had the quality of rich stifling velvet. I felt lost and a little miserable. Tim was still talking to Davina. They were sitting on the rim of the fountain together and she was stroking the still water at its edge into gentle ripples with the tip of her finger. Jocelyn and Simon were talking together as they wandered up and down the garden smoking cigars, tiny points of burning light in the night. Whatever reaction Maggie had expected from her host at her announcement at dinner, Simon had obviously disappointed her. His bland face had remained unruffled and he had merely smiled, rather bored, at her disclosure. She was talking now to Nigel, discussing people I did not know, laughing, touching his arm. I was sitting with them but I was an outsider, an observer who did not even speak their language and before long I rose with murmured excuses and tiptoed up to bed. I must have been asleep when Tim came up, for I never heard him.

When I awoke the room was cool and silvery with early morning light. Tim was already up and dressed in jeans and an open-necked shirt. He grinned when he saw me awake and came to sit on the bed beside me.

'Hi. Did you sleep well?'

I stretched in the soft silky sheets, my forebodings of the previous night forgotten, and nodded, holding out my arms as he bent to kiss me. But a moment later he was sitting up again. 'I'm going down to the cottage, Celia. I want to begin work at once. You don't mind, do you? Make the most of the sun and get a lovely tan beside their pool.' He ran his finger slowly down my breast.

I felt my nerves tighten. 'You're going to do a head of Davina?'

It wasn't really a question. I already knew the answer.

He nodded. 'She says Simon will pay for it for their anniversary and she can spare me a bit of time later this morning for a preliminary sitting so I thought I'd get straight to it.'

'Tim . . .' I reached out again and he caught my hands gently. Last night had been the first time we had not made love since our reconciliation, but what was the use of saying anything? It had all been said so often in the past. I just smiled at him, reached up to give him a kiss and lay back to watch him as he slung his denim jacket over his shoulder, winked at me and was gone.

Nigel Godson drove a British registration Lancia. I sat beside him in the front with Maggie Farquer, resplendent in a magenta jumpsuit, behind us, leaning forward with her forearms across the back of the seats as she directed us. She smelled faintly of gardenias.

We found it at last, a fourteenth-century farmhouse converted into a luxury holiday home. Sarah Cummins was the most beautiful woman I had ever seen. Elegant, ash blonde and charming she ushered us into the main room of the house and produced coffee and ricciarelli – delicious little almond biscuits – and it was only two minutes before I discovered that she knew Nigel as well as Maggie. It was an hour before Nigel and I could extricate ourselves from her hospitality and leave. I had not liked her; she was hard and I suspected clever, but with a hint of ice in her which touched us all. Even Maggie, who was effusive and voluble as she sat back on the Louis XVI sofa seemed a little uncomfortable.

Florence was hot and dusty and by mutual consent

Nigel and I agreed to forgo a trip to the Uffizi which we had planned and wander instead around San Lorenzo and down the Via Calzaioli towards the Ponte Vecchio. I had begun to like Nigel. He owned a smart gallery in Chelsea dabbling in art and antiques and was exactly the sort of man Tim resented, but he was also kind – a quality conspicuously lacking at the villa – strong and quiet and nobody's fool. And I sensed that his interest in me was real.

'How well do you know your brother-in-law?' Nigel asked suddenly as we examined some of the gilded leatherwork on a stall. I glanced at him, but he had retreated once more behind those dark glasses.

'I don't,' I said shortly. 'I've only met him twice in my life before and one of those times was the wedding.'

He said nothing for a moment, distracted as we wandered on through piles of intricately woven straw baskets, passed silver shops, silks and linens, antiques . . . Then he returned to his probing. 'Have you had a chance to speak to your sister at all?'

'What about?'

He looked uncomfortable. 'Nothing special. I just wondered how she seemed to you.'

I looked at him. 'I think she seems very tense,' I said cautiously. I was thinking of the last I had seen of her, wandering barefoot across the lawns after breakfast in the direction of the cottage, dressed in a simple Saint Laurent floating dress with a chiffon scarf draped over her hair like a 1920s film star.

He had taken off his glasses and I could see his face now in the blinding sunlight of the hot street. 'She's not happy, Celia. I don't think it's women – you gathered I suppose that Sarah used to live with him – I think it has something to do with his business activities.'

'You mean they're questionable?' I had a quick vision

of Simon in close conversation with Jocelyn Farquer, the man who had not, since I had arrived in the villa, addressed as much as one word to me directly.

Nigel shrugged. 'It's not my field of course, but I used to know old Simon pretty well and I get the impression he's up to something. Jocelyn and he are brokers of some sort in the City. Davina hates the Farquers, you know.'

I stared at him. 'I got the impression that Maggie was something of a bitch,' I said – I had also got the impression that Nigel disliked her intensely, 'but I haven't spoken to her husband. Not once.'

He laughed grimly. 'You wouldn't. He has no time for social niceties. He is one of those people who doesn't want to know you unless you are useful to him.'

'Touché!' I laughed. 'Why did they ask Tim and me to come do you think?'

Nigel looked down at me. 'Haven't you guessed?'

'I had hoped it was because of Tim's work.'

He grimaced. 'Perhaps a little. But something else as well.'

'To distract Davina?'

'Of course.'

'And you?' I was watching him intently.

'I am afraid my uses are very basic.' He smiled, suddenly humorous. 'I think I am the spare male to be used as distraction for any of the ladies who became too much of a nuisance. I thought when I arrived he had asked me to take Davina off his back – yes, I know it sounds pretty awful, but it gets worse. Now I think I've been asked to take care of you – so Davina can have your husband. I gather she's always rated her chances with him fairly high and Simon has never been a great performer in the sack so I'm told.'

I heard myself gasp. We were standing on the kerb, watching the noonday traffic roaring past in a haze of fumes and dirt. My head was spinning. 'I don't believe you! That's a wicked thing to say!' It was my own voice I could hear protesting but I knew what he said was true.

When we returned to pick Maggie up she dropped her little piece of news. 'I've asked Sarah to come back with us for dinner, Nigel. You don't mind waiting while she changes, then we can give her a lift.' It didn't cross my mind, then, to wonder how she would get back home again.

There was no one around when we drove up to the villa. The hall was cool and dim, the shutters closed as we trooped in and Nigel and I excused ourselves to go to our respective rooms to shower and change before meeting again on the terrace for drinks at six. Of the others in the party there was no sign and I vowed wearily as I climbed the broad sweep of stairs that I would not go to look for Tim in the cottage. Perhaps I was afraid of what I might find.

I showered and wrapped myself in a towel before lying down on the bed to rest. The walk around Florence had exhausted me and I was feeling very depressed at what I now realized was my sister's betrayal; I loved her, but I loved my husband too.

I must have dozed off for it was Tim who woke some time later. He was stripping off his shirt by the window, staring out into the garden as he did so. The sun had gone round to the side of the villa and the shutters were open now onto the balcony. I could hear a pigeon cooing from somewhere in the trees.

'How was work today?' I murmured. I didn't sit up.

He turned. 'I'm sorry, darling. I was trying not to wake you. It was fine. How was Florence?'

'Hot and dusty and very beautiful. But I missed you.'

He came to me then and sat on the edge of the bed. 'I

missed you. Let's work out a way of taking a day off and making a trip together shall we – just us.' He leaned over me and I felt the warm touch of his lips on mine, then slowly he pulled open the towel which was wrapped around me and ran his hands over my body. It was only the sound of the ormulu clock on the landing outside our room chiming six which brought me back from the warm sated dream in which I was lying, and reluctantly I pushed him away. 'Remember our aperitifs on the terrace,' I whispered as his hand began once more to stray between my thighs.

He gave a grimace. 'I don't give a damn about the terrace. I want my wife!'

And oh how I wanted him. But I slipped out of his reach and went to the mirror to do something about my hair while he showered and found a clean shirt.

It was only when I went to pick up his discarded shirt, lying on the thick Chinese carpet by the window that I saw the lipstick on the collar and remembered that when he had cheated on me his first reaction always had been to come and try to make it up.

Davina was wearing a red and gold sarong, her hair piled up on her head to show a pair of exquisite emerald earrings which I had no doubt at all were worth a fortune. She came straight up to us when we appeared and slipped her arm through Tim's. 'Where have you both been? We thought you'd got lost,' she said. She glanced at me, and I saw the suppressed triumph in her eyes. So Nigel had been right.

I glanced round for him, but he had not appeared. Simon was standing on the lawn talking to Maggie and Sarah and Jocelyn was sitting on the wall of the terrace looking out across the gardens. Feeling sick and lonely I went to stand beside him, my drink in my hand, content to be silent. But to my surprise he spoke to me.

103

'My wife is unbelievably stupid. Have you any idea at all what she's done?' He was staring down at the group on the lawn, his voice icy with contempt and I took a step away from him in surprise.

'What?'

He turned and stared at me and I wondered for a moment if he had realized that it was me he was talking to. His face was hard and bitter, his lips thin as he looked me up and down.

'Sarah was Simon's mistress before he met your sister,' he said quietly, 'and the only reason she has come to Tuscany is to make trouble for him. For Maggie to invite her here is the most crass behaviour, even for her.' His look of loathing encompassed his wife and Sarah as they stood on the lawn and I wondered briefly what they could be talking to Simon about so intensely. For a moment I had forgotten my own grief in the shock of his statement, but as I turned to look at Davina I saw her still clinging to Tim's arm and I wondered suddenly whether she would care at all what her husband did, or to whom. I looked back at Jocelyn.

'And Davina has no clue about this?' I asked softly.

'No. Maggie and Sarah used to run a boutique together and Sarah even met Simon at our place in Midhurst. They were together for about three years but Sarah was too interfering; she poked her nose in where it wasn't wanted just once too often and Simon got shot of her.'

'Jocelyn,' I looked up at him searchingly. 'Exactly why did he marry Davina? She's hardly his type.'

He gave a small hard smile at that. 'Why, my dear young lady, does any man marry at all?' He looked rather pointedly at my husband.

I swallowed, hoping the wave of bleakness which swept over me did not show in my face as I turned away from him and walked back to the drinks table. I was not going to let Davina see that I cared. I refilled my drink with an unsteady hand and then I saw Nigel appearing from the house at last; he came over to me at once and gave a small smile.

'So, the cast is assembled,' he commented quietly.

I sipped my drink. 'To play tragedy or comedy, I wonder,' I said bitterly.

On the lawn the sets of couples had changed. Sarah had wandered across to join Tim and Davina, and Maggie and Simon were walking back to join Jocelyn on the terrace. Maggie was smiling as she looked up in our direction.

'Nigel, come and tell my husband about that painting you mentioned to me, my dear. I would so love him to buy it for me.' She came up and slipped her arm through his, edging him away from me.

I didn't mind. I knew her for what she was now, a bored rich manipulator who made up for her own lack of love by playing with other people. I just hoped that Sarah's presence would deflect Davina's attention from Tim when and if Davina found out who she was.

Time passed; drinks were replenished. Nigel made one rueful face at me behind Maggie's back and then settled into conversation. On the horizon behind the pointed cypress trees the rim of the moon floated suddenly into view, pale lemon in an aquamarine sky. I felt myself shiver.

'Celia, are you all right?' I hadn't seen Sarah approaching.

I smiled. 'A footstep on my grave, that's all.'

'You must be careful not to chill. I've just been talking to your husband and I hear he is to sculpt your sister's bust. Do you think I dare ask him to do mine?' Her laugh was a silver bell in the thin evening air as she ran the fingers of her left hand over the line of her breast. It was somehow an obscene gesture. She had been drinking heavily since six, and her thick make up could not quite conceal the blurring of her features.

'I'm sure he'd love to . . .' I hesitated. 'He is very booked at the moment though . . .'

'I can believe it.' She was watching me with an intensity which made me uncomfortable. 'Your sister is very beautiful.'

'Yes, she is, isn't she?' I took a sip at my glass with stiff lips.

'I can see how easily she must have captured Simon; he wouldn't have stood a chance.'

'No.' I didn't know what else to say.

'And now she's captured your husband,' she went on quietly. 'Do you mind? Or does he always sleep with his models? Perhaps an artist's wife gets used to it?'

'No, you don't get used to it,' I had replied with more feeling than I intended and I hastened to cover up. 'There's no need. His interest is purely professional.'

'Although there are exceptions.' She was still watching me as she drained her glass. She refilled it from the table and I saw she was drinking neat vodka.

I gave what I hoped was a worldly smile. 'There are always exceptions to everything,' I said, but I was aching with unhappiness as we both turned and saw Tim slowly leading Davina back towards the terrace. Their footsteps left a dark track on the grass where the dew was lying and she was leaning on him slightly, her arm through his.

They walked slowly up the steps towards us and I saw that she was talking quietly so that he had to lean towards her slightly to hear what she was saying. I felt a sudden surge of anger. I turned and, putting my glass down on the table, I walked towards them, conscious as I did so of Sarah's eyes watching me. They stopped, still engrossed in one another and for a moment I don't think either of them realized I was there. Then they were both looking at me and I was sure that I saw guilt on their faces. I forced myself to smile.

'You look so cosy there is speculation on the terrace about when you're moving in together,' I said with a laugh which came out far too brittle. Davina released his arm abruptly, but I saw the quick anger on Tim's face and I cursed myself for having said anything at all. But I couldn't stop myself. 'You're in demand, darling,' I said to him lightly. 'Sarah is wondering if you will have time to sculpt her bust too.' I knew she could hear every word I said. 'I told her you come expensive.'

Davina had opened her mouth, but her retort was lost in the sound of the phone relayed out onto the terrace by an outside bell. There was dead silence, then Simon began slowly to walk towards the french windows. Behind him Jocelyn put down his glass and followed.

'Well!' Davina laughed abruptly. She walked across to the drinks table and began rather obviously to tidy the tray and screw the caps onto various bottles. 'I suppose this means we'll be late for dinner and Stephano will hand in his notice again. It happens about once a week I'm afraid.'

'Business calls?' It was Nigel's voice from the shadows. Davina tensed. 'I expect so. Business can't be left at home even here.'

I recognized the strained note in her voice and instantly my hostility lessened. I thought I recognized her play for Tim as a plea; a cry for help. I wanted to reach out my hand, to hug her as I used to do when we were children and would comfort one another when things became too bad to be borne alone. But the eyes she turned on me were hard and rejecting and I took a step back as if she had slapped me.

Tim came forward. He smiled at me, his usual warm special smile as though nothing were wrong. 'We can't ask Davina to risk losing so great a treasure as Stephano; I suggest we go in and start to eat without Simon. I'll take the blame if he gets violent.' His smile took in everyone as he gestured to Davina to lead us into the candlelit dining room. There was no sign of Simon and Jocelyn. The double doors to Simon's study were closed; when we had come down earlier they had stood open.

We had finished the Parma ham garnished with figs and had already begun on the veal escalopes before the doors opened and Simon and Jocelyn reappeared. They both looked angry as they took their places and I found myself unwillingly catching Nigel's eye. He winked at me.

'Bad news?' he asked innocently.

Sarah laughed. She had already finished a second glass of Chianti. 'It must be bad,' she said, slurring her words slightly. 'It takes more than a bear market to make our Simon flinch.' She leaned forward across the table to put her hand on his. Her gold bracelet clanked heavily against the cut glass. 'That's right, isn't it, honey bunch?'

I was watching Davina's face. She had refused to look up as her husband came in, toying with her food with her fork, but now I saw her staring at Sarah in disbelief. She opened her mouth to say something but before she had the chance her husband spoke.

'I'm afraid it looks as if I'll have to nip back to London for a couple of days.' He cleared his throat. 'Awful bore. Sorry. But Davina will entertain you all.'

'And you, Joss?' Maggie was watching her husband across the table.

'Not Jocelyn.' Simon answered for him. 'Jocelyn has done enough damage.'

There was a moment of complete silence. Then Sarah started to laugh.

I cornered Davina in her bathroom. It was an amazing place of ornate marble and gold illuminated now by cruel hidden lights. She looked haggard as she bathed her eyes.

108

'What the hell is going on here?' I perched on the edge of the bath. 'What has happened to you, Davina?'

She looked up at me, her face wet. 'Did you know that Sarah woman used to be Simon's fancy piece?'

I nodded.

'Maggie's a cow. You know it was she who asked her here. I detest her.' She had drunk more than usual and her face beneath the heavy streaked layer of make up was flushed.

Privately I agreed with her. 'You haven't answered me, Davina. What is going on here?'

She shrugged. 'What do I care? Simon never tells me anything. I just have to sign things; and entertain his guests.' She was peering into the mirror now, her shadowed eyes expressionless. 'And you'd better mind your own business. Don't tangle with Simon.'

'How long has it been like this?' My sympathy for her had returned and I wanted to touch her, to comfort her. But I was not prepared to risk another rejection. She stared down at the mosaic floor.

'Ever since we married. I've wanted to see you often but I didn't dare ask you. I didn't want you to see what I had become. I could bear the thought of you and Tim as long as you were unhappy. It meant you were no better off than me. You see what a horrible person I am?'

There was a long pause. I closed my eyes wearily. 'And when you saw we were happy, you thought you'd take him for yourself, is that it?' I asked at last.

'You're my sister. I thought . . .' She stopped in mid sentence. Then she turned to face me. 'Oh Celia, you shouldn't have come.' And she began to cry.

*

Tim went into our room ahead of me. He didn't turn on the light. As I closed the door he came up to me and put his arms around me in the dark.

'Celia. What is it? What's wrong?'

'I talked to Davina. She thinks we ought to go. Can we, Tim? Please. Tomorrow. I know it's a disappointment but you'll get work from other people. You're good. We don't need to rely on Simon for any commissions.'

I felt him tense. He was stroking my hair gently. 'Celia, you can go if you want to, darling. But I can't. Don't you see?'

The room was very dark. The maid had pulled the curtains across the windows when she came in to turn down the bed and it was stifling. I pulled away from him wordlessly and went to open them. Outside the balcony was black. The brilliant moonlight flooded past the villa and focused on the lawn. The fountain was still playing.

'Do you love her?' I asked softly. I leaned on the stone balustrade and looked down.

'Who?' I felt the anger in him, the resentment which always came when I questioned him and I knew I could not fight it this time. What was the point? Tim came out onto the balcony beside me. 'Don't run away, Celia. I'm beginning to think you must be paranoid or something. Who do you think I'm having an affair with this time?'

'Davina.' I could hardly bring myself to say the name.

'Oh for God's sake. It's always the same, isn't it? The moment I show interest in a woman you imagine I've fallen into bed with her. What's the matter with you?'

What indeed? How could I explain to him how much I loved him; how much I feared to lose him; how much I had looked forward to these summer months in Italy as a second honeymoon? And now I saw the whole frail structure of my dream collapsing.

'You really mean it, Tim? You would stay here and let

110

me go home alone?' I didn't look at him. Below in the garden I saw a small glow in the darkness and I thought it must be a firefly. Then I realized it was a cigarette. There was someone walking slowly in the shadows of the trees.

'I've come here to work, Celia. And it's important that I do. More important than you know. Simon told me today that he is prepared to recommend me for a commission to do heads of all the members of a board he's on. It means security and freedom to work without worrying for a while; without you having to go back to that job. I'm not going to blow it, Celia, even if it means we can't be together. I don't want you to go. It's up to you.'

He turned and vanished back into the bedroom. A moment later I heard the door slam.

I could feel the hot tears burning my cheeks and I let them fall unchecked. The french doors below the balcony opened and someone stepped out onto the terrace. I knew it must be Tim. He would go to his improvised studio and work through the night, returning to fall into bed beside me at dawn. It had happened too often before after we had quarrelled. I did not call out to him. What was the point? He stepped out of the shadows of the terrace onto the grass and I saw him clearly walking towards the fountain. A figure detached itself from the shadows and joined him. A woman. The moonlight had washed the colour from her dress but I knew it was my sister. I watched as they stood talking then slowly they began to move, not towards the cottage but around the side of the house out of sight. Two minutes later I heard the sound of a car engine and the crunch of its tyres on the gravel of the long poplar-lined drive. Then there was silence.

I undressed and lay down on the bed, but my mind would not rest. I could not sleep and after a while I gave up trying. I rose and slipped on a thin sweater and some jeans.

111

The villa was in darkness save where moonlight slid through the windows on the staircase. I peered out. Our car had vanished from its place beneath the mulberry tree beside the wall. Behind me on the landing the clock chimed three. Tim had left the french windows open and I slipped out onto the terrace. I avoided the bright moonlight, following the dark shadows beneath the trees.

The cottage was in darkness, but the door was unlocked and I slipped in and at last allowed myself to turn on a light. The room was empty but for a large table and a couple of chairs. I recognized all the paraphernalia we had brought with us in the car. The plastic sacks of clay and plaster, the wire for armatures, the scalpels, the spatulas, the callipers and sketch books. Tim's overalls hung on the back of the door and the room already had the cold oily smell of the clay. On the table I could see the outline of the head beneath its cloth and I moved over to uncover it.

He had made a lot of progress. Davina stared out at me, her lips enigmatically smiling, her eyes still a blind sightless sketch in the glistening clay. I stared at it for a long time, then I covered it again and moved across to the stairs. The cottage had only one bedroom and it was fully furnished. The bed had been slept in. Beside it the bathroom was also fully equipped with toiletries and cosmetics. I unscrewed a bottle of cologne and sniffed it. It was spicy and rather strong. I did not recognize it.

A bell pealed in the silence and I froze. Then I realized it was the telephone beside the bed next door. I tiptoed across and hesitated as it rang. Then cautiously I lifted the receiver. A voice was talking in fast Italian on the other end and I realized suddenly that it was an extension from the main house. I was about to replace it when a second voice cut in. It was Simon and he sounded once more very angry. Holding my breath I sat gingerly on the bed and listened.

They were speaking in English now. 'I told you not to ring me!' Simon's voice hissed down the line.

'The deal is taking too long!' the Italian cut in. 'You have only twenty-four hours. Then I pull out.'

'You can't pull out, remember? Your currency is being held in my wife's name,' Simon snarled. 'I fly to London tomorrow. The transaction will be completed on schedule.'

'And if she asks any questions?'

'She won't. She never does.' Simon's mirthless laugh floated from the receiver in my hand. I could feel myself beginning to shake as I listened in disbelief, and for a long time after he had hung up and the line was empty I sat there, the phone still in my hand.

I could see the light on in his study as I tiptoed back across the lawn towards the french windows. I had no wish to meet Simon and I held my breath as I crept in. Then I realized he was not alone. Davina was with him and they were having a furious row. There was no question of them hearing me; they were making enough noise to wake the whole villa. The doors to his study were half open and I could see them both clearly. Simon was fully dressed still, but Davina was in a négligé and I could see from the stark paleness of her face that she had removed her make up. She looked as though she had just got out of bed and I wondered suddenly whether like me she had been listening on the extension.

I crept upstairs without them seeing me and peered out of the window on the landing. The car was still missing, and I realized bitterly that my husband's midnight rendezvous had been not with my sister but with Sarah Cummins.

Simon was missing from the dining room when I plucked up courage to descend at about nine, but the others were

113

there, all except Tim. Maggie smiled at me. 'Is your divine husband at work already, Celia?' she asked.

'He's been at it all night,' I heard myself reply. I was watching Davina as she got up and went to the urn on the sideboard to pour herself a cup of black coffee.

She raised her eyebrows. 'How dedicated,' she said tartly.

'But I don't know where. He drove off with someone at about midnight,' I went on quietly, 'and the car's not back yet.'

Maggie and Nigel were listening intently; Jocelyn was engrossed in the *Financial Times* and did not look up. I saw the coffee overflow into Davina's saucer. Her face suddenly turned white.

'The bitch!' she said. 'The bloody bitch!' She put the cup down and flung her napkin on the floor.

There was a telephone in the hall – an ornate affair of gold and white – and she picked it up angrily. 'Maggie, what is the number of that woman you brought here last night?' she yelled through the door.

Maggie was smiling quietly. 'I wrote it on the pad by the phone,' she answered softly. 'I figured someone from this house might want to call her.'

Davina was connected almost at once and I listened in disbelief. This was my husband they were fighting over. Sarah Cummins had arrived at the house, bent on revenge on Davina for stealing her man, as she saw it, and in order to do it she had decided to steal Tim from her. Wordlessly I stood up and went to stand in the hall behind her, listening. There was no question that Tim was there, but he was refusing to come to the phone. After five minutes' vicious tirade Davina slammed down the phone and whirled round. She found herself face to face with me and for one second she had the grace to look taken aback. Then she smiled. 'Don't look like that, Celia. If you were any good

114

at all with men you'd be able to keep him, wouldn't you! You deserve to lose him!' She ran to the staircase and vanished up it.

I was stunned. For a while I could not move, then I was conscious of the dining room door closing softly behind me, shielding me from the staring eyes within. An arm went round my shoulders. It was Nigel.

'Come on up to my room. I've some brandy up there,' he said quietly. I went without a murmur and sat on his bed sipping it until I had stopped shaking. His arms were round me, comforting, holding me close. I hardly noticed when he took the glass from my hand and set it down on the bedside table, then his lips were against mine and I felt myself lying back on the pillows. 'I'll take care of you, Celia. Forget him. He's not worth it,' he whispered, tickling my neck with a curl of my hair, wound round his finger. He looked down into my eyes with such concern and kindness that for a long time I lay still. I felt secure and safe. I was wanted. 'Oh Nigel!' My arms went round his neck and I was sobbing at last.

We lay like that for a long time and it was only the sunlight crawling across the carpet towards us until it threw a brilliant hot beam across the pillow which brought me to my senses. I pushed him away and sat up.

'Nigel. What shall I do?' I looked miserably down at the floor. I should have told him then what I had overheard on the phone, but I was afraid. Afraid for Davina but afraid of her too and I hated her at that moment almost as much as I hated Sarah Cummins. And myself.

Nigel did not try to touch me again. Getting up he poured another tot of brandy and put it into my hands. Then he walked across to the window and stared out. 'Let me take care of you,' he said. 'There is no point in staying with a man who makes you so unhappy, Celia. You can fight for years, but he's not going to change. Do you want

115

to waste your whole life on him? He's not worth it.' He walked back and stood looking down at me. 'You're a hundred times more beautiful than your sister, Celia. You're natural; you're unspoilt. Don't let them corrupt you. Let me take you back to London.'

On my way back to my bedroom I listened at Davina's door. I could hear her sobbing and I raised my hand to knock. Then I lowered it again. There was nothing I could say to Davina. I had to think. I had to make up my mind what to do.

For a long time I lay on the bed in our bedroom staring at the ceiling. The house was completely silent around me. Nigel was going to drive down into Florence after lunch, he said, but I had declined his invitation to go with him. I wanted to be alone. His words were ringing in my ears. 'Do you want to waste your whole life?' Was that was I was doing?

The phone number was still on the pad by the phone in the hall. I sat down on the carved chair by the table and stared down at the scribbled figures for a long time before, hesitatingly, I picked up the receiver and dialled.

'*Pronto*.' The voice which answered was that of a stranger.

'Can I speak to Tim?' I said slowly, and groped for the Italian words.

There was a long silence, but he came in the end.

'Tim!' I tried to keep my voice calm. 'Tim, I must speak to you.'

'Can't it wait till tonight? I'm working, Celia.' He sounded exaggeratedly patient, like an adult humouring a fractious child. Something inside me seemed to break and I knew I was fighting; fighting for my marriage and my self respect.

'No, it bloody well can't wait,' I hissed down the phone. 'You get back here, Tim, and meet me at the cottage. I've got to see you now. I've found out something you've got to know about. Simon is involved in some shady currency deal and he's using Davina. You've got to tell me what to do. She's the one who is going to get into trouble. Now, get here.' I hung up before he had time to reply.

There was a sound behind me and I turned to see Simon himself standing in the dining room doorway. His arms were folded and he was watching me. 'I wonder what sort of trouble that could possibly be?' he said quietly, with a small smile. 'Perhaps you would come into my study a moment, Celia. It's time you and I had a short talk I think.'

He ushered me into a carved rococo chair by the fireplace. Then, half leaning on his desk he turned to face me. 'What exactly have you found out?' he asked. His face was quite bland and unthreatening, and yet suddenly I was afraid.

'That you treat Davina like dirt,' I replied. I had no intention of telling about my eavesdropping.

'I see.' He waited a moment, then he went to a cabinet beside the fireplace and produced a bottle. 'Campari and soda?' He put the glass in my hand. 'What do you intend doing about it?' A smile played across his lips for moment.

'Do you know what happened this morning?' I asked him suddenly, looking down at the glass in my hand without seeing it. 'Your ex-girlfriend has gone off with my husband because she wanted to hurt Davina. Don't you think that is rather funny?' I heard myself laughing, a high nervous sound which bordered on hysteria. 'Is that why you asked us here? So you could procure Tim for your wife and distract her from your illegal activities?'

I could have bitten my tongue out. His face had not altered but I saw the knuckles whiten on his glass. Slowly he raised it and drank.

117

'So. I ask you again, what have you found out, sweet sister-in-law?'

'Enough.' I stared at him defiantly.

There was a long silence. He set down the glass and looked at me thoughtfully. 'Do you love this husband of yours, Celia?' he asked.

'Of course I do.' It was true. It was agonizingly true.

'Then I suggest you keep very quiet about whatever it is that you think you have discovered, *cognata mia*, or I will break Timothy's career. Do you understand me? I can do it, you know. I'll see to it that he never gets another commission as long as he lives.' There seemed to be no animosity in his voice, no violence, just calm certainty. And I believed him. I stared at him, my heart hammering uncertainly in my chest as I set my glass down without tasting the drink.

'You bastard.'

He bowed in acknowledgement as though I had paid him a compliment.

When Tim returned Sarah was with him. The car crunched to a halt on the gravel outside the villa as I was descending the stairs from my room in search of a cup of coffee. I had had no lunch and my head was aching violently. I stopped dead as the ornate doors swung open and they appeared on the threshold. Sarah was laughing as the soft jacket thrown across her shoulders caught on the elaborate arrangement of flowers in the hall and a spray of stephanotis fell to the floor. Tim looked at me intently for a moment. The anger which had shadowed his face as he caught sight of me was replaced by concern. 'Sweetheart, are you all right?'

I glanced at the dining room door which stood open.

Beyond it Simon was still in his study. 'Come to the cottage,' I whispered. 'I must see you alone.'

Sarah was watching me. I saw a slight sneer flicker across her lips. 'Go on, Tim. I shall speak to Simon. I know exactly what this is all about. He tried it once with me.' She kissed her fingertips and laid them quickly on his lips. Then she went through the door and closed it behind her.

In the cool of the cottage Tim held me for a long time before he would let me speak. Then slowly he pushed me away, holding me at arm's length. 'I was only sketching her, you know. It never crossed my mind she was trying to make Davina jealous.'

His eyes held mine steadily and I knew that I believed him.

'And Davina? Did she have any reason to be jealous?' I asked softly.

'What do you think?' He was holding me tightly again and his lips on mine were urgent and demanding. It was a long time before I remembered my excuse for bringing him back to the villa.

'He said if I told anyone he'd see you never got another commission, Tim,' I whispered when I had finished telling him what had happened.

Tim laughed softly and the sound sent a shiver up my spine. 'I think I'm prepared to risk that,' he said.

Half an hour later I was packing when the door of our room burst open. It was Simon and his face was puce. 'Get up,' he said roughly and he bent to pull me from the bed where I was sitting. 'You silly bitch. You thought I didn't mean it? You thought you could double cross me, is that it?' He yelled at me. I heard a door open in the distance and I guessed it was Davina's.

'What do you mean?' I pulled away from him angrily. 'Take your filthy hands off me!'

'Simon, let her go!' It was Davina in the doorway. Her voice had risen to a scream.

'You told Sarah. She's just confronted me with my plans downstairs. She thinks I'm going to cut her in.' He gave an unpleasant laugh. 'I told her to go and screw herself.'

I wrenched my hand free. 'You're mad. I haven't told Sarah anything. I haven't spoken to her. She must have guessed.'

'I don't care how she knew,' his face was ugly. 'But there's nothing she can do. No one can, because it's too late and my plans are always foolproof.' He turned to look at his wife, then swung back to me. 'If you want to stop your sister going to jail you are going to do as I say for the next few hours. That is all I ask.'

Davina and I stared at each other. Her face was white and pleading.

I subsided onto the bed. 'What do you want me to do?'

He lifted my bag off the side table and wrenched it open to look inside. Then he threw it in my lap. 'Get downstairs and wait for me in the car,' he said.

In the hall the spray of fragrant white flowers still lay on the Bokhara rug where Sarah's jacket had flicked it. I bent and picked it up then I went out and climbed into the blue Alfa Romeo which stood outside.

He took the hairpin bends of the mountain road with screaming tyres as we swooped down towards Florence. The glare off the white road reflected through the windscreen and I closed my eyes.

'Where are we going?' I asked wearily.

'England.' He did not look at me.

My eyes had flown open. 'England!'

He chuckled suddenly. 'I told Davina that if anyone wanted to see you alive again they had better keep very quiet about what they know.' He glanced up at the driving

120

mirror and smiled at himself. 'You could say, *cognata mia*, that I am using you as a kind of hostage.'

A wave of nausea swept over me and I felt myself clinging to the sides of the seat. The palms of my hands were clammy with fear.

'You're going to kill me?' I whispered in disbelief.

'Of course not. I don't want a murder charge hanging over me, Celia. I'm not that much of a fool. But they don't know that do they!' He laughed out loud. 'And I know you will behave because of what will happen to your sister – and your beloved husband – if you don't. You are merely an insurance policy, my dear. I have a plane waiting at San Giusto and like any good tourist you carry your passport in your handbag. So we should have no more problems.'

'I don't believe you. You're kidnapping me!'

'You are hardly a kid,' the scorn in his voice flicked at me and I flinched. He was right. I was no kid, and I understood perfectly that I had no choice but to do everything he said.

The Learjet was waiting on the tarmac near the terminal buildings, a beautiful glittering bird, poised for take off. Within twenty minutes we were cleared and in the sky.

I remember little of that flight. Europe lay beneath a haze of thin cloud which flattened the countries below into a tableau of white. I did not know when we crossed the Alps; I did not know when we crossed the Channel, but suddenly we were losing altitude and Simon himself took the controls from his pilot as we began to circle southern England. Gatwick was wet and glistening beneath a summer shower and very crowded, but Simon took my arm and guided me through the formalities with the minimum of fuss. Then we were in the chauffeur-driven maroon BMW swooping down the lush green lanes of Sussex.

Two cars were parked outside his Queen Anne mansion, an XJ6 and a sleek Rolls and he chuckled when he saw them. 'You see, I don't even have to go to London. They are here to meet me. You will excuse me, Celia, for half an hour or so, I know,' he said as he handed me out into the soft mist of the rain. 'This business won't take long.' He showed me into a pretty drawing room, furnished in pale greens and greys – Davina's favourite colours. 'Sit down. Help yourself to a drink,' and he was gone. This time I poured myself half a tumbler of Scotch.

There was nothing I could do. Outside the window the rain lent the countryside the smell of sweet grass and bruised velvet roses; somewhere a blackbird was singing undaunted. The house itself was very quiet.

Later I heard the cars leave. I did not move. I was too weary. When Simon appeared he was smiling. 'Celia. What about some food? Forbes has left steaks and champagne in the fridge.'

I followed him into the gleaming kitchen.

'How long do you intend keeping me here?' I asked. The house was quite empty, I discovered; his staff lived in cottages on the estate.

'Not long. You'll find a spare room that's comfortable – and I assure you I shan't bother you.' He eased the cork expertly out of the bottle and caught the bubbles. 'I find sex greatly overrated as a field sport.' He handed me a glass. 'Unlike so many of your contemporaries.'

I ate the steak and sipped a little of the champagne and then excused myself. Climbing the stairs slowly to the pretty chintzy bedroom which had been allotted to me, I kicked off my sandals and fell, fully dressed, onto the bed. It was barely half past nine.

Below me in his study Simon sat alone in the dusk with his telephones and his Telex and a new bottle of Scotch.

I was awakened by the sound of shouting. Somewhere

a door banged and there was a rush of feet. I sat up disorientated for a moment, then I ran to the door and looked out. It was pitch dark in the body of the house but I could hear the sound of shouting, muffled now, from downstairs and barefoot I ran down towards Simon's study.

Tim and Nigel were in the study with Simon and all three men were shouting.

'Tim? Oh Tim!' I ran to him and fell into his arms.

'Are you all right, Celia? Don't worry, the police are on their way.' I heard him reassuring me as his hug closed over me.

Nigel was grinning. 'I bought some air tickets when I went down to Florence yesterday,' he said good humouredly. 'I was hoping I could talk you into eloping with me, Celia. But I found myself eloping with this reprobate instead!' He punched Tim on the arm and both men laughed.

I stared from one to the other bewildered. 'Davina told you where I'd gone?'

'She told us everything,' said Tim grimly, 'including Simon's nasty little threat and Nigel here persuaded Jocelyn to fill in the rest. There was quite a show-down after you left.'

Simon broke in. 'You're too late, Armitage. If you've called the police it's too late to stop the deal. And it is Davina who will suffer if anyone does. And you. I'll break you for this. Ask your wife. I'll see you never sell so much as a flying duck to go on somebody's wall!'

Nigel turned to him slowly. 'Shut up, Simon, old boy,' he said tolerantly. 'You don't know what you're talking about. I'll see to it that Tim does all right. I do have a certain influence, you know. If you remember, that is the reason why you bother to know me at all.' His tone dropped in heavy sarcasm. Then he turned back to us. 'Now you two, I want you to get going. Take yourselves off to a motel or somewhere for the rest of the night. Borrow his car, he won't mind, and Uncle Nigel will take care of things here.'

Only when we had been driving for about half an hour did Tim tell me what had really happened. Jocelyn had convinced them that there was nothing they could do about Simon's activities. Davina was implicated too far and Simon too clever, so they had not called the police. Simon's only punishment would be a few hours' sweating until he realized that he had got away with it. Men like Simon always win.

'Davina's leaving him and I've told her she can come to us, Celia, do you mind?' Tim's hand groped for mine on the seat beside me. There was a long pause as we both peered through the windscreen wipers at the road ahead. I could feel the tears pricking at my eyes. 'I didn't sleep with her you know,' he said at last. 'You do believe that, don't you? It's you I love, and always will.'

I believed him.

The motel we found was small and shabby and the most beautiful place on earth. We were soaked from running from the BMW into the chalet and we had no luggage save my handbag with my passport, and we were both deliriously happy.

Trade Reunions

Jackie looked at her watch and then at the phone. Another half hour and Sue would be home from the cinema to relieve her, unless Bob and Phil were back by then. She glanced at the message pad. Two addresses so far this evening. Not bad, considering how hard it was raining!

The twenty-four-hour plumbing service had been her brother Phil's idea when she had joined the firm. The only rule was that she didn't go out on night jobs alone, which was fair enough by her. Instead she took it in turns to mind the phone with Sue.

She drained the dregs of her coffee and looked regretfully at the paperback on the table, finished twenty minutes before. If only it had lasted the evening because there was nothing worth watching on the box and if she made any more coffee she would begin to look like a Beautifully Blended Bean . . .

She took the phone call with her usual slight sinking feeling. Nightcallers were always dodgy: on the defensive for ringing late; or desperate; sometimes hysterical; sometimes downright abusive as if it were her fault; almost never what you would call routine. She picked up her pencil and waited.

And for the first time in her short career as a plumber it happened. The customer the other end of the line was someone she knew. She kept her voice carefully impersonal as she repeated his name and address.

'Someone will be there within half an hour, Mr Peters,' she said reassuringly.

She was smiling as she hung up and tore the page off the pad, folding it into her jeans pocket and when Sue appeared she was ready to leave.

'Only the two calls tonight, Sue,' she said happily. 'And the boys should be back soon, so I'll be on my way. I'm exhausted.' And she was out of the house and into her mini van before Sue could delay her another minute.

Stamford Avenue was much as she remembered it, quiet, respectable, really rather pleasant houses, not all that far from the school where John Peters and she had been sixth formers together. Number 35 was different though. Shabbier, not quite so imposing – or had it seemed so marvellous then because she had always seen it through rose-coloured spectacles?

Stupid, to feel her heart thumping again after all this time, just at the sight of his house. It wasn't after all as if she had even given him a thought in ages.

She pushed the gate and heard it squeak slightly on its hinges. Then she rang the door bell.

He was obviously waiting for the ring for the door opened almost at once. 'Thank God,' he said, 'come in quick!' Then his mouth dropped open. 'I'm sorry,' he said. 'I was expecting the plumber . . .'

She was used to it. Her bag of tools and the flat tweed cap she wore over her long chestnut hair usually convinced people in the end though. She walked on. 'That's right,' she said. 'I'm the plumber. Now, where did it happen?'

She kept her face straight with difficulty. He was wearing jeans rolled up to the knees and his feet were bare – and obviously wet. He looked distraught.

'Upstairs in the bedroom. I was nailing down the carpet and one went through this pipe under the board.'

'Have you turned off the water?'

He had not recognized her yet. And why should he? After all it was what, five years, and the light in the hall wasn't too good. She realized suddenly that there was no furniture. Just a ladder and some paint cans.

He was staring at her, but not with recognition or adoration. Just plain horror. 'I didn't think,' he said. 'I was trying to seal it off with towels . . .'

They found the main stop cock reasonably fast – not fast enough, she noticed sadly, to prevent a nasty brown stain appearing on the immaculately decorated ceiling of one of the rooms, but if a man didn't know where his own stop cock was then really she could not wonder if his house came to rack and ruin.

She followed him up the stairs.

The bedroom was a shambles. He had at least rolled the carpet back and torn up the boards. But the cavity beneath was full of soggy towels. Shaking her head she began to pull them out and pile them in a dirty revolting heap beside her on the floor.

'Nice new installation,' she commented critically. 'Been doing the house up I see.' She opened her bag and brought out the blow lamp and some spare lengths of copper pipe. Then she glanced up at him under her cap. Some stray wisps of hair had escaped and hung around her ears. He was staring at her.

'Jackie?' he said at last. 'I don't believe it!'

She grinned. 'You'd better. For the first time in your life you need me, John Peters.'

'But you went to university. You were going to teach . . .'

She made a face. 'Didn't anyone tell you that teaching jobs are hard to find?' she said, rummaging in her bag.

'You'll probably find lots of plumbers with English degrees these days. I did an apprenticeship and went into partnership with my brother.' She laid out her tools in a neat line. 'Do you live here with your parents?' she went on.

He seated himself on the end of the bed, still staring at her. 'No. They've retired down to Bournemouth. I'm buying the house off them. I teach at the old school now . . .' He looked down, suddenly abashed. 'Pure luck I got the job I expect . . .'

He had asked her out for the first time in the spring term of that last year at school. 'There's an exhibition I'd like to see at the Hayward Gallery. I thought we might go up by train and have a meal afterwards,' he had said. He was quite the best looking boy in the school then; tall, broad-shouldered, with a shock of fair hair and was considered by the girls of the top forms the supreme catch of the season.

Jackie was stunned by the invitation. Quiet and shy by nature she would never have dared so much as hope. She did not realize then the impact her coppery hair and green eyes could have on the opposite sex. Her eyes were nearly always fixed on her thumbed copies of Keats and Chaucer, so to raise them and find the smiling figure of John Peters standing before her was a considerable shock.

The day in London was a success. She had adored the exhibition and forgetting her shyness had blossomed under his attention. By the time they were ordering the hors-d'oeuvres she was madly in love.

Her work suffered of course, but not a lot. Being in love can help with the art of unravelling Keats or the sonnets of Shakespeare. Only John didn't see it that way. She was fun and a good doubles partner at tennis. That much he did not dispute. She was the right person to take to the cricket club dance at the end of term and fitted well with his old red MG but she did not particularly inspire his work; he was studying pure maths and physics.

He never asked her to his home. She knew where it was because once or twice she had quite by chance, of course, walked the dog down Stamford Avenue. That was how she knew the immaculate front garden with the row of standard roses and the shiny blue front gate.

To celebrate the end of A levels they had gone together on a picnic in the MG. He had prepared the food, in a real hamper; chicken, salad, wine, and they had stopped by the edge of the river and spread their rug on the bank. The water was cool and gentle against her toes.

'Where will you go if you don't get into Cambridge?' she asked him, lying back lazily, her arm across her eyes to keep out the sunlight.

'Cambridge,' he replied.

'You're pretty confident,' she retorted. Her own first choice was Bristol, a million miles away from Cambridge.

'There's always the vacations,' he said softly, for the first time since she had known him, reading her mind.

But vacations had come and gone and she had not seen him again. The anguish was lessened by the new faces, new places, by lectures and by the theatre, but always somewhere in the back of her mind she had kept alive the memory of John Peters and his old red MG.

'I never thought I'd see inside this house,' she said cheerfully as she wielded her hack-saw.

'I didn't bring people home.' He was watching her, fascinated. 'It was too distracting.'

'You were a real pig, you know,' she went on, neatly lifting out the damaged piece of pipe. 'I broke my heart over you that summer we left school.'

He gave a sheepish grin. 'Me too. But I was afraid you'd come between my work and me. I was always terrified I'd run into you in the vacations. One look at you and I'd have been a gonner again.'

She sat back on her heels. 'Should I be flattered?' She had never even guessed he felt as strongly as that.

'You should. I saw you as a *femme fatale*. *Fatale* to my career that is.'

'As a teacher? Here!' She was incredulous.

He pulled a face. 'No. I had something a bit more exciting in mind then. Research. The States. That sort of thing.'

For a moment they stared at each other. Then she burst out laughing. 'Looks as though we both came down to earth with a bump!' she gurgled. 'Poor John. Always so impractical!'

'You're married now, I suppose,' he said after a minute.

She shook her head. 'A career girl me. And you?'

'No. No one would have me.' He was surveying the shambles around them despondently.

'Not even for your good looks and your cooking?' She was teasing him now, remembering how he had grudgingly admitted that it was he and not his mother who had put together the food for their picnics. He was, she had heard later, a notable chef. But he never washed up.

She carefully measured out the new length of pipe.

'You,' he said, retaliating at last, 'couldn't boil an egg in those days.'

'Still can't,' she said cheerfully unabashed.

She was looking for her matches. They weren't in her pockets, or her bag or her jacket. He was watching speculatively.

'Lost something?' he asked at last.

She could feel herself blushing slightly. 'Matches,' she said. 'For the blow lamp.'

'Oh. I see.' He didn't move. 'I'd have thought a really efficient plumber would have had several boxes.'

She glanced up at him under her eyelashes.

'I've a confession to make. I shouldn't really be here,' she said.

'I thought not. What are you? A secretary or something?'

For a moment she was speechless with indignation.

'No, John, I am a plumber. A real plumber with a piece of paper to prove it. The reason I shouldn't be here is because Phil and Bob don't let me go out on night jobs alone.'

'I'm glad to hear it.' He was watching her closely. 'So, how come you're here?'

'I didn't log it in the book.' She bit her lip, trying not to laugh as she saw the knowing look on his face. 'I'm willing to trade, Mr Peters,' she said softly. 'You cook me a meal and I'll fix your central heating for free. How does that sound to you.'

'Pretty good,' he said. 'I don't think I can fault that bargain.' He stood up. 'Providing that you take off that appalling cap when you're eating!'

It was five minutes later that she found him in the kitchen. He was whistling.

'John,' she said. 'You've forgotten something.'

'Oh?' He turned and looked at her enquiringly.

'Matches.'

'Oh yes, matches.' He reached a box down from the dresser. Then he put his hands behind him. 'Not included in the bargain, of course. Matches are extra.'

She stuck her tongue out at him. 'It's your central heating. I can always go away and leave you to freeze.'

He grinned. 'I'd complain to your boss. Come on. They're not too expensive. One small kiss. For old times' sake.'

131

She thought for a moment. 'Payment deferred till after supper?'

Nodding he held them out to her. 'Payment deferred. Though there might be a bit of interest accruing by then of course.'

She laughed. 'I'll risk it,' she said.

All You Need To Do Is Smile

Once when Celia was about eight years old, her mother had said: 'You'll never keep your boyfriends, darling, if you look as grouchy as that when they speak to you,' and she had laughed and fondly punched the boy in question on the shoulder to comfort him for her daughter's disdain. Her cousin Michael it had been, Celia thought, frowning as she probed the memory.

Strange that she should think of that now, so many years later, as she walked slowly from the post office up the village street. Her mother's voice was vivid in her ears as was the memory of her own anguished embarrassment and her burning hatred of the unfortunate Michael.

But she had been right, her tall distinguished mother; Celia hadn't been able to keep her boyfriends and now, true to form she had lost her husband as well.

'It's not your fault, Cee,' he had said ruefully as slowly he packed his cases. 'I blame myself. Something went wrong somewhere. Perhaps it would have been OK if I hadn't met Louise. We might have struggled through and made it work but now there's no point. I'm sorry.'

And he had gone.

Bruised and alone she had refused to cry, to question fate. She continued to exist; to light the autumn-bitter driftwood fires in the cottage grate, to feed the cats, to collect the mail and the groceries every week at the village post office and walk the two miles back along the saltings home. But now there were seldom any letters; the post had always been for Don. For a week or two after he had gone they had continued to come, the letters and the packets and then abruptly they had stopped almost overnight. So presumably now they all went to his new address, his and Louise's, and all his colleagues and his friends knew that he had left Celia and no longer lived in the cottage at the edge of the ocean. The post which had accumulated she put into a drawer unopened. He had left no forwarding address.

She stooped beneath the heavy rucksack full of tins and packets and eased the shopping bag from one hand to the other. Soon now the winds would come, lashing the tides higher and higher up the beach, tearing the surface sand in spindrifts from the path, hurling rain and spume against the windows. That was when in any other year they would have put up the shutters and ruefully left their home for the worst three months or so of the year and gone to stay with Celia's mother in the town. But not this year. Celia was not going to tell her mother that Don had left her. She deliberately stopped her weekly phone call from the post office and wrote instead, a stilted, hearty little note which she knew would fool no one, and she posted it in the little box in the pebble wall beneath the shop window before turning for home.

Already it was growing dark and grey clouds were scudding in across the sea, trailing icy showers in their wake. Behind her the young man who had been buying stamps in the post office came out and banged the door, pulling the collar of his jacket round his ears before setting off after her up the street. His boots rang on the stone echoing beneath the blank walls of the cottages. The holiday-makers had gone now and most of them were empty. The fishermen lived further back in the lanes and alleys out of reach of the corroding air of the sea.

Celia hesitated, conscious suddenly of the hurrying steps behind her.

'Excuse me?'

She stopped and looked back. He had pleasant wavy hair and a shy grin which reminded her of someone: Michael. Of course, he was like cousin Michael who had complimented her on her pink dress all those years ago and been so rudely rebuffed. That's why the memory had returned unbidden. She smiled uncertainly. 'Can I help you?'

He grinned, pushing the fair hair out of his eyes as the first cold shower swept over them.

'I hope I can help you actually. Can I carry something? It is Celia Scott isn't it? I'm Brian Fraser, a friend of Don's. Did he tell you?' He was too busy lifting the pack from her shoulders to notice the smile freezing on her lips.

'Did he send you?' She stayed turned away from him, gazing out across the salt grass towards the sea.

'Send me? No, I haven't seen him in years actually. I thought I'd surprise him. How is he?'

She began walking again. Her shoulders straight now, not flinching as the rain misted across her face. The terns were wheeling and crying over the tide beside them. Brian walked beside her, the heavy bag swinging easily from one shoulder. Glancing at her he grinned.

'It's some place you've chosen to live! Trust Don to find a hide-out like this.'

She forced herself to smile. 'We love it here.' She had to tell him, make him turn back, send him away.

She walked on. 'It's a long way from the station. Did you take a cab?'

He grinned. 'I hitched. Not affluent enough for anything else I'm afraid. Actually,' he stopped and faced her,

135

his face suddenly troubled. 'Actually I'm on the scrounge. I wondered if you and Don might be able to put me up for a few days and . . .' He looked down at his scuffed canvas shoes. 'It's a long story,' he added quietly.

A squall of wind grabbed the rain and flung it at them threateningly, moaning across the shore line. Celia shivered. The stove would have gone out and the cats would be huddling disconsolately by it, waiting for her to come and light it, waiting for her to talk to them. She talked to them a lot now; there was no one else to talk to.

She grinned at Brian, wiping the streaming rain from her eyes. "Course you can stay. Come on. Let's hurry.'

He lit the stove and stacked away her tins and took Linnaeus on his knee and drank hot soup as the shutters rattled and the lamp smoked. Then he looked at her and smiled. 'Where's Don?'

'Not here.'

'I can see that. Where is he?'

She shrugged. 'He left me for another woman. It's the oldest story in the book.'

'Do you care?'

She opened her mouth to protest, to assure him, to emphasize her love and then she stopped, watching the black paws stretch and flex on the rough denim on his knees. 'He likes you,' she said irrelevantly. 'He won't go to many people.'

Brian went on staring at her and she knew she had to answer. 'I'm numb without him,' she said at last.

His long gentle fingers were playing with the fur behind the cat's ears. 'You can't stay here on your own surely.'

'I have Linnaeus and Kizzy.' She smiled wistfully. 'I talk to them. And then I have my painting.'

He did not turn to look at the half-finished seascape on the easel. 'You're quite famous, I believe.' He did not make the statement sound sarcastic. He was stating a fact.

'I've had a few exhibitions,' she replied, guarded.

'And Don was still studying the seaweeds and the crabs?'

She smiled for the first time since they had seated themselves beside the stove. 'As usual. So this place suited us both.'

'Where has he gone, do you know?'

She shook her head. 'Her name is Louise.'

He stood up then, putting the cat down in his place on the chair, went over to the easel and stood looking at the painting on it. For a long time he said nothing then he turned, his eyes narrowed. 'Have you touched a brush since Don left?'

She could feel herself colouring. She bent and fed some sticks into the stove. 'I've done some sketching,' she said at last, defensively.

She watched as he walked around the room, turning canvases to face him, flipping over the sketches in the portfolio under a chair.

'You said you'd explain what you were doing here,' she said at last into the silence. Her voice was brusquer than she intended.

He straightened up abruptly. 'You're entitled to that.' He fumbled in the front pocket of his jeans and brought out a flattened pack of cigarettes. He did not offer her one. 'I would rather have told Don,' he said after a pause, his back to the shuttered window.

'Well, you'll have to make do with me.'

'I knew Don at college.' He struck a match and held it out for a moment, staring, waiting for the flame to steady. 'We were good friends once. I liked him.'

'And since?' She was watching him closely.

'Since, he went his way and I went mine. He went on to do a doctorate and became an expert on seaweed, I became a drifter.'

'You must have kept in touch, to have known about this place.'

He shook his head, absently putting the spent match back in the box. 'Someone gave me the address a year or so back; I never followed it up.'

'Till now.'

'Till now.' There was a long silence. 'I'm in trouble, Celia.'

'I thought perhaps you were,' she said softly. 'What sort?'

For a moment she didn't think he was going to answer. He threw the cigarette unsmoked into the stove and went back to perch on the edge of his chair. Behind him Linnaeus began to purr.

'Shall we say I borrowed some money? I need to pay it back.'

Celia stared at him, her stomach tightening. 'How much?'

'A hundred quid.'

She closed her eyes, feeling the heat from the stove beating against the lids. Don would have given it to him, would have shrugged and cursed him and given it to him without any questions. But Don was not here and she had no money.

When she opened her eyes he was looking at her. He smiled. 'No, Celia, I couldn't take it from you anyway. Don't worry. I'll think of something. I usually do.'

He was still like Michael. The hair, the smile, that disarming, gentle smile. 'Are the police after you?'

'I don't know. I shouldn't think so. It wasn't quite that bad. I didn't rob a bank or anything. If I had I hope I would have done a bit better than a hundred lousy quid.'

She stood up jerkily and picked up the coffee pot which stood on the stove. 'They would never find you here. No one would.' She swung round to face him. 'Don't tell me any more, Brian. I don't want to know about it.'

He reached down at his feet for his mug and held it out to her to refill. 'I'll go. If you want me to.'

She straightened up and stared stiffly past him at the shuttered window, listening to the scream of the wind, the crash of the waves against the sea wall beyond the saltings. There wasn't another human being for two or three miles.

'No. I'd like you to stay.'

Kizzy liked him, purring and flirting her tail as she wove intricate patterns around his ankles.

'I like coquettish females,' he said laughing as he bent to stroke her and Celia, watching, felt a sharp pang of jealousy.

'Most men do,' she said, unconscious of the longing in her voice.

He glanced up. 'You don't find it easy, talking to men, do you?' It wasn't a question.

She shrugged. 'Is that how it seems to you?'

'That's how it seems.' He grinned. 'We're only people, you know.'

She knew. Only too well. 'You'll never keep your boy-friends, darling,' the phrase came back again echoing in her head, the words pounding against her skull. Her mother had kept her boyfriends all right, after her father had died, flirting, giggling, simpering at them, hiding her brain, her talent, her ability. Anything to keep her escorts attentive, producing even now a new one every winter for her and Don's inspection. Celia at the age of seven had vowed never to be like that. She would giggle and flirt for no man. Ever. And she glared at Kizzy who had closed her eyes in ecstasy as she was tickled under her chin.

'I expect I drove Don away,' she said suddenly, her eyes meeting his in defiance.

And it was then, amazingly, that he had kissed her lightly on the mouth, his hand on the point of her chin, his eyes open and laughing. 'I doubt if you did,' he said softly. 'All you need to do is smile occasionally. I've seen you do it. I know.'

Perhaps it was the fact that he was not perfect which gave her the confidence she needed. She saw him not as a male, to be challenged and defied, but as someone who needed her help. As he himself had said he was, after all, only people.

She relaxed and unchallenging and unchallenged she did, almost without realizing it, begin to smile. The wind did not seem so cold now with someone else to share the blaze from the wood stove and she ceased brooding about Don, concentrating instead at last upon the beauty of the present, not the disasters of the past. Brian taught her that.

'Treasure what was good, forget what was bad,' he said, as together they watched an aquamarine sunset. 'That way, when he comes back you'll have a future together; something to build on. Otherwise you'll only destroy and tear down what is left.'

'When he comes back?' she turned and looked at him, her face illuminated by the pale light from the sky.

'When. If.' He was still trying to sound impersonal. 'Take what comes as it comes, Celia, and draw on it. Use it to make you strong.' He reached for her hand and held it and suddenly he could not pretend indifference any more. 'You know what I want. I'm hoping he never comes back.'

And he kissed her again.

*

Was it months or was it only weeks he stayed with her? She lost count in her new strange happiness, pouring out her confidence on canvas after canvas, not thinking at all of the decision she might have to make if Don returned. For the time being there was no word from him and that was enough. She no longer thought of him as her husband. Perhaps she never had, properly. Only now, for the first time in her life, was her whole being centred around a man. And it was not humiliating or servile. It was fulfilling. She felt complete at last.

Brian would stand and watch her at her easel, studying the fluent lines of her body as she wielded her brush or the palette knife, smiling slightly at her unconscious beauty, realizing that against all the rules − his rules − he had begun to love her, and as she sensed his eyes on her and looked up he would exchange with her a quiet smile before turning away to the stove or the cats, not wanting to distract her.

But he knew it could not last. He had watched the emergence from her shell, felt her relax and bloom beneath his hands; he realized her new dependence on him and he knew he could not allow it to continue. His own conscience was too stern. He had no right in her house, no brief to give her advice when his own life was such a mess.

'How long will it take you to finish that painting, Celia?' He was leaning against the door, feeling the buffet of the wind against his shoulder through the wood. He aimed the ash from his cigarette at the stove, frowning.

'A week perhaps. I don't know.' She did not look up as she spoke, squinting at the canvas, her thin face framed by its tangle of ash-blonde hair. Brian forced himself to look away.

'As quick as that?' Bleakness swept over him for he knew this painting would be the last he watched. He bent

141

to pick Kizzy up from her nest in the chair and buried his face in her fur.

'You're going, aren't you?' Her quiet voice behind him made him swing round. He looked into her eyes, the cat still in his arms.

'Sometime. Yes.'

She held his gaze for a moment. Almost, but not quite, she heard her mother's voice but the pain in his face was too plain. This time she understood. She smiled and held out her hand. Her fingers met silky black fur and secure against his chest Kizzy began to purr.

Three days later he was gone.

She awoke to find the pillow next to her cold, the kitchen door swinging gently in the icy sunshine. The glare from the crystalline sea hid the path across the saltings, but somehow she knew he was already long out of sight.

For a long time she stood there clutching her towelling robe around her in the cold wind, then, slowly she turned back inside and closed the door. But the house wasn't empty as it had been when Don had left. It was still warm and welcoming and full of happy memories, and bereft as she was she knew she could continue with her painting and her life, for this time she had not driven anyone away.

She found his note pinned to her easel:

I wanted to stay for ever. You know why I couldn't.
When I've settled my debts I'll come back to see you.
Then if you're still alone and you want me, all you
need to do is smile.

The Bath –
A Summer Ghost Story

In the long, narrow back garden behind the house the grass they had so carefully tended through the spring was rapidly turning, beneath the children's feet, back to the dust from which it came. Cathy's anxious watering, walking up and down with a long-spouted can, refilled eight solemn times from the tap in the kitchen, did nothing but turn the dust momentarily into little swirling eddies which promptly vanished. If only they could use a hose pipe, but they had been banned until further notice. It hadn't rained for five weeks.

She turned from the kitchen window with a sigh. Ben and Sarah were occupied at least. Perhaps she could snatch a cup of coffee and five minutes with the paper before the children's onslaught resumed.

The crash outside in the street made her leap to her feet. A huge lorry had backed up the cul-de-sac of Edwardian terraced houses and deposited an enormous yellow skip almost outside their front door. She stared at it, watching mesmerized as the man uncoupled the heavy chains. Behind her two small heads pushed against the front window beside her, noses flattened against the glass.

'We heard the noise from the garden, Mum.' Ben's eyes were shining. 'Is it ours?'

143

Cathy was indignant. 'No. It's not ours.'

It was the new neighbours'. Liz knocked on the door half an hour later and introduced herself.

'I am sorry about the skip.' She seemed genuinely embarrassed. 'When I ordered it, I had no idea it would be bigger than the house!' She ran her fingers through a shock of short brown hair. 'It's only for a couple of days – while we gut the place.'

Cathy shooed away the children and offered her a cold drink. 'Is the house in a bad state? Ours was already more or less modernized when we moved in. We were lucky.'

Liz drained the glass of orange with apparent enjoyment. 'The place is a tip. I doubt if it has been touched since it was built. I only hope we haven't taken on too much!' She gazed reflectively into the empty glass. 'Come and see what we're doing if you like.'

One look at her children's faces told Cathy such an invitation could not be missed.

They told Tony about it later. 'There were still gas lamps on the walls, Dad. No electricity. Not anywhere. I didn't know there were houses without electricity!' Ben, a true child of the twentieth century, had been shocked speechless by the thought of there being nowhere to plug in the TV.

'You should have seen it, Tony.' Cathy had loved it. 'It was like walking into the past. Oh, it was dirty and everything, but the detail – the stained glass, the carved wood, the ornate shades on the gas lamps. It's a crime it's all going to be thrown away. There was the most wonderful old bath with wrought iron scrolling on it and beautiful ornate legs.'

'Sounds like you, my love.' Tony smiled at her fondly. 'Shall I take a turn with the watering can, while you put the kids to bed?'

Cathy cringed. A part-time feminist – part-time

144

between taking the children back and forth to playschool and cooking and cleaning – she had taught herself like so many of her friends to loathe what she considered sexist remarks. 'No, my love. You take a turn putting the kids to bed. Then you can roll up your trousers and show me your legs.'

'OK, sorry. Point taken. It was a joke.' No longer upset when his attempted compliments were rejected, Tony raised his hands in rueful surrender.

Two days later, when the bath appeared in the skip, Cathy could bear it no more. She went next door.

'You want it?' Liz looked at her amazed. 'You want that old bath?'

'I'll buy it from you.'

'No, no. We've thrown it out. You can have it and welcome. Where would you like it?' Jim, Liz's man, was vastly amused. 'I'll get our builders to put it round in your garden, shall I?'

Solemnly the huge iron bath was marched in through the front door, across the living room, through the kitchen and out of the back door into the hot dusty garden. They left it, standing forlornly on what passed for a terrace outside the kitchen window. Then Cathy rang Tony at work. 'I know you'll think I am quite mad, but . . .'

When he had stopped laughing, he told her she was, quite mad. 'You don't seriously want it installed?'

'I do, Tony. Please. After all there is room. The bathroom is big enough.'

'Cathy, you are out of your mind. We have a beautiful modern bath! And it matches the basin. It matches the loo for that matter.'

'The loo is next door,' Cathy retorted, 'so it hardly matters what colour that is. Anyway, I intend to paint the bath. It will match as well as the old one, I promise. Please, Tony. You wait till you see it. It will be magnificent.'

As she hung up she knew she had slipped disastrously down the scale in their relationship. To want the old bath was an illogical 'feminine' act. She had to convince Tony of its interior design possibilities or her personal five year battle for female equality would be lost on a momentary impulse.

The plumber they called to install it thought she was mad as well. As did the children. 'Mum, it's horrible! It's dirty and all black and grey at the bottom, and YUKKY!' Sarah was in no doubt at all how she felt about it. 'I will not sit down in it. I will NOT!'

Cathy was beginning to feel rather desperate. Family revulsion and ridicule were all very well in small quantities, but in such unanimity they were beginning to worry her. Doggedly she worked at the bathroom, throwing open the windows to the hot July night as she painted the outside of the bath a beautiful olive green to blend with what was left of the modern suite and resurfaced the pitted, stained inside. The result was dramatic and very effective. Pleased with herself, she called Tony and the children for an inspection. They were all watching TV and were not too keen on leaving their programme. With much protesting they solemnly trooped upstairs and crowded into the bathroom.

'Not bad,' Ben was grudging. 'At least it's bigger than the old bath.' The little boy had to stand on tiptoe to see over the edge.

'It's twice as big, you dope.' Cathy ruffled his hair affectionately. 'You'll be able to swim in that! But not yet. We've got to let the enamel dry.'

'I must say, they built man-size baths in those days!' Tony said with reluctant admiration. 'Even I will be able to stretch out full length in that! No more excuses about dirty knees because they never get under the water.' He grinned. 'We're not getting a Victorian loo next, by any chance?'

She shook her head. 'Pretty curtains, and perhaps a mirror from the junk shop on the corner – they've got one there which would be just right. He's had it standing out on the pavement for days; it's not expensive.' She glanced sheepishly at her husband. 'Old pine would be perfect, wouldn't it?'

'I dare say.' Tony frowned. 'But we're not made of money, love . . .'

She bought it, guiltily, after knocking the price down by a fiver, comforting herself with the thought that she would soon be working again. The mirror was perfect. Staring into it, she could see the whole bathroom behind her. The room had once been a bedroom so it was large; there was room for a chair and the old chest she had stripped the year before down to the warm soft honey-coloured wood. The new curtains blew gently in the hot breeze from the garden. From the trees at the bottom of the road she could hear the gentle moaning of a wood pigeon. It was very, very hot. The house was quiet. The children had gone out to play and Tony was at work.

Cautiously she touched the new enamel of the bath with her finger. It felt hard and cold. Impulsively she put in the enormous brass plug and turned on the taps. Dragging off her T-shirt and jeans she pitched them into the straw clothes basket, followed by her bra and pants. The draught from the window was cool on her skin as she pinned her hair up on top of her head. A mist of steam shaded the mirror and she rubbed it absentmindedly with her fingers as she reached for the bath crystals Liz and Jim next door had given her. 'As a sort of launching present,' Jim had said with a grin. They still thought her mad, although they had been in to admire the bath.

Behind her there was a shadowy disturbance somewhere in the mirror. She stared into the glass, puzzled. Some of the silvering had gone and parts of the image were indistinct and blurred, but there it was again – a light movement behind her in the room. She turned. There was nothing there. Only the gentle whirl of steam and the glittering patterns of water. Guiltily she turned off the taps. It would be wrong to try and fill such a big bath with the water shortage so bad.

She lay there a long time, luxuriating in the these days unaccustomed luxury of a daytime bath, then slowly she climbed out and dried herself and, dropping the towel on the carpet, began to rub some lotion lazily over her body.

As she balanced one toe on the chair, stroking the lotion up her legs she suddenly had the strangest feeling that she was being watched. She spun round, grabbing the towel, holding it tightly over her breasts, but there was no one there – only the cheerfully gurgling water spiralling out of the plug hole and, outside the window, the pigeon still crooning in the heat of the afternoon. She told herself she was a fool and, wrapping the towel round her, ran through into the bedroom to dress.

In the end the children loved the bath. There was room for both of them at once, together with Ben's fleet and they could still re-enact the Battle of Trafalgar with sound effects. Tony grinned at his wife as they stood for a moment listening in the kitchen. 'You sit down and have a cold drink. I'll sort them out.'

He disappeared upstairs and was still missing half an hour later. The sound effects had if anything worsened. Cathy smiled. The bath was obviously a success.

At half past ten that night Tony went upstairs yawning, while Cathy sat watching the end of the film. After it had finished she sat for a while on her own, relishing the silence and the cool. Upstairs the house was unbearably hot. When at last she followed him up, the light in the bedroom was already off and she could hear the gentle sound of snoring.

148

She smiled sadly. They were often too tired to make love these days.

She ran a cool, shallow bath while she undressed and stood naked while she brushed her teeth. Outside the closed curtains the night was very still.

The appreciative chuckle was almost drowned by the sound of running water. Spitting out the last of the toothpaste she rinsed out her mouth. 'I thought you were asleep,' she said over her shoulder. 'I'm glad you're not.' She turned, expecting to see Tony. The room was empty. She peered into the bedroom. He was exactly as she had left him, snoring.

Puzzled and disappointed she went back into the bathroom. She was obviously hearing things.

She was vacuuming in the bedroom next day when she smelt the pomade. The rich, spicy scent was drifting into the room from the bathroom next door. She sniffed appreciatively, then, puzzled by its source, she switched off the cleaner and looked into the bathroom. As always in the heat the window was flung wide. The room felt steamy as if someone had just had a bath and the exotic smell was very strong. She stared round, feeling the little hairs on the back of her neck stirring slightly. Then a shriek from one of the children downstairs distracted her and she turned away. When she came back, crisis over, half an hour later, the smell had gone.

That night she and Tony were going out. The children had refused to go to bed; the baby sitter was late and long after they were supposed to have left she was still desperately putting on some make up. She was leaning towards the mirror in the bathroom, squinting slightly as she stroked the mascara onto her lashes, when she caught sight of a movement out of the corner of her eye. The room seemed steamy and hot and faintly she could smell it again. The sweet spicy smell. She peered harder and her eyes widened in astonishment. Someone was in the bath. In the mirror she could see the water swirling around his middle, thick with suds. He was lying back watching her, an expression of quizzical amusement on his face. For a split second she saw him, saw the handsome, heavy-set face, the mutton chop whiskers, the wavy chestnut hair, the broad shoulders, the slightly plump hairy chest, then he was gone. She spun round with a gasp, staring into the bath. It was empty. She swallowed hard, trying to calm herself, but her heart was hammering furiously somewhere under her ribs. Cautiously she stepped towards it. She reached out and ran her fingers over the enamel. It was cold.

'Come on, Cathy, we're going to be late.' Tony appeared in the doorway. 'For God's sake, you're not even dressed!'

She stared at him blankly then without a word she turned back to the mirror. As she hastily finished her make up, the bath behind her remained bleakly cold.

She didn't say a word to anyone. In retrospect she wasn't afraid. She was really quite amused. Half of her – the rational half – knew she must have imagined him and yet – the smell of his hair oil, the steam, the gentle sound of water dripping into the deep, warm suds. They were so real! Real enough to stop her wandering round the upstairs with no clothes on! She would grab her bath robe and knot it firmly round her waist before going into the bathroom. When she actually had a bath it was different. She put in the plug and filled the bath, almost daring him to appear. But she knew he wouldn't. As she climbed into the two inches of water they were now allowed in the tenth week of the drought she knew she was alone. It was when she had her back to it, thinking about something else, glancing absent-mindedly into the mirror that she saw him.

But he only came when she was naked.

Testing him, half daring, half afraid she left her towelling robe on the bedroom floor and walked nude into the bathroom. She could feel herself self-consciously holding in her stomach and pushing back her shoulders, walking with a studied grace she had no time for in her real downstairs life. She did not even glance at the bath. Holding her breath she went and stood at the window, looking out across the parched gardens, feeling the clammy, thundery heat touching her skin.

It took a moment to pluck up the courage to look at last into the mirror.

He was there. She could see the clouds of steam, smell the soap, the spice, hear the splashing of water as he lifted a sponge and thoughtfully squeezed it over his broad chest.

Forcing herself to stand still she stared into the mirror until she caught his eye. He smiled and raised an eyebrow appreciatively and then, slowly, he winked. When she turned he had gone.

'I wish we knew something about the history of these old houses,' she said to Liz a few days later.

Liz nodded. They were side by side in her house stripping wallpaper on the landing. 'I do know something about ours, actually,' she said. 'It belonged to Ned Basset. He was a famous music-hall artist. "A notorious rake and a ladies' man", as that idiot at the house agents described him. I'm glad I never knew him. He sounds exactly the type of man I should detest.'

'A male chauvinist pig of the worst kind, no doubt.' Cathy found herself smiling as she agreed. 'Ned Basset,' she echoed after a moment. 'So that was his name.'

'Why, do you know something about him?' Liz ripped a strip of torn wallpaper off, screwing up her face at the dust.

'No.' Cathy threw down her scraper. 'Nothing at all.'

She didn't tell Liz about the bath. She didn't tell anyone. She knew Tony hadn't seen him; nor, she was certain, had the children. He was her secret. Her admirer. Perhaps he was her fantasy.

Was that it? Was he just a product of her imagination? The creation of a woman who had been conditioned by the age she lived in to reject compliments from men as sexist and unwelcome when deep down inside she craved them? Without realizing it she looked at Tony and smiled. That night they made love for the first time in weeks.

The next day after she had taken the children to play-school she came back and walked upstairs to the bathroom. She stood looking down at the bath. It was cold and empty. The enamel was dry. The room was just as usual, the children's toothbrushes lying on the basin, a streak of gaudy striped toothpaste decorating the soap, a wad of hairs in the plug hole, flecks of shaving soap on the mirror behind it, a pile of discarded clothes on the carpet. A towel lay near them, still damp, tangled and already a little smelly. Cathy felt a wave of depression sweep over her. Oh yes, she needed a fantasy. What woman didn't?

But she didn't want him to be a fantasy. That would be a weakness on her part; an admission of defeat. She wanted him to be real.

There was only one way to find out the truth.

Liz laughed. 'It's crazy, isn't it? We throw out that bath, and you make it so nice that you can invite people to come along and try it!'

'Only while your new bathroom is still disconnected,' Cathy said, all innocence. 'I thought it would be a change from the plastic bowl you were telling me about!' She had tidied the bathroom, laid out fresh towels, put a small bowl of roses on the windowsill.

Of course, it might not work. He never appeared when she was actually taking a bath, but sometimes afterwards, when she was drying herself . . .

And Liz did have, when one came to think about it, a

rather buxom figure beneath her habitual overalls. The kind of figure a rake and a ladies' man might appreciate. If he were real . . .

Liz took her time. Cathy could hear her singing cheerfully. There was a lot of splashing and afterwards the sound of water running away. Then there was a long, long silence.

When she reappeared Cathy looked at her hard. 'Was everything all right?' she asked as casually as she could.

'Fine.' Liz smiled. 'But what on earth was that fantastic exotic smell up there as I was getting dry?'

'Ah,' said Cathy with a smile. 'I've been wondering that myself . . .'

A Private Ceremony

She had slept in the room for nearly three weeks before she noticed that one strip of wallpaper was upside down. A spider showed it to her.

Lying gazing at the wall she saw the sunlight in the fine lace web. Behind it a rose hung stem upwards, its petals drooping. Lazily her eye followed to see leaves and buds and further blooms suspended as though by invisible wire over the creamy void. It hurt her to see the flowers thus. It seemed incongruous and cruel; a stroke of fate which left them for ever vertiginous, outcasts among their fellows on the wall.

Now she could no longer come into the room without her eyes immediately straying to this corner by the window. When someone moved the spider's web she was really very angry. It seemed the flowers' only redemption that they had been selected by the spider as the nearest thing to nature in the room. Now nothing distinguished them any more, save their own oddity.

Sitting at her mirror, brushing out her long hair, she heard again in her head the voice which haunted.

'The trouble with Samantha is of course that she is a teeny bit different from the rest of us, haven't you noticed?'

Her eyes as she gazed at them were a pure expressionless blue. They saw much. The silver-backed hairbrush made her arm ache. It was too heavy. But she kept up the

154

endless strokes, listening to the crackle, watching the fine floating strands as her hair took on a life of its own around her head.

'Never, but *never*, brush your hair a hundred times, darling. It's death, positively death, and *so* Victorian.' She heard in her head the voice of the posturing little man who tended her hair and she brushed on harder than ever. This hairbrush had been made to brush hair a hundred strokes. It would be mortified if used to do less. When she had finished her hair then she would polish the brush. It seemed only fair.

In the mirror, in the corner where the silvering had gone in tiny freckles, she could see the angle of the room behind her. The casement window stood wide and she could see a fine mist of rain drifting over the garden below. The window still shone with wet and the pale green carpet beneath it darkened slowly as it grew damp. She could smell the grateful earth as its fragrance rose up in response to the rain.

Her roses, the upside down roses, could never smell like roses. But then they would never rot and grow black and die either.

She slammed her silver brush down on the dressing table glass and reached to clasp a bracelet around her slim wrist. Flinging off her dressing gown she stood naked on the carpet, throwing back her head and feeling the silky weight of her hair on her shoulders. It was strange that one was not allowed to appear naked before the world, even when one knew that one was beautiful.

She stood before the open window and felt the icy mist of rain on her warm skin.

A man stood outside in the garden, in the rain, his hair plastered blackly to his head, his tweed jacket heavy with moisture. He was standing looking up at her, not noticing the rain any more.

She smiled down at him and raised her hand. Then she moved away from the window and zipped herself dreamily into gold and embroidered chiffon. The spider was spinning again, she noticed suddenly, slightly further down the corner but still carefully, precisely, on the misplaced wallpaper. She watched fascinated.

She knew the man in the rain. In less than three weeks he would be her husband. His ring was on her finger; his kisses in her hair. Was it those she had been trying so hard to brush away?

The moth, its delicate finely traced velvet wings whirring ecstatically, stood no chance. Samantha put out her hand to ward it off, but she stayed the gesture in mid air, arrested by the sight of the diamond ring on her finger. It mesmerized her with its rainbow prisms and when she looked again the moth was caught. The spider's paralysing jaws were ready, and the straitjacket of fine spun silk. The spider embraced its victim tenderly, lost in caressing the silky fur on the tiny quivering body. How quickly beauty and freedom and life itself were lost.

She turned away, revolted and suddenly afraid.

The days passed. Showers of rain swept the gardens and terraces. From time to time she saw the man again standing beneath her window. In the corner the web was deserted, the moth no more than a frail dust caught in the still-sticky threads. The spider had gone.

Now when she stood at the window she kept her dressing gown on, clutching it to her, shivering.

Then she left the house in a haze of goodbyes. When she returned she would be its daughter. The web would have closed around her and the time for dreams would have gone.

In the taxi she looked into the mirror in her powder compact and saw that the haunted blue still shadowed her eyes. Where was their expression and their life? Her soul was shut down, secret, protected. It must be kept separate now or he would possess it as he must possess her.

She could not understand, suddenly, why she was afraid now. She recognized him as her friend. He was kind and gentle. He had not tried to rush her, had carefully controlled his own swelling waves of emotion. He recognized her fragility. He would treasure and protect her as a piece of fine porcelain. Again the voice spoke in her head:

'Samantha is a teeny bit different from the rest of us . . .'

'I'm not, I'm not,' she screamed silently. 'I am the same. I feel, I need, I fear. But I am trapped within myself. I am Rapunzel within the tower. He stands in the garden, at the foot of the wall, but he will not climb. He does not know that I have let the ladder fall. He strokes my golden hair, but he does not grip it, does not climb.'

The train carried her back to London where the rain smelt of soot and the plane trees wept in their concrete prisons, here and there their roots breaking free of tarmac and flagstone only to shrivel and waste in the dead air.

Her flat was dark and empty, a refuge she had always thought, for her soul. But her soul would not be comforted. It sought a mystic union now and would be satisfied with nothing less. Here where the wallpaper was immaculate, where no spiders dared to defile, where no mists of rain could spatter through the window glass, she had built for herself a temple of virginity. And she knew now what must be done. She picked up the telephone and dialled his number.

'Meet me at the station,' she said. Her voice was smiling. This time she needed no luggage; no gold bangles; no chiffon. No hairbrush save the wind.

He did not understand. He thought she had forgotten something. Never before had he seen her smile like this. His heart grew warm as he met her eyes. Now, she saw, he understood at last.

They drove up onto the moor. Still the rain surrounded them, misting the windows of the car, soaking the bracken and heather, filling the upturned bells of tiny flowers till they hung their heads beneath the weight of the water, and spilt it, nectar-like upon the ground.

Once more she felt the weight of her hair on her shoulders, the cold rain upon her warm body. She saw in his face delight and hope as she turned to him, her arms outstretched, at one with the soft wet earth, the grass and the heather. She felt his hand gently, hesitatingly on her golden hair.

Her eyes as she scanned them anxiously in her mirror in the train going home had a new depth of violet in the iris. She tore open the windows of the flat, bought armfuls of roses and trimmed her pure white wedding dress with blue.

She took her hair, tangled from the wind and heather, to be restyled and giggled as the voice said, 'But darling, the wind is death, positively death.' The posturing little man wanted her to wear her veil, but now she insisted on a garland of rose buds, entwined with the white moorland heather.

In the church the carol of gladness soared up into the vaulting and her heart with it. With him at her side and their own vows already made this formal binding no longer held any terror. It blessed the bond they had pledged in the rain with public ceremony. Her eyes and his held one another and knew their own secrets.

As she changed in the room with the rose wallpaper she drew apart from her attendants. While they fussed and gossiped over tulle and silver she looked for a new web. There was none on the wall, but outside, where a watery sun shone on marquee and grass, she saw in the angle of the window, a new, more delicate web, hung with diamond raindrops. It had ensnared nothing but a wisp of thistle-down.

Satisfied, she returned to the voices. Let them say what they will, she and he were one; he did not find her different. He understood the way she thought. He had not laughed when she told him about the spider and the roses, but caressed her hair with his lips, wondering and gentle. Sympathetic to her needs he had made her glad by cancelling secretly the tickets for the south of France, people and society, and planning instead for a continuation of their private ceremony.

Soon, entertaining done and friendship appeased, they would leave for the far, empty north. Among the mountains the deep, reflective lochs and the purple heather they would find one another again. There they would nurture too the first foetal moments of the child she knew would be conceived. This room, she vowed, would be its nursery.

The Green Leaves of Summer

Grass the colour of young beech leaves stood high in the valley when the young man came to Cae Coch. Megan, her eyes blue with the freshness of forget-me-nots, would go quietly through the wood, down the way the brook went and peer through the hazel brakes to see him. He was tall and his skin was pale. She had never seen a man with pale skin before and her eyes rounded at the whiteness of it. The men of the hills had their faces reddened by the wind and tanned, young, into coarse leather. This man was smooth and she imagined his skin silky and cool like the keys of Dai Morgan's new piano.

Each morning Jeff would come out of his grandmother Lewis's cottage and sniff the sweet air with disbelief. After a city childhood and youth he had not dreamed such air could exist. He sometimes sensed the eyes watching from the wood beyond the brook and would peer into the undergrowth, wondering what small animal was hidden there. Never did he see a movement, save where the wind stroked the leaves and made them dance.

'Jeff, his name is,' Megan whispered to herself as she watched him. Raymond the Post had told her mother that, winking, as he put the parcel from Swansea on the scrubbed wooden table.

Today, as she watched, Jeff was wearing a dark green jersey, warm and soft. He must be cold inside himself she thought, to need the warmth of lambswool in the summer sun. She crouched lower and took a step forward.

It was shy she was or she could have taken eggs to Cae Coch, or warm bread from her mother's oven. She did gather roses once from the mossy ramblers on the back wall and tried to dare to take them down to the old lady, but then she gave them instead to her mother.

Often she sat with her books in the warmed stones of the ruined farm over the valley. It was quiet there. She felt secure, the crumbling wall with its curtain of ivy at her back. She did not look up as the shadows of the clouds chased one another over the hillside and a buzzard soared, mewing, out across the empty air.

The pony's hoofbeats must have been muffled by the grass for when he spoke she dropped her book with the fright of it.

'Hello,' he said. 'What a lovely place to read.'

The ride in the wind and sun had whipped a delicate shade of rose into his ivory cheeks.

Megan felt her hands begin to shake. Stupid it was when she had dreamed so often he would speak to her.

'May I sit with you for a moment to rest the pony?' His eyes were dark and secret like the eyes of the romany folk over by the town. Without waiting for her answer he lifted a long leg easily over the pommel of the saddle and slid to the ground. The pony dropped its nose to the sweet grass and blew gustily. 'Are you Megan?' he asked, sitting next to her.

She nodded shyly. 'How did you know my name?'

'Raymond the Post told me.' He smiled. 'I'm staying here for a few months' convalescence. I've been ill.'

'Are you better?' Her enormous blue eyes were turned to gaze at him, full of sympathy and concern.

'Much, thank you. The air is so good I'm eating like a horse now.' They both turned as the pony tore up a mouthful of weeds and stood champing them on her bit. Then they laughed.

'Is it buttercups you eat then?' she asked quietly.

'Even buttercups.' Unnoticing he had put his hand on hers. It was warm and dry and friendly. Without speaking they both gazed out across the valley towards the distant mountains to the west.

'My parents are coming over next weekend. You and your mother must come down and see them.' He looked down at the glossy curls of the girl beside him. 'I dare say your mother knew my mother when they were children.'

'Mam never said.' She screwed up her nose to think. 'She goes to Cae Coch sometimes, for a chat like, but she never said.'

There was silence again. Then he rose and went to take the pony's rein. 'Will you walk with me a little way, back to the stables?'

She shook her head, suddenly shy again and took up her book. 'I'll stay here a while if you don't mind, to read a bit.'

He shrugged and smiled and mounted the pony which laid back its ears and took a last defiant mouthful of buttercups. The small hooves made no sound on the grass as he went.

'Oh yes, I knew Sarah Ann,' her mother said thumping the dough with a floury hand. 'A fine madam she was. Got into trouble she did with one of the Jones boys from Llangoed, then she went to Birmingham. I never heard from her after that. Granny Lewis never talks about her and I never asked.'

'Will you go down there Saturday and see her?' Megan ran her finger round the edge of the jam pot on the table and licked it delicately.

'Take your hands away, girl.' Her mother slapped at her, scattering flour. 'Indeed I will not. I doubt if I've anything to say to Sarah Ann Lewis after all these years. And you'll not talk to that boy again, Megan. Like mother, like son, no doubt.' She snorted and turned the dough again, punching it.

For three days Megan took her books to the ruin, sitting, the pages blowing on her knees, her eyes fixed on the track at the edge of the wood. But Jeff never came. The fourth day she crept down the wood to the back of Cae Coch and waited to see him come out and breathe the fresh air.

A car was parked in the yard. When he came out there was a girl with him. She was tall and slim and had stylishly cut red hair. Megan could hear the sound of her laughter from across the brook. It was English laughter: strident, confident, and as she laughed the girl slipped her arm through Jeff's and clung to him possessively. Megan, in spite of herself, looked down at her own thin brown hands. She could almost feel the warm touch of Jeff's fingers again.

That girl would wear nail varnish and have smooth oval nails without a crack. Megan knew that. Her jeans were elegantly cut and her shirt immaculate.

Jess glanced up at the trees as though he felt the eyes watching him again, but already Megan had slipped back into the dark of the wood, her sandals making no sound on the leaf mould beneath the trees.

She went back to her books, and back after two days of rain to the ruins of the farm. She sat on the stone wall to be out of the damp and wrapped herself tightly in her jacket against the wind.

Although she did not watch for him any more she knew when he came out of the trees. It was a different pony.

163

Behind on his sorrel came the girl, her head tied in a headscarf, her stirrup leathers too long.

Megan hunched her shoulders. He should not have brought the girl here. This was *her* place.

'Hello, Megan.'

She did not look up.

'Megan, I want you to meet my fiancée, Rose.' She heard him slide from the saddle. 'Aren't you cold up here in this wind, Megan?'

'I'm used to the wind, Jeff, thank you.' She looked up at last.

The girl, Rose, had not moved from her saddle. Her face was wary. Megan could see she had light blue eyes and gingery eyebrows. So the colour of her hair was real then. The slim fingers holding the rein were manicured. The nails were coloured; she had been right. They glowed a delicate shade of plum. Megan noted the sapphire with bleak satisfaction. So she hadn't got a diamond then.

There was no talking today; no need to rest the ponies. The sorrel pawed the ground, impatient to be gone. When they were out of sight, Megan closed her book. Quietly she slipped down into the wood to make her way home.

She didn't see Jeff again for many days but she thought of him in spite of all she could do to stop herself. Nor did she go to peer through the hazels at Cae Coch. The farm too was spoiled for her now. She took to rambling on the mountain, watching the sheep as they wandered through the bracken and gorse.

It would soon be time for her to go away to college. She put the date away from her. The rest of the summer came between her and that day. Her last freedom. She climbed higher towards the rocks and took deep breaths of the air, storing them up against a time when she would see the great open mountain sky no more.

She saw the galloping pony a great way off and stood to watch as he rode recklessly up the pony path, great clods of peat flying up from the thundering hooves. This time he was alone.

'Megan,' he called as he reached her. 'I've not seen you for ages.' He slid from the saddle and grinned at her. Now his skin was almost as brown as hers.

'You still have the book under your arm, I see.' He smiled, his dark eyes lighting with silver.

'How is your fiancée, Jeff?' she asked, not wanting to say it, not wanting to know. She saw his face fall, his smile go.

'She's well, thank you.' He sat down on a lump of rock and then he smiled at her again in spite of it. 'She's gone back to Birmingham now.'

'Has she indeed?' Megan felt her own heart lighten a little. She sat down beside him. The warm wind stroked her hair back from her face. He looked at her for a moment, then his fingers went gently to her forehead.

'You have lovely hair, Megan. Soft and shiny like nut-brown silk.' His eyes were serious as they looked into hers. She felt the message of them pierce right through her and she knew what he wanted so badly.

'Is it loving me on the mountain you're after?' she asked him direct, and she saw his eyelids droop in assent. His hands slowly strayed to the top button of her shirt, undid it, and the next. Gently, with his warm hands, he stroked her breast.

Towards the end of summer when the evenings were drawing imperceptibly in there was a wind; a storm from the west which brought with it the message from autumn that the leaves were doomed to fall from the trees as they turned colour and sent late harvesters scurrying to collect in the last of their store.

Then it was that Jeff told Megan he was leaving Cae Coch. She had borrowed his comb and was kneeling in the soft-brown leaves within the walls of the ruin, combing pieces of grass out of her hair.

'Back to your Rose?' She smiled up at him wistfully, still combing. He nodded, his eyes pained. He had expected her to cry. He buttoned his shirt and went to tighten the girths of the grazing pony.

'Will I see you again, Megan?' He asked it over his shoulder half afraid to turn, to see her face.

'I'll be here till I go.' She smiled enigmatically, slipping his comb into her own pocket. Without a word she began to walk back down towards the trees.

He stood and watched her go, gently stroking the pony's muzzle. In his heart there was already an ache of emptiness he had never felt before.

When he went two months later to her cottage Megan had left for college. In vain Jeff pleaded with her mother for her address.

'No son of Sarah Ann Lewis is going to follow my daughter,' she cried adamantly, hand on hip.

He walked back slowly through the wood to Cae Coch, his heart heavy with longing. The track he followed came out in the trees at the back by the brook, the place he had always thought he felt eyes watching him in the mornings. He smiled gently. So it had been Megan, that shy fawn of the woods whom so often he had tried to glimpse through the trees.

166

He groped in his pocket for the little box. Inside lay a ring, a tiny diamond on a band of white gold. The large sapphire, returned with such venom, had more than paid for it. He kissed the cold stone and put it back in his pocket.

Megan wilted beneath the dark city skies, but she worked hard and tried not to think of the mountain and the brook. Above all she tried to forget the image of the grazing pony and the buttercups.

Her first vacation she spent in Swansea with her Aunt Bethan. The next she went to London and met her mother for a three-week stay in a small hotel in Bayswater while they visited the shops and museums and had tea with Great Aunty Elen who lived in Richmond.

It was not until the sweet summer winds were blowing again over the mountains that she returned home. Granny Lewis had died at Easter and Cae Coch lay empty, the windows already broken by boys from the village.

Megan laid aside her new town clothes and climbed at long last back up to the ruined farmhouse. The stones of the mossy wall were familiar against her back as she sat reading in the sun. The gable wall had fallen some time during the winter and already the nettles were poking up thickly amongst the scattered stones, but she felt happy here; relaxed and safe again. No one else would come to sit beside her on the warmed stones.

She read through the long warm afternoons, watching only sometimes as the shadows of the trees lengthened across the path out of the wood the way he used to come with the pony.

The first storm of the autumn tore some slates off the roof at Cae Coch, leaving a gaping hole. The gate was hanging off its hinges.

Sadly Megan walked down out of the trees and stood in the yard for the first time, looking round. Raymond the Post had told her that it belonged to Jeff now. But he had never been back to see it. Never come back to the mountains.

She heard a soft whinny and shivered in spite of herself. It sounded like a ghost from the past. The sorrel pony was tethered to the fence behind the lean-to, out the back of the cottage.

She stood for a moment, uncertain, overcome with shyness. Then she turned and ran back towards the shelter of the wood. For a brief second she turned back to peer through the branches not letting the hope come. The yard was deserted and silent, the past a whole year away now. Sadly she made her way up the hillside, away from the brook towards the ruins of the farm.

Whistling, Jeff came round the corner of the cottage, his shirt sleeves rolled up, a hammer in his hand. He looked at the sorrel pony, munching sleepily at the net of hay he had hung for it and then he stiffened. Was he being watched? He turned towards the wood, his eyes scanning the pale-green hazel brake hopefully.

'Megan?' he whispered softly. 'Megan, are you there?'

The leaves rustled to the wind, but there was no answer.

Slowly he turned to the rucksack lying inside the door of the cottage. At the bottom was wedged the small ring box. He hadn't looked at it for many months. The diamond winked and gleamed in the silent sun and he gazed at it for a while, his head a little to one side. Then, his mind suddenly made up he stuffed it deep into the pocket of his jeans. Hitching his jacket over his shoulder he vaulted the fallen gate and set off into the wood and up the hillside towards the ruined farmhouse she had loved so much.

Encounters

I knew it was a mistake as soon as I held out my hand.
His eyes behind their polite disinterest were mocking.
He raised my fingers ostentatiously to his lips, then delicately, almost fastidiously, turned aside to sip his champagne; to rinse away the taste.

'Of course I know Jessica. Why it can't be more than
five years since the trial.' Smiling, his teeth were immaculate as ever. I had a vision of the dentist's bill when he
had them straightened. 'You knew she tried to murder me,
surely?' He still held my hand and as I tried to pull away
his grip tightened fractionally.

Our hostess's eyes became like marbles. A greenish
tinge had appeared around her mouth and I felt a wave of
sympathy. I tried to smile a reassurance.

'I expect he'll show you his scar if you ask him nicely.
No, Sara, you guessed aright. You don't have to introduce
us.'

My fingers, draining of blood in his grasp, were beginning to tingle uncomfortably. If I had had a glass in my
free hand I could have dashed it into his face. As it was I
reached forward for the centre button on his shirt. The
scar was so small now. The incision appeared to have been
made with such precision. A professional, considered thrust
aimed, so the prosecution had maintained, with callous and
cold-blooded premeditation. I felt a ridiculous giggle well

169

up inside me and, unable to control it, let it burst forth like a hiccough. Abruptly he released my hand and groped for the button, concealing his wound.

Sara recovered some mastery of the situation. 'Well, dears,' she said with commendable sang-froid. 'Shall I leave you to talk over old times, or would you rather be parted at all cost?' She smiled, but not with her eyes.

His, on the other hand, were sparkling. Their appeal was irresistible. 'Let's talk, Jess,' he said. He took two fresh glasses from a passing tray and handed me one. 'There are things I want to know.'

'And I. My record of Verdi's *Requiem* for one. My begonia rex and the spaghetti jar from Habitat.' I sipped and he smiled. I let the bubbles effervesce for a moment against the roof of my mouth.

'Hostages to fortune,' he said. 'But you can come and get them whenever you like. I've taken cuttings from the begonia and I have the *Requiem* on tape.' He put his head on one side. 'Was it premeditated, Jess? I've often wondered. You must have hated me so passionately.' Shaking his head he took a gulp from his glass. He always closes his eyes when he swallows. It's an irritating habit when you're talking to him.

'Did you never look up in your *Anatomy*? X marked the spot I was aiming for. Only I could have missed so many vital organs so completely.' I lowered my lashes modestly and he nodded, understanding.

'You should have tried poison. It's the woman's method.'

'You can't have forgotten already that I do not like feminine compromise?'

Silently I applauded as he intercepted a tray of canapés.

'You take the plate and I'll help myself to enough for both of us.' He eyed my hand. 'You don't have a Borgia ring, I suppose?'

I raised an eyebrow. 'I was not expecting to meet you, and anyway, second attempts are so boring.'

'I agree.' He said it so heartily that I laughed.

It seemed natural then to head conspiratorially for the tables at the side of the marquee and sit down together with our plate and our drinks. Catching my eye he raised his glass and grinned. 'To the past before it went wrong,' he said and I drank to it with him.

We had, once upon a time, lived together for five years, he and I. We shared a love of Italian food and music. I suppose we shared a love of begonias. We certainly both enjoyed the making of our life and love together as we had enjoyed painting the flat the glorious plums and russets of autumn – 'So very sombre, my dear,' my mother had said once, but I could tell she was impressed.

We had stripped article after article to the basic wea-ther-beaten pine and scoured our Cretan holiday haven for local wares, till our home was sophisticated and cool and I was secure in my liberated mutually-free relationship.

Then he had gone away to a medical conference. The day he was due back the doorbell rang and a woman stood there, tall and dark, her skin tanned and oiled.

'You must be Leo's sister,' she said, walking confidently in and throwing down her bag.

It was as much of a shock to her. She had known him only three months, but this holiday, for her the culmination of their relationship, had involved no conference that she could recall other than with one another.

We circled each other like cats. Then, our anger turning in despair on Leo, we kicked off our shoes and drank a bottle of gin, sitting together on the sheepskin rug, gazing through blurring eyes at the sunburst of corn in the fire-place.

It was her bitter suggestion that he deserved to die. And she admitted it at the trial, I never could decide whether from motives of self-sacrifice or malice.

Leo had not come back that night – perhaps some secret qualm had warned him of the passions that were smouldering beneath those plum and aubergine ceilings as I staggered round the flat after she had gone, tearful at last, to find a taxi.

When he came back the next evening and sat down to read the *BMJ* I gave him, silently, three minutes to explain. Then, as he closed the magazine to turn the page – he never laid a book or paper flat on the table as he read – I stood up and leaned across the table. It was laid, although I had prepared no food. I remember my sleeve catching at the carefully folded napkin as I stuck the stainless steel delicately through his sweater.

He had looked so surprised. Then the customary mocking glance had returned and he had said, 'Darling, Jess, was I late for supper?'

He had phoned for the ambulance himself before he collapsed and I in a fit of masochistic rage rang the police. I wanted reaction, drama; I wanted I suppose to be vindicated. I gave myself up and was half disappointed when they did not appear with handcuffs.

Then the game ended. They let me see Leo in hospital. We had a row, the first we had ever had, and I could remember even now, gazing at him across the canapés, how he had called out in despair, 'All right, Jess, if that's the way you want it, I'll press charges. I'll bloody well press charges.'

That was the last time I had spoken to him, till now.

'Did you qualify in the end, Leo?' The 'incident', as the police psychiatrist called it, had occurred four months before he sat his finals in medicine. He certainly looked respectable now. I eyed his immaculate morning suit.

'Indeed I did.' He grinned. 'Our little brush with the gossip columns does not appear to have harmed either of our reputations, I'm glad to say.'

I blushed. I was recognized now as a photographer and my name, the part of it I used these days, was occasionally to be found in glossy magazines beneath portraits of society personalities.

'You know what I do now?' I had been convinced that I no longer existed for Leo in any respect. The certainty helped me to bear my shame.

'My dear, I do have a certain proprietary interest in your career. Perhaps you have forgotten who lent you the money for your first decent camera.' He smiled encouragingly.

I couldn't help laughing. 'It was less than £5!'

'But you never paid me back.'

'I thought it was a present.'

'Oh.' He considered for a moment. 'Yes, perhaps it was.'

Behind his shoulder the creamy canvas of the marquee billowed slightly and a shadow was silhouetted by the sun.

'They make a very nice couple, don't you think?' I bit into some flaky pastry. 'Are you a friend of the bride or groom?'

'The groom's father. We're with the same hospital. How about you? Have you known them long?'

We were talking as strangers again. I shook my head. 'I was here to photograph the house. I know Sara, the bride's mother, through work.'

He laughed. Again those beautiful teeth. 'And she didn't know about your murky past?'

'I don't usually tell people.' I hesitated and then catching his eye and holding it, I found myself grinning ruefully. 'I'm not very proud of that effort.'

'Of course you're not. You botched it. You were never

one to crow over a failure.' His face was suddenly inscrutable but I thought, I hoped, he was still smiling inside.

Our glasses were charged and we rose to listen to the speeches. I stood bemused by champagne and the heady fragrance of trodden grass, surrounded by best dresses and hats in the cream twilight. Leo was beside me, tall, strong – alive. And then there was a surge of clapping and laughter, the formation changed and Leo was gone. I gazed round, trying to see him, but nowhere was there a sign.

I drank the next toast without enthusiasm and, bored with speeches, edged discreetly towards the entrance.

The garden was gaudy with roses and deserted now that everyone was crowding into the marquee. I could see a fountain playing at the end of a grassy walk. At the centre the slim bronze figure of a girl stood gazing down into the water, water trickling from her fingertips and her tresses and from the fronds that curled around her ankles.

I walked slowly towards her, my heels sinking into the velvet grass. I knew Leo wouldn't follow even if he'd seen me leave.

I sat on the surround of the fountain and lazily trailed my hand in the water. The afternoon was very still. In the distance there was a burst of shouting and laughter from the marquee. I ignored it.

I sat there until the light began to fade. After a time I realized that people were wandering around again. The speeches must be over. Then they began to disappear and, remotely, I heard the revving of engines as one by one the guests began to depart. One of those cars would contain Leo.

I hadn't told him that I was to fly to the States. Why should I? The next morning I boarded the jet at Heathrow and left England behind, leaving a cool hazy morning for the shimmering hothouse of New York and my own wedding.

I had a premonition that my marriage was doomed. Perhaps it was the thunder and lightning that raged round the slender spire of the wooden New England church as we exchanged our vows. Perhaps it was the helpless adoration I felt for George. A love like that could not be allowed. The gods are not sentimentalists. So when the end came I was almost prepared. The small plane he was flying from New York to Montreal dropped out of the sky and buried itself in the flaming glory of the Vermont fall exactly three months and four days after we were married.

When I came home the tawny of the English autumn wrapped itself gently around me like a familiar comforting arm. I walked in the mist and rain until the ache was dulled, then hesitantly I resumed work.

I had been staring at his back for some time. Perhaps it was the set of the shoulders. Perhaps it was the angle at which he held the *BMJ* over his head to ward off the streaming rain that held my attention. I was fascinated to see the water dripping from the page almost with deliberation into the perfectly angled upturned collar of his coat.

There were three people between us in the queue. I stood painfully hoping he would turn; dreading that he might turn. I wanted to run away, but I wanted my ticket for *Trovatore*.

Agonized, cold, wet, I shuffled on in the queue through the doors of the Opera House and across the foyer, regimented, obedient, hypnotized. Then I was gazing through the glass at the man in the ticket office. His gold-rimmed spectacles were slightly askew. A tiny puff of cotton wool supported one side of the frame over a red and swollen ear. He looked harassed.

175

'Ah yes, the lady in blue. Miss Ferindale. One ticket in the stalls. It has been paid for. Thank you. Next.' He pushed an envelope towards me and I took it.

I stood and looked at it. Then I looked for Leo. He had gone.

I arrived a little early and slipped into my seat while the Opera House was still half empty. The cool, clean sawdust smell from the stage hung in the air, then as the rows filled it was replaced by the scents of wet coats and expensive perfumes and people hurrying straight from work. An elderly couple side-stepped past me and settled in the seats to my right. The left-hand seat remained empty until the orchestra began to tune up. Then he came as the lights were dimming, wrapped in a heavy gaberdine raincoat. Not Leo.

The half glance I gave him told me I could sit back and relax. Obviously Leo's nerve had failed. The stranger had not even looked in my direction. But in the first interval he smiled.

'Leo had to go to the hospital,' he said. 'He said I could take you out to dinner and then I must deliver you to the flat later. I understand there is some plant you have to collect.'

The begonia.

It was a pleasant meal. The young man, a colleague of Leo's but specializing in paediatrics, played his part as escort well. I enjoyed myself. Until the coffee came.

'I wouldn't have put you down as being particularly homicidal,' he said, his hazel eyes serious. 'Of course, psychiatry is not really my line at all, but you seem quite rational to me. Have you ever felt the urge to repeat your violence?'

'Not very often.' I sat forward in my chair and began

to toy with the fruit knife. 'Do I gather that Leo's feeling nervous?'

He smiled enigmatically. 'Cautious perhaps.'

He called the waiter and then escorted me firmly to a taxi. He did not leave my side until we were standing outside Leo's door that had once been my door too. Then with a handshake and a stiff little bow he turned and left me.

The ceilings had been painted white. As Leo opened the door and I composed my face to greet him, I noticed the fact automatically. And I was pleased.

Nothing of my personality remained in that flat. Even my begonia, which stood ostentatiously on the table by the door, had changed. It had grown gnarled and whiskery and one of the umbrella leaves had blighted and curled up at the edges.

'It was kind of you to water it for me.' I might have been away for a week's holiday.

Leo acknowledged my thanks with composure and showed me to a chair by the fire. The hearth had been opened out and the glowing coals were sending out a radiant smokeless heat. I noticed that some of my carefully stripped furniture had been repainted. Some antiques and bric-à-brac had been introduced and the Greek island look had vanished completely. It was, I had to admit, very attractive in its own way, but not, I thought, entirely Leo's taste.

'Are you married now?' I asked as he handed me a coffee cup. He unscrewed the cap from a quarter bottle of brandy. I did not expect him to nod and when he did I did not expect the sharp wave of jealousy which flowed over me.

'Do I know her?'

I was relieved to see that it wasn't the tanned beauty who had incited me to murder. I gazed at the photograph he put in my hand. She was delicate and fair and had the gentle eyes of a dreamer very much in love.

'Can I meet her?' I gazed round, half expecting her to appear, but the door to the bedroom was closed. I knew suddenly that the flat was empty. Taking the glass from Leo I looked up at his face. His gaze was fixed on the photograph in my hand, and his eyes reflected exactly those of the girl.

Suppressing with difficulty the lump that persisted in rising to my throat I took a sip of brandy and set the frame down on the low table.

'I want to make love to you, Jessica.' He took my glass and cup away and sat down next to me, holding my hands. His eyes were sad, not searching, not demanding; just holding mine.

The bedroom was too tidy. I followed him to the bed and then stood looking down at the coverlet. There were no signs in the room of her presence. No make up, no slippers, no photographs, no lingering whisper of perfume.

And there were no signs there either of the time I had shared Leo's bed. It was a different place now. The rugs were changed, the pictures were different except for one. Glancing at Leo I felt myself smile just once. He had kept the hand-coloured print I had bought him of two goldfinches clinging to a head of thistledown.

'Why didn't you move?' I asked at last.

'I liked it here,' he replied.

His fingers fumbled as he unbuttoned my dress and as he slipped the material back across my shoulders I saw him stare and hesitate and frown.

'God, Jess. I must have had too much to drink.' His hands dropped to his sides and with a defeated little shrug he sat abruptly on the bed.

I stood before him for a moment and then, wriggling back into my dress I began to rebutton it. Perhaps he, like me, had had a vision of another, more recent love. I had been Leo's for so long, but my months with someone else had effaced the memory of Leo's hands and Leo's kisses. It was as though a stranger sat before me.

I brought his glass of brandy and my own from the drawing room and sat beside him on the bed.

'I've been married too, Leo. My husband is dead.'

His eyes filled with tears and I knew then for certain that he had lost her. I did not ask any questions and after a while we rose and went back to the fire. The bedroom door was closed behind us.

We talked of many things. Of our lives and careers, of old friends and memories, even of the trial and the horrors that surrounded it. On my third brandy I found myself giggling over the solemnity of the judge. He had turned out to be the grandfather of the dental student who had helped us with the beautiful ceramic tiles we found for the bathroom.

As the fire grew cold and the red, glowing coals faded to clinker I found the silences between us growing longer. I was too tired to move. My head began to roll on my shoulder and when Leo gently took away my glass and covered me with a rug I made no protest. I was content to be there.

The kitchen I found was almost unchanged from five years before. Leo had always been a keen cook. Evidently his wife had not challenged him on that ground. I found the coffee beans in the same place; the grinder was an updated model. I cooked his eggs and put the rolls in the oven while he shaved and in the fragrance of the cooking breakfast felt myself five years younger.

Looking for the butter I found two bottles of her nail enamel in the bottom of the fridge. When Leo wasn't looking I slipped them down behind a dresser drawer. It was better that he try to forget.

He drove me home on his way to the hospital, with my begonia, my spaghetti jar and my *Requiem* neatly stacked in a cardboard box on my knee. I would rather have left them.

'Will you come again, Jess, one day?' His smile was sad but genuine.

'I'd like to Leo. I'd like to very much.' He drew up outside my flat and sat for a moment gazing wordlessly through the windscreen. Then he got out and came to my side of the car.

Helping me out he pinched my cheek suddenly. 'I forgot all about the need to hide my knives. You must have lulled me into a sense of security.'

As I carried the box of treasures up to my flat I was feeling happier than I had for many months. And I had left another hostage to fortune behind me. In an envelope on the mantelpiece in Leo's flat I had put a five pound note and a message, 'Thanks for the loan', and my phone number.

The Touch of Gold

Pushing open the door the boy peered cautiously round it. The room was empty. On the bed, his uncle's suitcase lay with its lid thrown back, some clothes spilling over onto the patchwork counterpane. The curtains had been drawn against the brilliant afternoon sun and the room was a twilit cavern, scented with spice and pomade. He could hear the desperate rustling as a butterfly beat its wings, trapped somewhere between the curtains and the broiling glass.

Glancing back over his shoulder to make sure the passage was empty the boy tiptoed into the room. Lifting aside the heavy material he pushed open the casement. The frail wings beat against his cupped palms for a moment then the creature was gone out into the sun, leaving a dusting of gold on his fingers. He pulled the window to and slipped back through the curtains, holding his breath.

Full of curiosity, he looked round in the gloom. On the chest of drawers lay silver-backed hairbrushes, keys, pencils and a jar of some sort of cream. He unscrewed the lid and sniffed, wrinkling up his nose.

He hesitated before touching the suitcase. Then quietly and efficiently he went through it, searching the pockets, looking beneath every folded garment. He didn't know what he hoped to find. Some sweets perhaps or interesting photographs.

181

His eyes rounded in amazement when he found the sovereign. He held it for a moment, hesitated, then slipped it into the pocket of his shorts.

It was hard to remember to walk quietly, to shut his uncle's door, to stroll off casually towards the stairs. His gym shoes squeaked on the linoleum. He could hear his mother clanging saucepans in the kitchen and his uncle's drawling tones coming from the front of the house somewhere. Perhaps he had cornered one of the choirboys on their way to practice and was boring him with one of his interminable stories. His father would be in the study writing his sermon.

Stealthily he made his way out into the garden, his hand cupped protectively over his shorts' pocket. Sitting in the long grass behind the beech hedge he at last looked properly at the gold coin. He had never seen one before, never held one. He gazed at it and turned it over in his palm.

Then suddenly the awful realization came upon him that he had stolen it. He was a thief. In spite of the sultry heat he grew cold. His hand began to shake and unthinkingly he hurled the thing from him. It fell somewhere in the grass.

Hiding his head in his hands he sat for a long time, thinking. He knew what he must do. He must return the coin to its place in his uncle's suitcase. No one would know it had been taken. Only God.

The boy looked heavenwards and fearfully, fervently, hoped that God was busy somewhere else this afternoon. There had certainly been occasions when He had missed other misdemeanours, after all.

On hands and knees in the long feathery grass he began to search for the sovereign.

Peering between the cool green stems he covered every inch of the ground near him. Then methodically he crawled

in circles further and further away from the small patch of
flattened turf which showed where he had been sitting.
His anxious eyes flitted over stones and a piece of amber
glass, a ladybird and finally, miraculously, a glint of gold.
It turned out to be a butterfly; perhaps it was the same
butterfly. His head ached. His shoulders ached. Trickles of
perspiration ran down his back and his shirt clung to him.
His nose itched from the grass seed and his eyes watered
as he forced them ever closer in the green twilight between
his hands. The shadow of the hedge lengthened over him.
It formed a darkness so black he doubted that he would
ever see again.

Blindly, exhausted, he climbed to his feet. It was no
good, he would never find it. Tears trickled down his
cheeks leaving clean trails in the dust beneath his eyes.
Then he spotted the gold piece shining in a patch of dap-
pled sunlight ten feet from him.

He clutched it to him and ran as fast as he could for
the house. The shadows of the tall yew trees in the churchyard had already engulfed the small vicarage: it was as dark
as night in the hall and he almost collided with his father
who was emerging from his study.

Up the stairs two at a time he ran and listened for a
moment, his heart thumping, at his uncle's door. All was
silent. Turning the handle he pushed his way into the room
and looked round.

The suitcase, closed, stood on the floor by the dressing
table. The hairbrushes and things had disappeared. Everything seemed to have been packed away. Hesitating, he
wondered what to do. He could hide the coin in the room
and hope people would think it had got lost. But his conscience told him otherwise. He must put it back. Silently
he pulled the heavy case flat on the floor and tried the
catches. They were unlocked. Relieved, he threw back the
lid and slipped the sovereign back into the pocket where

he found it. It was hard to reshut the case. He struggled to push the clothes down and to strain the lid back into position. The more he tried, the more untidy the contents seemed to become.

He sat on it, but his slight weight was not enough. He was so intent on his efforts that he almost missed the sound of heavy footsteps in the hall. Heart in mouth he left the case and fled to the heavy curtains, slipping through them as the door opened and his father and his uncle came in.

'I have something for the boy.' His uncle's voice had an affable confident boom which had always endeared him to the nephew. 'I'm sorry not to have seen him at all. Explain why I couldn't stay, there's a good chap.'

The boy heard the puzzled exclamation as his uncle saw the open case and unhappily he pictured his angry face. But no further comment was made. He heard a faint scrabbling and then his uncle spoke again, slightly breathless. 'Here we are. A sovereign for him. I know he'd like it.'

The boy, red-faced and unhappy pressed himself further back behind the curtain. With a slight click the window swung gently open as it had for the captive butterfly. He clutched wildly for a moment at the heavy material as he felt his balance go, then he fell, with a frightened shout, towards the scented flowerbeds in the garden below.

The Helpless Heart

Mark was standing in the warm evening sunlight gazing up at the front of the house. Watching him a little anxiously from behind her billowing curtains Susannah saw him hesitate for a moment before raising his hand to push the door then, walking slowly like a man in a dream, he disappeared out of her sight into the shadows below her window.

She was waiting for him at the top of the stairs when he reappeared in the hall and she stood quite silent until, glancing up, he saw her framed against the landing window. At once the preoccupied expression on his face vanished and she breathed a quiet sigh of relief; the magic was still there. He ran up two at a time and kissed her on the forehead and then held her at arm's length to see her better. On tiptoe she came only to his shoulder.

He followed her into her room. It was pretty and pastel-shaded, he saw looking round, feminine like her; the walls were hung with prints of flowers, festoons of blossom filled the vases on the table and bookcase and the shaggy rug was littered with her sewing. The flat was cool in the breeze from the open window.

Quietly she took his hand. 'I am glad you came, Mark,' she said softly.

Had she met him only two days before? It had been at a party which had been held in the big conference room at the offices where he worked. Long tables laid out with food and drink had been dragged across the length of the room and she scrutinized them anxiously from her corner. She had been feeling nervous about the party all day because she had supervised the catering and seen that all was ready; now it was up to the contract waitresses to cope for the rest of the evening. She eyed them critically; they looked smart and competent. She took a deep breath and pushed her fair hair back from her forehead. She knew she looked all right; she knew the food was good; so why was she worrying?

They began to arrive: the businessmen, the reps, the cool supercilious secretaries and at last, surreptitiously still rubbing little bits of wallpaper paste from beneath his finger nails, Mark. She didn't know why she noticed that one man amongst so many others. Perhaps because he too looked a little ill at ease. She watched him walk to the bar and collect a drink. Then he carried it into a corner and, sipping repeatedly, began to observe.

Susannah had known no one there at all except the managing director who had given her the job. He smiled at her distantly and bowed. She smiled back a little wryly, tempted to thumb her nose at so much pompous authority but not daring. It was then she caught Mark's eye and knew that he had read her mind. Glancing down she smiled, a little embarrassed.

He came over. 'Are you thinking what I'm thinking?' he asked easily.

'I'm afraid so,' she said.

'Are you with the company? I haven't seen you before.' Mark could not take his eyes from her face and a flutter of excited unease arose somewhere below her ribs. She took another sip from her glass. 'Actually I'm the cook. Free-lance. I arranged the food for the party.'

He didn't seem to be listening.

186

'I expect you work here?' she tried again, wanting to see him smile. They were jostled suddenly by a surge of loud-talking men and Mark slopped his drink a little on the skirt of her dress.

'I'm sorry.' He was jerked from his reverie abruptly. 'Here, let me.' He produced a handkerchief and dabbed her skirt. 'I'm Mark by the way,' he said glancing up at her, obliquely, almost on his knees at her feet.

'I'm Susannah,' she said, and he smiled.

For the rest of the evening they talked and laughed, inseparable; companionable; feeling as if they had known one another for years and he, realizing at last who she was, complimented her on her cooking, doing more than justice to his share as they talked.

Then the crowds began to thin. 'Do you have to stay behind to clear up?' he asked.

She shook her head. 'Not this time, no. I'm coming back in the morning to see to things.'

'But it's Sunday tomorrow,' he objected.

'I know. I don't mind.'

'In that case, can I give you a lift home?'

She would have liked so much to say yes, but she had a car. She felt panicky suddenly. She hadn't even known his surname, then.

But later, as the party finished he had offered to walk her to her car, opening the door for her as she stepped out of the hot stuffy building.

'I can never understand how people can lock themselves up in smoky rooms like that when it's so lovely outside,' she commented over her shoulder to him as he followed her, talking wildly to hide her nervousness and stretching her arms above her head, shaking her hair to rid it of the smell of smoke.

He smiled. 'It can't be the company tonight. It must have been your food.'

187

'Flatterer.' She walked ahead of him across the asphalt. Her car was parked with its nose almost in the dark sootiness of a privet hedge.

She paused and turned to look at him and hesitated for a moment. He was looking down at her, a frown on his face. Wasn't he going to say anything? The silence lengthened. Desperately she spoke up again, her voice sounding too loud in her own ears. 'Perhaps I'll see you around?' she hazarded, with an attempt at a casualness she didn't really feel. She wanted so much to see him again.

'Oh I hope so.' He took her hands in his and held them tightly, his eyes seeking hers in the dark.

He was going to kiss her. Susannah took a small step towards him, raising her face imperceptibly to his, but he released her quickly, as if afraid, and stepped back. 'Drive carefully, Susie,' he called as he turned away.

She stood still for a moment, unbelieving, disappointed, then she began to grope in her purse for her car keys.

The next day Susannah let herself into the office with a pass key she had been given and went into the room where the party had been. She wrinkled her nose in distaste. Dirty glasses and plates, overflowing ashtrays, crumbs trodden into the carpet, everywhere the stale smell of exhaled smoke and musty conversation. She threw open the windows and began to clean up, plodding methodically through the job, stacking, scraping, emptying. Resolutely she did not allow herself to think of the tall handsome man who had talked to her so caringly the evening before and who had left her so abruptly.

It was a long time before she realized that he was there. He was watching her through the glass door of the office. She took a deep breath to steady herself and raised a hand in greeting.

He opened the door. 'I had to come to collect some papers. Do you want some help?'

She smiled. 'I'd love some, but it's a dreadful mess in here.'

He shrugged. 'For you, ma'am, I'd brave the Augean stables if you asked.'

They had both laughed so easily together and it had taken her half the time with his helping her.

'Susie, I want to see you again.' At last he had said it. 'Soon. Tomorrow, if you can.'

And now he had come. Susannah watched him looking round her room, hungry for details of her life. She smiled again, understanding. She longed to know about him, too. But not yet. She liked him still to be a little mysterious; a stranger whom destiny had brought to her door. He told her that he had booked a table, she picked up her coat and they went out together.

They drove through the bright evening to a restaurant she had never been to before, she talking, a little puzzled by his long silences, and intrigued; he wanting to touch her, his hand straying every now and then to hers, not really listening at all, just happy to be close to her. He was already certain in his own mind, although she didn't know it, that what he wanted was a future linked indissolubly with that of this exquisite, fragile girl.

It was a dark, intimate restaurant, the tables barely lit by smoking night lights, hidden from one another by high-backed settles. Susannah sat opposite him and every now and then, as they talked, his hand would stretch out and gently, with a finger only, touch hers across the deep-crimson cloth.

'Would you like to come in?' She looked up and smiled at him at the door of her flat when he brought her home later.

For a moment his gaze met hers. Imperceptibly he nodded, but he said. 'I shouldn't.'

'Why not?' Her voice was gentle. She reached out to him and he came.

He watched as she filled the kettle at the sink and plugged it in. 'There's a drink if you'd like,' she smiled at him, but he shook his head.

'Coffee's fine.'

She knew he wanted her.

In the sitting room he smiled and put down his coffee cup and looked at her so long she began to feel strange – almost dizzy – there was such an intensity of feeling in his eyes. Then he put his arms around her and she let him kiss her.

She heard the little clock beside her bed next door chime midnight. He heard it too. Gently he pushed her away. 'Your coffee's getting cold,' he whispered, inexplicably sad.

She slipped to her knees on the soft carpet and sipped her coffee, leaning against his legs. His head was lying against the sofa back, his eyes closed in the lamplight. She couldn't know that suddenly and unwillingly he was thinking of Annabel.

Two days before, on the day of the party where he met Susannah, he and Annabel had at last bought the new wallpaper for their flat. She had chosen it and he was content to watch, knowing her eye for colour and her quiet taste. He had smiled at her fondly as she pulled out first this roll and then that until at last she had decided and turned to him for confirmation.

'Are you going to help me do it?' he asked as they paid for it, scrupulously half each.

She nodded. 'I'll do the painting round it; you do the

papering, Mark. Remember? You said you could do a better job than the men who did our bathroom and I seem to remember a small bet?' Her dark hair was curling into her eyes and he had longed to push it back for her, but his arms, like hers, were loaded.

They had worked hard and by mid-day she had painted a door and one strip of the paper was up.

'It'll dry flat,' he murmured hopefully as she came to inspect his handiwork and she hadn't criticized it.

'It'll be lovely,' she had said. 'I'll go on painting while you're at this party tonight. They shouldn't allow office parties on Saturdays. Do you really have to go?'

He hadn't wanted to go. If he could have thought up an excuse he would have used it. But this time, this once it was important that he be there. 'It has to be on a Saturday because the German delegates will be flying back to Frankfurt tomorrow. It's boring, I know, but there might be some good contacts there.'

'I know your kind of good contacts! Curvaceous, sexy Fräuleins!' She smiled at him.

That was the joke between them, just as when he said to her every so often, 'One of these days you'll marry one of the fat directors of that firm you work for, Miss Conway,' and she would solemnly nod and compute their salaries on her fingers. She wouldn't, of course. Mark and she might not be married, but he was the man in her life and had been for nearly five years.

That afternoon when he was wrestling with the second strip of paper she had slipped out for a while.

She walked slowly to the surgery, feeling the warm June sun on her hair, acutely aware of the colours and shapes of things in the road, as if her faint anxiety made her more alive. The waiting-room was nearly empty and it was barely fifteen minutes later before she was once more

191

in the road. The test had been, against all probability, positive.

This time she was thoughtful as she walked and she saw nothing of the summer trees. It was strange that she did not wonder at once what Mark would say. Perhaps because she knew instinctively that what had happened would in a way make no difference; her future, as it always had been, was in her own hands – her future and now that of the baby. Decisions, if they had to be made, were her job and she was not afraid of them. Not usually. Unnoticing she broke a twig off a lime tree as she passed and twirled the stem in her fingers.

Mark and she were a partnership. They shared their lives and their home, but at the same time they respected each other's rights as individuals. Whatever she decided – and she knew that ultimately he would say that the choice must be hers – he would respect her for it when she told him. If she told him. She snapped the twig abruptly and threw the pieces into the gutter.

The future did not seem to be clear. There were so many aspects to face: to tell him, or not to tell him; to have it or not to have it; to have the child and then let it go perhaps, to someone else.

She and Mark had never seriously considered marriage. Their relationship suited them both as it was and she knew he valued it for its freedom. But now?

Her tongue suddenly tasted blood in her mouth, sharp and salty and she realized she had been chewing the inside of her cheek as she walked. She hadn't done that since she was quite a little girl.

She walked a long time before turning at last, as she began to feel tired, for home. Her only decision was that she would do nothing – not yet.

Strangely she began to notice things again now; her heightened sense of perception had returned with that one meagre resolution – to do nothing. The trees were again brilliant in their cloak of summer green, the last of their blossom white and creamy, with bees clustering to suck, their buzz droning above the cars. As she turned back into the main road she saw a couple walking towards her. The girl, obviously pregnant, turned to the man and laughed up at him with such trusting joy in her face as they walked that Annabel found that she too was smiling. She hugged herself a little and against all reason felt ridiculously happy.

Mark had left for the party at about six, not guessing anything, and Annabel, strangely contented, reached for her brush. 'I'll only look in at the party for an hour or two, and be back in time for supper,' he said as he left.

She stroked the paint onto the skirting board in long even strokes, concentrating on making the creamy ridges merge and glisten into a smooth flat strip. She almost decided to tell him when he came home. Something kept telling her that he would be pleased with her news. She pushed her dark hair out of her eyes with the back of her wrist and easing her cramped position a little, painted on. Behind her the clock struck nine.

Annabel stopped at last, finished cleaning her brushes and pressed the lid back onto the paint tin. She was exhausted but the painting was finished, all but the door. She could do that tomorrow. She glanced at the clock; it was after eleven. She frowned. Surely Mark should have been home long since?

Shrugging she went to turn on the bath. They didn't worry about each other as a rule. It was part of the way they lived. After all, office parties and office colleagues were a hazard they both lived with and on the whole ignored. It made for a free, happy relationship, and today's news should – would – make no difference. She flung open the bathroom window and leaned out, taking a deep breath of the fragrant summer night and wondering idly if Mark were still there, and she felt a wave of pity at the thought of him, bored but dutiful, still making polite conversation to the delegation from Frankfurt.

She was asleep when Mark got home. He let himself into the flat quietly and stood in the hall smelling the cloying tangy wet paint. Then, creeping into the kitchen he poured himself a glass of milk. He was restless, and he didn't feel in the least bit sleepy. The bathroom was a little steamy still and rich with the scent of bath essence and talcum when at last he began to undress and he let it relax him deliberately, standing a long time looking down into the clear water as it ran into the bath, allowing the reflections and the swirling transparent bubbles to mesmerize and soothe him, making his mind go mercifully blank.

Annabel was lying naked beneath the sheet, her dark hair tossed in a shadowy web on the pillow in the moonlight, an arm half across his side of the bed. He stood and gazed at her for a long while and then gently, so as not to wake her, he eased himself into bed.

Leaving the coffee perking quietly on the stove the next morning Annabel pulled on her jacket and slipped round the corner to the shop. Hot rolls and the Sunday papers were their special treat each weekend and they took it in turns to go out and buy them.

Mark was still asleep when she carried in the tray. She smiled at the sight of him so vulnerable with his face relaxed, half smiling in his dream. She set down the tray and dropped a kiss on the end of his nose. Lazily he opened his eyes and grinned up at her.

'Hi.'

'Hi. It was your turn, you know, but I went as you were so very asleep. What on earth time did you get in?'

194

Remembering the events of the night before he pushed himself up in bed. 'Midnight, I think.' He hesitated guiltily.

'It must have been a good party after all.' She was breaking open a crusty bread roll, buttering it, unscrewing the jar of honey. There wasn't any need to look at his face; she trusted him absolutely.

'It was quite fun.' He reached for the paper.

'Did you have a look at my painting when you came in?' She handed him the roll. This time, glancing up, she saw the look of guilt.

'I came in so late, Annabel. I'll go and see in daylight.'

'It doesn't matter. Not much to see, really; it's just a bit fresher, that's all.' She felt absurdly hurt.

They read and ate in silence for some time and then at last Annabel got up. She glanced at him again. 'Are you going to get on with the papering? We could finish that room today, between us.' She was collecting their plates.

Mark glanced at his watch. 'Annie, I'm sorry and I know it's Sunday but I've got to slip back to the office this morning. I was supposed to bring some papers home yesterday and I forgot. I won't be long.'

He did not look at her as he spoke.

She wandered into the kitchen when he had gone. She didn't as a rule spend much time cooking, but today she wanted to do something special. She began to search through the cupboards and the fridge and then when she started to lay the table and set wine glasses she realized why. It was today, after a special meal, that she would tell him.

The quiet happy assurance of the evening before had gone. That morning she had awoken early and lain in bed, gazing at the cool sunlight through the thin curtain, thinking. She had wanted to wake Mark then, tell him everything, ask what he wanted her to do, feel his comforting arms around her, but she had stopped herself in time. It wasn't like her to want reassurance and she lay puzzled and a little frightened, watching the hands of the clock tick round until it was time to get up.

He was late for lunch. She drew the cork from the wine bottle on her own and sipped a glass as she stirred the gravy, hypnotized by the circling creamy brown vortex beneath her spoon, thinking about Mark. When he came at last she could sense at once that something had happened and she knew she could not tell him now. He was elated and yet, as he refused to meet her eyes, in a strange way he was almost surly. She poured his wine, disappointed and watched him eat. Her own appetite had gone.

'You've remembered Bernard and Joy's dinner party tomorrow night?' she said at last, to break the silence.

He looked up and frowned. 'Oh Annie, I can't make it. I forgot to tell you. Something's come up at the office. We shall be having a meeting till all hours, I'm afraid.' He looked so ashamed as he spoke, tapping his knife on the plate until the gravy splashed across the cloth, that she shrugged her disappointment aside.

'It can't be helped. I know you're very busy there at the moment. I think I'll go though; I enjoy their evenings.'

'Yes, you go. Enjoy yourself, Annie. Please.' He was almost over eager. He put his hands on hers for a second. His skin was ice cold.

Annabel didn't enjoy the dinner party as much as she had hoped. She was too blatantly the odd one out; the single woman suddenly cast by the wives there in the role of predator. She might have laughed at the situation and flirted with the husbands deliberately if Mark had been there to egg her on; if Mark had known. But of course if Mark had been there she would not have been alone.

She smiled to herself climbing into her car. He would laugh when she told him; and next time he would see to it that he was at her side, mocking and teasing, there to enjoy the jokes with her.

She drove home fast, glancing at her watch. It was nearly midnight. He would be back by now. The flat would be warm and cosy, with Mark probably watching the late show on TV; perhaps a hot drink warming on the stove. She would tell him; now.

She parked the car and ran upstairs to their door.

'Mark?' Her key turned impatiently in the lock. 'Mark, I'm home.' The flat was in darkness. Puzzled, she clicked on the light and glanced round. He wasn't there. She went through to the bedroom to see if he was already asleep but the room was cold and empty. 'Mark?' she called again. 'Mark?'

For the first time she felt a tremor of unease.

Susannah was sitting with her head resting sleepily against Mark's knees. She was unbelievably happy. Still she could not bring herself to believe that this man could have fallen so deeply and so painfully in love with her so quickly. She was frightened too; vulnerable in her own sudden defencelessness. She felt his hand on her hair and she looked up at his face, strongly shaded in the lamp light as they smiled at each other. He set down his coffee cup and slowly pushing her head away he stood up and reached down for her hands. She let herself be led, trembling a little, into the bedroom. Deliberately he pulled back the counterpane and sat down on the blanket, still holding her hands, drawing her close so that she had to stand near him, her knees touching his. Gently he reached up to touch a curling tendril of her hair, which had fallen between her breasts.

He felt overwhelmingly protective towards this girl. She was so fragile, so defenceless; she brought out in him a strange almost fatherly feeling; the need to look after her, a feeling which he had never experienced before with Annabel and which he found exciting and stimulating. It was undeniable. He stroked her breast, feeling her shiver a little at his touch and then slowly he pulled her down beside him on the bed.

Annabel was sitting on the floor of the sitting room, her chin resting on her knees, her arms wrapped around her legs. She had turned on the television for company but she wasn't watching the screen. She had been deciding what to say to Mark. She could not carry the burden of her knowledge alone any more. He had to know. Now. She was uncertain and vulnerable and she needed him. She knew it was out of character and it was frightening to feel herself so undecided and exposed, but whatever his problems at the office, and ever since yesterday she had known that he had them, she knew he would help her. Her hot chocolate grew cold beside her and a skin formed on the surface as the minutes ticked by and she waited for him to come home.

She didn't turn round when at last she heard Mark's key. He crept in, not wanting to wake her and stopped abruptly as he saw her sitting on the floor, her narrow shoulders hunched as she gazed at the television in the corner.

'Hello,' she said wearily. 'How was the meeting?'

'OK.' His own voice too was colourless. 'The dinner?'

It seemed like a hundred years ago. 'Boring. Your drink's in the saucepan.' She turned then and watched as he went across to the kitchen, his feet dragging as if he were intolerably tired.

'Mark?' She scrambled up and stood in the doorway

behind him as he lit the gas, nerving herself. 'There is something we must talk about. I can't put it off any longer.'

He looked round. He knew she was right; they had to talk. He could not pretend with her, or let things drag on. She deserved far more than that and seeing the pain and doubt in her face he knew that she must have guessed something at least of the conflict that had been going on inside him for the last three days. He swallowed hard and for a moment he glanced away, unable to meet her eyes. He couldn't bear to hurt her and yet he knew it would be more cruel to deceive her. They had never lied to one another; never hidden anything.

Bewildered by the emotions within him, not certain suddenly what he should do or what he was going to say he forced himself to look at her again. There was a long pause. Then impulsively he held out his hands.

'You're right, Annie; we must talk.' He hesitated.

She swallowed. Now that it had come to it she was afraid. He might think she was going to use the baby as a lever to make him marry her; he might try and force her to get rid of it. Suddenly she knew she wanted to keep it more than anything in the world.

Why, when she loved and trusted him so much did she have this strange feeling of foreboding? Why, now that he was here, had she begun to feel so very cold?

She took a deep breath, but before she had time to say anything he had rushed in ahead of her.

'Annie, as you've guessed there is something you have got to know. There is something I must tell you. I wasn't at a meeting this evening at all . . .'

Unnoticed by either of them the milk stirred and began to rise in the pan on the stove.

She looked at his face and suddenly she knew. The anguish, the uncertainty she saw there were not because he had guessed her secret; they were there because he had one of his own. Her mouth went dry and she began to shiver uncontrollably.

The boiling milk hissed angrily over the sides of the saucepan and put out the flame. Automatically she released her hands from Mark's and pushed past him to turn off the gas. She was still shivering as she stood with her back to him, looking at the puddle of milk on the enamel round the gas burner.

'What do you want to tell me?' Her voice was tight with fear.

'Annie, we've lived together a long time. I've always thought – well, assumed – that we'd go on like that, but . . .' He stopped, fumbling for words, his eyes on her tense narrow shoulders. He wished he could see her face.

'Annie, we've never thought about marriage, either of us. We've always agreed that we're free. It's been a good relationship . . .'

He broke off again.

There was a moment of silence.

'It's over, is that what you're trying to tell me?' To her horror Annabel could feel unheard-of tears welling up into her eyes. She gripped the edge of the cooker until her knuckles whitened.

'There's someone else, Annie. I never meant it to happen. I still don't know how it did. But I feel so much for her. So suddenly. It's as if she's been waiting there all the time; I don't understand it. I've been so happy with you. I care for you so much, but this – this is different. I can't explain.'

He pressed his hand to his forehead in despair.

'How long have you known her?' Still she didn't face him.

'We met at the office on Saturday.'

'Saturday! That's three days!' At last she turned and her large grey eyes seemed enormous in the pinched whiteness

200

of her face. 'We've been together five years, Mark. Doesn't that mean anything?'

'We're not married, Annie.'

'Not married!' She still looked stunned. 'That doesn't mean there is no commitment! It doesn't mean we don't belong to each other. I love you, Mark.' Her voice had begun to tremble suddenly.

He turned away, unable to face those enormous eyes.

'Mark.' She followed him into the sitting room. 'Have you slept with her?' Suddenly it was terribly important to know.

'I want to *marry* her, Annie.' Absently he bent and switched off the crackling blank screen of the television.

Slowly she walked to the window and pushed back the curtain; the narrow strip of lawn was bathed in moonlight. She knew she had only to tell him, now, about the baby, but something stopped her.

'I suppose you want me to move out?' She took a deep breath to steady herself. 'Have you fixed a date for the wedding?'

'Annie, Annie.' His voice was gentle. 'I haven't even asked her yet. I'm the one who must move out. This is your flat as much as mine. More perhaps.' Unconsciously his eyes went to the half-repapered wall. They never had finished the room. He bit his lip unhappily.

'I don't think I want to talk about it tonight, Mark. I can't face it.' Annabel ran her finger along the lower edge of the window frame. It came away dirty, but she didn't notice. 'We'll sort it out tomorrow somehow.' She faced him slowly and tried rather feebly to smile. 'It's all come as rather a shock, I'm afraid. I never guessed. I'll be able to think better, later.'

She walked numbly past him, ignoring his hesitant out-stretched hand, and went into the bedroom. He turned to follow her automatically and was brought up short as gently she pushed the door closed in his face.

He didn't go home the next evening. He went to Susie. He was late and tired. All day at the office he had found his thoughts straying back to her – never once to Annabel. Once or twice he had broken off in mid-sentence with a puzzled colleague, unable to remember anything but the ash-gold glints of Susie's hair or the grey green of her eyes. Then at last he was at her door and she was standing there smiling and he could forget everything but the touch of her lips and the faint haunting scent of her perfume.

'I'm sorry I'm so late.' His arms were round her at last, as slowly the door swung shut behind them. It was a long time before he pushed her away.

She glanced up, half shy suddenly, and smiled. 'I'm so glad you're here, Mark. I was afraid that perhaps you weren't going to come back.' Since the night before she had been going over in her mind the scene in the bedroom, unbelieving, hugging to herself the memory of what had happened and of the things he had whispered to her as they lay in each other's arms on the bed. Still she could not bring herself to believe that this was really happening to her.

'Susie,' he whispered. 'Would you mind if we didn't go out? I'd rather have a snack here this evening.'

'That's a lovely idea, Mark.' She had to stand on tiptoe to kiss him unless he bent to meet her. 'What about a salad and some cheese? And as it happens, I've a bottle of wine.' She was very happy.

When at last he went home again the following evening. Annabel was sitting at the desk, a cup of cold coffee at her elbow, gazing in front of her with unseeing eyes. Mark frowned. Her hair was unbrushed and she was wearing an old pair of threadbare jeans.

'Annie?'

She turned to him, her face unmade-up and white. 'I've been trying to sort out our finances, Mark. They seem to be a bit entangled,' she began tonelessly.

'Annie, I rang you at your office. They said you hadn't gone in.'

'I didn't feel like it. I . . .' she hesitated. 'I was a bit sick this morning. I think I must have a touch of gastric flu.' Her eyes gave a flash of defiance.

'I came to collect my things. Don't worry about the money, Annie. I'll go on paying my share of everything for the time being.' She heard his words, but they were one dimensional; impersonal. She wanted suddenly to hit him.

'Don't be so bloody reasonable, Mark!' She got up, pushing the chair so hard it crashed into the wall, marking the new wallpaper behind it.

She wanted desperately to touch him, too. To feel the reassurance and comfort of his arms. But he, now, was the last person she could turn to. She wrapped her arms around herself defensively and went to stand by the window. 'You'd better pack. Don't worry, I won't smash up the place after you've gone. Anything you can't take now will be perfectly safe.'

'Oh, Annie. You know I don't think anything like that.'

The phone rang. Automatically she put out her hand and lifted the receiver.

Mark watched her answer and saw her face tighten with pain. 'It's for you,' she said quietly. 'A lady.' She put the receiver down on the table and walked past him into the bedroom, closing the door behind her.

*

'Who was the woman who answered your phone?' Susie asked curiously when he arrived at her flat.

Inexplicably he was angry with her.

'It's none of your business, Susie. How did you get my home number?'

'I'm sorry.' She was puzzled and then afraid. Suddenly she didn't want to know who it had been.

He sat down heavily on the edge of the kitchen table. 'Please, Susie, can I have some coffee? I've brought all my cases up and I'm tired.'

She wanted so much to do as he asked, to trust him, to forget the sadness of the voice she had heard on the phone. She bit her lip. 'Please, Mark. I have to know who it was, don't you see?'

He sighed. 'She's my sister. Who gave you the number anyway?' Strange, how he found it easier to lie to her than to Annabel.

'Your office gave it to me this afternoon. I wanted so much to hear your voice so I rang; I knew you wouldn't mind. Or at least, I thought you wouldn't . . . But you haven't got a sister, Mark. You told me, remember?' Her words tailed away. She could feel herself beginning to panic and desperately she tried to steady herself.

'All right, Susie. I suppose it's better for you to know the truth.' He ran his fingers through his hair. 'I have been living with someone; sharing a flat if you like. It was she who answered the phone.'

'Have you known her a long time?' She forced herself to speak steadily as she turned away from him and picked up the kettle, filling it automatically, her fingers fumbling with the plug and switches.

'We were together about five years, I suppose.' He spoke quietly, his eyes on the floor. 'She and I, well, we were different. We were very good friends and,' he hesitated, conscious suddenly of his enormous disloyalty in dismissing Annabel so casually, 'and, yes, we loved each other, of course we did, but we never thought about marriage. I've never thought of marrying anyone before. Not until I met you, Susie.'

She wanted to cry.

'I'm sure she must have thought of marriage, Mark.' Her hand was on the handle of the kettle, feeling it grow warm beneath her fingers. 'If you've been together so long she probably half thought of herself as married to you already.'

Slipping off the table he began to fiddle uncomfortably with a spoon on the dresser. 'All right, if it makes you feel better to know, Susie, I think she did.' He was silent for a minute. 'But what can I do? I want you. I love you. I want you to have my children and I've never felt that way about Annabel. I'd never even thought about it before.'

Susie pushed past him out of the narrow kitchen and went to stand in the middle of the sitting-room floor, looking down at his cases. 'Oh, Mark, why did this have to happen? It's all spoiled somehow. I never wanted anyone to get hurt by our love. It's too perfect for that.'

'Sweetheart.' He was behind her, his hands on her shoulders. 'Forget about her, she's my problem. I will be as kind to her as I can. She must have realized though, deep down inside her, that our relationship was going nowhere. If she's honest with herself she'll see that. She might be glad of the chance to meet someone else now, who will marry her and make her happy.'

Susannah glanced round at him hopefully. 'Do you really believe that?'

He smiled a little desperately and nodded.

'Will you see her again?'

'I must, Susie. I've still got a lot of stuff to collect and I can't – ' he hesitated, 'well, I can't just walk out on her. Not after five years.'

'No, of course not.' She shrugged off his hands with an impatient little gesture and went to turn on the electric fire. 'Funny,' she said in a strange high voice. 'It's cold suddenly; I thought it was supposed to be summer.'

Annabel had tried to eat a boiled egg but the runny yellow yolk congealed on the spoon and made her feel sick again. She felt hungry; empty inside and a little light-headed. Glancing round there were already signs that he was going from her life. Pictures; the hammer which for some reason lived on the bookcase, the clothes scattered untidily over every room in the flat – all had gone. A lot of the furniture would too, she imagined, eventually. Her mind skidded sideways at the thought and she found herself clutching the table as though it were about to get up and walk of its own accord out of the door.

She stood up and immediately flipped open a cigarette box on the desk. It was empty. It was months since she had smoked, but tonight . . . She began to bite her thumbnail. If she had the right change she would go to the machine on the corner. But there were practically no coins in her purse.

'Oh, Mark!' She found herself sobbing his name suddenly into the silence. She took a deep breath trying to steady herself.

The clock struck ten. She forced herself to go and turn on the bath and stood watching the water, eddying beneath the steam. She pushed her hair out of her eyes and glanced in the mirror. She was as slim as she had ever been. She supposed it would be a long time before it started to show.

For the first time in months she slipped on her nightdress afterwards. Then she lay in bed trying to read, but the print danced and blurred before her eyes.

*

'Annie.' When she heard his quiet voice she froze, her fingers clutching the book till it warped in her grasp.

'What have you come back for?' She refused to let the tiny whisper of hope surface.

'I thought I would get some more things.' He came in. He was frowning, his face was strained and sad. He stood for a moment looking at her and then he sat down at the edge of the bed, groping for her hand.

'Annie, I'm sorry.'

'So am I.'

'Can we still be friends?'

She raised her eyes to his and tried, not very successfully, to smile. 'I expect so. Later. Not yet.'

He nodded dumbly, not releasing her hand. 'We've had some good times.' There was a long silence. 'I haven't seen that nightie before. It's pretty.' He grinned a little.

'I didn't often wear them, did I?' She tried to smile again. But it was no good. Then suddenly his arms were round her and his lips were on her hair as she flung herself sobbing bitterly against his shoulder.

Susannah was pacing up and down her room, her mouth dry with fear, at every turn going to the window and peering out behind the curtain. It had begun to rain. There was an ominous roll of thunder and the street lamp in the forecourt below blurred and crystallized through the streaked glass. She walked across the room, pausing at the kitchen door, staring unseeing at the kettle for a moment, then she turned and retraced her steps, skirting the suitcase with a sudden pang of misery. She shouldn't have made him go back tonight. She shouldn't have *let* him go back. She wasn't sure if she had ever had Mark's love at all, not his real love and now she might never know. It had seemed so sincere, so real and yet how could he have done

207

this, lying to her and to this other woman, this Annabel? But no, she comforted herself. Some instinct told her that his love had been genuine. His eyes could not have lied.

She glanced at her wristwatch. It was twenty to twelve. She couldn't expect him yet anyway. He had to drive there, talk to her, load the car, drive back . . . She went to the window again and lifted the curtain as a flash of summer lightning lit the sky.

'I must go, Annie.' Gently he pushed her back on the pillow. 'Please, darling, don't make it more difficult.'

She sat up and reached for her thin dressing-gown as a distant rumble of thunder broke the silence.

'You're right,' she said. 'I'm being silly and hysterical. Not at all me.' Her voice sounded cold, quite unlike herself. 'Shall I help you pack or something?'

'No, thank you.' He went to the window and pushed back the curtain. 'It's raining so I won't take much. If you don't mind, perhaps I could come back tomorrow after work.'

'If you like.'

'Annie . . .'

'Please Mark, stop it. It would be so much easier if you were just plain nasty to me.' She was pleating the skirt of her dressing-gown with shaking fingers.

'But I . . .'

'Get out, Mark. Please.' She had her back to him. 'I can't bear this hypocrisy another minute. Take your cases and go back to her.' She paused. 'You really only came tonight to appease your conscience, didn't you?' She faced him at last. 'There's nothing in those cases you could have needed that badly.'

'I couldn't bear to think of you on your own. I had to make sure you were all right.'

'Well now you've seen. I'm fine.' Her voice was trembling a little.

'Annie. We never . . . Well, we never discussed marriage or anything, did we? It's not as though . . .'

'Goodnight, Mark.'

'What I mean is . . .'

'Goodnight, Mark.'

She heard him hesitate and then go, as she stood by the window, her arms protectively across her stomach, watching the silhouettes of the rooftops against the flickering sky. Not until the front door had banged behind him did she move. Then slowly she reached up onto the wardrobe for her own big suitcase. One by one she began to drop her books and her clothes and bits of make-up into the case. Wherever they went, she and the child within her, they would have each other. One day, perhaps she would give Mark her address; he had the right to know. But not yet.

'Oh Mark, darling, you're soaked through. Here let me help.' Susannah had been waiting for him at the open door of her flat and her face, so recently white and strained, was suddenly happy in its relief. 'You've been such a long time.'

He smiled wearily. 'It didn't take long, Susie. I've just been driving around in the rain.'

'Oh.' She was chilled by his tone. 'Well, come on; I've got a stiff drink poured for you. You must be exhausted.'

He sat down on the edge of a chair, his drink clasped loosely, his hands between his knees. His face was grey with fatigue and she knelt quietly down to be near him, not daring to say anything.

'I can't do it to her, Susie,' he said after a long silence.

Susie climbed to her feet and walked away from him, determined he shouldn't see her face. She went to the window and threw it open. The rain had stopped. There was already a grey lightening of the sky in the east.

'You and I have known each other such a short time, haven't we?' She tried to keep her tone light, although she suddenly felt sick with apprehension. 'If only we had met years ago.'

'We could have been happy, Susie. You're the only woman I've ever really wanted to marry.'

She knew he meant it.

'We still could, Mark?' Her voice, trembling with hope was so quiet he could hardly hear it.

His knuckles whitened on the glass as he shook his head. 'It's not just that; there are so many reasons it couldn't work. Life's not that simple.' He took a gulp from his glass as the first cautious notes of a sleepy bird echoed across the room. In a moment it was silent again. 'Love like this, that we feel for one another, it is self destructive. It must be. It would devour us, Susie, in time and devour itself too.'

'Don't decide too hastily, Mark,' she whispered. 'Please think a little longer.'

But he had thought. For that hour, driving round peering through the rain-streaked windscreen at the black sky he had thought again and again. And realized with an unexpected feeling of relief that real though his sudden infatuation with Susie had been he could not, could never, change the love he felt for Annabel; the protectiveness which Susie had first aroused in him had now strangely transferred itself to Annabel, wrapping her round, making her safe, wanting so much to comfort her for the hurt he had caused her. It was strange to think of her as vulnerable and fragile and alone, but this evening he had realized that she was all of those things. He could not think how he had not seen it before. Susie had known him so short a time she would, he hoped, soon forget, without too much pain. Annie was different.

He had known then that he had to go back. Nothing had really changed. Annabel was the woman he loved and she needed him. Suddenly and inexplicably she needed him.

He drove home in the pale green dawn, the car window down so he could hear the full-throated roar of the birds greeting the day. The roads sparkled from the night's rain and the heavy trees bowed under their frosting of raindrops. He parked, climbed stiffly out of the car and quietly shut the door, taking a deep breath of the clean air. For the first time in an age he felt light-hearted.

He ran up the stairs three at a time and slotted his key into the lock. The room was as he had left it a few hours before; a few boxes and cases still piled by the wall ready for him to collect. He crept over to the bedroom door, picturing her lying there, her dark hair a blackbird's wing across the white of the sheets. He would wake her with a kiss and beg understanding and forgiveness.

But the bed was empty and neatly made. The room was unnaturally tidy, the dressing table bare and dusted. It was as though she had never been.

He sat on the bed, kneading his eyes with his knuckles while the joyous chorus of birdsong flooded through the window; mocking him.

Slowly, he stood up. He took off his jacket and walked back into the sitting room. Behind the sofa she had stacked all the wallpaper. Sadly he picked up a roll. At least he could finish the decorating for her.

Two weeks later Mark let himself into the flat after work and glanced round wearily. The room looked good now that it was finished. Annabel would have liked it so much.

211

Wandering rather aimlessly into the bedroom he flopped down onto the unmade bed, his arm across his eyes. The silence and emptiness of the place oppressed him and he hated being there in the evenings. Later, perhaps, he would go out and find himself something to eat. He lay there for a long time, his mind a blank, and then at last as the light slowly faded he dozed.

He was awakened by the ringing of the phone. For a moment he lay still listening to the insistent sound coming from the room next door, tempted not to bother, then suddenly something made him throw himself out of bed. He ran, fumbled desperately with the door knob, wrenching it open and grabbed the receiver, his heart thumping, afraid the caller would hang up before he could answer.

'Mark?' Her voice came from a long way away. She had not dared to hope he might be at the flat. 'Mark, I had to talk to you; are you alone?'

His relief and happiness were so great that for a moment he couldn't reply and in the long silence he heard her again. 'Mark, are you there? Mark? . . .'

The Indian Summer of
Mary McQueen

'Mary, Mary, quite contrary,
How does your garden grow?'

Mary McQueen murmured the words to herself languidly as she stood at the veranda door, gazing through the mesh out to the barren, puddled lawns and the dripping maples. The rain was pouring straight down, a heavy curtain, never once slanted or scattered by the wind. She could hear the parched gardens gasping with gratitude beneath the weight of it.

Inside, the house was as hot as ever, humid and so uncomfortable that in another five minutes she would have to go and change her dress. She glanced back into the living room with its freshly laundered drapes and pretty summery chintz and she could not face the thought of dragging herself up the stairs.

If she did not look at the driveway where the gravel was rapidly disappearing beneath a sheet of slate-coloured puddles, for five whole minutes – not cheating – then, as she raised her eyes, surely she would see the biscuit-coloured Buick she had expected since breakfast, nosing in off the highway. She sat down on the rocking chair, her wrist dangling heavily across her knee. She immediately felt even hotter and more uncomfortable, but that way she could watch the tiny hands of the watch with the minimum of effort.

Dan McQueen had given it to her on the plane after they got married, as he took her up to the house in Vermont for their honeymoon. Then they had returned to live in New York. Fifteen years later, after deciding to make their home there in the soft woods and hills of New England Dan had inexplicably walked out. Mary had never suspected another woman.

'I have my English Mary,' he used to say, with nauseating frequency, at dinner parties. 'She's just about the greatest!'

Just about.

She had resented his work and his devotion to golf as did all the other wives at the Garden Club. But never had she suspected Dan, sidesman at the local church and co-organizer of the Lake Falls Arts Festival, of hankering after another woman.

Once, they had gone up to Tanglewood to listen beneath the great north American moon to Beethoven and Mozart. He had sat beside her on the grass holding her hand, trying to sneak little kisses like a boy of twenty. She had been so embarrassed. Dan was a man of fifty-six. But Dan did not like serious music – it was the organizing side of the Arts Festival he enjoyed, not the art – and they had not gone again.

She glanced at the watch once more. Two minutes more and she would look up at the rain-swept drive.

It was six weeks now since Dan had driven off with his bags to collect Sarah Walton. Mary could keep the house, he said. He would pay a regular allowance into her account.

He had been as excited as a kid going on holiday with his cases and, of course, his golf clubs. He had worn his new shirt and the silk cravat she had given him. She had had it sent from Fortnum's in London and she knew the label alone would have pleased him. That hurt as much as anything else; that he should wear her present when running away with another woman. It was as though he expected her to share his excitement, help him pack, even prepare the two of them some sandwiches.

'Don't you want to know where we're going, honey?'

He had sounded quite hurt and when she shook her head, wordlessly miserable, he looked upset and worried and took her hand rather as an anxious mother takes the hand of her child to feel if it has a fever.

She had waved him goodbye though.

That night, inevitably, Cyrus Walton had driven up complete with Californian wine and barbecued chicken. As inevitably after they had eaten he had expected them to go to bed together. Even in Lake Falls it seemed wife swapping could be viewed with equanimity if it salved one's hurt and avenged one's pride. But she proved contrary and Cyrus at last went home, hiccoughing and unfulfilled to his empty bed. She had sat a long time after she had locked up that night, considering whether she had been foolish and should have accepted his offer. Perhaps if he had been different she would have. But she had always found Cyrus the worst type of boorish male. She preferred her loneliness. Then.

The hand on the watch had traversed its full five minutes but she was reluctant to look up now and break the spell she had woven.

She could hear the rain pounding down onto the leaves and the roof and the gravel outside, but no scrunch of car tyres. She would wait another two minutes, she bargained with fate, and then go in if he hadn't appeared and fix herself a cold fattening drink.

After all, it had not been such a definite arrangement that he arrive this morning. She pictured again the square jaw, the fair untidy hair, the piercing eyes which seemed to see her soul, of the man with whom she had shared martinis and lunch on the plane down to New York three weeks before.

They had got talking, as people do on planes. He helped her with her seat belt and adjusted the air conditioning. Then they had a drink and relaxed.

By the time they had reached cruising altitude they had been chatting like friends; by the time they approached LaGuardia they had both felt, she was certain, that they *were* friends.

They were both pressed for time, but parting had seemed inappropriate and too hurried. Then she had remembered the new car, a biscuit-coloured Buick, which he was to pick up on this trip and drive back north. 'Come by, won't you?' She had asked and he had agreed. They had held hands for a moment and exchanged glances, she had thought, of significance and promise.

The two minutes were up. At last she raised her eyes again to the dripping garden. It was curtained by the falling rain, scented, beautiful. It smelt, she thought, like every beautiful smell there had ever been, but it was empty of life.

Getting up from the rocking chair she went through to the kitchen. Ice cream in the freezer. Maple syrup in the cupboard. Soda somewhere. To hell with the inches.

Then abruptly she slammed the carton back into the freezer. No. Bravado aside, she wanted a cup of tea, however hot it would make her feel.

Then she would go up and change her dress. And if she had a quick shower as well, he would probably arrive then. People so often call when one is in the shower.

She snapped on the radio as she waited for the kettle to boil. A phone-in show was on, as always, with lonely women pouring out their hearts in the seclusion of their kitchens to the public anonymity of the air. American women have such shrill voices, she thought suddenly with a shudder, and they are always complaining. But that, after all, was the purpose of the programmes. Suffering in silence may be dignified and English but was it any better for one's peace of mind? She thought not.

She switched off and looked instead out of the back window over vistas of dripping bushes and trees, down towards the lake. She and Dan used to keep a boat down there. Then, two years before, he had suddenly announced he was too old and sold it. It was the first time he had done anything like that without consulting her and she had been heartbroken, both for the boat itself, which she loved and for the precedent which, she had felt somehow even then, might bode evil for the future.

She made the tea with a teabag in her cup and carried it, steaming, up to her bedroom. It looked out over the front of the house, so she could see him if he came.

If he came?

So she was having doubts now. She sat down at the dressing table and wondered for the first time whether he would come at all. She had been so certain. She had even bought a new dress for the occasion. She glanced sadly at the bed where she had thrown it, crumpled and damp with perspiration.

If only the rain would stop. If only she dared run down to the garden, naked. If only there would be a premature frost.

As she did every day of every summer she thought nostalgically of the summers at home in England with the cool fresh winds and early morning mists and felt homesick once more for her happy girlhood.

If I had stayed at home, she thought again, where would I have been now? And what would I have been? Not, certainly, a middle-aged American matron, husbandless and hunting for a man.

She gazed up at herself in the mirror, suddenly appalled. Is that what she was? Is that what she, who so despised the other man-hunting women she had met, had become?

She scrutinized her image carefully. She certainly looked the part. Her hair showed no thread of grey and every strand was immaculate, her hairdresser saw to that. Her tights came from Lord and Taylor, her dresses from only a few select couture shops. Even in that boat she had not been really casual. Her slacks were tailored cleverly to conceal any broadening of the hips which might have shown and her jackets were without exception long enough. She had always been careful not to chip her nails gardening or on the jetty.

She stood up. Why in a temperature of over 100° and with the humidity unbearable was she wearing heavy make-up and tights at all? To impress a man she had picked up – oh yes, Mary, face the fact, that's what you did, she thought – picked up, three weeks ago on a plane ride to New York. For three weeks she had been living in a breath-less pause like a teenage girl with her first infatuation. It was shameful, shallow and childish.

Looking back at the mirror she caught herself blushing with embarrassment and she felt suddenly more contrary than she had ever felt in her life before.

Falling on her knees in front of the highboy in the corner she pulled open a heavy drawer. There, neatly packed away in tissue and lavender were some of the old clothes which she had never brought herself to give away to the Garden Club bazaar. Pulling them out she heaped them on the floor around her, searching through the well-remembered garments.

She couldn't make up her mind between the dark blue cotton shift and the slacks and cotton shirt. Both were a little shabby and badly needed pressing. Both had been hers when she had first come to the States so very long ago.

She showered and removed her make-up and slipped at last into the shift, unwilling to try the test of time and her constant slimming by putting on trousers which she had worn as a girl.

Then she stood bare-legged and barefoot before the mirror. The dress was creased and faded in the creases and shabby and the wrong length for today's fashions but her legs, she decided critically, were perhaps not too bad. Her hair was all wrong. It was formal and stiff and, she suddenly realized, the colour was too hard for her face.

She brushed it hard, trying to dislodge the careful style, but it would not be disarranged.

Ten minutes later she was in the rain, her feet delightfully chilled in the cold grass, her shift black with absorbed water and clinging to her skin, her hair bedraggled, untidy and quite styleless. She cut armloads of roses, the raindrops still on their petals and watched the gentle curves of their leaves fill with more rain as they lay in the basket on the grass at her feet. She wondered if Sue Beckstein could see her across the lawn from her kitchen window. If so she would probably call up the local sanatarium.

She laughed aloud at the thought, shook her head so the raindrops flew, then picking up her basket she almost danced back to the house.

Her hair dried into tight little curls, with wisps and loose ends around her eyes. She stripped off the dress and threw it in the tub. Recklessly she tried on the old slacks. They still fitted after all those years.

She rummaged in a drawer and found a copper-hammered pendant which went with the throbbing green of her shirt, then still barefoot she ran downstairs to arrange her flowers. Dan had always discouraged flowers indoors because he reckoned they gave him asthma and hay fever.

The biscuit-coloured Buick arrived at ten after three. Mary was lying reading in the hammock on the veranda and hardly looked up as she heard the tyres on the drive.

The rain had stopped at last and he stepped out on the wet gravel to a fitful sunshine. All around the sky was still heavy with black thunder-clouds.

'Hi,' she called. 'I wondered if you'd turn up.'

He hesitated and then came towards her, at first slowly and then sprinting up the veranda steps.

'Have a cold drink,' she said with a smile. 'I'm sure you can do with a rest. My husband gets back about four. Perhaps you'd like to stay and meet him?'

They drank soda together on the veranda, he uncomfortable and formal with tie and shoes and she relaxed and happy and untidy. The seam on her left hip started to go a little as she hitched back up into the hammock but she didn't think he noticed. She saw him eyeing her unhappily as he laboured with polite conversation and remembered how he must have pictured her. Cool, friendly, immaculate and sophisticated. A rich woman on the make.

A little giggle escaped her and she tried to smother it within her glass.

'What's the joke?' he asked, embarrassed, suspecting her.

'Me,' she said and sipped her soda demurely.

He stayed only half an hour, anxious, without seeming so, not to risk meeting her phantom husband.

She waved him goodbye and then stood for a long time gazing after him.

That night she fell asleep on the couch by the open window, listening to Brahms' *Requiem* on the hi-fi. The next morning she drove downtown and made a reservation for a fourteen day round trip to England.

If they'll have me back, she thought, I'll stay.

She bought Levis and sneakers and, studying herself in her mirror at home, decided she looked good in them. Not mutton trying to be lamb, but artistic and intelligent.

She had the piano tuner come by and dug out all her old music and classical records. She read Walt Whitman and Emerson, Salinger, Burroughs and Mary McCarthy and replenished the tubes of paint in her paintbox. She had always meant to paint the fall; that after all had been the reason she had first come to visit the States as an art student way back. After she met Dan she had painted less and less as his social interests took up her time. Besides he thought her Bohemian and although he had said nothing she had felt herself discouraged.

She threw all the garbage and accumulated junk out of one of the guest rooms, set up her easel and began to paint again. She took her records up there and the kettle and wondered how she could have wasted her life for so long.

Slowly, by a fraction of an inch at a time as though not believing the chance she gave it, the grey began to appear in the roots of her hair. Bravely she ignored it and began to plan her trip to England.

Then with the first frosts Dan returned. He drove up beneath the reddening leaves sheepish and alone.

'I guess she and I didn't gel, honey,' was his only comment.

She was glad to have him back.

He noticed her hair, but said nothing. For two days she braved his puzzled looks and then she fled back to her hairdresser, who thought she must have been ill and congratulated her on her recovery.

Slowly she packed away her paints, brought the hi-fi back downstairs and forgot to practise the piano.

One day he said, 'Hon, I don't go much for those pants.

They don't suit the more mature woman.' Sadly she packed away her Levis, neatly washed and pressed, into the highboy. It was almost a relief to slip back into her smart clothes. She felt clean again, confident and immaculate. Her feet had had so much hard skin from going bare that she had laddered her tights when she first put them back on.

She missed the music and the painting. When Dan found her reading poetry he teased her; when he found flowers on the table he looked pained and sneezed. He said nothing, but she did not replace them when the petals dropped.

Arm in arm they attended parties and dinners as though nothing had happened. At first she tried to discuss things she loved and had rediscovered: poetry, music, the latest novels. But she met incomprehension and boredom. She remembered now why, so long ago, she had given up.

As though conscious of some loss in his wife which he could not name Dan suddenly promised her a trip to Europe in the spring. Quietly she slipped downtown and cancelled her own flight to England. With her returned reservations went the rest of her dreams.

The summer had been fun. But it was over. She knew the chance would never come again.

The day before the Garden Club winter bazaar she emptied the bottom drawer of the highboy, threw her paints and brushes on the top of the box of clothes and took the whole lot across to the jumble stall.

Her books she kept. That one small part of her, redeemed that summer and hidden in the guest room, she kept. That was all.

The Magic of Make Believe

She put the phone down and stared sadly down from the window thinking of Christmas things. Snow. Mistletoe. The hot chestnut man. Red noses. Mince pies. Noise. Quarrelling. Home . . .

'. . . We knew you wouldn't mind, Sue darling, as you'd be with Tony this year. Imagine! Christmas in New York with your sister! It's so exciting for us. And it's not as though you'll be alone, otherwise you could have come too . . .'

Her mother's tone was so apologetic, so guilty, so desperately hoping she wouldn't say the unthinkable – yes, I do mind. Yes, I'm hurt and lonely and miserable because Tony has left me and you're my parents and I need you.

When the phone had rung she had had the usual impossible hope which came with every call at home or at the office that it would be Tony. That, repentant, he was coming back to her, changing his mind as he did over so many things, suddenly and overwhelmingly, expecting to be hugged and forgiven and welcomed like a lost dog running home.

Slowly she covered her typewriter and picked up her tote bag. She smiled at the other girls. Her lips said the right words as she put on her coat and followed them into the lift, but her mind was whirling in a spiral of lost misery.

For the first time she was thinking: supposing he

doesn't come back. Ever. What shall I do? She had all this time been expecting him to appear in time for Christmas. She had known in some sealed, stubborn part of her that he had to come back. The certainty was as complete as the knowledge that her mother would be digging out the box of decorations and hanging them on the little spruce tree in the hall at home. But there would be no Christmas tree at home this year. And suddenly she realized that there would be no Tony either. This time he had meant it.

'I may be a while, Sue.' Tony had been standing in the hall of their flat, his raincoat shucked forward on his shoulders, the collar up, like Philip Marlowe after a particularly heavy night. She had grinned and raised her hand half heartedly, intent on what she was doing, not even standing up to give him a hug. Afterwards she remembered how he had hesitated, half turning back towards her. A thousand times she had asked herself what would have happened if she had jumped to her feet then and run to him and flung her arms around his neck.

But she hadn't. She had said, 'See you tonight.' Taken him for granted. Dared to be sure. Known, because she had an engagement ring on her finger, that he had to return . . .

But he hadn't. That night she sat up till one o'clock, watching and waiting, agonizing over what awful accident had happened, wondering when one rang the police and if one did what did one say . . .

She woke on the sofa, cramped and very cold, his last words ringing in her ears: *I may be a while.*

That was six weeks ago. He had sent a note.

'. . . I'm sorry but it wouldn't have worked. Forgive me and find someone else who will make you happy . . .'

Two days later when she came home from the office all his things had gone.

She pushed out into the noisy dark street, staring up at the coloured lights strung between the tall lampposts. Behind them the sky was never black in London. It was dun coloured. Muddy. The cloud reflecting the colour below it, mixing it and killing it with leaden overshadows. The sleet glittered on her eyelashes as all round her people rushed past elbowing one another in their rush to get home.

'*Sorry!*'

A particularly hard push sent her reeling towards the gutter, her boots slipping on the wet pavements and she fell, knowing suddenly that the wetness on her face was not sleet. It was tears.

'Oh Lord! Are you all right?' The man who had pushed her stopped and fought his way back against the crowd. He was tall, his collar also up against the wind.

He grabbed her arm and pulled her to her feet, swinging her back against the railings out of the way of the crowds.

'I'm . . . I'm all right,' she gasped, feeling stupid. Not wanting a fuss. Not wanting him to see her tears. Just wanting to crawl away and be alone. But impossibly he had gone down on one knee before her, raising the hem of her coat a couple of inches and looking at her muddy knees. She glanced down, her cheeks reddening with embarrassment and saw her tights were torn and a trickle of blood was oozing slowly down into the top of her boot.

He rose. 'That must be cleaned at once,' he said authoritatively. 'We'll find a chemist . . .'

'No, please. It doesn't matter.' She glanced up at his face for the first time. He had a tanned, rubbery comfortable sort of face. Youngish. Very young. Well, not much older than hers. A nice face.

He smiled at her. 'I don't often pick up strange women,' he said. 'But when I do, I do it properly.' He looked rueful. 'I was in such a hurry to get home.'

She felt absurdly left out and lonely suddenly.

'So was I,' she lied. 'There's no harm done, really. I'll see to it when I get home.'

'Bacillus *Clostridium tetani*,' he said absent-mindedly.

'I beg your pardon?'

'Tetanus. You must be careful and deal with that quickly. It's quite deep . . .'

'Are you a doctor?' She felt absurd standing there near the busy underground station, her knees bleeding like a child's, but she couldn't bring herself to leave. She had nothing to hurry home for now and he had a pleasant warmth, a kindness she wanted to be near for a moment longer.

A Salvation Army band was taking up its position near them. If they began to play carols she knew she would cry. She had to go. Now. She took a determined step away from him and let out a quite genuine yelp of pain as her left knee stabbed and throbbed as she put her weight on it. He caught her arm.

'A taxi is what we need,' he said decisively. He led her to the kerb and looked out into the road. She watched impressed as a cab appeared as if by magic from the almost stationary jam. Tony, for all his presence and *savoir faire* would never have managed to do that.

'Jump in,' he said. He climbed in beside her and leaned forward to slide open the glass portion behind the driver. The windscreen wipers were drawing refracted coloured arcs in the crystals of the sleet.

'Where shall I tell him to go?' he asked.

She gave him her address after only a second's hesitation. After all, he didn't look like a rapist or a murderer and Mrs Green would be in downstairs . . .

'What would you have said if I had lived the other end of London?' she could not resist asking.

'I'd have taken it on the chin, paid up and taken out a second mortgage on my flat.' He grinned and she found herself smiling back.

'You didn't tell me if you were a doctor,' she said as he sat back beside her, with a comfortable sigh. There was at least a foot between them on the hard slippery seat.

He grinned. 'Would that make it all right?'

'Make what all right?'

'Me, taking you home.'

'Probably not.'

'Then I can admit I'm not. My acquaintance with bacilli is purely passing, at the moment.'

She giggled. 'Are you going to tell me what you do do?'

'Must I? I'll tell you my name. It's Richard.'

'Mine is Sue.'

The taxi still had not moved a foot. Up ahead the lights changed from red to green and back to red. The driver glanced over his shoulder. 'I hope you're not in a rush, guv,' he commented.

'We've got all the time in the world,' Richard said.

Sue glanced at him accusingly. 'I thought you were in a hurry to get home.'

'I was. I hate being in limbo, between places. But now I'm here, which is somewhere. So I'm not in a hurry any more.'

He came up to the flat and poked around her drinks cupboard while she took off the torn tights in the bathroom and dabbed at her knees with cotton wool.

'One inch of decidedly-cooking sherry,' he said as she

returned to the living room, her elastoplasted knees safely encased in jeans, 'even less Sainsbury's whisky and a can of lager. I can safely say, either you are a dipsomaniac down to your last ten minutes' worth, or you are not a drinking lady.'

She laughed. 'I haven't felt very sociable lately. I'm sorry. Would coffee do instead?'

He shook his head. 'I don't feel I've made full reparation yet. I saw an off licence on the corner. I'll go and get something.'

He would not listen to her protests.

She stood and stared at herself in the mirror when he had gone. Her face was very pale and there were dark circles under her eyes, but there was a small sparkle in the clear blue irises which hadn't been there that morning.

He came back with two bottles of wine, a Chinese takeaway and a huge bunch of holly.

She stared.

'What on earth is that?'

'I thought you might get the wrong idea if I brought mistletoe.'

'But you didn't have to bring either!'

'I did.' He put the bottles down and stacked the paper carriers on the table. 'I've decided I've got to come clean and tell you what I do. Otherwise I'm here under false pretences. First, I'm not a doctor but I am a medical student, so I'm almost qualified to swab your knee myself. Next summer I shall be, exams permitting, and yours will be the first knee I touch professionally, I promise.'

'If the bacillus hasn't got me first.'

'Exactly.' He had found a corkscrew by himself and expertly drew the cork.

'Second, as this is the vacation and I am, in common with most of my species, hard up-ish, I have a temporary job. Namely, I am masquerading as one F. Christmas Esq. at the local big store.'

She stared at him. Then she burst out laughing. 'You're not serious!'

'Perfectly. I had only hung up my robe ten minutes before I met you. It's a jolly good job – with luncheon vouchers!'

They were half-way through the chow mien when the phone rang.

Sue climbed to her feet from her cushion in front of the coffee table near his and went to answer it, still laughing, unsuspecting.

It was Tony.

'Sue? Can I come and see you?'

She felt her stomach muscles clench uncomfortably. The receiver grew slippery in her hand. *Come home. Please come home.* The words screamed in her head, but she managed to control her voice with a supreme effort. 'Of course, Tony. What about tomorrow?'

'I had thought perhaps now . . .'

'I'm sorry. I'm busy tonight. Come tomorrow.'

She stood staring at the wall as she hung up, her hands shaking violently. Richard closed her fingers round the stem of her wine glass. 'Sip it,' he said quietly.

She obeyed and the world stopped spinning.

'That was my ex-fiancé,' she said after a moment.

'Don't tell me unless you want to.'

She went back to her cushion with a grimace. 'I think I do. Do you mind?'

She and Tony had met at a squash club in the City. She was swept off her feet by his handsome attentiveness, by his charm and his easy confidence and soon she was going with him everywhere, her blonde, blue-eyed prettiness set off by his dark hair and permanently tanned skin. He drove an MG and her parents had approved of him utterly. They had become inseparable and Sue was besotted by him, physically and emotionally obsessed by her first real affair.

'You still haven't told me what he does for a living,' Richard put in quietly.

Sue looked down. 'He hasn't actually got a job.'

'There's nothing wrong in that.'

'No, I don't mean he's unemployed. I mean he doesn't work.'

'Oh.'

There didn't seem any more to be said.

Tony took her to parties and dances and brought her first not-too-expensive presents, then expensive presents and moved in when her flat mate moved out and finally presented her with a sapphire surrounded by tiny diamonds as they chose the day three months hence when they would be married.

She looked down at the pile of empty cartons on the coffee table and laughed ruefully. 'Tony would have made me put this on plates in the kitchen and seal the cartons into a bin liner so they didn't spoil the ambience,' she said, gently self mocking.

Richard grinned. 'Why didn't I think of that? It sounds eminently sensible.' He reached for the bottle and filled her glass.

'My mother has started making lists,' Sue said quietly. Suddenly there were idiot tears in her eyes again.

'Mothers do.' Richard grinned, carefully not looking at her. 'My mother even listed how many hole-less socks I had when I started medical school.'

'How many were there?' She looked up, smiling through her tears.

'Three, as I remember.' He slipped off his shoe and stared reflectively at his protruding big toe.

She let out a gurgle of laughter. 'You'll have to do better than that when you get to Harley Street.'

It was nearly midnight when he got up to go. He walked slowly to the door. 'Can I ring you sometime?'

She nodded. 'Thank you for the holly and everything.'

He slipped back the lock and walked onto the landing. Then he turned and almost absent-mindedly dropped a kiss on her forehead. 'Don't forget to bathe your knees again,' he whispered. 'I realize I am probably too late to join the queue of your admirers, but I'm damned if I'm going to lose you to a bacillus.'

Tony arrived at seven-thirty precisely. He was carrying a sheaf of red roses.

'I've booked a table for dinner,' he said as he came in. He put his hands on her shoulders and gazed into her eyes. Then he kissed her. She felt her legs begin their customary descent to soggy cotton wool, but already he had backed away staring at her hand.

'You've taken off your ring.'

'I assumed our engagement was off, Tony,' she said. To her surprise now that he had let her go she felt perfectly calm. 'It's in the bedroom in its box if you want it.'

He bit his lip, crestfallen. 'Can't you put it on again?'

'I don't know.'

'Please. I want you to.' He took her fingers in his. 'Sue. I know I have behaved badly. I panicked. I needed space. Suddenly I saw the future all spread out before me like a long carpet. The wedding. The honeymoon. Bridge with your parents. Croquet or something with mine. Kids. Having to sell the car and get something sensible. Getting middle-aged. Going bald – what's so funny?'

Sue steadied her face with difficulty. 'I'm sorry, Tony. It just all sounded so unromantic.'

He grinned hopefully. 'Not really. The wedding will be nice and the honeymoon. And then. Well, it'll all be nice, I expect. Put the ring on again. Please.'

She shook her head. 'Not yet. Let's give it a bit more time. I think I need space too.'

'Sue. My parents have asked us to go down for Christmas. They'll expect to see you wearing it. Dad was furious when I said we'd quarrelled. He said I was spineless.' Suddenly he looked like a dog that had been kicked.

'We never quarrelled, Tony.' She bit her lip. 'Is that why you came back?' she went on in a whisper. 'Because your father told you to?'

'No, of course not. I'd have come anyway. Of course I would. Sue . . .' He reached out for her again. 'Come on, sweetheart.'

She gave him her hand. She went out to dinner with him and let him bring her home. Then she told him it was over and gave him back his ring.

The toy department was crowded. Children were everywhere, on and in and under the displays, evading harassed parents, screaming and crying and laughing with excitement. Sue looked at the lavish cardboard castle stuck with sparkling cotton wool at the end of the huge department. There was a queue of mothers waiting clutching the hands of their children. Had she really thought she would dare queue with them, without a child?

She paid for the small presents she had chosen and stared towards it again wistfully. Father Christmas might as well be in Snowland for real, she would get no nearer to him than this.

He hadn't phoned. Why should he? They had met once, passed a pleasant evening, laughed a lot and gone their separate ways. As far as he knew she and her fiancé had made up their quarrel and her life was once more complete. If he had thought about her at all.

Sadly she walked towards the escalator and let it carry her down back to reality and the office.

When she got home that evening a small packet had been wedged into her letter box. She gathered it up and let herself into the cold flat. The silver bells she had tied onto the holly in the vase glittered as she drew the curtains and turned on all the lights. She shook the sleet out of her hair and snapped on the TV for company and then turned the parcel over in her hands.

It was wrapped in white tissue and tied with ribbon. She wondered if it were from Tony to make up, but somehow something about it was not his style.

Puzzled she tore it open and stared. Inside was a tiny doll's first aid box. There was a note attached.

'I saw you through the windows of my castle and thought you might be looking for a bacillus-bashing kit. If you think a strong drink would be more effective, I'll pick you up about nine. F.C.'

She laughed out loud. Suddenly the evening had lost its bleakness.

The sleet had turned to snow since she had come home. She stood beside him on the front doorstep and stared out in wonder. In the street lights the air was magical. The treacly slush vanished beneath a crisp white crust which squeaked satisfactorily beneath their shoes and the air was a whirling net of cold.

She could not resist running her hand along the top of a car, watching the powdery whiteness caking and crumbling on her glove.

'You brought Snowland with you!'

He raised his eyes towards heaven. 'I'm never going to live that down, am I? Come on.' He caught her hand and dusted the snow off it. 'I'm going to be able to practise on your chilblains too at this rate. You're turning into a walking case book!'

The pub was crowded. Squeezed behind a small round table near the dartboard Sue sipped a shandy watching Richard play. He turned to her and raised his glass. 'Only one game, I promise. Is your fiancé waiting up for you?'

She was surprised by the suddenness of the question and looked down miserably. 'There is no more fiancé.'

He handed his darts to the man next to him. 'No more squash and Pimms and souped-up MGs?'

She shook her head, suddenly afraid she was going to cry as he sat down beside her, his burly figure squashing her on the narrow bench.

He put his hands on hers. 'The way you told it, he didn't sound right for you, Sue.'

'I know.' She sniffed hard, groping for a tissue.

'Come on. I'm taking you for a walk.'

They walked across the park in the whirling snow, his college scarf wound round and round her neck, his arm linked through hers as the dark disappeared before wave after wave of splintering whiteness.

'It doesn't often snow like this before Christmas,' she said, trying hard to be cheerful.

'It does when I'm in charge.' He smiled.

He took her home at last, exhausted, feet soaked through and numb, her nose and cheeks glowing.

On the doorstep he stamped the snow off his shoes. 'I'm coming in for five minutes only,' he said. 'I'm going to run your bath, prescribe you a night cap and, if I'm allowed, I'll kiss you goodnight.'

He was as good as his word, turning on the bath taps, then producing from his pocket a small bottle of whisky which he had bought in the pub. He put it on the sideboard. 'A slug of that with honey and lemon against the cold,' he said firmly. 'Then I must go. I've to be in my grotto again by nine in the morning.' He grinned.

He put his hands on her shoulders and drew her to him gently. 'Don't be afraid to cry, Sue,' he said softly as his lips came down on hers.

It was a warm, solid, comforting kiss, a bit shorter than she would have liked, she realized, as soon as it had stopped and quite definitely more-ish.

But he was fumbling in the cupboard for a glass. He made up her drink and carried it into the steamy bathroom.

'It's Christmas Eve tomorrow,' he said.

She nodded, feeling suddenly sick and empty.

'I won't have had my last sticky hug from my last toddling admirer till five.' He sat on the edge of the bath, testing the temperature of the water.

Firmly banishing the thought of Christmas Day Sue concentrated instead on wondering, since he was in such a masterful mood, if he were going to undress her as well. She rather hoped he was. The thought sent a small interesting tingle up her spine.

But he stood up again and moved towards the door.

'Get into that water before it gets cold. I've got to go now, but I'll pick you up at six with my tame reindeer. Unless you've got other plans of course?' He raised his eyebrows impishly.

There was a huge lump in her throat, but she could feel herself smiling blindly. 'I've no plans at all,' she said.

'Good. Don't bother to buy any food for the holiday. You won't need it,' and with that he was gone, leaving her in the warm bathroom with a glass of hot whisky in her hand. Behind her the flat door banged and she was alone.

She had to buy him a present, but how could she? She knew so little about him. In the end she bought a bottle of good wine – he seemed to be keen on drink and she suspected he probably knew about wine and on inspiration a pair of terrifying red, white and blue socks. He would never wear them, but they would bring his average of hole-less socks up a bit.

He was very prompt. She answered the door rather hesitantly, wondering if it were him, afraid he might have forgotten or changed his mind. But he was standing there in the same shabby coat, a broad grin on his face. 'I was tempted to borrow my red costume from the store, but I thought you might run if I did,' he said as he came in. 'Are you packed and ready?'

'Packed?' She stared at him with a small quiver of doubt.

'Of course. My mother would think it a bit odd if you turned up without a toothbrush. That's all you need though. We're very informal.'

'Your mother?' She was dumbfounded.

'That's right. The one who lists my socks.' He grinned. 'I've told her I'm bringing a girl home for Christmas.'

Sue looked down at her feet. 'But won't she assume we're . . . I mean, won't she think . . .' Her voice trailed into embarrassed silence.

'She'll assume nothing. She knows me better than that,' he said firmly. 'Now come on. This is all part of the therapy. A few days in the country.'

He drove a battered red MG. She stared at it in silence. Then she turned an accusing eye on him. 'You might have told me you had one too. And you were being so rude about them!'

'I'm never rude about Rudolph.' His eyes were gleaming maliciously.

'And since when has it been called Rudolph?'

'Since last night.' He tucked her case in the boot and helped her in.

The old house was already deep in snow as the car slithered its way up the drive. Sue loved it on sight, as she did Richard's mother, whom he introduced simply as Maggie and who greeted her with a kiss and a hug and pushed her into a rocking chair by a roaring log fire.

The ceilings were so low that the Christmas tree had to bend its head as did Richard when he waded through the two cats and three dogs sprawling before the flames to bring Sue her drink.

He grinned at her. 'No strings,' he whispered. 'Just enjoy yourself.' He winked.

While he was fetching logs from somewhere in the garden, logs that spluttered and hissed and exploded and smelt like summer nights by the Mediterranean, his mother sat down beside her.

Like her son she was tall, with deeply caring eyes and a warm smile.

'I'm afraid I haven't brought you a present,' Sue said awkwardly. 'Richard only told me we were coming here an hour or so ago.'

Maggie laughed. 'How like him. He told me a week ago.'

'A week ago?' Sue stared. 'He can't have. I've only known him a few days.'

'That's right. He rang up the night he met you and said there would be one extra for Christmas. "I'm bringing the girl I'm going to marry," he said.' She smiled. 'That's present enough for me, my dear, a thousand times over.' She stood up. 'I've been in a ferment of curiosity to meet you. But now I have, I'm so happy. Welcome.' She dropped a kiss on the top of Sue's head.

That night she had snuggled beneath the huge old-fashioned eiderdown and given up the struggle to evict a fat and very determined cat from the end of the bed when she was awakened by the door opening. A tall figure tiptoed towards the bed. She lay still watching as, with some difficulty it pinned a bulging stocking to the end of the counterpane with a huge safety pin. She heard a smothered curse as the pin must have driven into his finger and silently she managed to stifle a giggle.

Richard had turned back towards the door and was tiptoeing back towards the dim crack of light thrown by the landing lamp when she sat up. 'I never believed in Father Christmas before this year,' she whispered. 'Or since I was very very little. But I do now.'

He turned and came towards her. 'Go to sleep,' he said sternly. 'You're not supposed to have seen me.'

She held out her arms. 'Can I have a Christmas kiss?'

He sat down on the eiderdown and put his arms around her. He had just shaved and his cheeks were smooth and smelled of cologne.

'You invited me here under false pretences, didn't you?' she murmured, her lips against his. This time the kiss was of a very satisfactory duration.

She felt him smile.

'That would be against my principles,' he said softly.

'But you let your mother think you were going to marry me.' For some reason her chest had gone very tight and she couldn't breathe properly as she tried to see his face.

'Mother and I are always straight with each other. That's why we get on so well.' He smiled.

'But you didn't even know you were going to see me again.'

He smiled, touching her hair gently. 'I knew,' he said.

Several minutes later he started to stand up. 'I must go, Sue,' he said softly. 'If I stay any longer I may find it hard to leave.'

'But we're going to be married.' She started the sentence as a joke, but by the time the words had been said, spinning out into the silence of the old room beneath the thatch she knew they were true. The shortness of the time they had known each other did not matter. Tony, with all his show and his attraction did not matter. This was something so different, so right, that she was sure as she had never been, deep down, with Tony. Sure and content and very, very happy.

'Don't go yet.' She put her arms around his neck. 'Besides, haven't you noticed how unprincipled I am? I am already sharing my bed with one gentleman.'

In the distance, as Richard took her in his arms, the midnight bells began to ring, far away in the village. He kissed her gently. 'Do you think the other gentleman would move up if I asked him nicely?' he said softly.

And they both laughed quietly as, as if on cue, there was a deep contented purr from the end of the bed.

Destiny

On bitterly cold days I often went to the Palm House to warm up. Those heavy double doors were a passport to a tropical climate where hibiscus and bougainvillaea trail among the palms. My hands would come frozen out of my pockets, my chin out of my collar and I could walk tall and relaxed, breathing more easily after the paralysing cold outside.

Two lovely wrought iron spiral staircases lead up through the jungle towards the dome. One is marked 'up' and one 'down' and it was there that I met him. He was walking slowly, meditatively, down the 'up'.

Had I taken notice, had I had my wits about me, I would have been warned; I would have seen the danger signals within myself, but as it was I was unprepared and somehow it happened.

I saw the shoes first as I climbed with my hands on the curving rail. They stopped about four steps above me and automatically, because they were facing me, I stopped too. I lifted my face slowly, my eyes travelling up the jeans, clean but washed-out, the T-shirt – no rude or meaningful messages emblazoned in those days – with behind it a hint of muscular chest, a heavy lumber jacket and then a face. Automatically my eyes prepared themselves to slip sideways and simultaneously I sidestepped to pass him, putting out my hand to grab the central newel post. Of course he, at the same moment, did the same, and we both clung precariously on the narrowed end of the wedge-shaped steps, my chin nearly touching his knees.

There was a moment's silence, then as we both moved back to the outside edge of the stairway there was a muffled snort from above me.

'Say – do you tango too?'

I could feel my colour rising. I hate sarcasm in any form.

'This is the "up" staircase,' I muttered stiffly, my head now level with the furry edge of his jacket.

There was a soft slither of snow far above our heads on the glass dome and somewhere to my left a sparrow started cheeping plaintively in the frondy palm tops. I raised my gaze reluctantly – our relative positions on the stair left me at a neck-cricking disadvantage. He had brilliant blue eyes and a ski slope tan. His face was very serious. Not angry; just concerned and really very pleasant.

'You know, you shouldn't always follow instructions so blindly,' he said conversationally. 'Had you looked up you would have seen me already on my way down.'

'If you deigned to follow instructions at all I should not have needed to,' I retorted. I took a deep breath. 'Anyway. It is perfectly possible for us to pass. There is plenty of room for two.'

'Ah,' he said. 'So this has happened to you before?'

'Frequently. But usually people manage to pass without making an international incident of it!' It had not escaped my notice that he had some sort of mid-western accent.

'OK.' To my amazement he proceeded to sit down on the wrought iron steps. He reached into his jeans pocket, extending a long muscular leg past me in order to reach down into it. 'Let's settle this in time-honoured fashion, as when two heads of state confront on a battlefield!'

241

I fully expected him to draw a gun, but it turned out to be a coin. 'Heads I go back; tails you go back, OK?'

I gave a helpless sort of tolerant smile – the kind of smile one gives to a child when indulging it disgustingly – and watched him flip the coin. It disappeared into the sea of greenery around our feet.

'You're supposed to catch it,' I said acidly.

For the first time he grinned. 'I'll go and get it,' he said. He stepped lightly past me and proceeded to run down the stairs.

I stared at him, speechless. He couldn't be serious. But he was. He was coming right back up again, dusting soft black leaf mould off the coin.

It was his turn to look up at me and he did so shrugging. 'I guess you think I'm nuts.'

'Something like that.'

'Can I buy you a cup of coffee to make up for it?'

It was a tempting thought. I hesitated, and I was lost.

'All right, why not!' I laughed and solemnly we both turned and made our way down, passing straight-faced two hapless visitors meekly climbing up the 'up'.

We met twice more after that, by appointment – once by the frozen lake where the ducks skidded ridiculously with much complaint on the blue ice and once in the museum in front of a case of grotesquely ugly wax vegetables and we talked and laughed and I felt we had known one another all our lives. He was outrageous and irritating; irrational and domineering and I found myself liking him more and more until I knew that I could never live without him.

The third time he did not come. I walked for nearly an hour, my feet frozen, looking at the spiked fringes of frost which had turned every growing thing into silvered gorse and my heart was inexplicably heavy. I knew so little about him. His name was Peter and he came from St Louis and he was working in England as a journalist. I didn't even know his second name. It had seemed too conventional a thing to ask him. And he didn't know mine.

What I did know was what he liked to read: Walt Whitman and Donne; what he liked to hear: Al Jolson and Britten; what he liked to smell: wet earth and burning leaves; and that his favourite place, like mine, was Kew Gardens. And I knew that inexplicably his absence had left an empty place inside me.

I resisted the urge to go more often, to walk melancholy down the paths I had walked with him, to stand as the thaw loosed the water on the lake and watch the ducks or, ever, to climb again up the spiral stair towards the forest ceiling where I knew that now the spring had come a blackbird would be rapping with its beak against the glass. After all, what was he but a passing nod of the head, a smile in my loneliness?

Defiantly I put him out of my mind, this intruder into my consciousness and my calm. And I filled my life so I was no longer lonely and I was even happy, ignoring that strange unjustifiable emptiness which had settled somewhere below my left ribs.

The man with whom I spent my evenings now was a tolerant conformist Englishman whose names I knew – not only the first and the last but the middle three as well. We fitted comfortably together without rasping at each other's corners. I met his parents and he met mine. We ate strawberries and cream at Wimbledon and fish and chips in Leicester Square. We laughed tolerantly at one another's jokes and did not always have to interpret our deepest thoughts. Our taste in films was similar – and music. I gave him Brandenburg 1–3 for his birthday; he gave me 4–6 for mine.

And yet still that sneaking emptiness, that flickering,

243

subliminal vision as I woke at dawn that made me think I must have been dreaming of the spiral stairs at Kew.

We went to the Proms and twice I suggested concerts with Britten. The music was elemental; untamed. It reminded me of Peter. In the queues outside I found myself gazing, staring, probing the crowds with lonely eyes and I cursed myself for an ungrateful benighted fool of a woman; only a woman would be so crazy.

And of course he knew, my lover of the five names – yes, we were lovers by now – he knew there was something strange about me. Delicately he probed around the fringes of my secret and equally delicately I rebuffed him. There was after all nothing to tell. But I saw him watch me watching and I saw the heavy burden of uncertainty in his eyes and I hated myself even as I turned in the cinema queue and let my gaze wander over that sea of animated faces. All the wrong faces. And he was always there afterwards to comfort me, my lover, his arm almost apologetic around my shoulders and I would turn and stand on my toes to kiss his cheek.

I married him as the first coloured leaves pattered down onto the hot dusty streets. But still I could not tell and still he could not ask outright. Perhaps we both forgot. It was unimportant after all – a casual meeting in the cold of the winter when the blood was thin and vulnerable, a passing of strangers whose chemistries apparently fused for a time but who then were separated and lost to one another for ever.

I had a child, and then another. I took a part-time job which I turned into a business and I was fulfilled and satisfied. That empty gap was so infinitesimal now I did not realize it was still there. I was full of love – for the man I had married, my children, my home, my work, even for my dog. I had no time to think; no time to dream or brood upon my dreams and that was good save for the fact that time passed so very fast and I did not see it passing.

They went to school and I employed a staff to run my business. Their father and I talked and laughed: our faces made expressions over the breakfast table; our mouths formed words. We did not hear one another any more but we were content as in a stupor, lulled by our own narcotic dream.

So it was strange that after all the years I should have thought again of Peter – suddenly, yearningly thought of him with such an urgency that it could not be denied.

There was nothing to keep me at home; nothing to stop me going to Kew on that first day of snow, of a new, another, winter.

I walked slowly along the paths, not looking especially for him, not thinking, my mind an emptiness as, hands in pockets, I passed down the line of white queen's beasts, passed the iced fountain and climbed the steps towards the Palm House.

He was sitting on the iron staircase. I did not raise my head as I approached, climbing methodically step by step towards him. Then I stopped. My heart was beating fast like a girl's and I could feel the colour burning in my cheeks. Slowly I raised my head until our eyes met.

'Last time we tossed a coin,' he said. His face was a network of lines but the tan was the same, the blue eyes as intense, the costume the same too, though nowadays of course everybody wore it.

'Why didn't you come, that last time?' I said quietly.

'I had to cover a story in France. There was no way I could let you know.' He made a rueful face. 'I left a note for you later, pinned to the stairs here. I was so sure you would come back and find it. But I guess you never did. I came here every day too, after that, but I never saw you.'

He had come each day. And I had nursed my little pain

and refused to succumb and turned my back on him. I swallowed.

'I did come. I walked by the lake.'

'You're married now.' There was no ambiguity about the plain gold band on my left hand that rested on the white railing by his head.

Was that sadness I could see in his eyes? Suddenly my own were full of tears. 'I'm very happy.'

'I'm glad.' He did not say that he was too. 'And you still go up the "up" and down the "down"?' A glint of humour lit his eyes.

I nodded. 'You didn't quite have time to convert me – not completely.'

I wanted to touch him, to reassure myself that he was real and as if he understood he slowly reached up and put his hand over mine. 'I somehow knew you would come today.' Slowly he stood up. Still holding my hand he guided me down through the drifting summer fronds and out of the giant hot womb of the place into the whispering feathery snow and the tiny forgotten scar beneath my ribs opened, as his arm went round my shoulders, into a raw throbbing cavity and deep inside I could hear myself moaning as we walked through the empty silent gardens.

This time we did not speak. Perhaps it had all been said in the silence of the long years. He guided me beneath the heavy blue arms of the cedar and there he kissed me – the long slow kiss which had lingered unacknowledged in my dreams and I forgot at that moment my husband and my children; I forgot my past and my future – everything but this man for whom I had waited here by the lake for a hundred years as the frost made spikes of silver on the willows over the water. We lived a lifetime in that afternoon before I fled.

My courage was not enough to walk blindly out of the gates into the anonymity of the whirling snow. Now I knew his name and he knew mine and one day, I knew, he would call me to him once more and I would have to tear myself apart to heal the wound he had reopened in my breast.

Meanwhile, cowardly, I sought the comfort of my husband's arms and I knew at once that he understood again, as he had always understood, and our tears mingled in the darkness.

A Summer Full of Poppies

'   The surface of the moon must look like this. Imagine
...   the chaste huntress engirdled with barbed wire!
It is hard even to imagine it as it was before I was wounded
and went away. I remember it all mud and rain and cold
and smelling of mould and decay, and now it is a parched
desert with, where the fields used to be, behind the lines,
a scattering of poppies . . .'

Maria raised her eyes from the crumpled letter to the
dusty golden haze of the corn stubble which stretched
down the slope before her, across to the woods and foothills
in the far distance. There were poppies here, too, along
the hedgerows; great splashes of blood-red colour in the
dusty green and gold, and corn thistles, yellow patches in
the hedge, with (too delicate and thinly growing to be seen
from here) the pale blue of scabious and teasel.

The sun beat down on the shoulders of her thin
embroidered blouse and on the chestnut plait of hair carefully wound round her head but her hat, thrown carelessly
on the grass beside her, lay unnoticed.

'. . . Poor old Tom Kennedy has had a bad time. He's
lost a leg. They think he'll be strong enough to come home
by the end of the month and I've told him to look you up.
Do you remember I told you he has no family of his own
at all and I owe so much to him. Even now in that terrible
hospital he manages to be cheerful; the nurses all adore

him; I bet he gives them a bad time – teasing them I mean . . .'

There had been a photo of Tom Kennedy in James's wallet. He had shown her time and again the tall dark young man with widely-spaced light-coloured eyes and the new, so proudly borne uniform. 'I wish I could be like him, Maria,' James had said so wistfully as he sat, the healing arm still supported in its sling across his chest. 'He's such a good person, so gentle, yet so strong and always happy and cheerful.'

Maria had smiled at her young husband, her throat tightening at his vulnerability, his own unassuming and unrecognized gentleness. What business had these boys in a war?

She watched the shadow of a cloud race across the stubble towards her. It touched her with a finger of shivering cold and passed.

They had married when the corn, this same corn, was green in the field, she and James, he fumbling with the still-bandaged arm to slip the gold band onto her finger and smiling so bashfully in the neatly pressed uniform. She had been one of the lucky ones. She had married in that year of 1916; married the man she loved, known him for those few short weeks of bliss as his bone knitted and the shattered muscles drew together and slowly healed beneath the puckered white scar and then she had waved him goodbye, standing on the station platform, her arm aching as the small white handkerchief fluttered above her head. She waved long after the train was out of sight and only the smudge of smoke hung over the line in the still air.

'I'll try and be back for Christmas, my love,' he had said, as he bumped his bag into the carriage, his blue eyes twinkling down at her mischievously from the step. He was happy to be returning to his regiment, tired of the old men and the women and endless talk of war. They had no concept of what it was like out there and, though he sweated sometimes at night with the fear of returning and put his hands over his ears to block out the mind-breaking roar of guns, and the sound of screams, screams that had become for ever trapped within his own head, he could not bear any longer the inactivity; the knowledge that he, at home in England, no longer knew what was happening at the front.

He was sad to leave Maria. She was soft and golden and smelt of the new mown hay. He laughed with her and buried his face in her long chestnut hair, letting the scented weight of it run through his fingers like slippery water. But he never showed her the slim notebook in which he had scribbled his poems, those words from his own aching guts, twisted and moulded till they screamed like the sounds in his head and echoed the horrors of the trenches and the poignancy of those who prayed to come home and then knew as soon as they were there that somehow they could not escape; that they must return to the depths of hell of their own free will just as soon as they were able.

'. . . So many of the faces are new here, Maria, although a few of the old ones remain. Jones is here and Freddie Haytor and Timpson and Stuart, but I do miss Tom . . .'

Somewhere beyond Square Acre Field a column of smoke was rising straight up into the air, dissipating in the whiteness of the hazy horizon. Perhaps it was a rick burning, or a cottage chimney. She watched lazily, not registering curiosity or concern. Just watching and waiting as the shadows lengthened across the field. A wood pigeon began to coo, the soothing notes slurring into one another in the echoing woods. One by one slowly the stray yellowing leaves had begun to fall, accidentally, from the trees: the first unbelieved messengers of autumn.

She folded the letter into its worn creases and slipped

it back into the pocket of her skirt, brushing off the dusty grass. Already the sound of hooves from Patterson's wagonette had passed briskly on the road below. It was four miles to the station from the cottage she shared with her grandmother. James had lived there too for those weeks of their marriage. Maria smoothed the folds of her skirt and wedged the straw hat on her head, half listening for the whistle of the train, which when the wind was from the west, would echo across the country as it pulled out of the town and headed across the hills towards them.

The door had slammed as James rushed in from the road that day when he found out. He ran into the parlour where Maria's grandmother was sitting knitting socks for the men at the front.

'They've told me she was Richard Week's girl,' he shouted at the old woman, his eyes red-rimmed from the sun. 'That she was his long before she was mine. That she still loves him.'

The old lady laid down her needles and peered up, noting the hands gesticulating, the arms hanging free, their strength regained. His eyes were wild with grief.

'She's a pretty girl, James. You must have known she had boyfriends.'

He gestured impatiently, dismissing boyfriends as unimportant. 'I hear Richard was different. He was everything.' His face crumpled suddenly and he sat down beside the empty hearth, the line of unsunburned skin showing white where the folds of his cravat had loosened. 'I can't bear to think of her in another chap's arms . . .'

She smiled. 'She's yours now, James. That's all that matters. Richard has been in Flanders some time now. I believe he had already gone when she first met you.' She looked suddenly vague. Her eyes refused to meet his, slipped sideways and back down to her arthritic fingers and the tiring dark grey wool.

James understood then. Richard was away. She had wanted a man and as the one she loved was not there . . .

The quarrel they had that night was as unforeseen as it was unkind in its bitterness. Neither understood the passions that allowed them to hurl such insults at one another. They forgot the fears, the strains, the pent-up emotions with which they had been living and blamed one another.

That night alone in her bed, Maria lay crying herself to sleep as James, slamming the door, had walked out to stride until dawn over the fields towards the hills, his boots soaked with dew, his fair hair blown back from his face, his brain seething with an unforeseen jealousy which appalled him even as he recognized its force.

By some unspoken agreement neither spoke of Richard again. It was as though they both sensed a power to be released by his name which could tear them and their newly won marriage apart, and though James was often moved to do just that he refrained and forced himself to trust and love again.

As he turned to her on the step of the train she wanted to shout: 'It's not what you think, James; we never did anything; it's you I love now,' but her pride forbade it. If he really thought so badly of her, let him. She didn't care.

But she had written it down. Three times she had begun the letter; three times thrown it aside in her writing case until at last she had found the words to explain what there had been between her and Richard and what had passed. Nothing with him, however dear the memory, could equal the waves of happiness with James and the knowledge that she was his wife. And this although she had heard now that Richard had won himself a medal and promotion at the front.

It was only when her letter was posted at last that she stopped tormenting herself about what she might have done to James. His own to her, the letter in her pocket, had arrived some time later. She had read it again and again for signs of anger or remorse, unbending pride or forgiveness but the letter contained none. It was natural and friendly and being about other people was curiously impersonal.

She walked briskly down the lane towards the station, her skirt stirring small whorls of dust at her feet, her boots gathering a strangely matt film on the soft polished leather.

The wagonette would be there before her but it didn't matter. It could pick Tom Kennedy up with the luggage and then collect her on the way back from the station after the train had pulled out. In a way she was glad. She didn't want to have to see him climbing into the wagonette with his crutches and his stump and his wide-apart eyes, this man whom James had liked so much.

Tom Kennedy's letter had arrived only a few days after James's. '. . . I would so like to meet you, Maria, (may I call you Maria?),' he had said. 'I know James means to write to you himself but my transport has come more quickly than I expected or dared hope so I must risk my letter arriving unannounced. I have nowhere to go immediately and I would so like to stay with you and your grandmother. James said he was sure you wouldn't mind. How I envy him, lucky old Jim, going up to where the action is. But then I always envy Jim. For the last few weeks I've been envying him his lovely bride . . .'

> *I hear the thunder in my ears*
> *And weep aside*
> *For here there is no place for tears.*

It had been a surprise to her, the notebook. Of all the

scanty belongings they had returned to her it had been the most personal, that and her own unopened letter which had arrived too late. She had not known that he wrote poetry or how he felt about the war. Beyond a vague almost nameless terror for his safety she had not thought about the icy mud or the broiling sun or the guns. It was all beyond her comprehension, or was it just too terrible for her to try and comprehend? She could not decide which.

'You're one of the lucky ones, my dear,' her grand-mother had said to James over the breakfast things the morning before he left. 'You've had your terrible wound and God be thanked you've recovered. You'll not be asked to suffer any more. I feel it in my bones.' He hadn't suffered any more of course. He could have known nothing of the shell that exploded at his feet, nothing at all.

He had left a trunk in the outhouse for them to store for him, 'until we find our own home when the war is over'. There had been four days of blank misery as she realized she would never see him again and then suddenly on a morning of misty warmth and falling scented apples she remembered that trunk. Perhaps there was a message for her there. Perhaps part of him lingered, something, some way of recapturing him for herself. The key was in the drawer of the table in their room.

There was a powdering of dust in the black tin lid and she knelt in the rubbish of the shed and blew it off, gently polishing it with the sleeve of her blouse, tracing the initials of his name J. O. N. His middle name was Oliver. She had not known it until the moment they stood together before the altar in the little Norman church and exchanged the age-old vows, 'Till death us do part.'

She brushed the back of her hand across her eyes and inserted the key in the lock. It turned with ease and the lid lifted without any resistance. Inside, beneath a neatly spread newspaper were dozens of books. She pulled them out looking curiously at the titles, wondering why he had hidden them, not put them proudly on the shelves in their room next to her own.

Then she found his notebooks. Poems and stories, diaries and long descriptive passages penned in the rather careful sloping hand which she saw had not changed very much since he was a boy at school for there were some school books there as well. But after all he *was* still practically a boy. For ever.

She shut the lid of the trunk.

She had grown to hate the idea of Tom Kennedy. He had no wife, no parents alive to mourn him. His death would have hurt no one, while James's . . . James's death was intolerable. And she would have to tell Tom that he was dead.

She had put James's hairbrushes back on the small dressing table next to her own. There were one or two hairs caught in the bristles and somehow the brushes still smelt of him. She took his best shirt, the one he had left behind next to her dresses and skirts in the narrow cupboard, to bed with her and cradled it in her arms.

'Why, Maria, I'd have known you anywhere.' Tom beamed down at her over the wheel of the wagonette. He stretched down a thin brown hand and hesitating she shook it. 'Forgive me for not jumping down. I'm not quite up to gymnastics yet.' He gestured at the crutches tucked beside him and laughed. 'Oh God, but it's good to be home and here.

Come up beside me.' He swung her up to the seat without any difficulty. She tried to avoid looking at the leg of his breeches, neatly pinned above the knee. His eyes were grey not blue as she had imagined. But they were dreamy, like James's.

'James was killed, you know. The day after he got back to the front.' To her surprise she could say it quite without emotion.

His face folded and trembled for a moment like a girl's and he gripped her hand so tightly she felt the bones of her knuckles crack. She kept her eyes fixed on the rhythmical swing of the pony's rump beneath the long reins held so loosely in Patterson's hands.

'He was my best friend.' That was all he said.

He sat in James's chair by the empty hearth and took his place at the meal table and slowly he won them over with his charm and gentle humour. Maria's grandmother watched and nodded at him as she knitted and glanced from time to time at her granddaughter, noting without comment as the girl smiled and relaxed; hoping.

It was Richard Week who came home for Christmas to the manor, leaving the war for well-deserved leave modestly to display his medals and the attractively ugly shrapnel scar across his cheek.

Maria met him beneath gnarled apple tree branches white with frost in the orchard behind the mill. He seemed taller than she remembered, self-assured now, bronzed.

'Did you wait for me, my love?' His hand beneath her chin, his lips pouting towards her were too sure, too certain of their welcome. She raised her hand to push him away and he saw the wedding ring. His eyes widened and he whistled. 'I see you didn't. Too bad.' His breath came in frosty clouds to her face.

She lowered her eyes. 'My husband is dead, Richard.' She felt nothing any more for this young man. He was a stranger to her. Sadly turning away she retraced her steps towards the village leaving him staring after her, shaken. They had hardly spoken.

Tom Kennedy was waiting for her by the post office, leaning on his crutches, his face flushed with the effort of the walk in the icy air. He glanced at her keenly and meeting the gaze she blushed uncomfortably.

'Did you go to see this Richard Week?'

She didn't ask him how he knew but nodded miserably, wishing his hands were free so that he could put his arm around her. She had grown used to seeking comfort from Tom.

'I didn't know if I still loved him. I had to go and see him.'

'And do you?'

Shaking her head she turned her face towards the display of yellowing calico and linens in the post office window so that he shouldn't see the tears which threatened to spill over. She wasn't sure whether they were for the old Richard whom she thought she had loved, or for James.

'He told me all about it when he visited me in hospital, Maria.' Tom's voice sounded suddenly unlike him. She heard the tap and squeak of the crutches as he swung himself closer to her. Then she felt his hand, heavy, supporting his weight, on her shoulder. 'I am glad, Maria. I couldn't bear to think that you were deceiving him.'

Somehow she didn't resent the remark. Tom had the right to reproach her. He had been James's best friend.

'I wrote telling him the truth, Tom. He never got the letter; they returned it to me unopened.'

He nodded, understanding and squeezed her shoulder. Then he rebalanced himself upon the crutches and smiled, suddenly cheerful again. 'Come on, I'll race you home!'

In spite of herself she laughed.

I hear the thunder in my ears
And weep aside . . .

Together they read James's poems in the long evenings
after her grandmother had gone to bed.

'I promised James I'd take care of her if anything happened to him,' he had told the old lady. She was concentrating on turning the heel of the current sock and did not
look up, but nodding quietly she had smiled and approved
and Tom, seeing it, had taken courage. He could not
remember his own grandmother.

He brought in the dusty trunk from the shed and
helped her unpack it in her room, balancing against the
tallboy as he stacked the volumes side by side on the shelf,
frowning to himself in the concentration of getting the
spines neatly in line.

On the last day of his leave Richard Week came to the
door. Maria received him in the parlour while Tom helped
the old lady in the kitchen.

Standing awkwardly by the window with the line of
budding geraniums in their pots on the sill Richard asked
her to marry him. She thought she could hear in the silence
that followed the tiny squeak of rubbers in the passage
outside the door.

'I am sorry, Richard.' Her voice was clear, a little high
pitched from nervousness; too loud. 'But I shall never
marry again.'

In the shuffling and flurry of Richard's flustered prot-
estations and reluctantly disbelieving goodbyes she did not
hear the small sounds of the crutches in the hall as they
retreated to the kitchen.

'Oh, she doesn't mean it.' The old lady was cutting the
scones in half with a thin-handled knife, the blade polished

grey with age and scouring. She looked up at the crestfallen young man and smiled fondly. He was more of a grandson than ever James had been. She had known him much longer now, for one thing. They both had.

'She said that to Richard to ease his going. You'd not grudge the boy that? There's many may never come back from this war; he may be one of them. But I think if you give her time she'll maybe think again, Tom. For you. Just give her time.' She leaned over and patted his arm encouragingly.

He grinned. 'I'll give her all the time in the world if she wants it.' He swung himself round and out of the kitchen. This house was his home now. He had nowhere else to go; no one else to go to. For a moment he felt panic sweep over him. There was so much at stake. Then she was there looking at him from the parlour doorway, smiling, the copper lights in her hair high-lighted in the sun from the window behind her.

She held out her hand. 'Let's go for a walk, Tom, shall we? It's such a beautiful evening,' and her face lit with a gentle, reassuring smile.

Had he had a cap Tom would have thrown it into the air. He followed her out into the garden whistling and they were already half-way down the lane which led towards the mill before he remembered that the old lady had their tea ready in the kitchen.

A Face in the Crowd

Behind the bony silhouettes of the trees the sky was a limpid aquamarine; a crystal bowl carrying the reflection of a thin moon lying on its back.

Leaning on her elbows on the windowsill, gazing out, Jill shivered. The air was chilled and pure as it lay against her face and she welcomed its icy touch. Downstairs the clock in the inn parlour chimed again. Another hour had passed. Three more hours till dawn, she supposed, then the interminable wait until she could decently order coffee, then the whole morning, perhaps the whole day.

And if he didn't come? Supposing he had no intention of keeping their rendezvous? Supposing he was still 4,000 miles away and had never thought of her again? A breath of wind tiptoed over her flesh. She shivered and turned to pad back across the polished oak boards to the double bed. Climbing in she lay against the pillows and stared up at the dark ceiling, pulling the blankets up beneath her chin. She knew she would not sleep again that night.

'Jill?' Andrew had stopped her one day in the street outside Oxford Circus Underground. 'It is Jill Forbes, isn't it?' He had sleepy grey eyes and dishevelled hair which made her think he had overslept and rushed out without his breakfast. Later she discovered that he always looked like that.

'I'm sorry?' she stammered, confused by the grimly hurrying crowds and the relentless rain which blew in their faces. They were forced to circle each other as she kept slowly moving, late already and unwilling to stop for a stranger.

'You don't remember me?' He wasn't hurt or indignant; just amused. Then he reached out and took her arm and guided her away from the centre of the pavement into a wide doorway out of the rain.

She looked at him again, helplessly, glancing at her watch as she tried to recall his face.

'I'm sorry,' she said again, 'but I'm terribly late; I've a day off and I have things to do.'

'You have nothing to do,' he said laughing. 'You're spending the day with me . . .'

At least, that was how she remembered their meeting. Probably it hadn't been so simple. He had had to explain who he was – he had been a student at the same college as her brother Ted, years before – and he had had to go with her to take her passport photos, waiting outside the kiosk, laughing as she sat solemnly inside, then on to do some shopping. Only then, unable to shake him off, had she relented and they had gone out into the rain once more and had coffee together at a stall beside some park railings. She had still not remembered who he was; the circumstances where they must have met, yes, but his face? No.

She had cupped her hands around the thick grimy china of the mug beneath the awning which deflected the rain into a noisy stream and stared at him, disconcerted by the complete absence of memory. He had such an attractive face, such an attractive personality. Surely she would have remembered this . . .

'What are you doing now, Andrew?' she asked at last.

He grinned. 'You still haven't a clue who I am, have you? You really ought to ring Ted and check my credentials. I might be an impostor.'

She sipped her coffee. 'I'll chance it,' she said.

'I'm a marine biologist,' he said.

She stared. 'But Ted is a historian!'

'Such unexpected meetings!' He shrugged expressively. 'I live in a hut by the sea. Literally. I'm only in London for four days collecting equipment and working at the library. Then I go back to Scotland.'

So that was it. He was clutching at straws. A face he recognized in the metropolis; someone to talk to in a city of strangers.

They had lunch and they walked and she went with him to collect various weird and wonderful pieces of gadgetry from his college. They left them at the hotel and then she took him back to her flat so she could change before they went out to dinner.

On her bookcase was a photograph of Jerry. Andrew spotted it at once as he waited. 'Your fella?' he asked, holding it to the light.

'My fella,' she agreed.

'Will he object to your going out with me?'

Strangely it had not crossed her mind, but now she paused, staring over Andrew's shoulder at the familiar face of the man she loved. She hesitated. Then she said softly, 'Yes, I think he might.'

She felt even more guilty on Saturday when she had to put Jerry off, cancelling their usual supper-and-film, because it was Andrew's last day. But why should she feel conscience-stricken? After all, Andrew was going back to Scotland, to his deserted beach where his only neighbours were terns and crabs and kittiwakes and where his whole life revolved around the study of the tides. It was not as though this was the start of something serious.

She went with him to King's Cross, to help him find his sleeper. They had to stand very close in the narrow compartment.

'I wish you were coming with me, Jill,' he said.

'So do I.' She realized her eyes were filled with tears and turned away hurriedly. He was, after all, still a stranger.

Hands in pockets, her collar high against the wind, she walked back up the Euston Road; oblivious of the broad double tide of traffic which roared past her. In her imagination she was with him on the train, or already there in his shack on the edge of the rolling Atlantic.

Jerry called for her at six the following Wednesday. They were going to the Opera and in the Crush Bar in the first interval they met some friends of her brother Ted.

'Andrew Hamilton?' the tall thin young man who had been Ted's house captain at school and had then gone on to the same college, turned his pale blue eyes on her curiously. 'I'll say I remember him. Extraordinary chap! why do you ask?'

She explained, vaguely aware that Jerry was beside her, his knuckles white around his glass.

'Good Lord! Well, all I can say is you're well out of that encounter, Jill, old girl.' He paused to acknowledge someone in the crowd, his glass held above shoulder level to prevent it spilling. 'As far as I remember he broke a trail of hearts from Oxford to John o' Groats, then in the end he married some foreign lady, French or Italian or something!'

Andrew had not mentioned a wife.

As Jerry led her back to their seats he looked at her carefully. 'Sure it's only casual interest?' he said.

'Quite sure.' She smiled at him as she opened her programme at Act Two. 'After all, I'll never see him again.'

But he came back to London at Christmas. And she found out that she was in love.

When Jerry phoned she made some excuse not to see him and walked with Andrew through the noisy decorated streets, staring up at the huge tinsel snowflakes suspended from their wires between the tall office blocks. Then they bought hot chestnuts outside Foyles and wandered round the British Museum.

It was afterwards in a restaurant off Long Acre that he reached across the table and touched her hand.

'I'm staying at a friend's flat this time, while he's away.'

When she looked up and met his gaze thoughtfully, he smiled. 'Come back with me tonight, Jill,' he said.

She knew that if she accepted it would be a commitment; one she could not easily break, but her feelings for Andrew were so different from those she had felt for Jerry; deeper, more sudden and more painful, and she acknowledged at last, more real.

She looked up and found he was watching her closely. 'You know what I'm saying, don't you?' he said softly.

She nodded. 'I'd like to come.'

That afternoon she phoned Jerry from her own flat. 'I can't see you any more. I'm sorry, so very sorry,' she whispered.

There was a long silence. 'I suppose I've been expecting it,' he managed to say at last. 'I've known a long time. I think since that evening at the Opera.' There was another pause. 'Are you going to marry him?'

264

She gave a shocked little laugh. 'Jerry! I've only known him a few weeks.'

'It only takes a few minutes, love,' he said on the other end of the phone. 'Be happy, Jill. I'm always here if you want to talk.'

She stared at the receiver in her hand for several minutes after he had rung off. Then slowly she replaced it. Only then did she remember that Andrew already had a wife.

He was waiting for her in the next room. Sadly she took Jerry's photo up and looked at it, then she slid it into a drawer. 'Shall we go?' she said.

He understood her mood, not hurrying her, not even suggesting they go back at once to the friend's place. Instead they walked along the Regent's Canal, watching the raindrops digging pits in the slate grey surface of the water, shrugging into their coats against the wind, promising themselves crumpets dripping with butter before the gas fire as soon as it grew dark.

She liked the tiny flat in a house off Camden High Street. It was full of pictures and books and lit by impractically angled spot lights which threw shadows over the rugs so that she tripped and nearly fell on a hidden pile of magazines. The divan was covered by a faded dhurrie.

He kissed her long and hard before he began to unfasten the buttons of her blouse. Then, turning off the spots, he led her to the bed, lit now only by the gentle hissing flow of the gas fire and pushed her gently down among the heaped striped cushions, his arms around her, his lips warm as they sought her breasts.

It was daylight when he took her home.

In the car outside her place he took her hand and held it.

'I've promised to spend Christmas with my parents in Edinburgh, Jill. I can't disappoint them,' he said.

She looked down, not daring to let him see her face. 'Of course.'

'But I could come back a few weeks from now,' he went on. 'There's a little pub I know, in the Sussex Downs. I'd like to show it to you . . .'

She wasn't sure she could bear it that they must part so soon. The packing and the trail, almost familiar on this occasion, to King's Cross. He gave her a tiny Victorian pearl pendant for a present; she gave him the Grieg tape he wanted for his lonely evenings by the sea.

'You don't mean you're going back there for the winter?' she had exclaimed aghast. She had seen the photos now of his hut in the wild sea grasses and the dunes and the little boat beached high on the wet sand. His only light came from oil lamps; his music from an old battery driven cassette player.

'It's a two year project, Jill,' he said, 'and I'm only allowed away for a few days at a time. There are too many measurements to take, notes to make, things to do. You wait till you see it . . . You'll understand then.'

She remembered that conversation as they stood together in the sleeper saying goodbye and she thought again of the cold little shiver which had crept down her spine at his words.

'But I hate the sea, Andrew,' a little voice had cried deep inside her. 'I hate the sea and everything to do with it . . .'

The inn was old and rambling, snuggling in a fold of the hills, its thatched roof gold against the frost blue sky of winter. In the hall the grandfather clock ticked the centuries away in peace, to the gentle scents of burning applewood and baking.

Lying awake in his arms she heard the clock chime in

the warm darkness and she felt the tears come to her eyes at the pain of her happiness.

They spent their two days walking hand in hand across the sheep-cropped turf, feeling the icy wind in their faces, running sometimes for sheer joy, their feet hollow on the chalky soil, and the two nights they lay together on the huge goosefeather mattress lost in the wonder of their love.

As she nestled against him, her fingers tracing the line of his shoulders, holding him close, trying to see his face in the dark she prayed that the night might never end. The sharp ecstasy of their love and the tenderness which followed it had left her wakeful and she lay, listening to his even breathing as he slept in her arms and she wanted to hold him for ever.

There was no choice, though. He had to go, wrenching himself away from her, refusing to let himself see her tears. But on Valentine's day he sent her a pale yellow cairngorm set in a Celtic silver pin. 'I've booked us into the inn again for Easter,' he wrote on the card. 'Until then I'm counting each day. We won't waste a moment in London. Meet me at the station . . .'

It was a cold wet Easter, the buds still tight on the trees, the daffodils the only brave defiant challenge to a reluctant departing winter. Jill didn't care. The agony of the long wait was over and she was once more in his arms. To her the colour of the sky, the full gurgling muddy ditches were an irrelevance beside the man who was sitting opposite her at dinner at the table near the huge inglenook fire.

'Nine and a half whole weeks since I saw you,' she said.

They both laughed as though it were something funny she had said. He was watching the firelight flickering reflected in the smoky golden brooch at her throat. It set off the tawny colouring of her hair and eyes.

'We must always come back here,' he said. 'For our anniversaries and special occasions. It will be our home from home. When is your birthday?'

She smiled happily, picking up her glass of wine. 'Not till August. We'll have to think of something to celebrate before then. When is yours?'

It seemed strange that she didn't know.

'June,' he said.

Cancer and Leo she thought later. Fire and water. They can never mix. And she pictured again the pounding cruel waves and the desolation she had stared at in the photograph of the shore which he called home and wondered if she could ever bear to leave the city.

Something to ask him; something to tell him. And either or both could end their relationship; before it had really started. Was either worth it, she wondered? Was it really worth it for the sake of truth?

It was August, and she stared at him across the breakfast table near the open window. He was buried in the Sunday paper as unconscious of her presence as were the other men in the room of their table companions. The stamp of a husband perhaps?

'I know about your wife, Andrew,' she said softly.

For a moment he did not move. He did not hold his breath. His fingers had not tightened on the paper. Then carefully he folded it back at the page he was reading and put it down on the vacant chair between them.

She tried to read his face, feeling a cold sick fear settling into her stomach. Defensively she reached for her cup and sipped at the coffee scalding her tongue so that the tears came. But it did not matter; he was not looking at her.

'How long have you known about that?' he asked. He

was staring at the ragged torn fragment of toast on his plate.

'Someone told me just after I met you,' she whispered.

'And you never said anything?'

'I never said anything.'

'Why?'

'I was afraid of knowing for sure.'

He looked up at last. 'And now you are no longer afraid?'

She reached out her hand, tentatively, scared of being rebuffed. 'And now I no longer care, Andrew. I love you too much.'

His fingers had closed tightly over hers, but he was no longer looking at her. His face was troubled as he stared past her out of the window.

'Life never is simple, is it?' he said at last. 'We think because we ignore something, because we pretend it isn't there, because we leave it behind that we are free of it. But somehow, somewhere it is going to catch you up.'

'I said I didn't care, Andrew,' she persisted gently.

'But I care.' He stood up violently, pushing his chair back so that it rumpled the worn carpet. At the other tables there was an infinitesimal shocked silence at the interlude, then a studied refusal to allow it to ruffle the calm surface of breakfast time.

'I'm sorry you had to know about her.' He waved his arms in the air helplessly. 'As long as you didn't know that I had had a wife I could pretend I had not been through it all; pretend everything with us was fresh and new and real . . .'

'Andrew!' Jill protested, but already he had turned on his heel. He walked stiffly past the other tables and out of the room closing the door with a sharp click behind him.

Jill remained where she was, painfully conscious of the questioning stares that were being directed at her, clutching at one pitiful straw as the misery of their first quarrel descended on her.

'*Had* had a wife,' he'd said. Had, not have . . .

She forced herself to pour another cup of coffee and sat before it, not touching it for five more minutes. Only as the other residents rose and made their way out of the room did she too push back her own chair. She stood for a moment looking out onto the rose beds then resolutely she went up the stairs.

To her surprise he was there, lying face down on the bed.

'Andrew, it's our last day. Can you forget I mentioned it? Please?' She sat down before the dressing table and reached for her brush. 'I don't want to know about your past. All I want now is the two of us together.'

It wasn't quite true, but she would settle for it.

He rolled over and lay watching her, his arm across his eyes as though he was dazzled.

'You say that, Jill, but it will always be there in the background.'

'It always was, for you, Andrew,' she reminded him gently.

He gave a sheepish smile. 'I'd better tell you about it anyway. She was too young and I was too idealistic. We both expected fairy tales and found a grim reality we couldn't cope with. End of story.' .

She swivelled on the stool until she was facing him. 'End of story?'

He shrugged. 'You're right. Except for this residue of bitterness and disillusion. That stayed. I'm sorry. I love you, but I'm afraid of trying to make it permanent for us. Can you understand that? Like trying to trap a sunbeam. It's there till you make a move to hold it then wham, the world is dark.' He turned his head away. 'I shouldn't have led you to expect anything more from me, Jill. I can't give it.'

Later they walked, but no longer hand in hand. Somehow it was easier to put their hands in their pockets as if to ward off a cold wind. At lunch, though, the curious stares directed at their table by their neighbours anxious to know how the quarrel had progressed made them giggle. And suddenly the tension had gone. Jill felt the pressure of his knee against hers beneath the white starched cloth and, meeting his eye, felt her heart leap with relief.

They spent the afternoon in bed, both resolving drowsily that it would be best to say nothing more as they lay in one another's arms, realizing, after this their first argument, how fragile a thing love was; how easily it could be destroyed and how doubly precious it was for that reason. And for that brief afternoon and night their love reached a new height of passion and tenderness.

At King's Cross the following afternoon Jill knew, however, that things would never be the same again and she cried as she clung to him. 'Andrew! Oh Andrew!'

Firmly he unclasped her hands. 'It won't be long, love,' he said, 'I'll be back soon.'

But would he? Desolate she stood on the platform watching the long train snaking into the distance and she realized suddenly that she had not even got round to telling him how she felt about the sea.

Weeks later she was meeting her brother Ted for lunch. He was tanned and handsome, his hair streaked by three months of Kenya sunshine and she was proud of him as he escorted her to their table. He ordered for them, then he leaned across the cutlery and grinned. 'I met a friend of yours at Heathrow when I arrived.'

'Oh?' Unsuspecting she sipped the white wine she had asked for as an aperitif. 'Who?'

'Andy Hamilton.'

She became very conscious of the buzz of conversation around them, frozen as she was in a bubble of sudden silence. Cautiously she raised her eyes to Ted's.

'Oh?' was all she said.

'Nice chap. I haven't seen him for years. We had time for a quick drink and he mentioned he'd seen you.'

'Yes?' Her bleak answer was too quick; too casual.

He had been in London and he had not told her.

Ted was preoccupied with the arrival of their order and had not noticed her silence as she watched the waiter shuffling dishes onto the table.

Taking a deep steadying breath she said, 'What was he doing at Heathrow then?'

The plate of crudités gave her something to concentrate on so he could not see her face.

'He was off to some conference, I gather, on the west coast of America. High powered stuff. He won an award three months back for his research. Did you know?'

No, she didn't know. How could she? He hadn't told her.

The vegetables tasted like wet cardboard in her mouth, but she forced herself to swallow. It wasn't fair to Ted to spoil their reunion by crying. That she managed to contain in a short interlude in the Ladies' Room, dabbing her cheeks hard with her handkerchief and wishing it were still the fashion to wear thick concealing face powder. Ted did not look up when she returned. Instead he busied himself with the menu. When he spoke it was so casually she hardly for a moment heard his words.

'I rather gathered he felt he had messed things up with you,' he said quietly. 'A pity that. He's a good bloke, Andy.'

She found she could not speak.

He glanced up for a second and seeing her expression, hastily turned back to the menu.

'We all knew he'd made a mistake when he and Katya married. They were much too young. It only lasted about eighteen months, you know.'

She nodded, conscious that she couldn't hold the tears back much longer and that she was going to make a fool of herself in public. 'I didn't care about her, Ted. I don't care now.'

'What then?' This time when he looked up he held her gaze, forcing her to answer.

She shrugged helplessly. 'It's lots of things.'

'You never told him how you felt about the sea?'

She shook her head. 'The opportunity never came,' she whispered.

Ted frowned. 'Do you still get the nightmares?'

'No. Not for ages.' Her knuckles were white around the spoon she held. 'Anyway, it didn't matter. I'd have followed him across the Atlantic in a small boat if he'd asked me, Ted. But he never did. I told him I loved him. It was he who went away.'

'I told him about your dreams.'

She stared. 'You had no right!'

'I think I did, if your silly phobia came between you. But he said it hadn't. He said he knew there was something, but you had never talked about yourself. He assumed it was a man.'

'Oh.' Dully she slumped back in her chair. 'Is that why he never came back?'

Ted's eyes narrowed. 'He didn't say. It seems to me you never had a chance, him in Scotland, you in London. Why don't you go up to see him when he gets back?'

When he gets back? But how would she know?

*

She didn't want to phone Jerry, it seemed unfair. But he had said 'call me' and she was so lonely. He took her to the Chelsea Kitchen and was kinder than she had dared to hope he would be, listening to a story which she knew must hurt him if he still cared for her, yet unable to stop herself once she had started talking.

'How long is he away for?' he asked at last, picking unerringly on the most salient question.

She shook her head helplessly. 'I don't know.'

'Not even a post card?'

'No, nothing. Nothing for months.'

'But it's still on as far as you're concerned?'

She shrugged. 'How can it be? When he's so far away.'

Jerry couldn't help of course. All he could do was listen and buy another carafe of wine and offer comfort in his own way, taking her in his arms at her front door and kissing her gently on top of the head. 'Can I come in, Jill?' he asked.

She shook her head, but the knowledge that he still cared comforted her.

Later she crossed to her mirror and sat down staring at her face. How was it possible for her to love anyone so much? What strange chemistry had made her yearn for someone like Andrew when Jerry, sweet, kind Jerry who understood her, was there, loving her, waiting in the wings for a word?

'Stupid!' She said out loud to her reflection. She meant herself; her love; the whole world.

Three times she started to write letters to Andrew. Three times she tore them into little pieces and threw them out. What anyway was the point? She did not know where he was. His hut by the ocean was, she supposed, empty; perhaps abandoned for ever. She did not even know his parents' address.

Her only hope was the inn in the Downs and the

anniversary of their first visit a year ago. She clutched at the hope, writing to book the room because she did not have the face to phone with the lie that he would be with her.

A week before the date the snow began, falling overnight in a blanket on an unresponsive London, muffling the tyres, drifting for a few hours of beauty across the filthy pavements. The news carried hourly reports of the chaos in the country; the smothering and then the blocking of the roads and she knew she had the perfect excuse not to go. She listened to the weather forecasts, half willing the weather to grow worse to make the decision for her, knowing she would not have the resolution not to go.

She went.

The countryside was breathtakingly beautiful, the trees bowed down beneath their veil of white, the inn with a wraith of smoke from its chimney scenting the clear blue sky as it nestled into its fold of the Downs.

She was the only guest to arrive. 'I've put you in your usual room, dear,' the landlady said comfortably. 'Your husband coming separately, is he?' They had signed the register in their two separate names the first time. The next it had been easier just to use Andrew's.

The woman's face was kind and she produced tea and oven-warm scones and slid a hot water bottle into the huge double bed.

Jill forced herself to smile. 'I only hope he's coming,' she said. 'He's flying back from the States and with the weather as it is . . .'

At least the snow would cover her shame when he did not come.

She ate in their private parlour by the roaring fire and knew they were trying to cheer her with television and mulled wine while outside the icicles were daggers against the moon. She dreaded going upstairs alone.

Crawling back at last into the huge lonely bed she hugged the almost cold hot water bottle to her miserably, drawing her chilled feet up till she lay in a tight knot and finally allowed her tears to fall. He wouldn't come. She had known it all along. Their whole affair had been in her imagination, for him just an interlude to be ended as soon as he had realized she was serious, an encounter in the street that had led to a year of fun; for her a love which would stay with her for the rest of her life.

The cold dawn was filtering in at the window before she drifted off into an uneasy sleep listening to the sharp cry of an owl hunting over the snow-covered moonlit fields.

She was awakened by the landlady shaking her shoulders. 'It's your husband, my dear. Quickly! He's come through on our private phone. From America!'

The fire was out in the parlour and the room looked cold as she picked up the receiver with a shaking hand, her bare feet icy beneath her blue dressing gown. 'Andrew?'

'Jill. You are there. How are you, darling?'

Suddenly she couldn't speak. His voice from so far away sounded as though it were in the next room. 'I never let myself believe you'd be there,' he was saying. 'I told myself to forget you, but I couldn't. I decided a week ago to phone the inn. If you were there, I'd know you still loved me, if you weren't . . .' He left the sentence unfinished.

'I still love you, Andrew,' she managed to say at last. 'I had to come here . . .'

'Jill? Jill, love, don't cry. Oh God, I wish I were with you. Listen darling, listen . . .'

She could hear his voice repeating her name. Desperately she tried to pull herself together.

'Andrew, about the sea. It's only a dream I get. It doesn't matter. I'll learn to live near it – on it, if you want, I promise . . .'

'But Jill, that is what I keep trying to tell you!' There

276

was a crackle on the line and she heard his exclamation of annoyance. 'Ted told me about your dreams. I've had time to think. I've been a fool. And, oh so much has happened. Listen, darling, when it comes to it I can't live without you. I've been lost these last few months not knowing where you were or what was happening, not planning another meeting... Listen, Jill. I've been offered a research fellowship here in the States. I know we never discussed it, but would you be prepared to live over here—' his voice faded for a moment and distractedly she held the receiver away from her and shook it.

'Andrew? *Andrew!...*'

'Jill, listen darling. If you don't like the idea I'll turn them down. Can you hear me? Wait there! Don't move. I'm getting the first flight...'

She listened for a long time to the empty crackling on the line, staring around the room, then at last she hung up. The landlady had withdrawn discreetly and left her alone with the cold smell of the dead wood ash and the chill of the early morning still frosting the windows. But suddenly the room had lost its gloom and as she watched, in the earthenware jug on the windowsill, a bunch of winter jasmine caught the first tentative rays of the sun and turned to gold.

A Woman's Choice

It had happened after they went back to the States.

'No, no, no, Dan! It's just not on!' Maggie slammed her open hand down on the table in front of her, her eyes wide with anger. 'I knew you were going to suggest this and I won't do it. It's not fair to ask me.'

Dan looked up at her over the cup he held in both hands and gave a sheepish smile. 'OK, OK, so I'm sorry. I guess I knew it wasn't on. But hell, I had to suggest it. It might have worked.' He shrugged. 'Suzanne is –' he hesitated imperceptibly, ' – was my sister, after all. And those two kids are family.'

'I know and I'm sure that they're great kids. But Dan, we don't want kids! We've no time, no room for kids, that's why we didn't have any of our own, remember?' There was something like despair in her voice – and guilt.

'Sure, honey, sure.' He stood up and pushed his stool back from the table, meticulously folding his newspaper so that it fitted into his briefcase. He stooped and kissed the top of her head lightly. 'Don't worry about it. Ma and I will have to do something of course, what with poor old Roger having no family that we ever met – and, I don't know, I suppose they'll have to be taken care of back in Carson. Perhaps a neighbour or someone might take them in; I understand they're with one at the moment.' He was frowning as he straightened his tie at the mirror next to the kitchen window.

'Can't your mother have them, Dan?' She began to pile up the dishes and refold the foil in the cereal packet.

'You know she can't.' For the first time he snapped. 'She's too frail. Not that she wouldn't want them. She's always spoiled those two when she got the chance to see them but Carson is so far away. That's the trouble. Too far to know what to do for the best.'

He opened the door. 'I'll call you from the office, Maggie. Bye for now.'

She heard him walk through the hallway and then the front door slammed.

The kitchen was suddenly very empty and quiet. She dumped the cups and plates in the sink and left them so that she would have time to put on some make-up before leaving the apartment. Glancing at her wrist watch she groaned. Late again.

In front of the bathroom mirror she stopped and looked hard at her face in the cold unflattering glare of the strip light. Her skin was sallow and tired from lack of sleep and there were dark hollows beneath her eyes. She grabbed a bottle of moisturizer and began to pat it on with quick impatient strokes of the finger tips, trying to flatten out some of the lines.

Then as she watched she saw her eyes for no reason at all suddenly fill with tears, brim and overflow. 'Oh hell.' She groped for a tissue and dabbed at the little creamy rivulets on her cheeks, trying to stem the flow. 'Oh damn poor Suzanne and Roger; damn their poor bloody kids! Why did it have to happen now?' She sat on the edge of the bath tub and blew her nose.

It was two days since the midnight phone call from the hospital which told them the news of the car crash; barely thirty-six hours since Sue had died, twelve since hearing that, though Roger might recover consciousness, he would almost certainly have irreversible brain damage. Ever since, she had been haunted by the vision of the two small children waiting with the baby sitter for their Mummy and Daddy to come home. She dabbed at her face again and stood up, sniffing, reaching for the matt foundation she kept for disguising the dark rings. It wasn't as if she knew the kids. They had been babies of – what? – eighteen months and three months respectively when she and Dan had last gone to Carson on a visit. She shuddered remembering suddenly the horrible baby smell in the house – the buckets of soaking diapers, the sweet clinging scent of regurgitated milk. But what a happy close family they had been, with Roger over the moon with his little son and his pretty daughter and Sue, in her usual dream world but ecstatic over her bouncing babies.

She dabbed again at her make-up and drew an angry red outline round her lips, blocking in the lipstick. It was then, on the way home in the car that Dan had finally agreed with her about no family of their own. 'You're right, Maggie,' he had said, groping for her hand in the dark as they waited at a red light, 'I don't think I could face all that hassle and noise in our home. My God, those buckets and all those hours feeding them!'

She hadn't said that many houses were cleaner and more efficient than Sue's, half out of loyalty to her sister-in-law and half out of relief at his words; instead she had returned the pressure of his fingers and given a quiet sigh of relief. It had bothered her in the past that perhaps Dan really did want kids; that he had said he didn't just to make her happy and because he knew her career meant so much to her. He had always been so good with children, instinctively good, while she shrank from them, resented them as a threat to her independence.

Her career! She looked back at the mirror with a sigh.

She wouldn't have a career at all if she didn't hurry up, finish her face and leave the house!

She took a cab downtown to the studios and crept into her office via the coffee machine. Minutes later the phone rang. It was Dan.

'I'm going up to Carson tomorrow with Ma; I've fixed it here so that I can be away for two or three days. You'll have to make my excuses to Bet on Thursday.'

Bet, wife of one of the senior producers, and her dinner party, to which so many important TV people would go. Maggie hadn't given it a thought. 'Are you sure you wouldn't like me to come with you to Carson?' she said stirring the coffee aimlessly with the end of her ball point. She didn't want to go; to see those two small faces, the large eyes. At the thought the blotter on her desk blurred and went out of focus suddenly and she shook her head angrily – 'Sorry Dan, what did you say?'

'I say there's no need for you to come. They know Ma best of any of us, she's seen them each year at least and she was there only a few months ago; they wouldn't remember you – or me for that matter.'

Remember her? How could they? She had held each child gingerly, at arm's length, for a token few seconds before returning it thankfully to its mother's arms, and that had been how long ago? Five years, which meant that the children were now five and six respectively.

With a sigh she picked up the internal phone. 'Hi, Bet. I'm afraid we're going to have to take a rain check for Thursday. Dan's going to be out of town . . .'

At lunchtime she ate a yoghurt, then she slipped out to the supermarket for a bag of groceries. The humidity had built up unbearably in the streets as the sun blazed down on the glaring sidewalks. On the corner some kids were splashing round a hydrant; little kids, perhaps five and six. She stopped still and looked at their laughing little faces. Behind her a woman came out with a bag of groceries, saw them and screamed furiously at the children. 'Sal, Tony, you come out of there!'

Two sheepish faces turned towards her and, tee shirts dripping, they slowly approached her. She set down her carrier on the sidewalk and dragged a handkerchief from her purse to dry them. Then laughing she suddenly hugged them both to her, soaking her thin dress.

Maggie turned away, a lump in her throat and walked blindly back up the street.

Dan was away three days. When he came back he looked pale and strained, his handsome face wretched as he threw his case on the bed and opened it.

'I saw Roger for a few minutes,' he said as Maggie sat at the dressing table, pretending to brush her hair. 'He's still in a coma. The little ones are still with the neighbour but she can't keep them much longer; they're all in one room with her kids and they keep looking through the fence at their house and saying, when can we go home? . . .' His voice broke suddenly and he sat down on the bed, pressing his knuckles into his eyes. 'Ma wants to move down there, take over the house, keep it as a home for them, but hell, she can't. She was knocked out by all this. She started getting pains in her chest again.'

Maggie slid the brush to her other hand and went on brushing methodically, her eyes fixed blankly on the mirror.

'I spoke to Jim Baines at work today,' she said at last as Dan opened the cupboard, rummaging for a coat hanger. 'I asked him if I could work half time or at home if I had to. He said there shouldn't be any problem.' She went on brushing.

'So?' He sounded guarded, but she saw in the mirror that he was looking at her suddenly.

'So we've got a spare room with two beds.' She flung down the brush and turned on the stool to face him. 'We can't let them go, Dan; we can't let them be separated. I don't know anything about children; I don't have the first idea where to begin, but we've got to try, haven't we? We're the only hope they've got.'

The relief he felt at her words was apparent in every line of his body as in two steps he was across the room, his hands on her shoulders.

'Do you really mean it, Maggie?'

She nodded wordlessly and he drew her gently to him and cradled her head on his chest.

The airport was crowded. Maggie had arrived early to find a place to park and give her time for one last fortifying coffee before the flight arrival was announced. Then they were there. She could see Dan walking towards her, holding in each hand the hand of a child. For one terrible moment she felt a total paralysis take hold of her. What had she done? What about her job, her future, all her plans? What did she know of children and their problems? She didn't even like children. She had no experience of children – not even of nephews and nieces of her own. And now they were here and Dan had stopped walking and three pairs of eyes were regarding her – all solemn – all waiting for her to speak. Her mouth had gone dry.

'Hi,' she said.

Dan grinned. 'This is Mary-Sue,' he said, 'and this is Hal. Say hello to your Auntie Maggie, kids.'

The two pairs of eyes looked sullen and hostile. Neither child said a word.

*

She had made the new drapes for their bedroom herself and lined the cupboard shelves with pretty paper. On each bed lay a new toy. A doll for Mary-Sue and a truck for Hal. Sure it's bribery, she had said to herself as she had written out the cheque for them. Sure, but how else can I get them to like me?

Dan brought in the cases and together they unpacked the children's toys and clothes. The little boy soon forgot some of his reserve in the interest of seeing his toys revealed, arranging them himself in a row under his bed, but Mary-Sue sat on her pillow and watched, her thumb securely in her mouth. She had not said a word.

The first three days weren't so bad. Dan stayed home from the office to help and Maggie, who had to go to her own office at the studios in the morning for one more week before starting to work from home, found things not at all too bad. In the apartment the children played in their bedroom or sat in front of the TV. They came to the table when they were told and allowed her to put them to bed without protest. Dan took them to the park and bought them ice-creams and took Hal on his knee and told him fairy stories to which the boy listened with enormous round staring eyes.

Dan was a natural with the kids, Maggie saw at once with a little pang of jealousy. He seemed to know what to say to them, what to do and they took to him easily, showing none of the shy reserve they kept for her, instinctively sensing her own.

It was not until Monday that Maggie first had them on her own. Breakfast passed without a hitch. Neither child ate much at any meal, which worried her, but at least at breakfast they could be persuaded to take a bowl of their favourite cereal in milk. Then Dan kissed her goodbye as so often in the past, folding his paper, picking up his case, going to the mirror to check his tie.

'I'll call you later,' he said. 'See how you're surviving. 'Bye kids.' And he had gone.

She swallowed. 'Right. Hal and Mary-Sue, do you want to go and play while I do the dishes?' Her voice sounded too brisk, too hearty.

She turned to stack the plates and cups in the sink, ignoring the two small faces which turned to watch her. They were still sitting there when she had finished.

'Right kids, run and play now. Auntie Maggie wants to do some work.' And she walked out of the room leaving them still sitting on their stools at the breakfast table.

She had commandeered a table by the window in the living room as a desk. On it she had put the reading lamp and a coffee mug full of pencils and ball points. Briskly she unfastened her case and brought out the pile of scripts she had to read. As she pulled up the chair she heard the door opening quietly behind her.

'Hi,' she called, without turning round. 'Want something?'

There was silence.

She went on sorting the scripts for a few moments, then turned. They were standing in the doorway holding hands.

'Mary-Sue wants to watch television,' Hal announced in a piping voice.

With a sigh Maggie glanced at the blank screen in the corner. 'Must you, darling? Auntie Maggie wants to work just now. Could you go and play, just for a little while? Please. You shall watch it later, I promise.'

The children looked at each other. She waited for the words, 'Mommie let us watch it,' but mercifully they never came. Reluctantly the two withdrew in total silence. Maggie turned to her work. Or tried to. She found she read a page – then read it again. But even the second time she could not remember what she had read. Her attention kept wandering to the two little waifs at the other end of the apartment.

She threw down her pen and got to her feet with a sigh.

The children's room was ominously silent. She pushed open the door and looked in. Mary-Sue was sitting on her pillow her thumb in her mouth, her legs curled up defensively under her, watching Hal who had found one of the suitcases and was industriously stuffing all his toys into it.

Maggie stood watching them for a moment. 'Well, well, Hal, you're busy. That's a nice tidy boy.'

He looked at her solemnly. 'Me and Mary-Sue want to go home,' he announced clearly. 'We don't like it here.'

'Dear God, Dan, what was I to do?' Maggie sobbed that night after the children had gone to bed. 'They kept looking at me with those great sad eyes. Children shouldn't look sad. They should be laughing. I tried to tell them that their home would be here now, but they didn't understand.'

'It's hard, Maggie, I know.' Dan got up and shook an empty cigarette pack hopefully. 'Ma told them the whole bit about Mummy going to heaven, and Daddy being too sick to look after them any more, but I don't think it's sunk in at all. They cried. Of course they cried, especially Hal, but,' he shrugged, 'it's so difficult knowing what to say: to reassure without raising any false hopes.'

'I don't know how to cope with it, Dan. We shouldn't have said we'd take them. We could do more damage than good.'

He shook his head slowly. 'I don't think so. I think unobtrusive love and security are what they need now. We've got to give everything we've got, Maggie and expect nothing in return. That's the only way.'

She stood up and went to unplug the percolator. 'Pretty thankless task that is for me. It's not you that's had to give up your job – as good as. No, sorry, Dan. I didn't mean that. I guess I'm just so mixed up myself about it. I'm sorry for them; I want to cry every time I see them; I want to cuddle them and protect them and make the world go away and yet I don't dare. I'm not like you. I can't do it. I know they'll reject me.' There was a sob in her voice and she sniffed angrily, as he started to protest. 'Oh yes I do resent them, Dan. I don't want to. I know I shouldn't, but because of them I've almost certainly lost that producer's job I was after and they've put me on to wading through lousy scripts. And I can't even do that properly because the kids distract me. They distract me if they're there and they distract me if they're not there because I think they'll start packing again and leave or something.'

She ran her fingers through her hair in agitation, pushing it back from her hot face.

Dan's blue eyes were very sober. 'I didn't realize, honey. I thought you were a hundred per cent behind me in this. Maybe we shouldn't have done it.' He got up and took the percolator out of her hands, pouring two mugs of black coffee. 'It's not too late, Maggie. We can send them back, honey. It's not as though they're settled here yet.'

She shook her head violently. 'No, no. We must keep them. I want to keep them. I do really.' Accepting a mug from him she sipped it, quick gasping sips, blowing the steam from the nutty black liquid. 'I suppose I'm just tired and depressed after the strain of the first day on my own.' She smiled wanly. 'I'll get used to it. We've got to win through with them, Dan, somehow. Make it up to them for what's happened. That's all that matters now.'

Next day was easier. She worked in the kitchen while they watched TV for half an hour. Then she called them in to help her with the baking. Hal was full of enthusiasm, kneeling up on a stool, one of her aprons tied under his armpits and was soon merrily covered in flour. She glanced at Mary-Sue who was sitting next to him toying listlessly with a spoon. The little girl had great dark circles under her eyes as if she hadn't slept, although each night when Maggie had looked in at the children both had been lying still, breathing evenly in the little yellow-draped room.

'What would you like to do, Mary-Sue?' she asked, racking her brains. 'I tell you what. If we let Hal make the buns – he's good at buns – why don't you make us some peppermint creams and we can all eat one while the buns are cooking.'

She turned away casually to the cupboard, praying she had some peppermint essence as, over her shoulder, she saw the child watching her, interested for the first time.

That night when she went in to check if the children were asleep she found Hal had crept into bed beside his sister. She gazed at them quietly for a minute and then tiptoed out of the room without a word.

The next day was quite good. After TV Maggie suggested they each have one of Mary-Sue's peppermint stars and she was rewarded with a shy smile. Then they went to the supermarket and the children pushed the trolley for her and chose the food they liked best. Then they all went home for a hamburger lunch.

It was the first night that Dan wasn't there to help bath them and put them to bed. He was going to be out till late at a business dinner and Maggie planned to catch up on her scripts. As she towelled each thin little body dry and powdered it and pulled on the patterned pyjamas she longed to put her arms round the children and hug them.

Why can't I? she thought miserably. What's holding me back?

She dropped a quick kiss on each head. 'Run to your beds now and I'll come and tuck you in and read your bedtime story.'

Wearily she stooped to pull the plug and watch the foaming water run away. A small blue plastic dolphin grounded nose first in the soapy dregs and she picked it out with a wistful smile, shaking a gobbet of wet fluff from its snout and setting it in the soap dish, then she walked slowly into the bedroom.

Later she poured herself a large Martini and sat spread-eagled on the couch, her head thrown back against the cushion. The room was airless and she was tired out but she had to start reading the scripts. Half of them were due back – with verdicts – by the next morning. Hauling herself to her feet she put on a record, then she went reluctantly to the table by the window and sat down, the ice-misted glass in her hand, sipping as she flipped open the first folder.

Slowly it began to grow dark. She didn't notice; reading hard, the lamplight reflecting in the polished wood, she worked on, finishing one script, writing her report and opening the next. Outside the hot air beat up towards the windows from the sidewalk, reverberating with the distant noise of cars. In a minute she would get up, make herself a sandwich, fix another drink . . .

It was several minutes before she became aware of the small figure standing beside her just outside the circle of lamplight.

'Hello, Mary-Sue,' she said quietly, dropping her pen and stretching her cramped fingers. 'Can't you sleep, honey?' A surreptitious glance at her watch told her it was after ten.

The little girl shook her head wordlessly. Her face was haggard.

And then suddenly it was so easy to know what to do.

Maggie pushed back her chair and held out her arms and the child threw herself into them sobbing miserably. Maggie drew her up onto her lap and hugged her tightly rocking to and fro, overwhelmed by the wave of emotion which shook her as she felt the thin little body pressed against hers, the arms clinging round her neck for comfort.

It was a long time before the storm of crying passed. Then came the moment Maggie had dreaded for so long. The little girl, her voice muffled in Maggie's shoulder murmured, 'My Mummy's never coming back, is she?'

Maggie's voice was surprisingly steady as she hugged Mary-Sue close. 'No, sweetheart. She can't come back. That's why she's asked Uncle Dan and me to take care of you and Hal for her.'

They sat for a long time in silence – so long that Maggie thought the little girl had fallen asleep in her arms from sheer exhaustion, but when she cautiously straightened Mary-Sue sat up, yawning, her face still pink and crumpled from the tears.

Maggie gave her a reassuring smile. 'Was Hal still asleep when you came in, love?'

Mary-Sue nodded.

'Good. Then I tell you what. Why don't you and I go and get ourselves a midnight feast. I'm hungry and I'll bet you are too. What do you say to a sandwich and some ice-cream soda. A secret; just the two of us. Not telling Uncle Dan.'

'Or Hal?'

'Or Hal.'

Mary-Sue nodded without another word and reluctantly she slipped from Maggie's lap still clinging to her hand as they went through into the kitchen.

It was the strangest midnight feast. They sat cross-legged on the rug on the floor on either side of a fat red Christmas candle, dug out from the back of the closet, eating peanut butter sandwiches and brownies and drinking from tall icy glasses with coloured straws.

Across the street the neon signs flashed reflections on the dark wall of the kitchen behind the child and Maggie could see her clearly in the opal glow, her face solemn, her shoulder length silver hair hanging over two pathetically narrow shoulders in cotton pyjamas covered in pale blue elephants. Somewhere in the distance a police siren wailed, and always far below was the roar of traffic.

With a sigh she thought of the unread scripts on the table next door. They would never be done in time now; she felt a little twinge of regret. Then she remembered again the warmth and longing in the child's arms and she felt that perhaps after all they weren't so important. They could wait their turn.

She found Mary-Sue was looking at her suddenly and she smiled gently in the candle light. 'What shall we do tomorrow, eh?' she asked in a whisper.

'Make peppermint creams again, Auntie Maggie,' was the sleepy reply.

Flowers Shouldn't Make You Cry

The sun glittered on the water, refracting a thousand facets of diamond light as the river tumbled towards the west. It was very cold. Jane shrugged herself deeper into her warm coat and glanced up at the man at her side.

They had pulled up in the layby and kissed and then while Ian felt in the glove pocket for a packet of cigarettes Jane had climbed out to stretch her legs and peer over the hedge. The sight took her breath away. The meadow, nestling in the elbow of dazzling water, was carpeted with daffodils. There must have been acres of them, of the palest yellow and their rich, delicate scent was everywhere in the wind off the mountains behind her.

The sound of her delighted cry brought Ian to her side in a moment. He smiled at her and reaching down broke off a bloom and gave it to her.

'They're wild, you know,' he said. 'Quite wild. You'll see, there are acres of them near the farm.'

She looked down at the single perfect flower and suddenly her eyes were blinded by tears.

She shook her head quickly, gazing away into the distance so that he should not see, should not realize that she could still think with sadness about the man whom this time last year she had been about to marry.

*

Edward had bought the bulbs, string bags of them, all daffodils and together they had knelt in the sooty earth of his small back garden and planted them, brushing away the dusty dried sycamore leaves which had drifted over the fence from the road at the back. She scooped out pockets of soil, setting the bulbs in place and firming back the earth and after a while she sat back on her heels, brushing a strand of hair from her eyes with the back of a grimy hand. She watched him working, as carefully he dug out a line of neat holes down the edge of the path and she frowned slightly. She had been planting the bulbs in big, bold clumps, visualizing the blaze of colour when they bloomed. His would be regimented and orderly, a thin yellow line.

He was a tall man, older than she, with a cynical shadow at his mouth and eyes which intrigued and tormented her. It was there, even now, while he bent concentrating to firm in the bulbs. She knew that she would do anything for him in her love and forgive much if he should ask it, but there was a strange centre of aloneness in him which chilled her sometimes. It was a place she would never reach, a place completely apart, a place that belonged to the days of the week she did not see him, the evenings he spent away from her.

Perhaps she suspected then that somehow his destiny might not lie with her; that soon her hopes and her world might begin to crumble even as the soft earth crumbled between her fingers. She shook her head to rid herself of her thoughts. She must not allow herself to build things up, to allow them to assume too much importance. She must wait.

The bulbs planted at last, she had watched from the kitchen door as he darkened the soil with water before he kicked off his boots and together they had washed off the

293

earth, watching their fingers trailing black eddies down the sink.

Then his arms were round her at last and his lips on hers and for a while she forgot her fears and the bright rushing autumnal sky and the gently creaking door which swung to and fro in the wind.

In the end they went out for tea, walking hand in hand down the tow path before turning up the alley beside the pub and looking for the teashop by the church.

Their hands met on the checked gingham tablecloth and they had stared into each other's eyes, mesmerized, oblivious of the knowing looks of the three old ladies at the next table; that night she dreamed about him and the next, and then they met again to sit in the flickering twilight of the cinema, conscious only of each other and she feared again that the emotions were too strong, too sudden, their love too tempestuous. She knew she was obsessed and in her obsession the daffodils assumed a strange importance. They were a part of him; a part of her, planted by them both together as a promise of a future spring. The brooding bulbs in the earth of his garden became a symbol for her of their whole relationship.

In other gardens as winter began to release its hold she saw the hard green shoots hafting their way out of the frosted ground. But in the frozen space outside his kitchen door there was no sign. It had begun to matter tremendously that there should be one, the result of their joint efforts, a commitment for the future, something of hers which belonged in his world, something which was theirs together. And then it came. A first small spike, a second, thrusting up from the grip of the whirling snow which turned to water as it hit the path.

Edward was as attentive as ever, as loving, but somewhere deep inside there was still a core of separateness which made Jane uneasy. Her commitment was total. Surely his should be the same?

When it came, the moment she had so often feared, it was as if a lurking shadow had suddenly grown and darkened around her.

It was in the park where the buds on the trees and bushes were beginning to fill and the whippy gold green sallows by the lake were erupting into silver and pussy willow. She saw them across the water, Edward and the other girl. He was holding her gloved hand, gazing down into her eyes as she talked.

Jane stopped and watched them for a moment. Then, sick, she turned away.

'I saw you in the park today,' she said, her voice carefully unemotional as she climbed into his car that evening.

'Not me,' he said. 'I was in the office.'

She almost made herself believe him.

It was cold late spring. The pale green dilations which were the daffodils seemed to hesitate for an eternity before they began to swell at last into buds. She helped Edward decorate the kitchen and as they worked they left the back door open to take away the smell of paint. She could see the clusters of nodding points, the green shimmer above the dead earth and she planned to buy some tubs for geraniums later. If there was a later. And she ached with the fear that it might not happen, that the shadow might return. But for Edward there were no shadows. He was happy then, not suspecting her secret unease and it was while they were both working close like this in companionable silence that he threw down his brush and took her in his arms and kissed her.

'One of these days,' he said, 'I think I'm going to have to marry you.'

She hugged her happiness to her as she went on painting, not daring to show her joy too much.

His flat was big enough for two and slowly she found herself looking at it anew. He never suggested that she live there with him and somehow she never left any of her possessions there but secretly she dreamed. Here would go her grandmother's little chair, here her favourite mirror. She planned a colour scheme for the small dark bedroom with its ugly basement outlook and already in her mind's eye saw white trellis draped with clematis around the dustbins outside the window.

Once she crept into the bedroom alone and sat on the bed, looking around, thinking of colours; and it was then she saw it. A lipstick down behind the bookcase in the corner; she stared at it for a long time before she picked it up and then reluctantly she opened it. It was long and red and moist. A colour she would never use.

She left it on the table, swallowing her misery, inventing good reasons why it should be there, not daring to face him with it for fear of what his answer would be and later, after he had been in the bedroom to collect a book she saw that it had disappeared. She knew his swift action compounded some sort of guilt, but she loved him . . .

She would have preferred it if he had sprung the ring on her as a surprise – bought it or inherited it to place on her finger by moonlight or by the flicker of a candle. As it was he stopped suddenly as they walked down the High Street to collect her shoes from the mender and said 'What about it?'

She was embarrassed, unprepared, excited but flustered as the man behind the counter reached out a flock-lined tray.

On her finger the ring kept catching her eye as they

walked on to collect the shoes, a reminder that life can be very ordinary in its magic.

That evening she cut the first few daffodil buds and deliberately when he took her home she left her comb behind, her mended shoes and her jacket on the back of his bedroom door. It was a gesture of possession.

In the warmth of the flat the golden bells opened and filled the room with their fragrance. She came there every evening now and cooked on his stove and together they listened to his records, the bottom half of the dirty sash window thrown open onto the back garden so, from the tree in the road, they could hear the ecstatic carolling of a blackbird as the dusk fell and the flowers nodded palely in the dark.

She was very happy.

At last she dared to accept their love; she wanted to be with him all the time. She lay in his arms dreaming of the future, relaxed, confident, at peace.

But he leaned across her and turned on the lamp and looked at his watch, frowning.

'It's time you went, Janie.' His lips touched hers for a second. 'It won't be long now, before you're here, properly, for good, but now you must go.'

She sat clutching her knees as she watched him dress, feeling in some way betrayed, wanting him to stop, to turn back to her and take her again in his arms.

He found the car keys and then he turned to her. 'Come on, Janie. It's late. Don't forget I have to go to the office in the morning.'

So did she of course.

As she grew more confident in their relationship, so she felt more at home in his flat. She chose the material for the bedroom curtains in the lunch hour, secretly measured and made them and hung them while he was out buying some beer. They changed the room completely, making it bright and warm and now, a little, hers. But his polite admiration on his return, as he stood for a moment in the doorway looking, barely hid his anger at her presumption, and crying quietly in the bathroom later she realized she had taken too much for granted. She was still a guest, despite the promise implied by the ring she wore.

Edward spoke of getting married in the summer and, learning perhaps a little of his ways now, she knew better than to press him for a date. He would tell her she supposed when he so wished and she frowned, a tiny seed of rebellion taking root at last at her own passivity.

'We haven't decided yet, there's no hurry,' she said airily when her friends admired her ring and asked the obvious question. When she went home to her parents she had to take it off altogether – Edward had not agreed to go with her to meet them, although he had kissed away her hurt.

The back yard glowed with gold – clumps of dazzling colour and lines of waving heads along the short pebbled path. She thought again of her tubs and suggested them, laughing to Edward, expecting to be snubbed, but he agreed. They bought them that very weekend, humping sacks of soil to fill them and planting out the seedlings together. The garden was very pretty now but she knew, deep inside, that they were only playing house.

The other woman's name was Linda. If Jane hadn't gone to try to buy some ballet tickets and called off afterwards for a coffee near the box office she might never have known. They were sitting at a corner table.

Edward smiled, his eyes narrowed in the way she knew so well which usually made her heart turn over with love.

'This is Linda,' he said.

'I'm Jane. Edward's fiancée,' Jane repeated, putting out

her hand. She had recognized the brightness of the lipstick, the coat of the walker in the park.

They drank coffee, the three of them and laughed and joked and were at ease in their small talk, but something deep inside pained Jane so much she could scarcely swallow the hot sweetness of each sip.

He did not insult her with excuses. He kissed her later till her coldness stood no chance at all and told her he had fixed the date. She smiled and kissed him back but her happiness was chilled with apprehension; the game was spoiled.

There was no row, no scene when it happened. They had been working together in the garden, she showing him how to knot down the straggle of dying daffodil leaves to plant the summer colours between. Then they decided to go for a walk in the park.

The trees were heavy with new leaves rustling, as they walked hand in hand to the lake to watch the swans.

'I can't marry you, Edward,' she said quietly, gently easing off her ring. 'I'm sorry.'

'Is it because of Linda?' His face was stricken.

She shook her head. 'I can't explain. There is something wrong, my love. It wouldn't work.' The sleek white profile of the swan before her blurred and shimmered for a moment in her tears. She hadn't planned to say it; the decision had been quite impulsive and yet, now that it was made, she felt a strange sense of release.

Edward gazed out across the lake, his hands thrust deep into his pockets. He looked completely lost.

'Think again, Janie. Please don't decide just like that. Let's talk about it. Let's go home.'

But she had walked away across the park alone.

*

He sent her back the ring. 'Even if you still feel you could
never marry me, Jane darling, keep it please. To help you
remember the good times – and there were good times,
weren't there? . . .'

She smiled faintly and kissed the cold stone and put it
into the back of a drawer. She wouldn't need his ring to
help her remember.

She had met Ian when she had been at her lowest ebb in
the arid, empty days of the summer. Somehow she had
accepted the loneliness, the separate oneness of existence
and she had gone on living. Slowly she had found again
her friends from the time before she had met Edward, but
somehow their kindness, their understanding only touched
the surface of her being. Inside she was alone and crying.

The memory of the daffodils comforted her even then.
They remained. Deep in the earth they were drawing
strength back into themselves from their dying leaves and
next year they would come again, renewed and beautiful.
They would comfort Edward and give him pleasure and
perhaps remind him of the good times they had had
together. She had not guessed then that she too would take
strength from the dying of her love and that it would come
again.

It was in the picture gallery that she had first seen Ian;
he was standing gazing at a painting of some wild flowers
and they remained side by side for a while, rapt in the
painting, unconscious of one another.

Then slowly he had turned and looked at her and seen
the expression in her eyes.

'Flowers shouldn't make you cry,' he said gently and
strangely she had not been embarrassed that he should
have seen. They had walked on slowly together, pausing
before some paintings, passing others, companionable even

then when they were strangers and she had not thought it odd that he should buy her a cup of coffee. Later she had even smiled again, her tears forgotten.

She had agreed to see him occasionally almost against her will, resenting the involvement, determined not to risk unhappiness again. But there was no need for unhappiness, no need for reserve. Ian was the kind of man who possessed an essential quietness and kindness which reassured but did not demand.

'Remember the good times, Jane,' he had said to her with a sad smile when she had told him everything. 'Every beautiful woman needs memories like those. Don't try and forget. Build on your dreams.'

They returned to the gallery often and the flower picture became special to them. Each time they would go and look at it first and then they would smile and he would take her hand.

Ian was watching her twisting the crisp green stem between her fingers. He put his arm round her and pulled her gently against his shoulder. He had seen the tears at once as she looked at the daffodil, but he did not say anything. She would tell him what she was thinking in her own time if she wanted to. He had known from the start that he could never push her and he had never tried.

She dropped her head to the daffodil in her fingers and sniffed it sadly. She was picturing again the little back yard with its brilliant blooms. Was Linda there to cut them this year? Somehow she didn't think so.

Poor Edward. She hoped he was happy. One day perhaps she would meet him again and she realized suddenly that it would be without bitterness, without sadness for what might have been, for how could she be sad when she had found Ian and his love for her? With him there was never sick apprehension, never fear, nor hesitation. There were no doubts at all.

'You're the woman for me, Janie,' he had murmured once as they walked together through the early dusk. 'I'm only waiting till you recognize it, darling.' She did not tell him, then, that she already knew it.

Ian glanced at her sideways. 'Come on, it's getting late. My parents will be wondering where on earth we are. You're not shy of meeting them are you?'

She pulled up the collar of her coat against the wind. 'A little perhaps.' She hesitated. 'It's a big step, meeting someone's parents.'

A step that Edward had refused to take.

Ian laughed. 'You'll love mine, you'll see. Come on. Let's go home.'

When Edward had said those words, she had walked away.

They climbed back into the car and set off again slowly down the winding lane. She glanced at him, watching his fair hair blowing in the wind from the lowered window and found suddenly that she was smiling.

Footsteps in the Attic

They both heard it at the same moment. Somewhere upstairs a door banged and there came the sound of running feet.

Mike stood up quietly and picked up the poker. Glancing at Tessa he put his fingers to his lips. 'Wait here,' he murmured. 'I'll get them this time.' He tiptoed to the door and opened it.

The hall was in darkness. Cautiously he made his way to the stairs and crept up, stopping abruptly as the treads creaked beneath his weight.

Her face white, Tessa followed him as quietly as she could into the hall. She waited breathlessly, peering up into the darkness after him and it was several moments before she noticed that the front door swung gently ajar.

With a click all the upstairs lights came on. 'All right, come on out. I know you're there,' Mike roared.

Tessa gasped, but his challenge was followed by a complete silence.

A moment later he appeared above her and leaned over the banisters. 'No sign,' he called. 'Not a bloody sign. I don't understand it.'

'Did you look on the top floor?' She found that her voice was trembling.

'I've even looked in the airing cupboard. There is nothing there. Nobody.'

'The front door was open again, Mike.'

He ran down, the poker still in his hand and examined the lock, clicking it open and shut and running his hand down the door jamb. 'I don't understand it. I suppose it must be local kids playing around. One of them could have got hold of a key, I suppose, but whoever it is it's got to stop. I'll fix the door now and get some bolts tomorrow. And this time I'm going to ring the police.'

Tessa stood behind him, gnawing at her knuckle while he phoned.

'You're probably right, sir, about it being kids,' the duty officer agreed after listening to Mike's explanation. 'We have a lot of trouble with them and if, as you say, your house has been lying empty for some time they've probably found a way of getting in to play there. They could have been doing it for months and no one's spotted them before.'

'What did he say?' Tessa asked as Mike hung up.

'Pretty sure it must be kids,' he repeated. 'They're going to send someone out tomorrow.'

It snowed again in the night so any footprints the intruders might have left were obliterated and the CID men who arrived as Mike and Tessa were finishing their breakfast found nothing to give any clue as to who they had been.

'It gives you a funny feeling, doesn't it?' she said later with a shiver. 'To know there's someone wandering around your house. I don't like it.'

'You're not regretting moving here are you, Tess?' Mike had brought an armful of logs in with him after seeing off the policemen. He threw them into the basket in the corner and stamped the ice off his boots.

'Of course not. I love this house. It's not really so isolated – it's only the snow that makes it so quiet.' She opened the window to throw out the crumbs from the

304

breakfast cloth. 'Mike! There's someone out there now. By the gate,' she hissed suddenly. 'Come and look.'

He was behind her in a second, peering over her shoulder. Two men stood by the gate. One of them was pointing at the roof of the house.

'They look more like prospective buyers than burglars,' Mike muttered meditatively. 'Perhaps they haven't heard that it's sold. This is your chance Tess. We could resell quickly at a vast profit.' He grinned at her teasingly.

'Never!' She folded the cloth and put it in the drawer. 'Come away from the window, Mike. They'll think you're watching them!'

'I am watching them.' He opened the window again and leaned out. 'Hello! Can I help you?' he called, his breath smoking in the frosty air.

The taller of the two men raised a hand and tramped across the frozen lawn, his face reddened with cold above the upturned collar of his sheepskin jacket.

'When did you folks move in? The house was empty last time I saw it.' In spite of the irritation in his tone his face had a naturally friendly expression which Tessa found reassuring.

'Only a week ago,' Mike told him. 'I'm afraid you're too late if you wanted to buy.'

The man laughed. 'Not buy. Borrow maybe. Can we come in and explain?' Mike raised an eyebrow. 'I think you'd better. The door's round there.' He jerked his hand towards the side of the house.

Three minutes later their visitors were seated at the kitchen table and Tessa had the coffee on again. The red-faced man introduced himself as Pete Sanders. 'We're looking for a Georgian house like this for location shots for a film – part of a TV series. This one is just right. Beautiful, old, neat and surrounded by nothing – no telegraph wires that show from the front and, as I thought, empty!' He grinned expansively.

The other man was staring round the kitchen. 'Isn't it very big just for the two of you?' His abrupt question was curious rather than rude.

Tessa smiled. 'We're hoping to run it as a guest house next summer – or at least bed and breakfast.'

Sanders nodded. 'Perfect place I should think. Now. The thing is, I'm in a hurry. The shots I want require snow. If you'd agree I can get everyone up here today as soon as possible, because this snow's not going to last, I hear and my budge won't cover the synthetic variety. I usually give people a lot more warning than this when we want their house, but this is special.' He smiled winningly.

Mike glanced at Tessa. Her eyes were shining.

'Go ahead,' he said. 'It'll be fun. As you said, we're isolated and in this weather the neighbours haven't been falling over themselves to call. At least . . .' He hesitated. He had been on the point of talking about their visitor of the evening before – the third time they had heard him in the house – but he changed his mind.

Sanders had brought out some notes. 'All I shall want from you is that you keep out of sight. The house is supposed to be completely empty and our hero, played by Jim Dixon,' he glanced at Tessa knowingly, 'will walk up the front path – we'll have to brush out the footprints – he'll knock, walk round a bit, looking up at the windows, knock again, go back to the lane, get on his horse and ride away. OK?'

'Is that all?' Mike sounded disappointed.

'That's all.'

'The TV studios are only about twelve miles from here, apparently,' he said after he had escorted the two men back to their car. 'That's how Pete knew the house. He's had his eye on it for ages and he's been waiting for snow.

The rest of the series is more or less finished, I gather and it's due to go out quite soon. And – they're going to pay us!'

Tessa sat down opposite him. 'It'll be fun seeing ourselves on TV . . . Good advertising when we start the B&B . . . Mike, where are you going?'

He was reaching for his jacket.

'I said I'd clear away the empty crates round the side and shift the car into the barn. They'll be back in less than two hours. He said his men would do it, but I'd rather get it tidy.' He dropped a kiss on her head and hurried out.

The kitchen was suddenly very silent. She stooped and threw a couple of logs onto the fire and it blazed up, spitting frost up the chimney, filling the room with the scent of old dried apple. Upstairs she could hear Mike walking about, squeaking the boards, pushing furniture.

But Mike was outside. Only a moment before he had gone out of the back door.

Her heart hammering suddenly with fear she ran to the door into the hall and opened it. The front door was standing open, allowing the blinding snow-light to flood in across the floor and up the stairs. Mike must have let himself in and gone up for some reason.

'Mike?' she called, her hand on the banister. 'Mike, is that you?'

The house was completely silent again. She pushed the door shut and then cautiously she began to mount the stairs.

'Mike?' She stopped at the top and peered down the passage. There was no sign of him.

Then, distantly, she heard the car start, the engine coughing reluctantly as it was revved into action. Looking out of the landing window she could see Mike sitting at the wheel, the driver's door half open, his foot playing on the accelerator as clouds of blue smoke billowed round the car. She watched as he turned it and backed it into the barn, closing the heavy double doors before he walked back across the yard towards the front door.

She glanced round uneasily. 'Is there anyone there?' she called, her voice shaking a little, but the silence in the house had already told her that the bedrooms were empty.

She ran back down the stairs. 'You left the front door open, Mike and you know we want to conserve all the heat we can.'

He was riffling through the drawer in the kitchen table. 'Never touched it. I've just been putting the car away. A hinge is nearly off one of the doors on the barn. Have you seen my big screwdriver?' Exasperated, he slammed the drawer shut and went to peer at the clutter of tools on the windowsill.

'Mike, the front door was open again just now. And I heard someone upstairs. If it wasn't you, who was it?' Tessa swallowed nervously.

He turned to her at last. 'Upstairs. Are you sure?'

'I just told you.'

'Damn cheek! And in daylight too.' He picked up a heavy pair of pliers from the tools and went purposefully to the door.

Tessa followed him. 'I closed the front door,' she whispered. 'It was wide open.'

He went up two at a time and flung open the first door on the landing. The room was empty. So were all the others.

'No one here,' he commented as he closed the bathroom door.

'Look upstairs,' she whispered. The second, attic floor was dark and as yet empty of furniture.

Mike ran up, leaving her on the first landing peering after him. Minutes later he was down again. 'No, not a

308

thing. It must have been the wind. Perhaps when I opened the back door, the front blew open.'

She followed him down, unconvinced. 'I heard furniture being moved.'

'Boards creaking? All old houses are full of strange noises. We're just not used to our own yet. Perhaps all the noises we've heard have just been that – noises.' He shrugged. 'Look, Tess, I must get on shifting those boxes and tidying the yard. Sanders will be back with his camera crew or whatever they're called and we won't be ready for him.'

Tessa stood at the door for a while watching him, then she went to the phone.

'Mr Forbes? This is Tessa Gordon. Do you remember? You sold the Old Rectory to us. Did you by any chance give the keys to anyone else to come over, anyone who didn't return them?' The line crackled and she could imagine old Mr Forbes drawing himself up indignantly at his desk.

'Naturally the keys were given to any prospective buyers, Mrs Gordon. But they were always returned to my office. And after your husband bought the property naturally all the keys were given to him. May I enquire why you are asking?'

She smiled quietly in spite of her worry. 'Well, to be honest, Mr Forbes, we think someone has been in here a couple of times, coming quite openly through the front door. They must have had a key from somewhere.'

There was a moment's silence on the line and then the quavering voice asked, 'Have you actually seen anyone, Mrs Gordon?'

'Well, no, why?'

'I just wondered. Have you told the police?'

'Yes. They were out here this morning.'

'I see.' He cleared his throat. 'Mrs Gordon. I don't

think you should make too much of these incidents. I . . .
er . . . well, I seem to remember the vicar, old Mr Somerset, mentioning to me once or twice that a similar occurrence had happened to him. He . . . well, he seemed to think there was a perfectly natural and . . . er . . . happy explanation.'

'What do you mean?' Tessa was frowning. 'You mean he gave the keys to someone? Told them they could come in?'

'Well, no, not exactly. Look, Mrs Gordon, you must excuse me now, but I have a client waiting. Perhaps I might call on you one day next week when I'm over in your part of the world. I might just be able to explain.'

She stared at the receiver in her hand. He had hung up.

'Sounds as though he knows what it's all about, though,' Mike commented as they had a quick sandwich in the kitchen later. I hope it's not something he should have told us before we decided to buy. He's a funny old geezer, Forbes. He was very thick with the Rev. Somerset, too, I gather.'

They watched the arrival of the television crew with great interest, astonished at the number of people who seemed to be involved in the afternoon's work, their enthusiasm slightly dampened by the fact that they were expected to douse the kitchen fire at once, but mollified by an invitation to the mobile canteen which had followed the cars, vans and horse box into the lane.

'Now, no peeking,' Sanders instructed as a camera was being brought into position by the gate. 'In fact, why not watch from out here. You'll be able to see everything much better.'

They stood and watched as beneath the skilled hands of his men their house took on all over the lonely derelict

310

appearance which they had been at such pains for the last week to dispel.

Then at last when all was ready and every footprint banished from the lawn, a hush descended on the assembled company.

'It really is a pretty house, isn't it?' Mike whispered softly as they watched Jim Dixon, nattily dressed in Regency costume, mount the rangy black cob which had been backed out of the horse box and ride up to the gate as the cameras started to whirr.

The sun sparkled on the snow, winking in the windows. Suddenly Tessa stiffened. 'Mike, look! At the top. The end room. There's somebody there!'

Mike frowned up at the house, screwing up his eyes. 'Where?'

'There. There.' She pointed. 'Quick, stop them filming. It must be him. We must catch him.'

Her voice had risen sharply and she saw Sanders and Dave, his production assistant, frowning at her. The camera stopped and Jim reined in his horse.

'Problem?' he said, smiling down at her.

'There's someone there. Up there.' She pointed at the house.

Everyone turned to look but the windows were blank.

'Do you want a couple of the boys to take a look with you?' Sanders turned to Mike. 'Only, for Pete's sake, go round the back! Don't make any more footmarks, OK?'

Tessa bit her lip. 'I'm sure I saw a face,' she said as they watched the three men making their way cautiously round behind the barn.

'Could be a trick of the light, the windows are full of reflections.' Jim grinned at her reassuringly. 'Don't worry, if there is anyone there, they'll find him.'

There was no one and Tessa, scarlet with embarrassment, subsided behind Mike to watch the proceedings in silence.

It was growing dark when the last of the equipment was packed up and the cars and vans eventually rolled away. Tired, Mike and Tessa went back into the house and set about relighting the fire in the chilly kitchen, drawing the curtains against the twilit lawn which was now crossed and recrossed with slushy footprints.

'Tea?' Tessa filled the kettle at the tap and plugged it in as Mike knelt at the hearth, feeding kindling into the small new fire.

They heard no more from the film people until one night the phone rang. Mike went to answer it. He was gone a long time and after a while Tessa looked up from her book, gazing into the fire listening. She could hear him wandering up and down upstairs.

When at last he reappeared he was looking rather odd.

'What is it?' Her book fell unnoticed in her lap.

'That was Pete Sanders,' he said quietly. 'He wanted to tell us when the film was going to be on.' He paused. 'There was something else too. He said that the film showed quite clearly the face you saw at the window.'

Tessa gasped. 'You mean the burglar?'

'No.' He shook his head. 'No. Our other theory seems to be the right one. It was a child. A little girl.'

Tessa stared at him. 'A little girl?'

He nodded. 'In the end room on the top floor. That's where you saw it, wasn't it?'

'That's right. What bloody cheek! How on earth does she get in? Oh, Mike,' she suddenly thought of something, 'does that mean they'll have to do the film again?'

'No. There's no time. They can edit her out,' he said. 'Strange isn't it, though, that we found no one?'

He sat down beside her again. 'I suppose we ought to go and have another look round. I was thinking in terms of rowdy teenagers smoking pot up there or something, not a little girl.'

'I thought you were up there just now.' She reopened her book.

'Just now? No, I was on the phone.'

They stared at each other in silence for a second. Then reluctantly he hauled himself to his feet again. 'I just checked the door too. She must have got in some other way this time. Come on.'

The hall light revealed the solid oak door still securely shut and bolted. The house was completely silent. They stood looking upstairs for a moment, then side by side, they began to climb.

Systematically they searched the first floor and then they stopped, looking up the narrow attic staircase. 'Go on, you've got to look,' Tessa whispered. For some reason her voice had gone husky.

Mike walked up slowly with Tessa close behind him and pushed open the first door, clicking on the light. The naked bulb swung gently, reflecting in the back window panes. But the room was empty. As was the next.

'This is the one,' he whispered outside the last door.

He pushed it open hard and threw the light switch.

The room was empty. They both went in and looked around. The room was small with one square window in the eaves. Like the others it had a deep window seat and a wall cupboard in the alcove beside the empty fireplace and it smelled of damp and disuse.

They looked round carefully.

'This must have been a nursery,' Tessa whispered. 'Look at the wallpaper.' She pulled open the warped cupboard and peered inside. A few bits of broken china lay on

313

the dusty shelf paper and on one top shelf a heap of material. She reached up.

'Mike, look!'

Mike had been examining the window latch. He turned.

'Look. A genuine Victorian doll. Oh, isn't she beautiful?'

The waxen face was delicately painted and the dusty ringlets tied with threadbare blue ribbon.

'How on earth did she get here? I'm sure she wasn't here before.' She took the doll to the stark light and peered at her.

'Perhaps she belongs to the little girl at the window,' Mike said laughing. 'Come on, it's cold up here. Let's go down. There's no one here now.'

Tessa turned to follow him. Then she glanced down at the doll in her hand and she shivered.

She took it to the window seat and gently propped it in the corner. 'I think I'll leave her here,' she said.

She followed Mike to the door and then turned to glance back at the room, her hand on the light switch. The doll had fallen sideways on the window seat.

The house was very quiet. Mike had taken the car into town and Tessa was sitting at her sewing machine in the dark kitchen, the only light falling from the table lamp on the folds of the deep red curtain she was making. Outside it was snowing again. Standing up stiffly at last she turned on the radio while she made herself a cup of coffee. Then she sat down again to her curtains. The cheerful hum of the motor and the little warm patch of light which centred around her guiding fingers took all her attention and slowly she relaxed again.

The child must have been peering through a crack in

the kitchen door. She heard a smothered giggle and as she pushed her chair back in fright across the flags the sound of feet running up the stairs away from her.

She flung back the door and peered into the hall. The front door was closed and bolted.

Tessa went up the stairs two at a time. On the landing she stopped. There was complete silence from the top floor. She went on up, not giving herself time to think, heading straight for the nursery.

The room was empty. She hesitated, looking round. The doll was lying on the floor now, in the corner.

'Are you there?' she called. 'Come on. I won't hurt you. I just want to talk to you.'

She went over and picked up the doll. On its flaxen curls was a little wreath of daisies. They were real, the delicate petals tinged with pink. She carried the doll to the window and looked out. The garden was still inches deep in snow.

And then she understood. She glanced round and suddenly her hands were shaking. 'You live here, don't you,' she said out loud wonderingly. 'You're not one of the village children at all.'

She glanced down at the daisies in her hand and then gently twined them back in the doll's hair. Behind her the room was silent.

Below, in the lane, she saw a car drawing to a standstill. She frowned, wondering who it was and then she saw Mr Forbes, the house agent, climbing stiffly out. He stood for a moment gazing up at the house.

Carefully putting down the doll Tessa turned to go out and meet him.

She knew now why he hadn't mentioned the vicar's secret visitor to them before – and what he was going to tell her. She hoped he would know her name.

She wondered suddenly if Pete Sanders had kept the

315

edited bit of the film showing the face at the window. She hoped so. It might be the only chance she would ever have of seeing the dead child properly.

Someone to Dream About

How she came to fall from the horse she never really knew. She was galloping alone across the moors, her hair streaming out behind her, exhilarated by the huge, building masses of clouds on the horizon, feeling the electricity in the air, when suddenly she was conscious of a car travelling fast on the lonely moorland road some distance away from her. For a split second it distracted her attention – an intrusive, twentieth-century jar on her nerves as the sky was torn by the first wishbone of lightning – and in that second Moonlight swerved and, stumbling on a branch of wiry heather, threw Margot clear before falling heavily to the ground.

For a moment Margot lay stunned, feeling the first of the rain on her face, then, slowly, she began to climb to her feet, the exhilaration of the ride knocked out of her by the fall; her dream shattered.

Scotland had always brought out the dreamer in Margot. She would forget the image which was the Margot of London. Behind a desk as personal assistant to a high-powered financial director she was a competent woman, at ease with office technology, her hair bound sleekly to her head, her clothes businesslike, her shoes immaculate. There she was independent, seeking to taste everything the city had to offer: theatre, concerts, galleries, meals with carefully-selected men who shared her taste in food and wine – which often she would choose, not they. The men were purely decorative, to be kept at arm's length; her liberation total because she had allowed herself no possibility of involvement. That was how she saw it; commitment meant loss of freedom and to her, freedom was life itself.

At Inverglen she shed that image, as a snake sloughs its skin. There she found true freedom. She would put away the heels and the narrow skirts, let her hair loose and run wild. Then the thing she loved most, riding, became her obsession, every penny of her savings going to the hire of a horse for the whole of her holiday, while her London friends went skiing, or lounged on beaches in France and Portugal. And it was on the horse – a beautiful silver mare named Moonlight – that she would relive, secretly, all the fantasy lives of her childhood. She was Rob Roy, Flora Macdonald, Robin Hood, Boudicca, hero or heroine as the mood took her. Free. Alive.

If anyone had guessed about her secret life she would have died of shame. But there was no one to see her wild rides across the moors towards the high granite cliffs where the sea crashed onto rocks, slick with spray even in the gentlest weather. If her grandmother, Thea, guessed what went on in Margot's head, she never gave a sign.

It was a moment before Margot realized that the car had stopped a few hundred yards away and that a figure was loping over the heather towards her.

But he went straight to the struggling horse, his hands gentling the animal's fear, calming it as sweat poured off the satin coat, his strong, slender fingers feeling the animal's shoulder and on down the leg, not even glancing at her.

'Is her leg broken?' Margot heard her own voice, astonishingly calm, as she staggered towards the mare.

He looked up at her then, for a fraction of a second. His hair was plastered to his face, his jacket and shirt black with the now driving rain. The swift, dismissive glance told her that his eyes were violently blue and that they were blazing with anger.

'Small thanks to you if it isn't!' he snapped. 'Are you crazy or something? Riding at that speed over this ground – and in this light? Have you no common sense?'

'I'll ride my own horse on my own land how I damn well please,' she cried furiously. It was quite unlike her. She would never talk like that to anyone; it sounded absurd, arrogant and callous and she was none of those things. But for him now she would be all, and worse. 'What were you doing here, anyway?' she went on, her voice rising in the wind. 'That is a private road. If you hadn't been there and distracted me, it wouldn't have happened. She'd have been all right.'

Shock was beginning to hit her now. She could feel herself beginning to shake. Furiously she dug her hands deep into her pockets of her jacket. 'I'm sorry. I suppose I should thank you for stopping.' Her voice sounded ungracious and harsh.

'And walking on your land.' He was still bending down, his back to her, but there was no mistaking the mockery in his voice.

'That's right. On my land!' She suddenly wanted to cry. She ached all over from the fall, she was soaked through and very cold.

As if reading her thoughts he stood up abruptly and turned to face her. 'Are you all right?' he asked at last.

'Perfectly.' To her relief, her tone was remarkably steady.

'Good. Because this horse can't be ridden like this. You'll have to lead her.'

319

'I realize that.' She put her hand tentatively to the mare's muzzle.

He did not relinquish his hold. 'If this is your land –' was there a slight emphasis on the words? ' – you live presumably at Inverglen House. That's a couple of miles. You'll have to take it very slowly.'

'I'll manage.' She gritted her teeth and in spite of herself hesitated. It was the arrogance about him which made her hackles rise – but it was an arrogance which matched her own. Obviously and perhaps rightly, he despised her. That interested her.

'You still haven't told me what you were doing here,' she couldn't resist saying over her shoulder as she turned the mare.

'Correct,' he said. And for the first time he grinned.

'It sounds like Alan Macdonald,' Thea Locke said with a laugh when Margot told her grandmother about the incident. She was kneeling before the fire drying her long hair after the rain. 'I believe he's Canadian, in Scotland in search of his roots.' She smiled. 'A pleasant man, so I've heard.'

'A male chauvinist,' Margot muttered.

Thea suppressed a smile. 'Oh? What makes you say that?'

Margot hesitated, looking up through her hair. 'His manner.'

'And the fact that he is, I believe, good looking and, dare I say it, sexy?'

'Grandma!' Margot looked up with a grin.

'I may be old, but I have ears! And my memory's good.' The older woman smiled wryly. 'I am so sorry for you children today. So possessive of your feminist honour that when a knight in shining armour jumps up and down in

320

front of you, you turn your backs with a sniff. You need a man, my dear.'

'I do not.' Margot was furious.

'But romance?' Thea's voice was gentle. 'What do you do for romance?'

'I don't want romance! That is the point.'

As if conscious suddenly of the incongruity of her long, gleaming auburn hair, she swept it up on the top of her head and began stabbing at the untidy, still-damp knot with large hairpins. 'Is he on holiday here?' she went on, off-handedly.

Thea shrugged. 'Does it matter, dear?' she said.

A week later Margot was back in London and behind a desk, her eyes riveted to the screen of her word processor.

'How was Scotland?' Paula, her colleague, sat back in her chair with a sigh. 'I don't know how you can bear to come back here after all those acres.'

Margot grinned. 'One and a half acres, to be exact! The rest belongs to the National Trust for Scotland and other worthy bodies.'

On my land. Her own voice echoed in her head for a moment. What had possessed her to say it? He must have known. No wonder he had been so scornful. She punched at the keyboard indignantly. Why think of him? Who cares what he thought anyway? She certainly didn't.

He was waiting for her in reception. The soaked shirt was gone and he was wearing a tweed jacket. His hair, now that it was dry, was a sort of dark honey blond. But the eyes were the same. Piercing, direct, quizzical. And very blue.

'Miss Kinnaird?' He stood up as she pushed through the swing doors near him.

She froze.

'Perhaps you don't remember me?' He held out his hand. 'Alan Macdonald. We met in Scotland . . .'

'I remember where we met, Mr Macdonald.' She cut him short, trying to keep her voice coldly steady.

He lowered his hand, unruffled, taking in her smart skirt and jacket with a swift glance and then he reached into his pocket. 'I called on Mrs Locke last week, to find out how you were after the accident and when I told her I was coming to London, she asked me to give you this.' There was an envelope in his hand.

Margot looked down at it. 'I'm sorry you were put to so much trouble,' she murmured, suddenly at a disadvantage. 'I'm sure she could have posted it just as well.'

'She said not.' She could see the open amusement in his eyes. 'I don't know if you have any plans, Miss Kinnaird, but I was hoping you might let me take you to lunch.'

She could hardly refuse. If she did she would look ungrateful, even rude. 'You must let me pay for myself . . .'

'You can pay for me, too, if you like.' That was not what she had meant at all, but before she could draw breath he had stepped forward and, taking her hand, closed her fingers around the envelope. 'Come on. Take me somewhere nice and hugely expensive. I'm hungry.' Ostentatiously, he held the heavy glass door for her, then followed her into the street. She hadn't noticed the mischievous expression in his eyes.

The restaurant was packed and the tables smaller than Margot had remembered. She was intensely conscious of the proximity of his legs beneath the cloth.

'Did the horse recover?' he asked.

'She was fine, thank you,' Margot replied stiffly.

There was only the slightest trace of some transatlantic intonation in his voice, as he said to the waitress, 'The *entrecôte*, I think, with broccoli, beans and potatoes. And soup to start. The lady will have the same.'

322

Margot was silent for a full minute, trying to control her anger. By the time she was capable of speech the waitress had gone.

'I never eat steak,' she managed finally, with commendable restraint.

'It shows. With your colouring you should have glowing cheeks and shining eyes without dark circles round them.' With a raised hand he traced a line above her cheekbone, not quite touching her face. 'You are what our Scots compatriots call peelie-wally. Good hot soup and a steak is what you need. Why do you work in London?'

His directness was unnerving. 'Because my job is here.'

'Your family is in Scotland?'

'My grandmother is in Scotland.' She could feel all her muscles tighten warningly. The conversation was getting too personal, to the point where she usually began to withdraw; to raise the barriers. 'I go to see her as often as possible.'

'Which isn't often enough. She is very lonely.'

'How could you possibly think that?' She stared at him, genuinely astonished.

'Because she told me. I suspect that note of hers,' he looked pointedly at her bag lying on the table, where the envelope lurked, still unread, 'was an excuse to have me speak to you. And I think she wanted me to tell you that. I could think of no way of saying it covertly. I don't know you well enough yet. And I was never very subtle.' He grinned.

You can say that again, Margot thought. With a hard look at him she extricated the letter and tore it open: 'Forget all that feminist nonsense and hang on to this one. He's perfect.'

Her grandmother had written it in bold black letters across the page.

Blushing furiously Margot glanced up. He could easily have read it from where he sat.

'I think you are mistaken, Mr Macdonald,' she said coldly, when at last she had recovered her composure. 'My grandmother could not possibly be lonely.'

He looked at her for rather longer than necessary. 'And you?' he said. 'Are *you* lonely?'

'Of course not. I have London.'

She wasn't sure how he had managed to get hold of the theatre tickets. The play had been sold out for months. That was the only reason she went, of course.

It was in the rustling auditorium, expectant and hushed with excitement before curtain up, that she remembered to ask him the question that had been bothering her. She turned to him as the lights dimmed. 'Were you on holiday in Scotland?'

He closed his programme slowly, his eyes on the heavy red curtain with its swags of gold. 'Not a holiday,' he said slowly. 'I've taken over as manager for the trustees of the Inverglen estates.'

My land.

As the house lights went down she put her face in her hands.

'Perhaps we can go for a ride together next time you come up north,' he said quietly in the darkness. 'I know somewhere I can hire a horse, too.'

It was nearly a year before she went to Inverglen again. And Moonlight had been sold.

Miserably she went for a walk, hands deep in the pockets of her jeans, down the lane, over the burn and on to the moor where it led towards the cliffs. A westerly gale was bringing the long, white-tipped breakers rolling into the bay where they crashed onto the rocks. White horses, she thought sadly as she turned away.

Alan Macdonald had gone, too. Thea had told her that before she had even unpacked her case the night before. To a desk job in Glasgow. She felt oddly bereft. Part of her had, she secretly admitted, been counting the days until she saw him, until they could go riding together over the moor. Purely for the company of another rider, of course . . .

But the dream had gone with the horse, and these were no longer her woods, her moors, her cliffs. She was just another Londoner now, on holiday, on foot and lonely.

She spent the days walking, feeling the heavy Highland sun baking her pale limbs brown, fighting off the vicious horseflies which lurked on the moors, staring down from the cliffs and walking on the rocks at the sea's edge.

Then she found his number. It was written in large figures on a card beside the phone, with the Glasgow code beside it. It hadn't been there the day before. Slowly, she dialled.

'I just wondered how you were,' she said.

'Fine.' There was a pause. He wasn't going to make it easy.

'How do you like Glasgow?' She was furious with herself now for having rung.

'Very much.' There was another silence. Then he relented. 'You are up until the end of the month, I hear.'

'That's right.' So Thea had told him she was coming.

'Good. The course will be over long before that.'

'The course?' she echoed.

'Didn't Mrs Locke explain? I've been on a month's course here.'

'No. She didn't explain.'

'Ah.' She could hear the smile. 'I'll ring you as soon as I get back and we'll go for that ride.'

She had no heart to tell him Moonlight had gone.

But when he arrived it was on horseback, a second animal beside him. They were both bays. She met him at the door. 'So you know.' Miserably, she stroked the horses' soft noses.

'About Moonlight? I'm sorry.' He leaned down and handed her the spare rein.

Her horse was smaller, naturally.

He rode well and fast, but for the first time even on horseback she found she was her London self still; prickly, inhibited, resenting him. Resenting the fact that he had arranged everything without consulting her; taken the bigger horse; led the way.

When he reined in at last near a clump of larch and turned to wait for her, she found she was seething.

'Sorry. Did I go too fast?' He slapped his horse's neck gently. She could see the amusement in his eyes as he provoked her and suddenly she was laughing, too.

'You should know. You chose the faster horse.'

'And the bigger?' It was as if he could read her mind. 'I was always brought up to believe the lady rode the more delicate, the more beautiful, animal.' He raised an arm quickly as if to ward off her blows, mocking.

They both looked at the sturdy cob she was riding and laughed again.

'I *am* taller,' he went on conciliatorily. 'You have to concede that, Ms Kinnaird.'

'This animal could take ten times your weight.'

'Do you want to swap, then?' Already he was dismounting.

Suddenly, she didn't want to any more. She didn't want him to mock her. She wanted him to like her and she didn't want to see him on the ungainly cob.

He had tethered his horse to a tree and now he came to stand at the cob's head. 'Come on, get down.' His eyes were on hers, challenging. No longer amused.

Behind them she could hear the crash of waves at the foot of the high cliffs. The wind tore at her hair and the two horses had begun to fidget restlessly, mouthing their bits. The humour and banter had gone. Now there was real tension between them.

She didn't know what to do. If she obeyed her instinct and rode away from him she would look childish and spoiled. If she obeyed him and meekly changed horses, it would be not the victory she had intended, but some kind of defeat.

She met his gaze as squarely as she could and knew he was reading her thoughts, enjoying her dilemma. His expression spurred her into action. She slid quickly from the saddle, then, leaving him standing there, she took the path down towards the rocks where the sapphire water creamed in from the west, casting clouds of spray against the wind. She knew he was following her, but she didn't stop. Suddenly she was afraid of what would happen if she did.

But she had to. The narrow cove was beneath the tide, and at the edge of the rocky path she could go no further. Slowly, she turned. He was standing several feet from her.

'OK, point taken.'

'What do you mean?' The spray was cold on the back of her shirt.

'The choice of horses is yours.' He gestured back up the path.

'It doesn't matter. It doesn't make any difference.'

'Oh, but it does. It makes a lot of difference to you.' He took a step towards her. 'Just what exactly is bugging you, lady? Why the need for all this independence?' He was very close to her now. 'What are you trying to prove?'

Suddenly, his hands were on her shoulders and he was pulling her against him. Instinctively, her arms went round his waist. She could feel the warmth of his body beneath the plaid shirt, the hard muscles of his back as she looked up into his eyes. She was paralysed by the conflict of emotions which seized her. Longing, fear, desire – and panic.

More than anything, for a moment, she wanted him to kiss her – then it was over. Her fear and resentment returned and, pushing him away, she stumbled past him over the rocks and began to run back to the horses. This time he didn't follow her. He stayed staring out at the sea.

The office manager approached Margot's desk a week later. 'Miss Kinnaird? There is a visitor for you. I've put him in the conference room.' She was obviously impressed.

He was sitting in one of the leather-upholstered chairs, staring out of the high window at the distant dome of St Paul's. Rising as Margot appeared, he inclined his head slightly.

'I am here in my accustomed role of courier.'

'Courier?' she stared at him. Her heart had begun to beat faster.

'Your grandmother asked me to bring something for her.' He lifted his case onto the large oval table and opened it.

Margot swallowed. 'I'm sorry. It's unfair of her to bother you . . .'

'Not at all.' He smiled at last, his eyes brilliant in the tanned face, as he handed her a large envelope. 'I wonder if the advice is still the same as in her last note.'

She could feel her cheeks going scarlet as she looked up at him. 'My grandmother has a very strange sense of humour,' she said stiffly.

'She is also a very shrewd lady,' he retorted.

Margot snatched the letter from him and turned away towards the window. Tearing open the envelope she drew out a single sheet. Once again, the large, black felt-tip letters confronted her.

This is your last chance.

In spite of herself, Margot smiled. Shrugging, she held it out to him. 'As you obviously read the last one, you'd better see this.'

He scrutinized it solemnly.

'What do you think I ought to do?' she asked after a moment.

'Why don't you ask me out to lunch again, then we can discuss it.' He grinned.

'I can't afford to take you out to lunch again,' she said sharply. 'Not the way you eat.'

He laughed out loud. 'Then may I take you? It's quite fair that way. One round all.'

'Now you're making fun of me.' Strangely, she didn't mind.

'What on earth makes you think that?' he answered.

She was out of her depth. Disorientated. He was not a London man, he was part of Scotland, part of her fantasy world. But this – the briefcase, the dark suit, the assured way he ushered her into the expensive restaurant and commanded a prominent table – none of it fitted. Nor did the meek way she found herself deferring to his opinion as he ordered the wine – he did, she noted, know about wine.

'So.' Settling back into the chair he looked at her at last. 'What are you going to do about me?' She thought there was a smile behind his eyes.

'Is there anything I *should* do?' She managed an ascerbic tone.

'Oh yes. A great deal. You must try and relax. Enjoy my

company.' He grinned. 'I'm quite safe, you know. House-trained. Good with animals. Some people even like me.'

She found herself smiling. 'I'm sure they do.'

'And I'm very persistent.' His eyes were fixed on her face. 'Will you come riding with me again?'

The sudden swing of subject nearly threw her. 'If I do, do I get the choice of horses?'

'You can ride a bicycle if you wish. I don't care.'

She looked down. 'I did quite like the old cob.'

He grinned. 'I suppose we could draw up a rota,' he said, half-serious. 'Then we'd know where we stood.' His hand was on the table, very close to hers.

On the defence at once, Margot glared at him. 'I hate it when you patronize me!' she cried and he let out an infuriated groan.

'I am *not* patronizing you! For God's sake, stop being so prickly, I am trying to accommodate your every whim.' His hand hadn't moved. She stared at it.

'Are you?' she whispered.

He leaned forward. 'I know how important your dreams are to you,' he said gently.

She stiffened. 'Dreams are stupid!'

'No!' His eyes were on her face. 'Dreams are important. I don't want you to lose them. They are part of you. But only part. Reality must count as well. Even if it means compromise.'

'Compromise?' She looked up.

He laughed then. 'Not a word you tolerate with ease, I know. But it's one you must learn to use. I'm real, Margot. But I want to be part of your dream as well, if you will let me. You must find a way to make the two worlds come together. You must if you want to be happy. But only you can make it work.'

'But I don't know how.'

'Yes you do,' he said firmly. 'But if you get it wrong

330

now and again, I shall be there to help you, if you want me.' Gently, he put his hand over hers. 'It's up to you. You must decide.'

For a moment she didn't move – tensely waiting for the usual emotions to swirl round her, building the barriers which would keep her safe from the world. But nothing happened. To her surprise she found she was smiling.

Without a word, she returned the pressure of his fingers.

'We'd better draw up that rota,' she said at last.

A Fair Revenge

The *Lady Bird* swung easily to her moorings. I knew he wasn't there, for no dinghy bobbed behind her and all was quiet. Gently I rowed closer and tied my painter to the rail. It was Friday but still early. Practically no one was about on the estuary. I doubt if anyone saw me climb aboard.

The cabin door was padlocked. That was new. In the old days he never used to bother. I hadn't wanted to do any damage – not to the boat – but there was nothing for it if I wanted to get in. I found a screwdriver and levered off the lock with a horrible splintering noise which echoed across the placid evening water.

The cabin was untidy. That too was different. 'Leave her shipshape, Zoë,' always used to be his final comment every time we left.

There were signs of this new moll of his everywhere. Clothes; make-up; cheap novelettes; a tin of scented talcum powder standing on the chart table. Poor, poor Alec. What I was about to do was undoubtedly for his own good!

It took me about ten minutes to make a really good job of it. Every darn thing went into that canvas sail bag of mine. Bikinis – three of them, would you believe; shorts – the skimpy kind Alec always said showed just what a girl was bad for; sun tan oil – Alec never bothered with that; talc; books; everything I could be sure wasn't his. Carefully

I tied the neck of the bag and stood back to survey my handiwork.

The boat was a little tidier, but not tidy enough. Shipshape Alec used to like her. Shipshape I would leave her, just to show him what he was missing!

That took me a lot longer. The tiny galley was filthy and some of the pretty coffee mugs I had chosen as a present for the boat were chipped. 'Silly cow,' I muttered. 'Can't she do anything properly?' What the hell did he see in her anyway?

It was just as well I had found out what he was up to. If I hadn't seen him with Patricia a couple of times and someone hadn't told me he was bringing her down here for weekends I might never have suspected. I might have gone on believing his story that he had sold the boat and was studying in every second of free time.

With a cautious look round from the cockpit I lowered the bag into my dinghy and climbed in after it. I had half a mind to chuck the bag overboard, but thought better of it. For a start it might float. I tied up to the jetty and humped the bag up onto it. Where could I hide it then? I glanced around. The boat house? The churchyard? The bushes round the pub?

'Hello, Zoë!'

I leaped round and saw Alec watching me from behind a pile of timber.

'Hi.' I could feel my face colouring.

'I didn't know you still came down here,' he said. I could see him looking at me closely, puzzled. He knew damn well I had never been without him before.

'I like to keep an eye on the old place from time to time,' I murmured. 'I miss it.'

To do him justice he did look a little bit taken aback at that.

'Where's the lady friend?' I went on sweetly. 'I hear you have a new crew for the *Lady Bird*.'

He glowered. 'I told you, Zoë. I sold that boat months ago.'

'Oh yes,' I said, 'of course.' The sail bag was resting solidly against my legs. I shaded my eyes in the evening sun and looked across towards the moorings. I could see the boat clearly.

'Can I buy you a drink?' he asked casually, obviously trying to distract me.

'Why not?' I grinned, humping the bag up onto my shoulder. 'Can I dump this junk first? It's going behind the tomb in the crypt. A friend of mine is going to collect it – sometime.'

He raised an eyebrow. 'Strange place to leave it?'

I nodded gravely. 'I'm not sure when she'll be down again. No one will find it there.'

He waited in the church as I felt my way down the worn steps and stuffed the bag down into the dark corner behind the cold stone tomb of the duke of somewhere or other. Then we went to the pub. I felt enormously happy and not the least bit guilty.

We had a super evening. The drink became several, followed by dinner at the bar.

'Well, Alec,' I said at last. 'You haven't told me why you've come down here if you've no boat.'

He glanced at me sideways. 'I didn't say I had no boat, Zoë,' he said, chuckling. 'I said I'd sold the *Lady Bird*. I bought another – a Folk Boat this time. Do you want to see her?'

I went cold. 'You really sold the *Lady Bird*?'

'Yes. I told you.'

'And she's not yours any more?'

'What's the matter with you, Zoë? I sold her to some people called Gill and Harry. In fact they're over there.'

He waved across the bar and a man and woman came over. She was tall and slim and attractive and now, did she but know it, without a stitch of clothing to her name.

'Are you going out to *Lady Bird* later?' I asked casually as a new round of drinks arrived.

Gill nodded.

'Oh God,' I said.

Alec looked at me. 'Are you OK?' he asked.

I smiled. 'Too much to drink,' I said and I ran for the door.

He caught me up in the churchyard. I wasn't being sick. I was trying to break into the church.

In the end I had to confess. He laughed and kissed me. 'Pat never liked it here; and I haven't seen her for weeks,' he lied, but nicely. 'You know, Zoë, I was missing you. I'm glad you thought I was worth fighting for.'

He helped me hump the bag back to the quay. The tide had dropped and he had to kneel to reach their dinghy. As he was lowering the heavy bag the rope that held it must have slipped. It fell gently into the dark water, floated for a second and then disappeared.

Harry must have been close behind us and he must have wondered what we were up to as we struggled, horrified, to our feet, but he just grinned. 'We're off now,' he said, helping Gill into the dinghy. Then he piled their luggage in around her. They seemed to have rather a lot.

Alec and I stood speechless, watching. Then as Harry reached for the oars Gill turned and smiled at Alec.

'By the way,' she called, 'that charming friend of yours, Patricia, has been here all week waiting for you. She couldn't get into your boat, so we said she could stay in *Lady Bird* as we weren't there. I hope she's left it tidy,' and she raised her hand as they rowed away.

Milestones

It was a stupid place to meet. Why had they chosen it? The enormous soft sofa so discreetly placed beneath walls hung with dark damasks was too deep for her; she knew it before she sat down. Either she would have to perch on the edge, nervily uncomfortable, or she would have to sit so far back that her legs would stick out in front like a child's. She stifled a nervous giggle and glanced around. On the far side of the hotel lounge, acres of ankle deep pile away, another woman had solved the problem by reclining elegantly sideways. In her hand she held a martini, her glossy fingernails displayed talon-like round the glass.

With a slight shock Elizabeth realized the waiter was now standing, obsequiously patient, in front of her, the white napkin as stiff on his arm as his paper shirt front. His face was carefully bland, though she was sure he had noticed her suppressed hilarity. She was going to order, automatically, a pot of tea. Then she checked herself.

'Champagne cocktail,' she commanded and defiantly she sat down, drew up her legs and crossed her ankles on the cushions.

'Very well, madam.' He bowed and amazingly he disappeared registering neither amazement nor disapproval. Perhaps respectable middle aged females put their feet up on his sofas at teatime every day and ordered champagne.

Then she saw him. He was standing on the far side of the room. Only just in time she prevented herself from jumping to her feet. She pretended not to notice him, reaching for a copy of *Vogue* from the glass-topped table in front of her, opening it nonchalantly, glancing at the glossy improbable women who prowled across its pages.

The waiter arrived with her drink and she brought it behind the magazine with her. Why wasn't he coming over? Had he changed his mind? Could it be that he didn't recognize her? Covertly she glanced round a double page spread of exotically languorous net clad legs and watched him.

He was undoubtedly the handsomest man she had ever seen. Tall, tanned; middle-aged undeniably, but without an ounce of surplus weight on his frame; green eyed, fair haired – not enough white yet to touch the gold – with the bearing of a soldier as he stood there, his hands clasped behind him, scanning the room. Unbelievably he hadn't seen her. She saw his gaze flicker over the martini drinker, halt and return taking in, Elizabeth saw, those bloody talons and also undoubtedly the plunging breast-line of her dress. After a moment the woman was dismissed and his gaze began methodically to travel once again. Slowly it was coming towards her.

With an unexpected, almost fearful tremor of excitement somewhere just below her diaphragm Elizabeth slowly lowered her magazine and waited.

She had been a girl of seventeen, small, slim, a little too leggy perhaps to be pretty but with a mass of untameable auburn hair which carried only reluctantly and for the shortest time her studied attempts at the styles of the latest film stars, and she had been brown, brown from the sun and wiry with the farm work at which she was as good any day as the two land girls she worked beside; better, grandfather often said. And sometimes she had been glad to get away from the girls and from her grandparents and from the farm, up to the north woods on her own, watching the sunlight dapple through the leaves onto the soft beech mast and there she would retreat into a world which school had so recently opened to her and which the sudden irrevocable necessity of leaving had so abruptly closed. Sometimes it was Wordsworth or Byron, but most often it was Keats she had carried in the pocket of her dungarees, the flimsy edition in the cardboard leather covers which she had sneaked from the bookcase in the cold locked dining room. She would sit, leaning against the five hundred-year-old oak by Hereward's Pond, and recite the lines to herself slowly, fixing them in her mind. Sometimes the words had come aloud and the trees had mocked her embarrassment and dared her to repeat them more loudly still until in the end she had done so, proud of her gentle expressive voice in the echo of the deserted forests all around her.

He had been sitting on the other side of the water, his khaki uniform a perfect camouflage in the duns and shadows of the clearing and she would never have known he was there.

I cannot see what flowers are at my feet
Nor what soft incense hangs upon the boughs . . .

she had intoned slowly to the trees, her eyes filling with tears as she felt the beauty of the words and quietly, across the pond another voice had taken up the verse:

White hawthorn and the pastoral eglantine
Fast fading violets covered up in leaves . . .
And the coming musk rose full of dewy wine . . .

She sat up, scarlet-faced and saw a young man climb reluctantly from the shelter of the trees, brushing the dried leaves from his uniform. He walked towards her round the pond, stopping only when they were close enough to see one another's faces.

'We learned that one at school; I think I got it right,' he had said, and then, awkwardly, 'sorry, I shouldn't have intruded.'

She blinked away her tears and smiled. 'It doesn't matter.'

'It does. You were crying.' Closer now, she saw how young he was. Not much older than she, but still old enough to be in and to have lieutenant's pips on his arm. And because he was there and because he had caught her crying, she had told him everything. How her father had died at Comines just before Dunkirk and how her mother was a VAD in London and how she ached sometimes with the unhappiness and the unbearable beauty of life, and he had understood. And he had walked her slowly back to the farm at last as the time for milking drew near and by then she was laughing. At the gate she turned and looked up at his face. 'You didn't tell me your name,' she said quietly.

'Hugh,' he said. Touching her hand lightly with his own, there on the top of the sun-warmed five barred gate, he winked and turned away.

She watched him until he was out of sight in the lane and then she walked slowly to the farmhouse door.

She went on going to Hereward's Pond but she never saw him there again and slowly hope of doing so died. Perhaps he had been a dryad of the woods himself, conjured out of her imagination. Then, one day walking round the market, her grandmother's basket on her arm, she heard her name called and it was he. His face now was more tanned than ever hers had been and his blond hair was bleached almost white. His grin was the same though, warm and infectious.

She did not ask him where he had been or how long a leave he had this time. She lived for the moment, savouring his company. Ten days later he was gone again.

Everyone assumed they would marry. She assumed it herself, clinging in his arms below the stars, feeling the warmth of his skin through his shirt. She did not know why he did not ask her and it was not a subject she could raise herself. Nor did she let her grandfather or grandmother mention the matter on the rare occasions he sat down at their long table under the blackened farmhouse beams.

The last time she saw him was on a beautiful autumn evening in 1943 when he gave her, for no reason that she understood then, a bracelet, a gold charm bracelet, clipping the links around her wrist himself, raising her hand and kissing her palm and then for a moment holding her hand tightly in his. Only when he had gone did she have the chance to examine the charms. There were four: a silver threepenny bit, set in gold; a St Christopher; a tiny cat and a fish made from little links so that it lay, limply realistic, across her finger, its scales glinting like frost-touched leaves in the sunlight. When she looked up again her eyes were full of tears.

Two years later she married and moved away from the farm. Her husband was an architect and when he joined a partnership in London they moved to Holland Park.

In her heart she had never believed that Hugh was dead and yet she knew that had he lived he would have come back to her; two years was a long time to wait to a girl who had been barely nineteen when they had kissed goodbye that last lingering time; a lifetime to wait and a lifetime to mourn.

Gareth was a strange choice; a prickly difficult man who felt the world against him and the war a personal affront to his plans. But he loved her and she, receptive, lonely and romantic, saw him as some sort of crippled god who with her care and adoration would rise again to Olympian heights. Holland Park was the first step on that ladder.

Fourteen months after the marriage Michael was born and Gareth brought her a tiny golden cherub to go on her bracelet. She had, after they were married, told him a little about Hugh, partly because she needed still to say his name out loud to ease the pain of his going, partly because there had been so little there to make Gareth jealous; just a romantic dream and a bracelet with all the links, but four, empty. It touched her that Gareth was sensitive enough never to try to buy charms for the bracelet in his own name, only in those of her children who were part of herself and through her of Hugh.

Michael was followed a year later by the twins Margaret and Alexandra and two years after that by Colin; Colin, the only one to take after Gareth in every way – a haunted, unhappy child, sensitive to every nuance of life, suspecting always its worst conspiracy against him, clinging to his mother, jealous of his brother, resentful of his sisters but not, as his father was, clever enough to temper his torments with the fulfilment of a creative drive.

And yet strangely Elizabeth saw in him the reflection of herself and recalled through him, after years of forgetfulness, the agonies and beauties of growing up to feel in the very core of one's being the anguish of the world's pain.

She had never been unhappy with Gareth. Perplexed, often; numbed a little more each day by the repeated need to extinguish herself in the need to tend constantly the fire of his demands; tired, frustrated; but she had learned too, not because she wanted it that way, but because that was the way it happened, to live vicariously through her children.

Their careers were predictable. Michael did well at school and went on to university, a stable, handsome, charming boy. The girls both went horse mad and Mags, who cared little for learning, left school early and became a lad at a racing stable, while Sandy, who though not as clever as her brother was something of a plodder, vowed at the age of five to become a vet and twenty years later was in her final year at veterinary college, having looked neither to the right nor to the left of her chosen career.

Colin had followed his father and elder brother to Harrow. Two years later he ran away. Two more schools followed in quick succession. From the first he fled; from the second he was expelled for smoking cannabis and it was then that Gareth, taut, neurotic, consuming forty cigarettes a day, announced that his patience was at last at an end and withdrew all financial support.

Colin, and through him Elizabeth, reeled under the blow, unable to understand either his crime or the withdrawal, as he saw it, of love, and Elizabeth was powerless to help him. She had no money of her own to give. Her intercessionary powers with Gareth had grown fewer as his inner tensions had increased and the other three children closed ranks as siblings do against the outcast, sensing in him perhaps the cuckoo who given any chance at all would a long time ago have humped each of them over the rim of the nest.

And so he had drifted away. Elizabeth saw him sometimes and he rang her from time to time when he knew she would be alone – which was often now. Once or twice she dreamed about him; hard, unpleasant dreams which frightened her and left her in the morning with a splitting headache and a sense of doom not-quite-perceived around the corner of her consciousness, but there was no way of checking that he was all right and slowly she would forget the dream. Even when she had neither seen nor heard of him for several weeks, long schooled to silent waiting by his scorn when quite young when she had rung, worried, around his friends, she would resist now the urge to flap. They would, Gareth callously assured her, hear soon enough if anything happened to the boy. Colin was not one to submerge himself in anonymity should extremis come upon him. Elizabeth's worries about drugs she kept to herself. She knew Gareth's views and she had no wish to hear them attached to their son.

Time passed. Slowly the other children grew away. Sandy qualified and went to join a practice in Herefordshire, Michael married and Mags moved slowly from stud farm to stud farm around Newmarket, coming home once every month or so with enough dirty washing to fill her mother's washing machine four times over and Elizabeth resigned herself to becoming an observer viewing life, or so it seemed to her, through a sterile bubble through which once in a while she was allowed to push her hands. Gareth smiled at her now and then and swore when she forgot to get his new bottle of Maalox and resigned from several of his committees and became, much against his will, something of a TV pundit, discoursing on the architecture of modern Europe and flying off to Paris and Bonn.

And Colin it appeared still read the papers, for scarcely had his father's jet climbed out of the cloud-hazed spirals above Heathrow bound for a much heralded conference in Vienna, than he was tiptoeing across the lawn of the house, their third, still in Holland Park, and knocking urgently at the french windows.

Elizabeth let him in, guiltily glad to see him, hugging him to her for a moment as though she could give him by transfusion of will power alone a little of her strength.

Colin returned the hug and each for a moment was struck by the other's thinness.

'Hi, Liz, how are you?'

'Better for seeing you, Col.' She forced herself to release his hand, to walk away from him, wondering at this urge to cradle him which, even though he was a man, her youngest son stirred within her. Instead of looking at him she stared down at the Afghan rug, rippled a little by their feet, its lineny fringe tangled and flaccid, its colours warm only where the watery sun slanting through the front window touched it. She longed to pour herself a gin. 'Where've you been lately?' She tried to sound casual.

He had thrown himself down on the leather Chesterfield, all knees and elbows, and glancing cautiously at him she saw his shirt had lost a button and there was a dull shine of grease around the inside of his collar.

'Here and there.' He grinned wearily and sat forward, his fists locked, swinging down between his shins above the carpet. 'I need some bread, Liz.'

She sighed, hearing Gareth's voice echoing in her head: 'Not another penny until you get a fucking job,' and knowing she would not refuse walked, an automaton, programmed by mother love, to where her handbag lay on an armchair. She knew there was about forty or so pounds in it and she knew she would give him everything, even the loose change in her purse.

She knew he would be grateful; would return warmth for warmth and stay with her perhaps for a while. If she could get him to eat a few square meals while his father was away, that too would comfort her. She smiled down at him as he looked at the wad of notes in his hand, counting them between finger and thumb like a teller at the bank. Then he tucked them away into the top pocket of his shirt and buttoned the flap. His eyes, so like Gareth's were a brilliant cornflower blue. 'I need a hell of a lot more than that, Liz.' There was no smile on his face, only the hard, weary lines of a man twice as old as he.

Drugs? Gambling? Crime? The possibilities flashed through her mind as she faced him, not believing the hard shine of the eyes, the new cynical twist to his lips as he waited.

'Oh come on, Liz, don't tell me you haven't been salting away the housekeeping all these years. You must have thousands stashed somewhere.'

He didn't believe her. He didn't believe she had no private account, no hoard waiting to be spent gluttonously alone when his father was gone or divorced or dead, and there was no warm sympathy when, worn out at last by his browbeating she broke down and sobbed, only a calculating silence as he stared at her, knowing he must believe her.

But still he had not relinquished hope. He cast around the room, eyeing porcelain, the carriage clock on the mantelpiece, the rug itself and rejecting them in the knowledge that his father would miss them instantly.

'Your jewellery! There must be some jewellery you could sell.'

'No Colin, no . . .' Her voice came from a thousand miles outside her head, distanced by fear and disbelief. But already he was bounding up the long curving flight of stairs, his hand skimming the banister, and bursting into the bedroom.

Her jewel box lay on her dressing table, unhidden in spite of Gareth's oft repeated warnings about burglars, each piece inside warm from her skin, loved. She had never accepted much from him in the way of gifts but with each piece there was a memory, or an agony of its own.

With an exclamation of triumph Colin took the box and emptied it on to the bed. Pearls, lockets, rings, lay tangled on the sprigged pale duvet, and among them Hugh's charm bracelet.

Never, in all her twenty-five years as a mother had Elizabeth struck one of her children, but now as she saw those thin pale hands picking avariciously over the milestones of her life something inside her seemed to snap. In a quick sweep of her hands she had gathered up the things and thrown them, all jumbled, into her pocket and she faced Colin her eyes blazing. The slap she dealt him across the face sent him reeling backwards, the imprint of her fingers first white and then red across his cheek and mouth.

'Your father was right about you all along,' she shrieked at him, her voice dumb, the sound coming from her mouth belonging to a stranger. 'You are ungrateful; you are a scrounger; you're no good. No good at all. Get out! Get out! Get out of this house before I call the police!'

And he had gone. Later, when the tears had stopped, she realized how nearly he had hit her back. The cold fury on his face had been almost insane as he looked at her, but he had said and done nothing and with that sole scrap she would comfort herself in the months and years to come. He had done nothing. One deep shuddering breath and he had turned and walked from the room, leaving the house by the front door which reverberated defiantly behind him from the slam.

On 28th March Colin was arrested and taken to Marylebone Police Station charged with conspiracy to defraud and Gareth put up bail for his son. Three weeks later as he chaired a meeting at the RIBA Gareth had collapsed with a massive stroke. Forty-eight hours later he was dead.

Elizabeth saw the next few months through a pale veil of valium, surrounded, as Colin was convicted and sent to prison for five years, by a warm protective trio of children who treated her like rare Dresden, sharing her out between them in a layer of impenetrable cotton wool. Once or twice she tried to fight her way to the surface, sensing sunlight through the mist which swam above her head, but each time she sank again, drowning in depression.

She stayed with Michael the most. He had married and had a little boy and when all else failed to reach her she warmed to those tiny clinging trusting hands. It was in this house, at the long untidy happy dining table where breakfast lay in a shower of toast crumbs and splattered groats, that she had nerved herself to reach for the *Telegraph*, wearily unfolding it to face a further instalment of the enquiry into Colin's money-making débâcle, and seen a photograph of Hugh.

Stunned she stared at it. The hair, the eyes, the mouth – each had been sculpted and hardened and worn, but it was the same face. She glanced up guiltily at her daughter-in-law who was spooning scrambled egg into Crispin's mouth.

'If you'll excuse me, Ann dear, I'll take my coffee and the paper out on the porch for a while.'

She was quite unconscious of Ann's stare; of the excitement which had been betrayed by her voice, of the fact that her movements, which for months had been slow and dreamlike, were suddenly electric with trembling.

On the straw chair on the porch she arranged her skirt with care and, turning to the side table, poured the slopped coffee back from the saucer into the cup. Then, cautiously, she looked again.

The photograph stared out at her from the page, the eyes direct and challenging. Her heart thumped a little with fear and she lowered her gaze to the caption.

'*Major General Sir Hugh Denniston*,' it said, and below it: '*Army Representative to join Whitehall Committee*.'

Strange, that in all these years she had never known his full name, never known he was a war hero, a holder of the VC, that he had been repeatedly parachuted into

France, had been captured, had, dear God, been tortured by the SS, was married, divorced, the father of two children, had headed this committee, that committee, been in Kenya, in Northern Ireland, in Rhodesia . . .

A gentle hand on hers made her realize suddenly that she was crying.

'Liz? Liz, darling. What is it?' Ann was kneeling at her feet.

Those tears, floodgates of misery and happiness, had released the straitjacket which had held her for so long and, sitting there on the porch with the sunlight slanting through the dew-wet plane trees, her arms around her daughter-in-law and her warm sticky grandchild, she relived those moments by the pond in Hereward's Wood and looking up at the clear autumnal morning sky saw again the defiant crippled squadrons limping home, and progressing, knew that Gareth was dead and Colin was in prison.

It was Ann who rang him. His number had all the time been in the telephone directory.

She had waited until Elizabeth, newly alive, had gone to the hairdresser and then, her heart quaking a little lest the baby wake up and cry or the milkman call or Liz change her mind and return, Ann had picked up the receiver in her bedroom and begun to dial.

The phone was answered by a woman. Disappointed, Ann hesitated, then she asked for Hugh and he came to the phone. The woman was his daughter.

Somehow she had expected to be speaking to a dreamer and the incisive voice unnerved her. She began to feel a little foolish. Perhaps Liz had been right after all to dismiss laughing the notion of contacting him. Perhaps it was all much too late.

Floundering, the receiver slipping as her palm grew moist with embarrassment, she began her story. She began at the wrong end, with Gareth's death, when all the time she had planned to say 'Do you remember Hereward's Pond and a girl with red hair?', and the polite silence in the receiver rebuked her.

But he did remember. When at last she managed to say the right words the quality of his silence changed. She felt his stillness.

'Elizabeth?' The word sounded stiff and painful from his lips when at last she stopped gabbling and waited for a reply. That was all he said, 'Elizabeth.'

'Would you . . . that is, do you think you and she should meet?' she asked tentatively after yet another silence.

'Does she want to?' he asked, and she could sense the piercing interrogation of his eyes on the other end of the telephone line.

'She doesn't know I've rung you,' she confessed.

'She didn't want to ring herself, of course.'

'No, she didn't want to ring herself.'

It was Ann who suggested the hotel – the public place, the neutral ground – and who wrote the date in her own diary and then for three days was too appalled at her own temerity to confess to Liz just what she had done. And as she told her she knew at once she had been wrong. If Hugh and Liz should meet again, it should have been at the behest of fate in the cool secret thickets around Hereward's Pond, or perhaps it should never happen at all, allowing each to remember a young golden image of the other and a dream to treasure in their heart.

'I won't go,' she thought as she sat alone on the autumnal golden terrace at the back of Michael's house. I'll be ill. Or go away. I'll go abroad.

She had stood before the mirror inside her wardrobe door for a long long time, staring hyper-critically at herself: the hair still auburn but a glossy darker colour now than it had ever been naturally; the figure neat, slim, good legs – legs are always the last part of a woman to 'go' Gareth always used to say, and she had gone around for weeks studying the thin elastic-controlled limbs of old ladies. Her eyes were still clear and needed glasses only for reading and television and her skin was good, pale now and no longer tanned. It was inside that she had not changed. Inside she was still that dreamy, vulnerable girl of seventeen, but would he know it? Would he recognize her at all?

Hugh's picture was folded inside the lid of her dressing case and she took it out again and looked at it. They seemed to have worn well, he and she, but how much had they changed, really?

The *Vogue* lying open on her knee, she watched him approach her across the room. He had shown no visible sign of recognizing her but unerringly now he was threading his way towards her through the chairs and tables. And then at last he was standing before her.

'I thought you might not recognize me,' she said at last, looking up to meet his eyes.

'Why not?'

She shrugged. 'I must have changed. I feel different sometimes.'

'Better or worse?'

'Some of each. Won't you have a drink? I don't like drinking alone.'

He smiled, sitting down on the edge of the chair opposite hers, in the same movement beckoning the waiter and in some mysterious way conveying his order without even speaking.

'I tried to find you, you know,' he said. 'But your grand-parents had gone. No one seemed to know anything about you.' He gave one small shrug which to her betrayed more eloquently than the most poignant speech the agonized months he had spent searching for her when at last he had returned to England after the war. He gave a sheepish grin. 'This is one hell of a place to meet. I take it you don't normally frequent West End hotels.' He pronounced the word without an 'h'.

'It was Ann's idea, remember?'

'You get on well with your daughter-in-law?'

'Very. She's been very kind. Did she tell you my son, my other son, is in prison?' She had to say it quickly, to get it over with, to stop Colin's shadow hovering between them.

He leaned back slightly, reaching into his jacket pocket for a silver cigarette case.

'What for?' He tapped the cigarette on the case before returning the latter to his pocket and half turned to the waiter who, having set a double whisky down on the table before him, had produced a lighter.

'Fraud.' She sipped defensively at her champagne. 'It was all in the papers. It killed my husband.'

'I'm afraid I haven't seen the papers much. I've just come back from Zimbabwe.'

The gentle look he gave her told her he didn't mind. Not about Colin. He was part of her as were Gareth and Michael and little Crispin and the girls and all the last forty odd years.

'Your husband, what did he do?'

'He was the architect Gareth Sullivan.'

He frowned then, his glass half-way to his lips. 'But I met him. I met him several times. He was on a committee with me once,' and sitting forward, his elbows on his knees, he stared at her. 'All this time, Liz, and I never knew.'

Knew what? That she had married Gareth? That she was in London? That she was alive at all? All three perhaps.

He was watching her closely, reading her thoughts. 'Come on. This place is ghastly. Knock that back whatever it is – ' he was looking at the glass in her hand ' – and let's get out of here. I've got a car outside.'

She had forgotten he was so much taller than she. He made her feel delicate and feminine, almost girlish again as she followed him across the carpet. Behind them the woman with the glossy fingernails lowered her glass and stared after them.

She found a car outside, on the double yellow line, in the care of the doorman and affecting not to see the fiver which changed hands as the man opened the door for her she slid into the seat, waiting for a moment in that strange encapsulated silence for Hugh to come round and climb in behind the wheel. As they pulled effortlessly out into the traffic she leaned back and closed her eyes. She did not ask where they were going. She knew it would be the woods behind her grandfather's farm, now owned by strangers but mercifully preserved, where, at this time of year, the beeches were a cloak of gold.

As soon as she had got into the car she had spotted the tattered wartime copy of Keats in the glove pocket in front of her and quietly she smiled at the message. She wondered if he had remembered too the bracelet he had given her and gently as he guided the car into the traffic of the Cromwell Road she began to ease it down her wrist past the tightly buttoned cuff which had been so carefully fastened to conceal it.

The Magic Carpet

The day started badly.

'Why didn't you go into that first car park? There was loads of room.'

'Because it was so far from the fête. You know you hate walking.' Malcolm's voice had the patient note in it which always drove Ginny wild.

'I do like walking in the country, it's different, and look at this queue. We'll be here all day.'

The line of overheating cars crawling over the sticky tarmac was radiating heat beneath the blazing sky, while the procession of people strolling from the village kept safely, sensibly on the grassy verge in the black shadow of the heavy walnut trees. Ginny eyed them enviously. Her dress was sticking to her back.

'I've a good mind to get out and walk.'

'Why don't you, if you're going to be so grumpy?'

'All right. I will.'

She grappled for the handle of the door. Only when she was standing, slamming it shut, did she feel a twinge of conscience.

'Are you sure you don't mind me walking?'

'I don't mind. I'll meet you there, OK?'

The shade of the trees was heavy with bees and pollen and thick, humid heat. Her toes, bare in sandals, were pricked and stung by the grass vergey things which grew there. But at least it was better than the imprisoning seats of the car. Poor Malcolm. He was stuck there till he reached the car park. So much for an afternoon in the country. The idea of the little church fête had seemed such fun at the time – they hadn't dreamed there would be such a crowd. Distastefully she eyed the crawling vehicles, their heavy fumes polluting the country air.

A surge of excitement hit her as she came round the corner and saw before her the white marquees in the field, the khaki ex-desert army tents, the lines of booths with, in the centre, a tiny roped-off ring and everywhere the smell of drying grass with the sweetness of hay. Over a loud-speaker somewhere came music and as it was outside and a bank holiday she wanted suddenly to dance. She paid her ten pence at the entrance and then stood still uncertain what to do. How would she find Malcolm again? She walked cautiously in the direction of the car park. She could see the sun reflecting on the lines of windscreens behind a hedge.

Balls thwacked against the canvas backing to a coconut shy and she stopped to watch. 'Three goes for ten pence, love. Go on. Have a try.'

Why not?

Hitching her bag on her shoulder she took the three heavy balls from the man's hand and hurled the first one down the field.

'Bad luck, love. Two more goes.' Distracted, he was giving change to someone behind her. Her next go went wide. And the last.

She made a shamefaced grimace at the man and walked on. And then suddenly he was there, grinning, his camera in his hand.

'Malcolm! Did you come in by another entrance?' She was hoping he hadn't been watching.

'I saw you. Three bosh shots. How much did that little effort cost you?'

He was laughing at her and she blushed a little. 'I bet you couldn't do better.'

He couldn't.

They were even, now. Together they walked slowly into the white elephant tent. 'We might get something for the flat, Malcolm. There's so much we still need.'

'Like a dented warming pan or three chipped Victorian teapots, I suppose?'

Indignant she punched him in the ribs, then she began to push her way to the front of the gossiping women to where piles of exciting things were laid out on lines of flat trestle tables. All round the smell of trampled grass was very strong in the creamy twilight of the tent.

Strange, how two people with so much in common and so much in love could disagree so violently about decorating their first home. He wanted it light and airy; modern and functional. She had pictured it cluttered with Victoriana, draped and decorated, the windows festooned with lace.

'My goodness, Ginny, you need one of these.' His voice, mocking gently, was at her elbow. He had picked up a grimy watercolour in a fractured gilt frame. 'What is it?' He peered in the dim light. '*The Relief of Mafeking*, I think . . . Still it doesn't really matter much.'

She ignored him, her hand straying over the spines of a pile of books, glancing at the titles.

Reluctantly he relinquished the picture and followed her. 'Look, a novel by Mrs Radcliffe,' he exploded with a laugh. 'Ginny, my darling, that's for you . . .'

She was getting hot again, fed up with his teasing. In the distance at the far side of the table she could see a neatly folded embroidered tablecloth. As she pushed her way towards it, a gently determined hand reached out from the crowd and it was gone.

'That's your fault,' she flashed at Malcolm, suddenly. 'If you hadn't been fooling round distracting me I would have got that cloth. It would have looked lovely on the little round table.'

'Not my table with the melamine top.' His voice became suddenly threatening. 'No squalid cloth with somebody else's gravy stains is going on that. It's simple and perfect as it is.'

'It's not; it's . . . it's bare.'

'That's right. Bare.'

A woman came between them for a moment. When she had gone he was smiling again. 'Come on, Ginny. Don't let's quarrel. Let's go and see what else there is outside. This tent is getting too hot.'

They fought their way back to the entrance. Ginny was scowling. The tablecloth still rankled. 'That table needs something,' she muttered at his broad back as he pushed his way ahead of her into the sunshine.

'A pot plant, possibly. That is all,' he flung over his shoulder. 'Now forget it.'

A small child, red-faced and screaming, ran in front of them, the picture on its T-shirt grimy with melted chocolate.

'Come on, Ginny. I'll buy you an ice-cream.' He groped for her hand and together they made their way towards a booth with a long queue at the far side of the ring where two ladies, hot and dishevelled, unused to the problems of melting ice-cream and soggy cones, were battling manfully to supply the queue.

'What kind of pictures *are* we going to put in that room, Malcolm?' Her mind was still on the flat as they shuffled slowly over the browning grass.

'Perhaps one big one, over the couch. I haven't decided.'

'*You* haven't decided.' She repeated it just to make sure she'd heard aright.

He grinned. 'I know, Ginny. But if it was left to you we'd have fifty tatty old prints.'

'Better that than one painting on acres of white wall. With white furniture. Malcolm, it's going to look like an operating theatre!'

'Rubbish. It'll look very nice.'

They shuffled forward another place in the queue.

'It won't. Oh come on. It'll look terrible. It'll have no warmth. It'll be uncomfortable. Who'll want to sit in a room like that, on a cold winter's evening. No one.'

'I will.'

'Oh!' Exasperated she stamped her foot. 'Well, I won't. You can bloody well sit there alone.'

'Good. I will.' He grinned at her. 'Come on. We're nearly there. Do you want a pink one or a white one?'

'I don't want one now. I want a cold drink.' She pursed her mouth deliberately aping a small spoilt child. 'Come on. I don't want to stand in this silly queue.'

'Well I do.' The patient voice again. It snapped the last of Ginny's control.

'Well bloody well stand there then. I'm not going to!'

She was conscious of the shocked faces turned to her and the people hastily moving out of her way. Then she was alone, in the quiet green no man's land between the tents. She looked round for Malcolm following, but there was no sign of him. He had stayed stubbornly in the queue.

She stood for a moment, her hands absent-mindedly strumming a taut guy rope, examining the woven skeins of hemp. Behind her she could hear the music and the excited shouts of children. In front there was a narrow strip of grass and then a high hawthorn hedge silent except for the occasional sleepy note of a hedge sparrow.

As always her temper was gone as quickly as it had flared. She walked slowly back to the queue, her head held high. Malcolm had gone. She glanced round wildly, conscious of the interested glances of others waiting their turn for ice-cream, but there was no sign of him anywhere. In the ring a group of children were lining up for a race. 'Are there any more boys, seven to eight years old?' a megaphone boomed near her. 'Your race is starting next. Boys seven and eight years old, please . . .'

She began to walk slowly round the ring, her eyes scanning the crowds searching for Malcolm's blue shirt. Suddenly every other man there seemed to be wearing a blue shirt, but each time she looked again, heart thumping a little, for his face, she found another.

'Oh Malcolm, you beast. Where are you?' She felt suddenly angry. He had no business to walk out on her like that. None at all. She stamped her foot.

'Roll up, roll up. Come and try the hoopla. Roll up! Three hoops for fifty pence.' She was standing right in front of a stall. Behind it the vicar himself, his round face flushed and perspiring a little peered at her anxiously, his dog collar restricting, over shirtsleeves. 'Only fifty pence a go,' he said again, almost pleading. He was looking straight at her. Glancing round, embarrassed, she realized that there was no one else near the stall.

She grinned suddenly. 'What the hell,' she murmured and then clapped her hand, embarrassed, over her lips. She groped in her bag for the coin.

The vicar watched eagerly as she stood poised, the hoop ready to flick from her wrist. It skittered across the table and rolled drunkenly and uselessly away. 'Oh bad luck, my dear.' He sounded really quite upset for her. She aimed better the next time. The hoop fell neatly around a small packet of sugar cigarettes. She shrugged helplessly as the vicar handed them to her and slipped them, trying to keep her face straight, into her bag. The third hoop teetered, wavering towards the edge of the table and fell, half encircling, on the saucer of fifty pence pieces – the hoopla takings. They both laughed. 'You can't have that,' he said.

She had another useless go at the coconut shy and then wandered on down the rows of stalls, only half looking now for the blue shirt. She was beginning to enjoy herself. It was the turn of the little girls, five to six, in the ring.

A roar of laughter from a corner stall caught her attention and she wandered over. An old dresser, standing in front of draped sacking, was set up with old bits of chipped crockery. A man was hurling wooden balls at the plates and every smash was greeted by a cheer. She stood and watched for a while. It looked fun.

'Come and have a go. Come on,' the proprietor of the stall shouted, rattling the heavy balls in his enormous calloused hands. 'Get rid of all your frustrations, ladies and gents.' But the crowd was moving on, bored. In a moment they had gone and the stall was deserted except for Ginny. The man's shoulders slumped. He turned away, letting the balls roll from his palms into the box. Then he caught sight of her watching. 'Come on, darling. Want a go? Four for the price of three, seeing as it's you.' His shrewd eyes had spotted her new shiny wedding ring. He glanced left and right. 'Had a spat with your old man, have you? I've just the thing for you. See?' He bent and picked up a hideous jade green vase. He waddled over to the dresser and, sweeping a pile of broken china off with his arm, set up the vase on the middle shelf. 'There you are darling. That's him. Now. Take a good swing at it. Arm right back.'

Grinning she took the balls from him and hurled. The first smashed a plate on the edge of the shelf. It was the fourth ball which caught the vase full on its plump shiny belly. It rocked forward twice and then plunged from the shelf, smashing into a dozen pieces on the top of the dresser.

The man chuckled. 'Made you feel better, didn't it? Want another go?'

Ginny stood there, stricken. She hadn't meant it. She was shaken with guilt. Supposing she had harmed Malcolm in some way by smashing the vase. She hadn't really been pretending it was him. Oh please, please, Malcolm darling, where are you? She began to look round, lost again, searching desperately for his face in the crowd.

Puzzled, the man watched her for a moment. Then he shrugged. He waded through the broken crocks to the dresser and began to set up new plates and saucers, sweeping the debris from the shelves onto the old carpet laid on the grass below. Near the carpet was a sign. 'Carpet for sale. Five pounds.'

She walked quickly away, scanning the crowds again, searching everywhere for the blue shirt, aching to have Malcolm beside her.

In the ring it was the toddlers' race. Half of them were going the wrong way, but no one seemed to notice. The field was crowded. There were so many places he could be. In a tent, at a booth, walking like her in the crowd. Perhaps he had gone home without her? She was stricken with terror. Then she pushed away the thought. How silly. Malcolm would never do that, however angry with her. She set out to walk again, slowly, round the perimeter of the field, methodically glancing into every marquee and stall. It must be tea time, there were so many people clutching paper cups and sticky pink-iced buns. Wasps hovered over the litter bins.

She saw him at last back where she had started, standing arms folded, his feet slightly apart, watching two boys hurl wooden balls at the china on the dresser. There was a bemused smile on his face. The man had spotted him.

'Here you are, sir. Three balls for fifty pence. Small price to pay to get rid of your inhibitions, sir. Pretend it's your old woman, sir. Really put some beef into it.'

Ginny flinched. Surely he wasn't going to? She watched as Malcolm fished in his pocket for the money. Then he took the balls from the man. The first thwacked into the dresser back with such force that three saucers fell. The other two followed rapidly, shattering bowls. Malcolm was grinning. 'Thanks, chum. I needed that.' Then he was wandering off. He never looked round once.

Malcolm.

She stood and watched as he disappeared into the crowd and suddenly she found she was fighting back tears, screwing up her handkerchief in her fist. She felt desolate and abandoned as she was jostled out of the way by a big bouncing woman who had spied the stall.

'Come on, George. You've always wanted to smash the china. Come and have a go at this then.' The husband, equally big and bouncing, pushed after her and squealing with laughter the pair of them threw their balls at the dresser, hurling cheery insults after each shot.

Miserably Ginny gazed at the ground as the cascading china fell on the dim red design of the grubby carpet. It was a bit like the carpet in her parents' dining room. The kind she had thought would look so pretty in their flat, under the white melamine table . . .

She sniffed and blew her nose. Then, cautiously, she edged a bit closer trying to see the carpet better. Actually it was little more than a rug. But five pounds? It seemed too good to be true.

'Want another go, love? Come on, get it all out of your system. Four balls for you, wasn't it? Four for fifty.' He had spotted her at once.

She smiled at him uncertainly. 'Actually I was looking at the carpet.'

'Ah, I could tell you was a lady of discernment.' He slipped the balls into a capacious pocket. 'Real Persian that is. Woven in the desert and brought across the sands on the back of a camel I shouldn't wonder. Here, have a real butchers.' He held up the rope which held back the throwers so she could duck underneath and come closer. She walked with him to the dresser, feeling suddenly very exposed, blushing at the interested faces lined up behind her. Now that she was close she could see the carpet was horribly threadbare and torn. It was stained too beneath the piles of china. He stopped and with a flick of the wrist pulled it clear, pouring the crocks into a heap on the dusty grass. 'Look at that. There's real quality there. It's an antique you know. That's why it's a bit worn. It's an antique.' He glanced at her sharply from beneath his sandy brows and she found herself smiling suddenly.

'I can see it's old,' she murmured, seriously.

Her finger traced the pattern of little square stylized birds round the borders. She wanted it badly, however worn. She hesitated. Malcolm would kill her of course.

'Come on, darling. Make up your mind. There's people waiting to throw.'

'I'll have it.' She gulped a little nervously, wondering suddenly if she had five pounds in her bag.

Solemnly he began to roll it up, carrying it effortlessly under his arm. He threw it down on the grass just beyond the rope as she scrabbled in her purse. Four pound coins and a pile of odd loose change. He counted it carefully and then he grinned. 'Want another throw for luck? On the house?' But she shook her head.

The rug was surprisingly heavy. She heaved it up into her arms and then stood still. Malcolm had the car keys. She wasn't even sure where he'd parked the wretched car.

She couldn't wander round the fête carrying a carpet. What on earth was she to do? The trouble was she couldn't stop smiling. She was so ridiculously pleased with the thing.

She carried it away from the crowds to an emptier corner of the field where two oak trees stood, isolated from the woods behind the hedge. Nearby three girls were giving pony rides, leading the patient animals whose heads drooped lower and lower in the heat with a succession of breathlessly excited small children clutching their manes.

She set down the rug and carefully unrolled it on the grass, brushing off the bits of splintered china and goose-grass which still clung to it. It had a skimpy fringe on one side – at the opposite end the fringe seemed to have been shaved off. She stood and gazed at it proudly for a few minutes and then, experimentally, she knelt on it, brushing the threadbare pile with her hand. It was the first Persian rug she had ever owned.

'Don't tell me. It can fly!' Suddenly Malcolm was standing behind her, a coconut nestled in the crook of his arm. He was laughing at her.

She stroked it again. Protectively. 'For all I know it can. This is the sort of place one finds magic carpets.'

'What, at an Aunt Sally shy?' He snorted with laughter. Then he came and knelt beside her, reverently putting the coconut on the rug in front of him. 'Come on then. Ready to wish? Where do we want to go?'

He glanced at her sideways. 'I saw the rug too. I had a little bet with myself that you'd spot it. You know he's got another one down there already. Even more tatty, if that's possible.' He put his arm round her suddenly. 'Oh my lovely Ginny. You'll never learn will you, sweetheart?' He grinned again. 'Right. I'm waiting. Where are we flying to?'

'Just home? I want to see the rug down, in the flat.'

She couldn't keep the slight note of bravado out of her voice.

He was sitting cross legged now, palms down beside him on the rug, feeling the pile. 'I suppose we could mend it. If it were backed in some way it might not look too bad. Funnily enough these rugs can be dreadfully shabby and yet still look nice . . .'

She looked at him, her green eyes wide with astonishment. 'But Malcolm, it's old!'

He grimaced at her. 'I don't dislike old things on principle, love. I jut want to keep our flat in one style. As it happens I think a Persian rug or two would fit. It would look lovely under my table.' He glanced at her sideways. 'Perhaps you're right about that room. Perhaps it does need a little more colour to give it warmth. This would provide it, wouldn't it?'

'Oh, Malcolm!' She flung her arms round his neck and kissed him; 'Oh Malcolm, I do love you sometimes.' A thought struck her suddenly. 'I saw you at the stall, breaking china. Did you really think of me when you were doing it?'

'Of course. Every shot.' His eyes were twinkling mischievously. 'I'll bet you had a go too. And thought of me. Didn't you?'

She bit her lip, trying not to laugh. 'Well, there was this hideous green vase. And the man did say "pretend it's your old man".'

'Did you hit it?' he asked casually, lying back and putting his arm across his eyes.

She giggled. 'A bull's-eye.'

'But you're usually such a bad shot!' He sounded quite indignant.

'Ah, but I was provoked beyond endurance.'

'Just because I wanted an ice-cream?'

'That's right.' She lay back beside him and stretched

her arms ecstatically above her head. 'I am always provoked by ice-creams, especially pink ones.'

'And by white melamine tables?'

'Those too.'

He nodded sleepily. 'As long as I know,' he said. 'By the way. Did you see I'd won a coconut?'

The Proposal

'Have you time for a wee crack, Aggie?' Betty Anderson popped her head over the privet hedge and watched critically as her neighbour pushed two more tulip bulbs into the soft black soil.

Aggie Cameron straightened her back and wiped an earthy hand on her apron. 'What is it now, Betty? Have you yet more gossip for me, hen?' She didn't mean to sound impatient but she had been enjoying the peace of the crisp cold afternoon.

She knew, however, that Betty meant well and there was always the chance that the story would be about someone Aggie had actually met. Gossip lost its enjoyable edge if you did not know the people concerned. 'Come away in now and I'll put on the kettle while you tell me,' she said more softly.

She listened as Betty, her shoes rustling through the drifting leaves, made her way down her own side of the hedge out of the little gate and in through the identical one next to it. Then she turned and led her guest into the house.

Betty had at last learned not to offer to help. Aggie was not concerned that Betty would have made the tea in any one of a dozen kitchens. In hers, where everything had to be kept just so, no one touched anything. She did not like to be helped.

'Can I ask you something, Aggie?' She heard Betty's voice, slightly diffident, from the fire-side chair. 'How is it that you take so much care of the garden when you can't . . .' She hesitated, suddenly embarrassed.

'Can't see the flowers I'm planting?' Aggie finished for her. 'Och that's easy, Betty. I can smell, can't I? I can touch their soft petals and I can feel the green leaves trembling with the sap. I know you'll think I'm foolish, but I can almost hear the flowers sing as they hang their heads and rustle in the wind. And I can remember their colours you know.' She smiled gently, as she set the kettle down on the gas. 'I haven't always been blind. I can remember fine what a garden should look like in the spring.'

She groped for the other chair and sat down, waiting for the expected piece of gossip. For a moment there was silence and she sensed that her companion was inexplicably uncomfortable.

'What is it, hen? What's the matter? What is it you want to say to me?'

'Aggie. I've been keeping company with Roddy Mackay. I think you know that?'

'Aye. He's a fine man.' Aggie nodded sagely. She waited, her hands quietly folded in her lap.

'I think he's asked me to marry him, Aggie,' Betty went on in a rush. 'What am I to do?'

Aggie sat for a moment, her blue eyes fixed unseeing on the kitchen fire. Then she smiled. 'He's a fine man, Betty, as I said. But if you only think he's asked you and you're not sure what to do, then I think you'd best do nothing.'

Betty blushed a little and leaned forward. 'I think I love him, Aggie. I go weak-kneed and foolish as a schoolgirl when he comes to the house. It's ten years since my man died. I've not felt like this since I was courting him.'

Aggie rose stiffly and went to the kettle, her hand going without hesitation to the handle.

'Have you made up your mind what to say to him then?'

There was silence. Then Betty said. 'The trouble is Aggie, I'm not minded to leave my house. I've lived here too long. I've no desire to go up the mountain to Craigbeg.'

Aggie nodded. The two of them lived in pleasant little cottages and the gardens were beautiful. It took someone young and agile to live in the hills. Someone like her niece Alison and her husband. She remembered how they had gone for a drive up the glen and come back thrilled with the beauties of Craigbeg. They had even wanted, dreamily, to buy the place for themselves. How wonderful it would have been if they could live near her, close at hand. But Mackay had rudely refused their tentative offer for his cottage. And why not? He lived there himself. Now, if only . . . But Aggie firmly put the thought behind her.

'You'd best think about it, Betty. Don't say anything to the man, till you've made up your mind properly.'

It was four days later that Aggie, weeding by feel among the last blooms on the rose bushes by the garden gate, heard the deep cheery voice of Roddy Mackay above her.

'You're doing a fine job there, Mistress Cameron. I haven't seen such a garden in ages.' She heard her gate click and his step on the gravel path.

'May I have a word with you,' she heard him go on, his voice suddenly confidential close to her ear.

'Of course you may.' Aggie turned to him, wiping her earthy fingers on her apron. 'There's nothing wrong I hope, Mr Mackay?'

'Nothing indeed, Mistres Cameron, it's just that I have a wee bit of a problem and I'm no very sure how to solve it.'

There was a moment of silence. In the warm autumn sunshine, Aggie could hear the wistful song of her robin.

He was waiting for the stranger to leave so that he could hop back to the newly turned earth at her feet.

'The thing is, I think I've offended Betty Anderson. I've been going to see her fairly often, two or three times a week and then last time I went over there I must have said something to upset her. She's not said a word to me since. When I called yesterday and the day before, she didn't open the door to me, though I've an idea she was in.' Aggie could hear an aggrieved note slipping into the voice.

'That's strange,' she replied very cautiously. 'I know for a fact she has a great regard for you, Mr Mackay. Can you not think what it is you might have said?'

He kicked the gravel on her path and she heard him scratch his head noisily. 'I cannot and that's a fact. I mentioned to her that maybe her garden could do with a bit of a dig. That could have been it, I suppose. She said she wasn't strong enough to do it herself now she hadn't a man to help her. Well, I said, perhaps we could come to an arrangement. It doesn't do not to have a man to take care of your garden.' He paused.

Aggie smiled. 'There's no man to take care of mine either.'

'Och woman, but you do fine. You've no need of anyone. Betty now, she's not got the fingers for gardening. Such a fine patch it is, but her flowers are thin and poor and they're in all the wrong places and she hasn't a vegetable in the place.'

Aggie had always suspected as much. 'I know how you must miss gardening, Mr Mackay, living on that rocky hill yourself. I wonder, did you suggest some kind of permanent arrangement to look after her garden for her?'

'Well, I did and I didn't.' He shuffled his feet again. 'To tell you the truth I told her that I'd be happy to take care of the matter for her, if she'd allow me. Then she went

369

all foolish and giggly and said she'd have to think about it. Silly woman. I know she's enough money and I'd not charge her over much.'

Poor Betty. So it was as a gardener he had offered his services, nothing more. In spite of herself Aggie could not hold back a sad little smile.

'Did you mention money, Roddy Mackay?' she enquired innocently.

'I did not. I thought it should come from her.'

'Do you not think that maybe that's what embarrassed her?'

Again he scratched his head. 'Has she no money then?'

Aggie saw her chance. 'Aye, she's got money. She's got a fair bit tucked away and of course there's the house that's worth a lot too, with that good land. But can you no see man, it's an insult for a bonnie woman like Betty Anderson to have to pay a man to work in her garden. There are many as would do it for nothing.' She paused, waiting for a reaction.

'Are there so?' He was pondering.

'There are indeed. I know for a fact she would rather you were the one to help her and she knows how you love the garden but there she is, widowed, healthy, lonely.' Aggie emphasized each word carefully. 'It's my opinion she needs a man to look after her, Roddy Mackay. The garden is only one of the things that need taking care of.'

She broke off a stray tendril of weed and twiddled it between her fingers.

'She's wealthy, you say?'

'Aye, she is that.'

'And there are men, shall we say, courting her?'

'There are a few more than a wee bit interested.' Aggie smiled to herself.

'Is that so?' Roddy Mackay's voice was thoughtful again. 'Well, I'm glad I had this wee chat with you, Mistress

Cameron. Will you mind and not say a word to Betty about this please?' The gate clicked open. 'I'll come and have another word with her this evening.'

Aggie stood and listened to his footsteps as he walked purposefully down the lane. Then she bent once more to her roses.

The next morning Betty Anderson knocked on her door as Aggie was washing up her egg cup and plate.

'You know what I told you the other day, hen, about Roddy Mackay asking me to marry him?' She was breathless with excitement.

Aggie nodded quietly and began to dry a knife.

'Well, I wasn't sure what to do and so after I talked to you I thought I'd follow your advice and do nothing, to give myself the chance to decide, you understand and I avoided him, and I even hid behind the curtain when he knocked on the door.' She giggled excitedly. 'Well, last night he came over again. Straight in he came, without knocking even, with a great box of chocolates. He fair swept me off my feet. He said he thought I'd probably misunderstood his intentions, and that I should know he meant to make an honourable proposal. Oh, Aggie, he declared himself really well.' She stopped and waited expectantly.

'And what did you say, Betty?'

'Oh, I said yes. Och, Aggie, he's a really fine man!'

Aggie nodded thoughtfully and put away the last of her china. 'So will you be going to live up at Craigbeg now?'

'No, he says he'd like us to go on living here. He likes the garden, you know. It's always been his great weakness, gardening and there's no land worth the name at Craigbeg, he says.'

Aggie took down her tea caddy. 'Will you take a cup now you're here, Betty, to celebrate? When will the great day be?'

'Oh, soon, soon.' Betty was ecstatic. 'He said he'd bring down his gardening things in the van this week. He's no real use for them up there and he can make a start on the beds, he said.' She giggled coyly.

That evening Aggie sat down at her telephone and carefully dialled her niece's number.

'Is that you, Alison? Now listen. The cottage you liked so much at Craigbeg, I happen to know that it's coming on the market fairly soon. You'd be wise to make an offer at once.'

'But he said he'd never shift.' Alison's voice on the phone was indignantly puzzled.

'Well, something's happened to change his mind,' said her aunt quietly. 'He decided he couldn't live without a garden.' Smiling to herself contentedly, she hung up.

Spaces

The front door clicked behind her and she was outside in the quiet street. Above her the stars were crackling with frost as she walked resolutely into the darkness.

'You won't be too late, Faye?' Marta had said anxiously as Faye shrugged on her coat and Faye had turned to look at her, her eyes vague as she frowned, trying to listen.

'Don't wait up. I've got a key,' she managed to say as she groped for the door handle.

Outside she paused. Those were more or less the very words that Paul had used. She had not waited up but he had not used his key; not until three days later when he returned, collected a suitcase and packed nearly all his things.

'It's not working, Faye,' he said gently as she watched, too frozen to protest or to cry out. 'Better this way. We both need space to think.'

Space: the enormous, echoing emptiness which was the flat; the cold silence inside her heart; the beating of her quiet pillow against her ear drums.

In the end she had gone to Marta who knew the whole story and only then did she cry. At home she had not dared. Marta, always uneasy with emotion, resorted to practicality and made hot whisky and lemon and looked for her aspirin. Love at its nadir is a lot like flu. One aches;

373

one cannot bear to be touched; one shivers and longs for death.

'But it will pass, you know it will,' Marta whispered kindly as she tucked her into the spare bed and Faye wondered briefly if her friend was after all a little glad it had happened.

But now time had passed and she had thrown off the initial fever of misery. Her need was to be alone with the dull ache which had stayed with her.

In front of her the road led curving up the hill, the pale street lights flickering in the sharpness of the air. There were fewer of them now. Soon there would be none. She walked steadily, listening to the echo of her own footsteps and, in her head, to the echo of her life with Paul.

They had met in the dark; in a garden, escaping the heat of a noisy party where the disco threatened to bring down the walls and the smell of the wine cup and the cigarettes and the reefers sent waves of nausea across her shoulder blades.

'Too much for you?' the voice had said softly as she leaned against the moss-covered wall and breathed the scented silence.

He had materialized out of the shadows, a tall thin silhouette, slightly stooped at the shoulders and he stood several feet from her. There had been a long relaxed silence before they felt the need to speak.

She had not asked his name and only later, separated by a surge of dancers who spilled out of the french windows to the terrace and across the grass in a flood tide, did she realize she had not even really seen his face and she knew herself bereft.

It did not matter. He found her once more with calm certainty, took her hand and guided her over the gravel drive, through the parked cars, to her own which was up on the grass. Only in the pale interior lights as they opened the door did she at last see his face.

Weeks passed. At first he would not move in. 'You must be sure,' he said quietly. But the touch of his hands on hers and the touch of his lips left no possibility of doubt. She had fallen headlong through love to infatuation and worship.

It worried Paul. 'No one should love another person like this,' he said, holding her face between cupped hands, looking at her as if he wanted to memorize every detail. 'It is not right; the gods will become jealous as they did in stories.'

She did not believe him. She had laughed at first, secure in her shield of certainty and at last so was he, taking her in his arms and burying his face in her hair.

It was not as though she were a starry-eyed teenager. She held a responsible job; people relied on her judgement and skill. She had to be strong. But how, when her heart began to pound uncomfortably and her mouth went dry the moment he entered the room and all she wanted was to go down on her knees and serve him? Watching herself, her joy turned to apprehension and a strange amorphous dread.

She told Marta in despair and Marta stared at her.

'For goodness' sake, Faye! You are the one who went to the Equal Rights Commission to win your promotion! You can't let yourself down like this. You can't let *us* down.' She brought their coffee and sat opposite Faye, her pale face earnest and affectionate. 'You know as well as I do that it's only chemistry! Rationalize things. It's the urge to procreate and that's the last thing you want to do, for God's sake.'

She looked hard at Faye for a moment then passed her a cup. 'I bet *his* work isn't suffering,' she said softly.

Faye coloured in indignation. '*My* work isn't suffering!'

'Not yet. But you are. You are being torn in two. And why? You've got him. You're not fighting a jealous rival, are you? He loves you from what I gather. Why the hassle? You were so happy at the beginning.' She shook two sweeteners into the palm of her hand and glared at them before tossing them into her cup.

Faye lay back in her chair and closed her eyes.

'But he won't marry me.'

'Oh Faye, come on. Since when did you want to marry?' Marta slid forward to kneel on the floor and put her hand on Faye's knee. 'What has happened to independent womanhood? Independent equals un-dependent, remember?'

Faye gave a small shrug. 'That was before.'

'You really are in a bad way!' Almost admiringly Marta folded her arms and stared. 'There's no point in chaining yourself to the railings outside your front door and picketing him then?'

Faye laughed. 'No point at all. I'm a lost cause!'

'But you're frightened of him!'

There was a long pause. Then at last Faye raised her eyes and looked at her directly. 'No,' she whispered. 'I'm frightened of myself.'

The gods were jealous of course and one by one they began to load the dice. Little things at first, like working overtime – first Paul, then Faye. They tried not to mind.

'We both need an evening to wash our hair,' he said, teasing. But she knew his assistant was eager and beautiful and she sat watching the hands of the clock tick round till midnight, eaten up with anguish, unable to understand her own reactions. What had she to be afraid of? He had eyes, she knew, for no one else. Never before had she felt like this; she was vulnerable and scared; a little girl lost in the dark, groping for the hand which had been holding hers until it was wrenched away.

When her night to work late at the office came she sat at her desk, her eyes on the dark rain-streaked windows and thought of him at home, bored and lonely, and she had to stay an hour longer than she intended, just to correct what her straying thoughts had set wrong.

Then they were both at home again and it was daylight and as the sun shone she felt happy and reassured. The shadows belonged only to the lonely darkness, she thought.

It was her own mother who brought that darkness back, arriving with her matching Gucci suitcases and her aura of Givenchy to spend the weekend.

'Good heavens, but it's Paul Sandford!' she said. 'I remember you from when you were so high! But surely, you were married to Josephine Stapleton?'

'It didn't matter any more. That is why I didn't tell you,' he kept repeating, later. 'It is as though it had never been. We've been divorced for five years, Faye. She is of so little importance I had all but forgotten her. Besides, I didn't know you'd care.'

And she had thought they could read each other's souls!

They made it up of course, but the scar tissue was tender. The slightest touch was going to leave it raw and bleeding.

Spring turned to summer. As her nerves drew taut her body became thin and circles of exhaustion appeared beneath her eyes.

Paul traced them with a gentle finger. 'You're wearing

yourself out,' he said. 'I can't let it go on. For both our sakes.'

But he did. No more than she could he tear himself from her. They clung to one another, fending off the intrusions of the world which seemed to have become hostile and intent on hurting them. Once or twice at a weekend he pulled the curtains and drew her back into bed, knowing the front door was bolted and they would lie there tensely in each other's arms listening to the knocking of their friends.

The first autumn gales sent leaves cartwheeling down the gutters and they went away together for a week. By the sea, with its relentless grey pounding, like the beating of a heart, Faye felt a little reassured, as she did in the almost empty guesthouse where the landlady hid her curiosity beneath a layer of professional uninterest. Paul had agreed to call her his wife for that week only; for the sake of the good lady's susceptibilities and Faye clung to the pretence, letting it salve her wounds and gently fingertip soothe away the circles beneath her eyes.

The shingle beach tired their legs and the wind whipped colour into their cheeks and they both began to eat again, slowly savouring the food.

'I wish we could stay here for ever,' she whispered, her head on his chest as they listened in the dark to the metronome sea through the open window. 'Those gods of yours couldn't reach us here.'

His arms tightened momentarily as he stared up at the ceiling. The tiny pattern on the wallpaper had faded to a dusky shadow crossed by the black framework of the beams. It hung over them like a trap about to fall.

He could feel the prickle of icy perspiration in the small of his back suddenly; the terror as he counted the days they had left.

'What is it, Paul?' she had raised her head and was

looking at him, though she couldn't see him clearly. He clung to her, drawing her head down so she couldn't guess at his tears.

'Nothing, sweetheart. Nothing,' he murmured.

It had come between them for so long he had thought he could live with it for ever. Knowing that it was too late to speak he had kept silent. He had thought their love strong enough to smother his pain. But the unspoken truth inside him had grown and festered and had bred this claustrophobia which surrounded them. This was the cause of Faye's apprehension, though she could not know it and for Faye's sake it could not continue. The barrier between them had grown too high.

He told her when their train reached London, in the railway café over cups of grey coffee.

'When I divorced Josephine it wasn't just that it had never worked; it was so I could marry again. Her name was Clare. I thought I loved her, but I never really knew what love was, Faye, till I met you. You must believe me. She left me after a few months when we both realized what a mistake I'd made and I never saw her from that day on. I kept it from you because I thought I'd lose you. Because I lied to you . . . Because I love you . . .'

He did not look at her; did not watch as she stood up and walked numbly through the swing door and out onto the teeming concourse of the station.

When she got back to the flat at last it was after eleven. He was there, sitting in the darkness, his head cradled in his arms on the edge of the sofa. She turned on the light and stood looking down at him.

It had taken so long to find out what was wrong between them that for a while she had not realized that at last the problem was lying there in the open, naked, like the canker in a split apple. There had been no trust between them.

379

Ever. He had not trusted her with the truth. She perhaps sensing it had not trusted him at all.

'But it doesn't make any difference,' she said at last. 'It mustn't. You know that, don't you.'

That night was the only time he ever hurt her. Bruised and bleeding she dragged herself to the bathroom and was sick. Then she locked the door and huddled on the floor till dawn. When she awoke he had gone.

'He did it because he loves you?' Marta stared at her in amazement. 'My God, Faye, he could have killed you!'

But Faye knew the anger had not been directed at her. And she knew that her life would be a desert without his presence.

'All right, so I'm a doormat,' she said to Marta, later, and she managed to laugh at the disgust and disbelief on Marta's face. It had been harder to laugh at herself, to let her head make mockery of her heart, but she had forced herself to do it. It made her feel no better, but at least she knew she was still fighting.

Strangely it was to Marta that Paul went eventually.

'Go on, say it,' he invited her, sitting at her kitchen table as she turned a frosty back on him. 'You can't think of any names to call me I haven't called myself already.'

'Then I won't waste my energy,' she retorted, not bothering to turn from the sink where she was peeling potatoes.

'Are you expecting guests? Can I have a drink?' He picked up the half bottle of wine beside him and poured some into a mug.

'That's for cooking, it's yesterday's. If you want me to speak to her for you I won't.'

'Do you think she'd take me back?'

Marta turned, the peeler dripping starchy water onto the floor from her hand. 'You know damn well she would. You've bewitched her.'

'Somehow you make that sound obscene.'

'Perhaps it is.' She stared at him for a moment. Then she turned back to the sink. 'She told me about your second wife.'

'I've found her,' Paul said softly. 'I hired a private detective. I've found her and I've initiated divorce proceedings. There will be no problem there.'

Marta continued peeling. 'So. Should I be pleased?'

'I want to marry Faye.'

'Third time lucky you hope, eh?' She ran the tap into the colander and then ripped off her rubber gloves.

'Faye is my destiny, Marta.'

'Oh my God, Paul. Now you sound like a third rate movie!' She came over to the kitchen table and reached for a dishcloth, staring at him. There was a moment's silence. 'But you're serious, aren't you?' she went on in astonishment. 'You and Faye, it's as if it were something different from other people. Deeper.'

He grinned sourly. 'Romeo and Juliet didn't have a monopoly, you know. It can happen amongst the filing cabinets just as easily.'

Marta laughed. 'Touché. But tell me, why have you come to me?'

He glanced at the glass in his hand. 'Dutch courage perhaps? I never meant to hurt her, Marta. I've never struck a woman in my life.'

Marta sat down and poured herself some wine. 'Funny isn't it? People like me scream for equality, yet when a man hits a woman we act shocked as Victorian maidens, just because she's a woman. I told her she should have hit you back. Hard.'

He shrugged ruefully. 'Unfortunately men usually pack

a better punch.' He paused. 'Perhaps if she had, she'd have brought me to my senses sooner. I would have stayed. We could have talked it through eventually, now everything is in the open. As it is I can't blame her for not trusting me.'

'Nor do I.' She leaned back in her chair and scrutinized him closely. 'You look awful. When did you last sleep?'

He picked up the wine bottle and held it up to the light. 'Last night, in theory. Shall I go round and see her now?'

He split the dregs meticulously between them.

'Not now,' she said. 'Soon.'

Two days later Faye let Paul back into her flat. She gave a rueful smile. 'Have you lost your key?' she said.

'I didn't like to use it without your permission. I forfeited that right. Did Marta ring you?'

Faye nodded. That was odd. To use her of all people as a go between. 'I thought you knew she hated you.'

They were standing facing each other, not touching.

'She cares for you though.' He was taking in every detail of her appearance, feeding on her nearness. 'She must have thought you should see me. Either that or she was so adamant that you shouldn't that she made you angry and you did it as a dare!' He smiled at last and she felt her mouth go dry.

'Something like that, yes,' she said.

She had already decided not to tell him what Marta had said: 'For God's sake marry the guy and give us all some peace,' was the censored gist of what she had advised.

He stepped forward and took her hands gently. 'She told you that I'm divorcing Clare. As soon as I'm free . . .'

'No, Paul,' she interrupted him. 'Don't say any more. Wait until you really are free and then we'll think what to do next.' Gently she disengaged her hand from his. 'Come in properly. We can't stand here in front of the door. I'll make you some coffee.'

He watched as she walked to the kitchen door, her head high, her shoulders a shade stiffer than he remembered and he felt a pang of fear. Perhaps not till that moment had he realized just how much he had hurt her. But obediently he sat down and waited while she brought the tray with biscuits laid out carefully in the brown earthenware bowl as if he were a visitor. He didn't recognize the mugs at all, they had been bought as a gesture of defiance together with a dress and shoes and a large bottle of plonk to drown her sorrows alone. None had worked, but he was not to know that.

'May I not come back then?' he asked at last. He did not look at her face.

'I don't know, Paul. I want you to, but . . .'

'To hell with all the "buts", Faye. If you want me I'll come!' He put the mug back on the tray, then he leaned forward and took her hand, holding it so tightly that she winced and tried to pull away. 'Don't you understand, darling. Clare and I are getting divorced! There is nothing to come between us any more. Nothing. No more reservations; no more secrets and nightmares haunting us from the wings.'

Nothing, except her months of pain and her resolution to be strong so that never again would he – or any man – make her feel the anguish and humiliation to which such complete surrender had left her open.

She wavered. She raised her eyes to his at last and half unwillingly allowed herself to go to him.

Her resolution spun and dissolved. With him she was complete. More than anything she wanted him and she agreed that he could come back. But the pain was still there. She was hurt more deeply than even she had realized. However much she wanted to, she found she still

383

did not trust him; she could not let herself believe that the gods had finished their teasing and turned away to find another prey.

'Faye, you must believe me,' he pleaded. 'I only lied to you because I loved you so much. It will never happen again. The instant I'm free we can be married.'

She knew he was sincere and that his love was genuine, just as she knew her love for him had not changed. But she had no power to overcome her fears. They were involuntary and unwanted. She just had to hope that time would heal the bruises.

And time was what Paul did not give her.

'She's throwing my guilt back at me all the time,' he said to Marta one evening in despair. 'She doesn't even know she's doing it but it's coming between us like a brick wall ten feet high.'

'You've got to take him back unreservedly, or say goodbye to him,' Marta told Faye later. 'You can't go on turning this into a five act tragedy. It's making both of you unhappy. It's very unfair.'

'Unfair? To him?' Faye swung round on her.

'Yes, unfair to him. And to yourself.' Gently Marta hammered the point home. 'You are punishing him for something he had already punished himself for enough.'

Faye threw herself down on a chair. 'So, you're on his side now!' she said bitterly.

'I don't take sides. I watch from a safe vantage point. But I can see you losing him, Faye and it would break you up.'

For a moment they sat in silence. Marta searched desperately for something to say which would help, gave up and went to find some alcohol. It turned out to be the dregs of a whisky bottle. 'A snifter each,' she said triumphantly. 'Take him back without reservation, Faye. You can trust him now,' she said softly, 'and you can afford to trust yourself.' And she raised her glass.

But it was already too late. It was two days after that he got up as he and Faye were listening to a record in the dark sitting room, their eyes staring into the fire and dropped a kiss on the top of her head.

'I'm going out for a breath of air,' he said. 'Don't wait up. I've got a key.'

She sat unmoving for a long time after the sound of the music had died away. Then sadly she went to bed.

In the morning she was still alone.

And now, even staying with Marta she was alone and frozen in the spaces of her anguish. She walked on doggedly up the hill, feeling the cold wind lifting her hair about her ears, feeling the slight skim of ice forming on the pavements beneath her feet, her eyes used to the dark now, picking out details of sleeping houses, a wraith of pale smoke hanging still above a chimney and a holly tree, the berries glistening beneath a lamp, the red washed out of them by the pale light.

It was the first time she had allowed herself to think back to the day she and Paul had first met. They had not needed to speak then. What had gone wrong? Why was there this awful gulf between them now?

Slowly she turned and began to retrace her steps. Even if she had found the answer to her question it was too late. She had lost him a second time.

Marta has left one light burning on the table. The flat was very quiet. Dropping her coat on the chair by the door Faye made for the gently hissing flames of the gas fire and held out her hands to the warmth.

'Faye?' Paul was sitting in the shadows, so still she had not even seen him. 'Marta called me. She said I should come,' he said softly.

'Where is she?'

'In bed.' He held out his hands to her, smiling. 'I've done so much thinking, Faye. And each time I come back to the same answer. I still want you.'

She did not move. The shade of the lamp was angled so the light fell in a pool on the table. She could not see his face.

'I want you too, Paul.' She meant it.

'I'll give you time, Faye. I won't come back until you're ready. Just tell me when.'

'You're so sure?'

He chuckled. 'Destiny. I once told Marta you were my destiny.'

'She must have laughed at you.'

'No, funnily enough she understood. That's why she rang me tonight.' He stepped forward at last and took her gently by the shoulders. 'I'm going now. But I'll be waiting every second to hear from you. When you're ready, tell me.'

He didn't move to kiss her. He just stood looking down at her face and she felt herself strangely at peace for a moment, the pain and the doubt drained out of her. Giving a hesitant smile she put her hand on his arm. 'Don't go yet. Have some coffee, Paul.'

'If I stay, I'll find it harder to go later,' he said quietly. 'My self discipline is strained to the limit as it is.'

'I'll risk it,' she replied. Her mouth had gone dry just as it always had in the past and her heart had begun to pound uncomfortably below her ribs, but it was not with fear. For a moment longer she stood looking at him, realizing what had happened, then she turned away. She had been given a third chance; the gods had removed their veto. This time she could, and would, trust him with her life. She went into the kitchen and turned to the light, smiling.

An extra place had been laid at the table around a token cornflakes packet. Beside it was a note scrawled in red felt tip:

I shall expect there to be three of us for breakfast! M.

Faye laughed quietly. 'Just this once, Marta,' she whispered. 'I think we really will do as you expect.'

Marcus Nicholls

I was fourteen when it happened. But the memory still gives me nightmares, even after all this time. And still, when I go back to Camber, I avoid the stables if Duncan and Cathie are at home.

The summer had been unspeakably hot that year, with heavy thunderheads building up towards evening day after day, to deluge the countryside with humid storms which did nothing to clear the air.

I suppose if Aunt Flavia had been with us then, she would at once have said that the atmosphere was right for psychic activity; as it was, the three of us, Duncan, Sandy and myself, concentrated on staying in the neighbour's swimming pool as much as we could and on riding of course. We got up at six in the morning to ride before it became too hot and then turned the ponies out each day in the old orchard where there was plenty of shade.

Our parents felt the heat even more than we did, I think; our father worried about what the rain was doing to his standing corn and mother was worried about her mares – she breeds Welsh ponies. For us, although we helped on the farm and worked till we dropped, it was still the long summer vacation and we revelled in it. My brother Duncan was reading accountancy at university and Sandy was studying music. I was still at school, but there were weeks and weeks before I had to go back.

It was on Mother's birthday that Jan Fleming arrived to stay. She was Sandy's girlfriend – a lovely slim redhead whom I worshipped and hated and would have given my right arm to look like! And with her came a stranger.

'I do hope you don't mind, Mrs Nicholls, I really hope not; I knew you have lots of room at Camber Court and you've often said I could bring someone, so I wondered . . .' Jan's voice petered out, embarrassed and the stranger stepped forward. She too was tall and slim but dark haired, with enormous hazel eyes. Her mouth was rather large and her skin gypsy dark and I, standing in the shadows, saw Duncan's face as he watched her and I knew he had fallen for her on the spot.

'I'm Cathie Steuart,' she said in a low, musical voice. 'I'm a friend of Jan's from London and when she said she was driving down to the West Country I begged a lift. I certainly don't want to impose on you though . . .'

Duncan pushed past Mother hastily. 'We've plenty of room, Jan's right. Of course you must stay. Are you on holiday?'

She laughed. 'No. Believe it or not I'm here to work. I'm a photographer and I've got to photograph various houses – including yours – for a book a colleague of mine is writing about historic old houses in the west.' She glanced around. I could see her eyes taking in the carved oak staircase with its lovely half landing and the leaded windows which open onto the rose gardens at the back of the house. 'It's so beautiful here,' she said. 'I couldn't believe it when Jan said she was actually going to stay in the house. I just had to make her bring me . . .'

'You realize she's probably a burglar or a con woman or something,' Sandy said later to father, 'tricking her way into the house.'

But we all liked her immediately and it wasn't long before my parents had suggested that she make Camber her headquarters for the three weeks she would be in this part of the world.

I had already transferred my allegiance from Jan to her. After all, she was dark and so was I.

It happened about a week later. The day was overcast and the temperature up in the nineties all day. They were harvesting in the back meadow and the last of the corn to come in was being cut. Jan and I helped prepare the food and lay the long refectory table in the dining room for a large party for all the farm workers that evening. It was growing dark long before they arrived, hot and dusty from the fields, but soon the house was noisy with laughter and shouting.

Cathie had borrowed Jan's car again that day and gone over to Pincton Manor. Watching from my window I had seen her drive in at about nine and climb wearily out of the car with her bag of cameras. I heard her come upstairs and go into her room, then I heard the bath running. She came down to supper a bit late but looking very refreshed in pale red jeans and a cream linen shirt and I saw several eyes besides Duncan's on her.

Outside the window lightning flickered on and off and there were occasional low rumbles of thunder.

'Perhaps the weather will break properly this time,' my father was saying to someone down the table and I saw him wipe the back of his hand across his forehead. The enormous jugs of cider on the sideboard were already nearly empty. There was a burst of laughter from the far end of the room and the chink of cutlery and china – it was all very comforting and ordinary and happy.

The storm broke immediately overhead. One moment there was laughter and conversation and the heat coming through the long low windows which had all been thrown

390

open onto the garden and the next with a terrifying crash the heavens opened and the rain began to empty itself onto the house and fields. I saw more than one person look scared for a moment, at the sheer ferocity of that storm. It was hard to talk because of the noise of the thunder which was almost incessant, but after the initial shock of the noise most people went on eating and drinking as before. We didn't even have to close the windows, I remember, because the rain was coming straight down; it looked like silver green needles in the lightning flashes which lit up the lawn.

Then there was an extra bright flash, accompanied by a sizzle and a crack and the house seemed to rock on its foundations.

'That's a strike,' I heard my father say calmly. 'I'd better see what the damage is.' He walked out into the hall and pulled open the front door.

Mother rushed after him shouting, 'Henry, don't go out, you'll get hit, don't go out!' and Cathie, who had been standing near the door, ran after her.

I still don't know quite what happened. We could see straightaway that the east end of the stable range was on fire. It had a hay loft over it and it was very very old – about 300 years, nearly as old as the house. Mother screamed, 'My horses!' and everyone started to run.

Cathie was in front. She tore across the courtyard with Father and Sandy and Duncan just behind her, pulling open the stable door and disappearing into the smoky darkness.

Minutes later as the other men raced for buckets and ran round the back of the stable to reach the hay loft, which had great double doors opening away from the yard, two horses released from their stalls appeared at the door and careered panic-stricken across the courtyard towards the orchard. Then Sandy appeared, leading another which

391

he had blindfolded with a length of old rag. He pulled off the blindfold and sent the terrified horse off out of danger with a gentle push which sent it galloping into the darkness.

'One more,' I heard my mother saying, anguished. 'There's one more; Suki is in the box at the end, under the loft.'

Father was still inside with Duncan and Cathie as Sandy dodged round to help the men tackle the blaze from the rear. The rain was pelting down, bouncing off the cobbles, soaking our clothes and hair, turning shirts transparent against the skin.

And then I heard the scream. The most terrible sound I've ever heard. It went on and on.

The men running with buckets of water and Jan and Mother and I all stopped dead for a moment and looked at each other. I felt suddenly very sick.

The figure of a horse appeared at the stable door, lit up in a flash of lightning, her black coat gleaming in the wet, her hooves striking sparks of light as, ears back, she galloped half crazed out of the stable and away down the drive out of sight. I remember, even in my fear, vaguely hoping that the gate into the lane was shut.

Behind the horse I suddenly saw Father and Duncan appear at the door of the stable half carrying Cathie. She was sobbing uncontrollably. Father was ashen: he looked dreadful; so did Duncan. And Cathie was hysterical. Leaving her clinging to Duncan, Father came over. 'Beth, you and Jan take Vicky to the house quickly,' he said urgently to my mother. 'No one is to go into the stable; something's happened. The fire's out – they've pitched out all the hay now; there wasn't much in there luckily – but I don't want anyone going in there; not anyone, understand?' Already he was going back to Cathie.

'What is it? What's happened? Where's Sandy?' I could hear the fear in Mother's voice as she ran after him.

'It's all right; Sandy's round the side with the men. Go inside, please.' I could hear the strain in Father's voice as he snapped at her.

Duncan had his arm round Cathie. She was still crying brokenly as he tried to urge her towards the house. Another flash of lightning tore the sky open and I saw her face for the first time. I'll never forget the horror and anguish I saw there.

'Oh my God; oh my God! That poor man; oh God! Oh God!' She kept repeating it over and over. 'That poor, poor man. How could anyone; how could they? How could they?'

I stood still, shivering in the rain. What man? What was she talking about? Father had his arm round her too now and he and Duncan were half carrying her between them.

'Beth!' Father yelled after Mother. 'Ring Doctor Armstrong. Tell him to get here at once. And get that child inside!'

That was me!

I took one more look at the stable range and turning, ran after my mother.

Everyone else was still at the back of the stables, dealing with the fire, so the sitting room was deserted. Father carried Cathie in and laid her gently on the couch by the empty fireplace.

'Get the brandy, Vicky, please,' he said, seeing me standing nervously in the doorway, my eyes fixed on Cathie's limp form; her jeans and blouse were dark with rain and streaked with soot. In the hall I could hear my mother talking to Doctor Armstrong.

Cathie clung to Duncan and my father in turn. She was shaking so violently I thought for one minute that she must be putting it on, but one look at her face told me she wasn't. My own hands had started to shake as I poured out half a tumbler of brandy and took the glass to Duncan. He had his arm round her shoulders and raised her gently, putting the glass to her lips. She took a sip and then pushed it violently away.

'Christ! I could do with some of this myself.' Duncan took a drink from the glass and passed it on to Father. 'What do we do, Dad? He . . .' he hesitated, 'he wasn't alive, was he?'

Father shook his head and took another gulp of brandy. He held out the glass towards me and I ran forward with the bottle.

I felt sick. I was scared. Anything that could shake my father and my twenty-year-old brother like that had to be bad. And what had Duncan meant, 'He wasn't alive?' Who wasn't? Nervously I looked again at Cathie. Her normally tanned face was white. She clutched at Duncan convulsively.

'It was so awful,' she cried. 'The lightning came and I saw him there – three feet from my face. His eyes were open. Oh God. Oh God!' She was getting hysterical again, clinging to Duncan till I saw the skin of his forearm whiten beneath her grip.

'I know; I know, darling. I saw him too.' He was rocking her backwards and forwards in his arms as Mother came in with a rug.

'Keep her warm,' she said. 'The doctor is on the way. Now, tell me what's happened.'

For a moment there was silence as Father and Duncan looked at each other. Then Cathie, her voice rising desperately, sobbed: 'In the barn. In the barn. They've hanged someone. He's dead and his hands, oh God his hands . . .' Her voice had practically risen to a scream.

Mother reeled backwards as if she'd been hit and looked at my father.

'It's true, Beth. Duncan and I were right behind her. They've used the beam in Suki's stall; I'm surprised the horse didn't break out earlier. When we got there she panicked and flattened the wooden partition in the box. I was going to go after her when I saw it; we all saw it. The lightning showed everything for a moment. As soon as Armstrong gets here I'll get on to the police.' He sat down and put his head in his hands. 'Dear God. I went right through the war and I never saw anything so barbaric; never.'

It was a strange sight. The group of frightened, shaking people in their wet clothes, their hair flattened and blackened on their heads from the rain, their faces staring. Each time the lightning flashed the lights in the house dimmed for a second and flickered and then shone brightly again.

The doctor arrived in about fifteen minutes, roaring up the drive and swinging round to the front door where he left his car on the cobbles. He jumped out bag in hand and pushed through the open front door.

It didn't take him long to size up the situation. He gave Cathie an injection and ordered Jan and Mother to undress her and put her to bed with a hot water bottle. Then he went with Father and Duncan into the study. They shut the door.

I had been forgotten.

My curiosity got the better of me and I tiptoed out into the hall where I could hear them talking quite clearly as I sat on the bottom step of the stairs, shivering in my soaking shirt and jeans.

'I don't think he'd been there very long,' I heard my father's voice. 'The neck was obviously broken though. But to cut off a man's hands like that – ', his voice broke, 'words fail me, Armstrong.'

'Have you rung the police?' The doctor's voice was professionally calm.

'Not yet. Cathie was so hysterical and I wanted to get the women away.'

'Quite so. Well, if I may suggest, I'll go and have a look myself. No – you needn't come with me. I'm probably more used to these things than you; although, in this case . . .'

I could hear them opening the french windows, which overlooked the courtyard at the front of the house, and then their voices grew fainter and disappeared. Obviously Father and Duncan had decided to go with him.

I got up and slipped out of the front door. What I had heard nauseated me, but I was far too curious to be left indoors. I had to follow them. I saw the three figures striding through the rain towards the stable. The high loft door on this side was open too now and the bales of charred hay had been pushed down onto the cobbles. A man was standing up there with a pitchfork and I saw him raise his hand to my father in a thumbs up sign. The fire was well and truly out. Wisps of curdling steam crawled up through the loft doors and through the old red tiles but that was all. I could see the three horses from the stable standing on the far side of the courtyard by the orchard gate, sheltering beneath the old crab apple tree which overhung the wall. Beyond it our ponies were pale shapes in the dark.

I suddenly realized that there hadn't been any thunder or lightning for several minutes now. The storm was moving off towards the north east at last.

I wondered briefly what had happened to Suki. There was no sign of her. It scared me that my mother hadn't gone frantic with worry about her precious championship mare; everything was frightening that night and unreal. I shivered again in the dark. It was still raining hard.

I tiptoed across the wet cobbles to the stable door and waited, my heart thumping with terror. They had left it open and I could see the strong beam of Father's torch as he walked slowly down the line of stalls, followed by Duncan and the doctor. I knew the stable so well. The eight stalls and the old loose box at the end, Suki's box, with its blackened warped oak beam about ten feet off the ground.

Nothing could have made me take another step into that stable. The light stopped moving and I saw the three shadowy figures of the men stop. The torch beam raked up and down, roof to floor; I imagined it illuminating every wisp of hay in Suki's box – and anything else that was there. I shuddered at the thought. Then the light was joined by another. The doctor too must have had a torch on him. The two thin beams crossed and recrossed flashing up at the walls and roof; then all three men moved out of my line of vision into the box itself. I could feel the sweat standing out on my forehead as I stood there in the doorway, just out of the driving rain.

At first I didn't even notice the sound of hooves on the cobbles behind me. Then I heard a nervous whicker and turning, I saw the black pony standing, nostrils flaring, near the doctor's car. It was almost a relief to have to do something. I reached for one of the head collars on the rack inside the door and made my way out into the rain again.

To my surprise she came to me, pushing her head into my hands, almost begging for the head collar to be buckled round her ears. I stroked her rather nervously – Suki had a wicked nip and only my mother usually handled her – and discovered that she was trembling from head to foot.

I started to walk slowly towards the house and she followed without my having to pull on the rein, her head pushed hard into the crook of my arm and it dawned on me that she was probably as scared as anyone else by what had happened and that she was seeking reassurance, just as I was.

I met my mother at the front door. She had at last done the sensible thing and having put Cathie to bed and left her with Jan, she had put on a mac and gumboots and collected a torch. 'Vicky, you've caught her!' She reached out for the head collar. 'Is she hurt?'

'I don't think so.' My teeth had started chattering.

'Mummy. She's scared. She really is scared. Whatever happened in there – it's terrified her.'

'I know.' My mother was crooning gently into the pony's ear. 'I'll put her into the back paddock. And the other ponies with her. They'll be safe in there, and well away from whatever must happen.'

Whatever must happen? For the first time I thought of stretchers and police cars and ambulances racing up the long gravelled drive from the lane and I bit my lip as I watched my mother lead the trembling pony away round the corner of the house.

Then I turned to look back at the stables. They were still in the dark. I wondered suddenly why the lights weren't on. The fire presumably had fused the switches or something. Then I saw the thin beam of torchlight crossing behind one of the windows; then the next. Someone was walking back down the line of the stalls towards the door.

The three men reappeared, crossing slowly towards me, talking earnestly together. I waited in the hall, kicking off my wet shoes, idly inspecting my toe prints on the scrubbed flags.

The door opened and the three men appeared. 'I'll give the chief constable a ring, Armstrong,' my father was saying. 'I think this ought to go straight to him. Go on in and give yourselves a brandy. I'll be with you in a moment.'

Duncan and the doctor passed me, going into the sitting

room, and I heard the chink of glasses as I followed Dad to the study and stood in the doorway as he dialled.

'Hello? Bill?' He sat down on the edge of the desk and then realizing how wet he was stood up again hurriedly. 'Sorry to call you so late, old man, but I've a bit of a puzzle on my hands.' There was a pause, then he gave a short tense laugh. 'Yes. No, worse actually. Well, yes it was the storm in a way. No, I got the last of it in today, thank goodness. Listen, Bill. We had a bit of a fire in the hay loft – lightning struck a tree just behind it. We rushed over to get the horses out as fast as possible of course and we found something in there, Bill. A man has been hanged in there. What? Yes. In the loose box at the end. No, he was quite dead; no doubt about it I'm afraid. Three of us saw him: my son Duncan and myself and a girl who is staying with us. No, no idea who it was. No Bill, it wouldn't have been suicide; there's no question about that; someone had hacked off both his hands at the wrists. Yes.' There was quite a long pause as the voice at the other end spoke agitatedly into the phone. I could see the beads of perspiration standing out on my father's forehead.

'Yes, there was a lot of blood. But listen, Bill. He's gone. Yes – there's no trace of him now – nor of any blood. Armstrong is here and I took him over to see what he could do, but there is absolutely no trace of the body now. No trace at all. We were indoors for, I suppose, perhaps half an hour. But it's disappeared.'

I gasped and my father noticed me for the first time. He frowned and motioned me away, but I stayed where I was.

'It did cross our minds,' he went on into the phone, 'that the stables could have been fired deliberately to destroy all trace of everything – but then the tree was definitely struck. No question of that. Yes – so you'll come up yourself then? No, nothing's been touched. We've sent everyone else home now; they don't know what's happened. OK.'

He hung up and turned to me. 'The chief constable is bringing up a forensic team. He's getting them all out of bed if necessary.' He gave me a watery smile. 'I suppose it's no good telling you to go to bed, Vicky?'

I shook my head vehemently. 'I'd have nightmares, Daddy,' I said in a small voice and suddenly my eyes were full of tears.

I ran to him and he put his arms round me comfortingly. 'I know, love,' he said gently into my hair. 'I wish you hadn't heard – but there's nothing to be done till the police get here. Come and have a sip of brandy. It'll buck you up. Where's your mother?'

'With the mares.'

He nodded. 'Just as well to keep busy.' He frowned. 'She shouldn't be out there on her own, though.' He stood up, releasing me abruptly. 'I'll go and fetch her. Go through to Duncan, Vicky, and stay with him, understand?'

'You think they're still here, don't you, the people who did it?' My voice quavered childishly.

'Not for one moment. Don't think about it. Look darling, Dr Armstrong is going to give poor Cathie another shot before he goes. To make her sleep through into tomorrow. Would you like him to give you something?'

I shook my head and swallowed hard. 'No, I'm all right. Go and find Mummy, and I'll go and have a drink of brandy.'

I went into the sitting room and accepted a minuscule dose of brandy from the doctor and then I sat shivering on the edge of the sofa while the two men talked until my parents came in together. Then of course my mother took one look at me and packed me upstairs for a hot bath and a change of clothes, although she didn't insist that I go to bed.

The police arrived about half an hour later with search-lights and a large alsatian dog. They quartered the farm and nearly dismantled the stable block but it appeared that the rain, which hadn't eased for hours, had been heavy enough to remove any trace there might have been of tracks of any kind.

It must have been in the early hours of the morning that they eventually packed up and went. I had given in to my exhaustion at about midnight and crawled into bed, but I can't say I slept awfully well. My bravado, what there was of it, had left me completely in the loneliness of my bedroom, with its pale chintz curtains blowing so innocently in the open window and I left my bedside light on all night, pulling the thin single sheet up over my head. Somehow I still couldn't get the sound of Cathie's terrible screams out of my mind.

She came down next day at about mid morning, looking pale and shaken but otherwise more or less her old self. It was a glorious sunny day. The early morning had been white with low-lying mist as I looked out, but later it heated up again, until the temperature was as high as ever.

The farm returned to normal very quickly; or nearly so. The stables were searched again by daylight, but nothing was found. The hayloft was swept and repaired. It was as if nothing had happened at all. It was hard to believe by the next day that there had ever been a storm, or a fire – or a dreadful, insane murder. Except that no one was allowed to go out by themselves any more; there had to be at least two or three of us – even the farm men went about in pairs and we locked the doors and windows as dark approached, in spite of the heat. And the horses remembered. When my mother tried to lead Suki back into the stable she laid her ears back, her eyes rolling in terror and reared up with a terrified snort. They didn't try and make her go back in there again.

Cathie stayed with us another week and managed, with Duncan at her side constantly, to complete the rest of her photographs before she got ready to leave. She and Duncan arranged to meet in town as soon as his term started, and apart from the fact that it meant parting from him so soon, I suspected that she was very glad indeed to leave Camber Court. I was very sad to see her go. I liked Cathie enormously.

Nothing was ever found to give any clues as to what had occurred that night. There was no trace of any body; the poor man's description, as far as my father and Duncan managed to provide one, fitted no one who had been reported missing and as far as the police file went the murder went completely unsolved.

No one would ever have been any the wiser had it not been by the most extraordinary coincidence that we found out who the victim was. It was more than a year later when Father's Aunt Flavia arrived on a Christmas visit home from Canada. She was a tall, very upright old lady of, I suppose, about eighty, with brilliant blue eyes in her tanned face and a strong Canadian accent. It was tacitly understood by the family that no one would mention the horrible happenings of the summer before last but one night about three days after she had arrived when we were all sitting round the fire after supper, the incident was mentioned after all.

'Well my dears,' said Aunt Flavia, looking round with bright inquisitive eyes, 'have any of you ever seen the ghosts of Camber?'

She seemed disappointed that no one had, although we were all to varying degrees excited at the idea. I had often wondered if there might be a ghost or two at Camber but no one seemed to know. The house had belonged to our family for four hundred years although my father himself had been brought up in Canada and had only inherited it during the war when his uncle John and John's only two sons had all been killed, and although he loved it and felt it to be in his 'blood and bones' as he put it, he knew comparatively little about its history.

'There are two ghosts actually,' said his aunt, seeing that she had our attention. 'A lady who walks in the rose garden on summer nights and a little boy who runs about the upstairs corridors sometimes.' She looked round hopefully but none of us could claim to have seen either of them.

'How on earth do you know all this, Aunt Flavia?' my mother asked suspiciously. Aunt Flavia laughed.

'Very old books, my dear. My father left me lots of books which mention Camber. I don't know why he ever brought them out to Canada because they rightfully belong here. You shall have them all back when I die.'

'There must be a lot of history attached to this house,' Duncan commented lazily. He was sitting on the window seat, one leg up on the cushion in front of him. 'Cathie's book will be out soon; there's a whole chapter on Camber in that. I know Charles II came here once. Did anything else exciting ever happen here, Aunt, I've often wondered?'

She frowned. 'There was one time. At the time of the Monmouth Rebellion, against James II – do you remember? Judge Jeffreys and his ilk. There was a terrible fight here a bit later; young Marcus Nicholls, the son of the house, had fought for Monmouth at Sedgemoor and they captured him here in his own home. He was given a summary trial by some of the King's officers in the dining room here at Camber according to my book and they sentenced him to be hanged.' She paused, frowning for a moment. 'I believe he is supposed to have stood up and shouted defiantly at his accusers something about giving his right arm to serve King Charles's son and one of them said that in that case he would give Marcus the chance to give both.' There was a long pause. Then she went on. 'They cut off both his hands before they hanged him – somewhere in the outbuildings to the Court, I gather. According to the story he cursed King James and all his followers and said that if any of them or their descendants ever set foot in Camber again he would haunt them. They say he died very bravely, poor young man.'

She looked round. I don't know what reception she expected for her story but certainly not the stunned incredulity which showed on every face in the room.

My father stood up and reached uncertainly for a cigarette. 'When did you say this happened, Flavia?'

'1685 dear, after Sedgemoor. Why? What's the matter with you all?'

'This young man, Marcus. What did he look like?'

'I don't know. How could I possibly? There's probably a portrait of him in the house somewhere. Why?' She suddenly sat up, looking from face to face. 'You've seen him, haven't you?' She went pale.

I had suddenly begun to feel terribly cold. I moved nearer the fire and catching my mother's eye I saw she had begun to shiver too. The fine pale hairs on her forearms were standing straight up on end suddenly. I watched fascinated.

Father told Flavia the story from beginning to end and she listened, nodding slowly from time to time. When he had finished she looked up and gave a faint smile. 'Obviously this poor girl Cathie was the catalyst. She must be a descendant of one of the murderers – even of James himself – you said that her name is Steuart? What an awful thing.'

'I can't believe it.' Father relit his cigarette which had gone out while he was talking. 'I can't believe that that was an – apparition. I saw it. Duncan here saw it, it wasn't only Cathie.'

'But it disappeared, Dad.' Duncan spoke at last from the dim corner on the window seat. 'It disappeared without trace, without blood.'

'And it's still there.' Mother's voice was strangely flat. 'That's why Suki and the other horses still won't enter the stable, after all this time.' I hadn't plucked up the courage to either.

'The police dog knew,' Sandy added suddenly. 'Its hackles were all over the place and it growled and growled in that loose box and yet there was absolutely no scent for it to follow.'

'Are you going to tell Cathie this story?' Father suddenly turned towards Duncan.

'You must tell her,' Flavia said. 'She has the right to know. And the poor girl can't exactly have forgotten an incident like that. I don't know if it will help to put her mind at rest at all, knowing that, but she should know; she's part of the destiny of Camber.'

I wondered if anyone besides myself noticed the violent blush which coloured Duncan's cheeks as she said those words.

'Does it mean she won't be able to come back here without it happening again?' I asked quietly. She never had come back to Camber, although we had all been to visit her in London and gone to her parents' house in Bedfordshire.

Duncan frowned. 'Surely not?' He looked at Flavia, but she shrugged.

'What about an exorcism?' Sandy said suddenly. 'You know, bell, book and candle, the lot!'

'No.' Flavia rose slowly to her feet. 'No. Whatever happened here that night, has not, as far as we know, happened in 300 years before. It may not happen again for as long.

It may be that the thunderstorm and the fire had something to do with it; generating psychic energy or something. Leave it alone. That's my advice; leave it alone.'

'And the police?' Father stubbed out his cigarette and went to stand with his back to the fire. 'What do I tell the police? That the murder I reported witnessing happened 300 years ago and they'd better close the case?'

Flavia frowned. 'No, dear. Don't say anything to the police. They'll think you were drunk or something. It will have to go down on their files as unsolved. Leave it at that.'

And leave it at that we did. Except for one incident.

There was a portrait of Marcus Nicholls in the house. We found it hanging in a dark corner on the top landing where it had hardly been noticed before. It showed a tall, slim youth in riding breeches, one hand on the neck of a bony bay mare. He was a bit like Duncan to look at, I thought; the same nose and gently humorous mouth, but he had my eyes. Sandy pointed it out first. 'I say, look at that. We all wanted to know where Vicky got her big green eyes and dark hair. Well, there's your answer.'

I went back later to look at the portrait by myself. They were right. He did have my eyes. He looked friendly and kind and I could swear that he was watching me.

Everyone was busy in the garden that afternoon, gathering holly and ivy and mistletoe to decorate the house, so no one noticed when I slipped away.

The stable was deserted; the stalls swept and empty. Hardly anyone went in there any more as far as I knew. I took a deep breath, screwing up my courage and stepped inside. There was the age old smell of sweet hay and horses and dust and still a suspicion of the tang of burning.

Cautiously I made my way down the line of stalls watching the sunbeams slipping in through the high windows in the wall. I nearly didn't go as far as the loose box. My courage was ebbing fast.

Then I stood there, by the repaired partition which Suki had splintered. The door was still off, leaning against the wall. I looked in. The box was quite empty and absolutely quiet. A little patch of sunshine lit up the stone floor under the old blackened beam. Was it my imagination, or was there a brooding atmosphere about the place?

I swallowed. Then I went in. I produced from behind my back the small bunch of winter jasmine and frosted rose buds which I had cut in the bright cold of the garden and I knelt and laid them on the stone. Then I looked up. 'Please don't hate any more,' I said out loud. Was it just because we shared the same green eyes that I knew Marcus would listen to me? 'Please forgive. Go in peace and let Cathie come back to Camber. Please.'

I waited for a minute and then, feeling a little foolish, I scrambled to my feet and dusted the knees of my jeans. But somehow I felt better. I knew I wouldn't be afraid to come in there again.

The strength of the winter sun had woken a butterfly, which was trapped against the dusty window in the passage. I could hear it fluttering against the glass as I turned to go. Reaching up I pushed open the window and watched it soar up into the ice blue sky, then I walked out of the stable and made my way back towards the house.

Salesmanship!

Sylvia would insist on coming to the door and peering in as he worked. He didn't turn, but he could feel her eyes boring into the canvas, analysing the brush strokes, quartering the painting for new details. The sureness of his touch would falter and slow until he laid the brush down and waited, teeth clenched, for her to go away.

'Coffee, Sammy?' She was aware instantly that he knew her to be there.

'Thanks.' He bit the end of his palette knife and grimaced at the bitter stickiness of the paint on it.

'It's nearly finished, isn't it?' Her voice was breezy, encouraging, even patronizing.

'That's right.' Grudgingly he admitted it, stepping back to survey it himself.

'It's the best you've ever done.'

She always said that, silly bitch. If his paintings were so bloody good, why didn't they sell?

He'd asked her that once and she had looked at the ground and waved her hands apologetically, her cigarette shedding ash over the spare room floor. There was no carpet; a carpet would have been a concession to its spareroomness; boards confirmed its status as his studio.

'They'll sell one day,' she had affirmed and he had snorted.

'When I'm discovered, I suppose,' he commented sarcastically.

She brought him the coffee and he laid down his palette and sipped it. It was real. Sylvia refused to use instant and that irritated him too; real coffee upset his stomach. Mercifully she went away then and he heard the ting as the phone receiver was raised from the cradle. He relaxed. He had often wished there was a lock on the spare room door. Then he could have ensured his privacy. To put one on now at this late stage would be too hurtful for Sylvia, but if he had established a precedent for painting behind locked doors from the start it would have been all right. And it would have been so much better.

The painting was good; he gazed at it, critically, just bathing himself in his achievement. The brush strokes were sure; the composition controlled and interesting, the colour and subject . . . He smiled. The subject was exquisite. He closed one eye to get a better look at it and his joy survived even that test.

Later he went out. Only for a half. It wouldn't take long and, after all, it was Saturday.

When he returned Sylvia was in the studio and with her were two strangers, a man and a woman. All three were standing before the painting talking in hushed voices.

Sammy stopped abruptly, suspicious. He had never suspected her of bringing in her friends to gloat. He felt a suppressed fury that the woman should be so disloyal and took a deep breath, summoning up a scathing remark which would without being overtly rude, send them chastised on their way. But Sylvia forestalled him.

'Here *is* my husband,' she exclaimed turning as if she hadn't realized that he was there.

The two with her turned in unison and smiled uncertainly, almost guiltily, at him.

'These are Paul and Joy,' Sylvia gushed. That was

unusual for her. It meant she was unsure of her ground. 'They run the new art gallery in Chichampton.'

Inwardly Sammy stiffened. Outwardly he bit back his remark and smiled instead, holding out his hand.

'Your wife kindly asked us over to look at your work, Mr Korner.' Joy was obviously the spokesperson. She was tiny and slim, in apple-green jeans with a muted blue shirt knotted below a token bust line. 'And I'm so glad we came. They're fantastic.' Her expansive gesture taking in the whole room, including the windows he noted, nearly knocked her colleague on the nose. Paul dodged expertly, then he nodded long sufferingly, presumably seconding her opinion.

'We'd certainly like to take two or three for the gallery, wouldn't we, Paul?' She rushed on.

Again he nodded.

'This one on the easel; it's powerful. We must have it. Do you have a framer?' In the fascination of watching her bobbed hair flopping enthusiastically in time with her speech, Sammy missed the question. Then he noticed Sylvia looking worried. It was an unusual sight and he pulled himself together rapidly to find out why.

'I'm sorry,' he smiled, he hoped with all his charm. 'I missed that question.'

'Your framer, dear,' Sylvia hissed. 'She was asking about your framer.'

'I haven't got a framer,' Sammy commented candidly, still distracted by the hair. 'I've never sold any of the paintings and for ourselves we've always made do by just hanging them up as they are.'

He saw from Sylvia's black look that he had said the wrong thing. Of course he should have implied that he sold lots of paintings and that he had a tame framer. They could always have found one later. But it was too late.

Joy did not seem worried by his naivety. On the con-

410

trary, she seemed even more delighted. 'It is so exciting to make a *discovery*!' she pronounced earnestly. 'Our very own discovery. I am glad you came in and asked us, Mrs Korner. We might never have seen your husband's work otherwise.'

Sylvia looked contrite. As well she might, thought Sammy. But he couldn't help being pleased with her. So she really had had faith in him. She hadn't just been flannelling all this time.

He listened in a daze while Joy named dates and discussed, apparently with herself, the technicalities of mounting and presenting the paintings she wanted. She wrote down the name of a framer for him – strange, he thought, she had close-bitten nails like a little girl – and then she and Paul had gone.

He and Sylvia stood looking at each other in the hall.

'I hope you don't mind, Sammy.' Sylvia sounded rather scared. 'I knew they'd be interested. It seemed so silly not to try to sell some of your paintings. We could do with the money.'

Sammy winced at the last remark but on the whole he was prepared to forgive her even that. After all she was the one who had dared. Half shyly he put his arm round her and planted a hesitant kiss on her cheek. She giggled and after a second moved away.

He went back up to the studio later, clicked on the light and drew the cheap cotton curtains. The painting on the easel stared at him reproachfully. Was it really finished? Under normal circumstances he might have pottered around adding the odd touch of paint here and there for days, but now . . . 'Don't touch it, Mr Korner; I forbid you to touch it; it's *perfect*.' The sound of Joy's high-pitched voice echoed for a moment in his head. Don't touch it! His own painting! He wandered restlessly round the room looking at other pictures; thinking, staring. Unconsciously he picked up the afternoon's palette and dabbed at a still life leaning against the wall. As the paint made contact he jumped back guiltily. After all it was going to be framed. It couldn't go with wet patches on it. He put down the brush miserably.

Then with resolution he went to the easel and lifted down the painting. It was finished and that was that. The time had come to prepare another new, virgin canvas.

Half an hour later he sloped downstairs and sat down on the sofa next to Sylvia. She was concentrating on the television and didn't look round, but after a moment or two her hand, crawling hesitantly across the cushion, sought his and held on. Her eyes remained glued to the screen where unbelievably a large coffee jar appeared.

'That's it; that's what I wish you'd buy.' Sammy was momentarily stirred to enthusiasm. 'Look, look!' He tugged at her hand.

'I am looking!' She sounded cross and Sammy scanned her profile anxiously.

'I do like real coffee, love.' He hated the apologetic note in his voice. Why couldn't he just tell her? 'It's just that it doesn't like me.' He shrugged helplessly and impassively she watched the screen which was now promoting with equal vigour the nutritional properties of a well-known chocolate bar.

He sighed.

When he wandered into the kitchen to boil the kettle she didn't seem to notice. He left a cup of tea, a peace offering, on the table beside her and crept back up the stairs.

Ten minutes later the painting was back on the easel, a corner wiped clean and a new idea under way. What the hell did Joy know about it anyway? A painting was a living, breathing, changing thing until it was actually sealed under varnish and left to hang in the dust.

His tongue protruding a little between his teeth he worked hard. Occasionally he hummed a little. His tea grew cold; the top filmed over unnoticed.

At closedown Sylvia looked in and watched in her accustomed manner over his shoulder for a while; but she was gone, yawning, before his arm had a chance to falter this time. He was relieved. If she had spotted what he had done she might have come right in and given an opinion. That would not have been welcome; not at the moment.

He worked hard, concentrating on every brush stroke. By two o'clock the painting was perfect; Joy would never have recognized it.

Sammy stood back as he cleaned his brushes and smiled. He was a satisfied man.

By half past two he was in despair. The realization had just dawned on him that he could never part with it; no, nor any of the other paintings which had suffered those rummaging critical hands. They were part of him; a very sensitive part of him. Supposing someone bought one and then became so used to it they never even saw it any more? Sammy groaned out loud.

He crept into the bedroom and fumbled for the light switch beside his bed. Sylvia always awoke in a fury when he crashed around in the dark, trying to be quiet. With the light on she merely awoke indignant.

'I'm sorry, love,' he whispered automatically as she stirred. 'I'll only be a jiffy.' There was paint on his shirt cuff. Guiltily he rolled it up, sleeve innermost and pushed it under a chair.

'I'll bet you altered that painting.' Her voice was sleepy, but her eyes peering over the duvet at him were intense.

'I had to, Syl.' He sat on the bed to take his socks off. 'The balance was all wrong. I've got it right now, though.'

413

'I'll bet you something else too.' She pulled herself up on one elbow.

'Oh?' He felt foolish sitting there with one sock on, one off.

'You won't let her have it in the end. Nor any of them, will you?'

To his surprise she was grinning. 'I never said that, Syl.'

'You didn't have to.' She leaned across and put her arm round him affectionately. 'It's written all over your face, you poor booby.' She kissed him and then lay back on the pillows watching as he removed his other sock.

'I'm going to tell you something, lover.' She never called him that except when she had overspent the house-keeping money or broken one of his mother's best crystal glasses.

He wished he'd got his pyjama trousers on. He felt too vulnerable sitting there in his pants.

'What?' he asked cautiously.

'You never noticed that one or two of your paintings – well, six actually – were missing, did you?'

He sat up straight, frowning. 'Missing?'

She nodded. 'I sold them. Oh, I kept the money for you. I just never dared tell you, somehow.' She looked miserably hard at her finger nails and took an absent-minded bite at one of them.

'You what?' He had grown cold.

'Sold them. I've watched you, Sammy. You look at them and fiddle with them and alter them and talk to them even. Then, wham! They're leaning against the wall. You look at them twice then they're turned face in and you forget them. It's criminal. They're forgotten. And they're begging to be hung up somewhere to be looked at.'

To his astonishment a great tear welled up in one of

414

her eyes. It teetered on the rim for a moment and then overbalanced, splashing down onto her cheek.

Sammy swallowed hard. 'I never noticed,' he whispered. It was the most terrible treachery. 'I never even saw that they had gone.' He was silent for a moment. 'I remember every painting I ever painted.'

'Of course you do.' She sat up again. 'But Sammy love, they're four or five deep round the walls, some of them. Oh Sammy. They deserve better. They deserve to be seen.'

'You sold them through Joy?' His voice was still hesitant.

She shook her head. 'I only met Joy this morning; well, yesterday morning now.' She corrected herself. 'The others I took to a gallery in London.' She took another bite at her nail and Sammy winced.

'How much did you get?' He couldn't help asking.

'Fifty each for the two little ones. Seventy-five for three others and £150 for the *Forest Fire*.' She looked at him sideways to see how he was taking it.

'I was fond of the *Forest Fire*.' He was mournful.

'It's nearly five hundred pounds, Sammy.'

'I always thought I'd change it so that the trees were silhouetted against the sky more.'

'Well four seventy-five anyway.'

'I suppose you sold the *Marionette*? I was looking for her the other day. I thought the strings ought to be tangled.'

'She fetched seventy-five pounds, Sam.'

'She'd have been so much better if I'd had a chance to work on her some more.' He got up at last and found his pyjamas. 'I suppose you want commission for handling the sales?' He turned round suddenly and appeared to be quite serious.

Sylvia smothered a giggle. 'I wouldn't say no, lover.'

She waited while he disappeared into the bathroom.

When he was sitting next to her she turned to him. 'I do care about the paintings, Sam. I'm sure they went to good homes, you know.'

Biting his lip Sammy lay back and switched off the light. 'Of course they did. I'm just being silly, I know it. But that's the way I am.'

'And Joy can have the pictures she wanted?' She was almost wheedling.

'Sometime, I suppose, yes.'

Sylvia gave a big sigh of satisfaction. 'As long as it's sometime, Sammy, there's no hurry.'

She turned over and settled herself for sleep contentedly. She knew exactly how long it would take! And this time she would claim her commission. She had already worked out just how much it would cost to buy a smart portfolio for carrying Sammy's paintings. Not for him of course. She was the salesperson in this family. She smiled in the darkness. Poor Sammy. She really must try and remember to buy a jar of instant coffee for him. First thing on Monday morning.

A Quest For Identity

When Katherine was seven she wanted to be a nun. She fingered her mother's coral beads lovingly, as a rosary, and threaded to them the cross she bought with her pocket money and chose herself from the black flock tray in the window of the second-hand shop on the corner. It was of chased silver, wafer thin and very holy. At the bottom of the garden, deep in a most secret place among the sooty privets, she had made from an old orange box an altar and there she played at churches, her head draped in the mantilla of an old dressing-up shawl.

At boarding school there was a chapel; stark, serviceable and compulsory. She threw herself into the daily service with fervour, mouthing the hymns in a reverent whisper, half disapproving when her friends heartily shouted the well-worn verses and screwing up her eyes during the prayers in an effort of concentration.

Confirmation classes begged from a reluctant father – 'You're not serious are you, Kate? All that mumbo-jumbo!' – were a bitter disappointment. Held in the cold chapel when other less dedicated people were at prep, the only sound save for the chaplain's bored voice, was the agonizing embarrassment of her own stomach rumbling.

But the day of confirmation itself was a success. The pretty white dresses and veils, the beautiful illuminated postcard from matron, mother in her best hat; and the bishop. The bishop was quite beautiful and she almost fainted with excitement to feel his hands upon her head. She accepted the glow of happiness within her as a genuine inspiring experience and knew that at last the mystery she sought had come to her. Her first communion in the cold spring morning, light-headed from lack of breakfast, excited and half-afraid, maintained the wonder and the exhilaration.

But as the months passed so did her resolution. Getting up early on Sunday was all very well in the summer but on foggy winter mornings it was a different matter. By the time she left school she had stopped going to church in the holidays altogether.

At university she read philosophy and deliberately abandoned the one religion in the quest for the truths of many. The search left her interested, well-read and with a BA, but without faith. And she no longer felt the need for it. Her life was full of material things; of work and play; of friends and men; of parties and books and fun. There were no more long evenings leaning elbows on sill, gazing from her bedroom window at the infinities of heaven. She shared her bedroom at the flat with three and peace was a non-existent commodity even in the depths of night. The agonizing soul-searching quest of the teenager had been replaced by the complacent confidence of a healthy young woman. If her soul still cried out for succour she firmly ignored the call. She rejected faith now as consciously and outspokenly as she rejected her parents' standards and values as being bourgeois, old-hat and faintly ridiculous.

George was an atheist. And at first everything that George said and did had the ring of absolute truth in her ears. She gazed into his eyes and hung adoring on his every word.

'It's ourselves that count, Kate. We are what we are and life is what we make it. No rational person can believe

418

our course is dictated by a bearded old man in the sky.'
He put his arm round her waist and squeezed her playfully.

'You're right, it's up to us.' Dazzled by his smile she
followed him to parties and dances. She entertained for
him and ended up darning his socks when she moved into
his Notting Hill basement. Her parents threatened to wash
their hands of her but both secretly came, each not telling
the other and swearing her to complicity in their guilt, as
they looked around the two dingy rooms with the stuffing-
less sofa, the clothes horses draped with towels and the
uncompromisingly small double bed. Her mother brought
her a bunch of chrysanthemums and michaelmas˜daisies
the colour of the smoky autumn sky and the scent of her
tweed skirt was of bonfires and new-mown grass.

Kate cried when her mother had gone. Her free-think-
ing independence hinted suddenly of squalor.

Then came Mary Thomas with whom she had been at
school. Sweet angelic Mary, whose gym tunic had never
been creased and stained was exactly the same, if a little
plumper. She was not, as Kate had secretly expected,
impressed and envious of *la vie bohème*.

'Oh Kate, how awful.' Mary looked round with blatant
and sincere horror. 'That dreadful man. How does he
expect you to live like this? Oh Kate, can't you leave him?
Why do you stay?' She turned over the dusty books on the
mantelpiece with fastidious fingers and touched by accident
a mouldy piece of cheese which Kate had put down a few
nights before and unaccountably lost.

'I love it like this,' Kate countered indignantly. 'This
is the life I've chosen. I meet interesting people; I read
interesting books. We save our money to go to the theatre
and concerts. George is not interested in material possessions and I agree with him.'

'I suppose he'd think I was a bourgeois old hen then.'
Mary smiled gently, but the expression in her eyes made

Kate think again. Mary was laughing at him. She saw his ideas as ridiculous and silly. 'It must be just like being a student still,' she went on, and Kate was confirmed in her opinion. Mary was quietly confident in her own way of life and in her eyes she and George were irresponsible children. The idea shocked Kate very much.

'What a boring cow she must be!' George shouted with laughter when Kate told him of the visit. 'I'll bet coming to see us is the most exciting thing she's done since she left school.'

'She's had a baby, George.' Kate did not mean to sound reproachful. It was wonder she felt for the experience her best friend had had which she could not share.

'Well, there's no great virtue in that. She's just adding to the population problem.' Unimpressed George threw himself down in the chair and put his feet on the table. He had brought the *New Statesman* home and was at once immersed in it.

'But George, she's happy. Really happy, and . . .' Kate groped for a word, rejected it as trite and cosy and then unable to find another, reluctantly produced it. 'She's fulfilled.'

There was another snort of derision from behind the paper, but no further comment.

Kate retreated to the kitchenette and began to open tins. Mary would undoubtedly by now be preparing a nourishing and wholesome meal for her family, made with real food; her saucepans probably matched and her kitchen would have come entire and co-ordinated from the pages of a glossy magazine.

Kate looked up at the greasy grey wall behind the cooker. Once she had begun to wash this corner and her efforts had ended sharply and distinctively in an uncompromising black line. The shiny road safety poster disguised nothing. She had given up not even half-way through the job and it showed.

Depressed she poured the contents of her saucepan into two bowls and carried them to the table where George's feet still rested, side by side, showing a hole in the shiny sole of one shoe.

'Has anyone ever told you that you behave like a peasant?' she said with unexpected venom. He peered over his paper and slowly removed first one and then the other foot from the table.

'Yes, you, honey, with boring repetitiveness. But you've never told me how you're so sure the nobs don't stick their plates of meat on the Chippendale.' He picked up his spoon and started eating ravenously. 'Or did *mummy* tell you?'

She hated the way he emphasized the word, debasing it to sound cheap and silly by a mere flicker of inflection. His occasional bitter sarcasm, always aroused if he thought she was getting at him through his background, usually reduced her to tears. His tone was too acrid not to be genuine.

Turning unhappily from her own food she rummaged under the cushion for a packet of cigarettes. She had given up giving up. 'I'd like to go out for a meal, George. Somewhere nice, just for once. Could we?' She blew a cloud of smoke in the air and pushed her hair back from her eyes. It was unwashed and stringy. Mary's had been immaculately styled. She checked her thoughts abruptly. It was almost as though she were jealous, which was unthinkable. She renounced her parents' way of life absolutely and that, after all, was the style Mary followed. It might work for Mary, but not for her. 'Please, George.'

He looked up suddenly, hearing the note of desperation in her voice. 'Katie, love. Of course we can, if it means that much to you. Candles, wine, dancing – the lot if it will make you happy.' He scraped his bowl and eyed hers speculatively. 'Aren't you hungry?'

'You have it.' She ground out the cigarette and threw herself down on the sofa. 'I'll have some coffee in a minute.'

'She really got under your skin today, didn't she?' He got up at last and ruffled her hair gently. 'Are you having regrets about living here?'

'No, of course not.' She reached for his hand and pulled him down on the sofa with her. 'It's just that I miss some things . . .' She broke off helplessly, looking round at the torn wallpaper, the shabby furniture, the threadbare rugs. It was as though for the first time she had seen them through her own eyes. Before she had always seen them through his. When her parents came she had been consciously on the defensive, but Mary's open criticism had caught her unawares, unguarded.

'It's not very nice, George, is it? Be honest.' She gazed at him intently. But he just shrugged.

'To *be* honest, Kate, I never notice. It suits me fine. It's cheap and it's warm and it's convenient. What more do I want?'

What more indeed?

On her way back from work the next day Kate hesitated in front of the greengrocer by the station. On the pavement lay ranks of potted bulbs, houseplants and buckets of golden daffodils. She eyed them longingly, trying to ignore the exorbitant price tags pinned to them. A florid young man came out of the shop wiping his hands on his overall.

'Can I help you, love?'

He stood in front of the flowers as if to prevent her even looking at them unless she meant to buy. Wordlessly she shook her head and turned away.

Three days later George had to go away to attend a conference. It was the first time she had had to sleep alone in the flat and she found herself lying gazing up at the ceiling in the dark, listening for all the strange city noises which now suddenly seemed hostile around her. The flat itself was hostile. It was George's, but for the first time since she moved in it was not a vehicle for George's dominating personality and without him there, without his belongings scattered to the four corners it was dead and dull. Of her own personality and her dreams it reflected nothing at all.

She sat up in bed suddenly and turned on the bedside light. What were her dreams? Where was her personality? Wrinkling her forehead to think better, she gazed at the paisley design of the old eiderdown. A sharp quill was sticking through the material near her hand and absent-mindedly she pulled at it, watched as the delicate white feather drew through the tiny hole and opened like a flower in her hand. It was soft and pure and rather poignant.

At school she had dreamed of being a grown up. When she had stopped wanting to be a nun she had wanted to be a nurse, then in turn a riding instructor, a vet, a secretary with beautifully manicured nails, an artist and a concert pianist. But when the careers mistress, realistic, short of time and possibly of insight, intent on actualities had probed into the subject she had had to admit, even then, a lack of any real purpose.

It was taken for granted she would go to university – her grades had always been good – but her choice of subject, philosophy, had been a surprise to everyone. Kate could explain neither the origin nor the depth of her interest, but her examination results proved that this was indeed her subject. Graduation had brought the return of reality. Decisions could no longer be deferred. Or could they? Her contemporaries hoped for a career in TV or publishing or journalism and she had half-heartedly drifted with them. But of course she had failed her interviews; the keen young men saw at once through her veneer and spotted her lethargy and indecision. So she reverted to a quick course in shorthand typing and then as she had been at last about to face up to some half-hearted self analysis she had met George. Unbelievably he too had been doing a typing course, although his was part of a master plan for his career. They had compared their speeds and later mockingly their legs and agreed that hers were the more likely to turn a boss's head.

But her job at last was very ordinary, undemanding and boring. While her social life was an exciting and exhausting round of parties she had not minded this. Work was somewhere she could surreptitiously relax. She had usually completed her day's quota of letters by lunchtime. She was never stretched. Lately she had begun to question the point of it all. She adored the theatre and concerts. She was fascinated by some of George's friends, although more and more she was finding them pretentious and opinionated. But she had to admit to herself at last that, when she had time to think about it, like now, she found her home life boring and squalid.

She had, however, no complaints about sex, and that in itself was beginning to bother her. Was she hanging on to this life merely because George was good in bed? She hugged her knees and gazed thoughtfully at the washed-out amoebic shapes on the quilt. Where was it all leading? Was she going on like this for years, dragging at George's heels? And another thing: she missed the solitude of being an individual, even while amongst a crowd. George was too possessive to allow her that freedom. He didn't do it intentionally. It was just his way, but it was stifling her, that and the boredom at work.

She awoke next morning in a state of rebellion. She rang the office and said she had flu. (She still, childlike, crossed her fingers when she told a blatant lie, however expedient.)

Then as soon as the shops were open she went to the greengrocer. Before he had even set his wares on the pavement she had bought two large earthenware pots of hyacinths. They were half opened into lush heavy white heads and already their scent as she carried them home was overpoweringly exotic. She set them down near the phone and then reached for her address book.

Mary seemed astonished at her request, but agreed quite amiably to meet the 10.50. Kate felt guilty as soon as she hung up. She wanted to impose herself on someone else's life. She wanted to borrow some of Mary's serenity. She wanted quite simply to steal a day for herself; and that day had to have the essence of perfection within it. It had begun with the new treasured feeling of aloneness and with white hyacinths. It continued with a taxi: the plutocrat's barouche, as George called them, she remembered defiantly as she settled herself back on the broad seat. The bus queues lined the road as they went past and she had an irresistible urge to thumb her nose at them. But she did resist. She had stood dirt-splashed on the edge of the gutter in the nine o'clock queues too often herself to fling insults in their poor resigned faces.

Victoria was a palace of promises; the train, as it fled into the spring countryside, a magic dragon, a princess's carriage, a mystery tour. She gazed at the tiny pale green buds on the trees, the yellow whip-lash branches of the stirring willows along the line and ignoring the other passengers began quietly to hum to herself.

The train, a conspirator in her list of happy things, was on time as was Mary with her mud-splashed estate car with the silky spaniel in the back, the baby in the baby seat and shopping next to it. She leaned across and opened the door.

The set had fallen out of Mary's hair, Kate noticed as she climbed in and she felt a ridiculous sense of being let down. The immaculate clothes had been replaced by stained jeans, and a broad kimono top, beneath which she might or might not be pregnant of a baby elephant, lacked even a suspicion of the Harrods' account which had so shocked Kate before. Kate had a horrible suspicion suddenly that perhaps Mary wore her best clothes for 'going up to town'.

Mary put her foot flat. 'Got to get home before the washing machine stops,' she said apologetically. 'Otherwise Gerry's shirts will crease. If you'd rung last night I'd have done them then.' She swung the car off the main road into a narrow high-hedged lane.

Kate raised a deprecating hand. She wrinkled her nose. There was a mingled odour of dog and regurgitated milk in the car which filled her suddenly with nausea and she closed her eyes wearily. The *joie de vivre* which had given her the impetus for the day had gone. She was suddenly limp and drained. She followed Mary into the house, loaded with shopping and therefore unable to fend off the inquisitive spaniel from her white trousers.

Basically the house was all she had hoped and expected. It was pleasant, detached, attractive, with a gnarled fruit tree on the lawn and mossy grass sprouting through the paving stones of the drive, but her call had obviously caught Mary unawares. The hoover lay in the hall surrounded by looped flex. A duster and tin of polish sat on the hall table and she glimpsed baskets of washing in the kitchen.

Mary straightened up from putting the baby in its bouncing chair. 'I'm sorry about the mess, Kate. It's lucky it was you. I knew you wouldn't mind. If you had been Sally or someone like that I'd have told you not to come.'

Who was Sally? Kate groped back in her mind to school days and vaguely pictured a tall girl with buck teeth and freckles.

'She's married a baronet, you know.' Mary puffed slightly as she bent to collect a squeaky toy from beneath the sideboard. 'He's very nice; they came to dinner last week, but I could see her looking round to see if I'd dusted on top of the pictures.' She giggled and Kate relaxed a little. That giggle made her feel more at home. So did the sight of the kettle going on. But Mary's remark rankled a little. I wanted you to bother for me, a little voice cried out inside her somewhere. I do care what it looks like. I wanted it all to be perfect.

'And had you?' She didn't mean her voice to sound quite so weary.

'Had I what?' Mary was putting hot milk in the coffee and Kate shuddered. She had imagined the steaming sauce-pan contained some concoction for the baby.

'Dusted the pictures.'

'Sugar? – Yes, of course I had.' Mary giggled again. 'I even dusted the cat that evening.'

Kate spent the rest of the morning as a bystander feeling very much in the way but constantly being reassured: 'I know you won't mind, Kate; I must get it done. Just let me finish this then I can sit back and relax. No, no. I don't want you to help when you've come for the day.'

The baby's lunch was dreadful. Mary spread sieved apples liberally all over its face then to Kate's horror she sat down on the kitchen chair, and heaving her shirt up to her chin, proceeded to expose a heavy blue-veined breast. The baby seized hungrily and painfully, Kate saw aghast, at the raw nipple. My God, I'm a prude! she thought to herself. She was not sure where to look. There was nothing beautiful in the sight of mother and child. The one seemed ungainly, the other obscenely greedy and the expression on Mary's face, if totally unembarrassed, was anything but placid.

'The dog's trying to get into the cupboard, Kate. Clout him for me, will you? And turn down the peas while you're up, there's a dear.'

But at last it was all over. The baby was put to sleep in its pram after its nappy had been changed, mercifully out of sight and not on the kitchen table as Kate had gloomily expected. The dog was put out, the housework at last seemed to be if not finished, then suspended, Mary produced some expensive sherry and the lunch began to smell as though it were nearly ready.

Mary sat down and smiled with relief. 'All under control at last, so we can talk.' She eyed Kate with disarming directness. 'How's George?'

'Away for a few days. I was browned off alone in the flat. I hoped you wouldn't mind me coming.'

'Of course not.' Impulsively Mary leaned forward and put her hand on Kate's. 'I thought perhaps there was something wrong. You looked so lost and unhappy when I saw you in London.'

'I did?' Kate was shocked. 'Well, I'm not, or at least . . .' She hesitated. 'I'm not unhappy, Mary, and I love George dearly, but perhaps you're right about being lost.' Shrugging, she held out her glass for a refill as Mary uncorked the bottle again. 'I feel sort of empty; purposeless.'

'Have you and George ever thought of getting married?'

It was strange, thought Kate, how married people so often leaped on that idea as being the true panacea. She shook her head violently. 'He doesn't believe in it and I, well, I don't think I believe in it either. Not with him.'

Mary glanced up shrewdly. 'Keeping your options open? That doesn't sound to me as though you're wildly satisfied with him, or it would be "George for ever, right or wrong".'

'Is that how you feel about your husband?'

'Gerry?' Mary laughed. 'I'd never really thought, but I suppose I do in a way. I'm very happy here. I have a good man to live with, a lovely child and a nice house. I'm awfully lucky.' She stopped for a moment, frowning and then went on. 'But it's more than that. I've stopped striving after impossible goals. Most of my dreams are realizable – perhaps not now, but one day.'

Kate was pleating the tablecloth between her fingers. 'At least you still have your dreams. That's my problem. I seem to have lost all mine and my ambition. But not because I'm content. I've given up or lost interest; I'm not sure which.'

She glanced up under her eyelashes and saw Mary absently studying her finger nails.

'Perhaps that's part of growing up; what they call maturity.' Mary, getting up to strain the peas into the sink, was enveloped in a cloud of steam.

'No, it's not. There's something else wrong. Something deep down inside me. I think it is George in a negative sort of way. When I'm with him I don't bother about things; nothing seems to matter.' She noticed what she was doing to the tablecloth suddenly and tried to quickly flatten out the creases.

'George dominates you too much; he's killing the real you.' Mary put a plate before her. 'I told you before, you ought to leave him. Now stop worrying about it for a bit and eat.'

After lunch they walked in the fields, Kate in borrowed gum boots, the baby in a kind of back pack on Mary's shoulders.

'Do you still believe in God?' Mary asked suddenly, in the companionable silence as they watched the spaniel running figures of eight in the meadow grass.

'I'm not sure.' Kate answered without thinking and then stopped short. Two weeks ago she would have said no. Two years ago she would have said no.

'I do. It helps you know. One is no longer so terrifyingly alone.'

They climbed the stile and set off up the edge of a field.

A delicate shadow of green lay across it; spring stirring deep in the soil.

The route Mary took led them back over another stile into the ancient churchyard. Rooks were busy in the budding beeches behind the belfry and the sun was slanting through the lichened stones, showing up eroded inscriptions.

'I often rest here for five minutes.' Mary sat down squarely on a tombstone. 'It's peaceful here. A good place to collect one's thoughts. You ought to look in the church. It's got a beautiful medieval screen.' She sat and watched, the panting dog at her feet, as Kate wandered to the door and lifted the heavy latch.

The church was shadowy and very cold. The thin spring sunlight was filtered by the windows to throw ice-diamond facets onto the worn pavings. Slowly she walked up the aisle. She hadn't been inside a church since Mary's wedding. She tried to remember when she had last prayed. It had been a selfish prayer; a please, please, make it all come right prayer and it had got nowhere. It was illogical to pray to a God in whom one did not believe. It was not even permissible as a safety valve, just in case He might exist. But what if one had genuine doubts?

She raised her eyes to the agony of crucifixion in the east window. For six hundred years men and women had knelt in this church before that image. She could feel their prayers and their peace around her. She could almost smell the incense which had not been burned there for four hundred years.

Thoughtfully she slipped into a pew and, half-embarrassed, knelt. But her mind was still empty of prayer. She searched for the long-familiar words, hesitating as her lips fumbled silently and then gave up. There was too much turmoil still inside her.

Mary was wandering around reading the tombstones

when she came out at last. They made their way back to the house in silence.

Only when they had drunk their tea and were watching the baby kicking happily on the rug before the fire did Mary allude to her long wait in the churchyard. 'Did it help at all? I often go there to be alone.'

Kate smiled. 'I suppose it did in a way. It's a long time since I sat on my own to think like that. I've got as far as recognizing that it's not intrinsically my lifestyle that's at fault, although that is depressing me too. It's something inside me.' She picked up a rattle and shook it tentatively. 'You're right. Being with George is suppressing my will to live as an individual. He scorns faith in God; he denies the old standards and while I'm with him I agree with him. But I think deep down inside perhaps I've been yearning back towards them all this time. I've been allowing him to think for me and act for me. I've let him make all the decisions, even for my conscience, just as I let him decide what music we're going to listen to.' She looked up at Mary and grinned. 'You know that's why I came to see you today. I think I'd already made up my mind, but I needed someone to tell me I was right.'

That night when she walked wearily up the dark streets from the Underground back to the flat she found she was thinking deeply about her childhood again. She recalled with envy that early burning certainty in things which had so guided her daily life.

She paused by the phone to sniff the hyacinths and then, going into the bedroom fell on her knees beside the bed. In the trunk wedged beneath it was a carved sandalwood box. She pulled it out carefully and gazed for a moment at the design on the lid. Then she opened it. Nestling in a bed of cotton wool were her few pieces of jewellery and beneath them all she found the little silver cross. She held it in the palm of her hand for a moment, remembering the glow of security and otherworldliness it had always given her. Surprised, she found a little of the feeling remained.

Inexplicably, George brought her back a delicate Indian silk scarf when he returned and even more inexplicably he admired the hyacinths without once commenting on her extravagance in buying them. He even offered to help paint the flat but she still told him she was going.

'Kate, why?' He took her hands and gazed at her, shocked and horrified.

She shrugged. 'It's hard to explain. There isn't anyone else or anything like that. I just feel terribly restless.' She felt her resolution wavering at the sight of his anguished face. She had not really thought that he would mind much beyond the first irritation at the inconvenience of losing her.

'Will you come back?' He was beginning to look lost. 'Please Kate, will you come back?'

Again she shrugged. She turned away, hating herself for the pain she was giving him. 'Shall we just say I need to be alone for a while. I've chucked the job. I'm going down to Cornwall for a couple of weeks.'

'And then?'

'And then I don't know.' She turned back to him and smiled, a little sadly. 'Don't worry about me, George. I'll keep in touch.'

Standing high on the cliffs above the grey seas, her hair tangled by the wind, she realized fully at last that she had been right to seek her freedom. She missed George dreadfully, but she was free to make her own decisions and formulate her own plans.

'What are you going to be when you grow up?' They had asked her at school. Well now at long last she was about to find out the answer to their question.

Such A Silly Thing

Molly drummed her fingers on the breakfast table, looked at the clock on the mantelpiece, compared it with her wristwatch, and with an impatient sigh threw her paper on the floor.

From the window she could see the garden, flattened and sodden with the endless pouring rain. The thunder had passed. It had gone with the darkness and with it some of the humidity, but the room was still airless, in spite of the slightly open windows. There was a puddle on one of the sills she noticed vaguely, where the rain was being driven in. She let it stay.

When the doorbell rang at last she jumped. The house had seemed so empty, so quiet save for the rain on the paving outside.

Bill was grinning widely. 'Sorry I'm late, Molly. The car wouldn't start.' He shook himself like a dog and stepped into the porch. She could see a line of droplets running down his unruly forelock. One dropped onto his nose. She resisted the temptation to touch it with her finger.

'I'll fetch my bag, darling. Hold on one minute and I'll be with you.'

'Better bring your brolly!' She heard his voice echoing up the stairs after her as she ran to her bedroom. She stood looking round, her heart pounding. Her handbag was downstairs on the hallstand; her case too. She had packed last night after James had gone to bed. She looked down at the two identical beds, virginal beneath their white candlewick.

James had kissed her goodbye this morning as usual, about three inches in the air somewhere above her head as she sat over her coffee, passed her *The Times* – he took the *Financial Times* to the office – and strolled, humming gently, into the hall. She heard him mutter something about the rain and rattle the walking sticks in the stand, trying to extricate his umbrella. He swore gently, very unusual for James, and then from the sudden silence she knew he had gone. He always managed to shut the front door without a sound. There was nothing else to hear but the rain dripping down onto the terrace outside the window. She had poured herself another cup of coffee, a thing she seldom did and opened the paper to the Court page as though today were just like any other day.

'Come on, Molly, where are you?' Bill's voice broke through her thoughts and she jumped guiltily.

Poor James. He was going to be very upset in his own quiet way when he found she had gone. She took the envelope from her dressing table drawer and laid it gently on his pillow. Poor James.

Bill was waiting in the hall, her handbag in one hand and her umbrella in the other. He proffered them, one eyebrow slightly raised. 'Better bring a coat. It won't always be as hot as this.'

'Oh, I forgot.' She turned towards the stairs again, but he grabbed her hand.

'Never mind, sweetheart. Come on. We're late as it is. I'll buy you a coat.'

She slammed the front door and followed him across the soaking gravel to his car. The morning smelt of roses and grass and wet, wet earth.

In the car he turned on the radio. Then he leaned over

435

and kissed her. 'Mine at last,' he muttered, taking her hand. 'Dearest Molly. I've waited so long for this moment.'

She wormed her hand out of his grasp. 'Not here, Bill, please. Someone might see.' She patted her hair nervously.

She should have left the note downstairs on the mantelpiece. The bed was too personal; too pointed. What if Mrs White came today instead of Friday? She would see it and guess. The wretched woman might even read it. Perhaps she ought to go back and move it – but already the car was driving away. She sat back and closed her eyes. It was too late to go back. She must stop thinking about James. It would probably be days before he even noticed that she had gone.

She opened her eyes and watched the road through the labouring windscreen wipers.

Bill glanced across at her. 'I know how you feel, darling. It's a big step. Are you scared now you've done it?'

'If you know how I feel, why do you ask?' She didn't mean to snap.

Don't look so hurt, Bill, she thought to herself. You're supposed to be carrying me off on your charger, remember? You're taking me away from all this to a new life. You've swept me off my feet, remember?

She groped in her handbag for cigarettes and then remembered she had given them up. How strange. She hadn't made that mistake for weeks now. James had made her do it. 'I can't bear to hear you coughing like that, Moll,' he had said. 'Please darling, for your own sake.' He had taken her hands and looked into her eyes with such tenderness.

She shook her head angrily. Why did she keep remembering the good things about him?'

'Have you got a ciggy, Bill?'

''Course.' He changed gear expertly. 'In my left hand pocket.' He raised his elbow so she could reach.

Didn't he care about her health then? She lit one and took a long draw on it. It left her convulsed with coughing and she stubbed it out angrily.

'Let's stop for coffee somewhere, Bill, please.' Her voice was more urgent than she had intended and he looked at her, quickly anxious.

'Can you wait five minutes? There's a roadhouse about four miles further on. A good place.'

A roadhouse! James always took her to the best hotels for coffee so she could use the powder rooms in comfort. She wondered suddenly whether Bill would expect her to use public lavatories on their long drive north and she shuddered.

The roadhouse was red brick, impersonal and crowded. A coach had just discharged its occupants outside the door and Bill and Molly had to wait half an hour before they were served with their coffee. Then at last they were on the road again.

Bill sensed he had made a mistake. 'I've planned a really good stop for lunch, Molly, in Grantham. Then I thought we'd stay tonight in a pub about ten miles further on. We don't want to drive all day on our first day; or be too tired on our first night, do we?' He felt for her hand and squeezed it gently. 'I'm sorry about that last place. I've never seen it crowded before.'

'It doesn't matter.' She smiled at him. She must make some effort. Poor Bill.

Lunch was good. The restaurant was small and intimate and the food delicious. Molly relaxed at last, gazing into Bill's eyes across the brandy he had insisted on buying her.

'I shall fall asleep drinking like this in the middle of the day,' she murmured. He had lovely eyes. They were what had first attracted her. An intense blue of the kind that usually faded in middle age, surrounded by thick black lashes.

'Your ancestors must have been Irish,' she had said to him once, but he had laughed.

'As far as I know none of them have ever been further west than Hertfordshire,' he had teased her. And she didn't ask any further.

She wondered briefly why she had never wanted to know about Bill's family or his past. She should be curious about everything to do with the man she loved. Was it that she was afraid of what she might discover? Not that he was bad, but that he was good; too good. She wanted to imagine without being sure that there was something disreputable about Bill. It was not such fun being carried off by a respectable man. James was a respectable man.

Bill had started well. He had brought her flowers and chocolates and a tiny filigree pendant and stolen her glove and her hanky. He had carried her to the summer house at the Barnabys, that first time they had made love, gently ignoring her half-hearted protests and he had stopped her conscience with kisses. He had phoned her and written and played games of hide and seek to meet her in London when she went up with James, giving her an orchid as her prize when she had found him.

But now?

He had suddenly become diffident. Nervous. Almost half-hearted. Now that she was here with him she could sense all was not as it had been. He was not dashing any more.

She glanced at his profile. 'Let's do something foolish, Bill. I want to be mad this afternoon.' She put her hand on his knee, willing him to smile and mock and change his sober Rover into a rearing, bit-champing white stallion.

'Careful, Molly. You'll distract me while I'm driving. Wait till we get there.' He was frowning through the windscreen. The rain hadn't stopped.

She slumped back in her seat, disappointed.

They were registered as Mr and Mrs at the inn. It was a pretty room with pink chintz curtains and a wide bed. The ashtray on the dressing table had been emptied but not washed. Molly wrinkled her nose at the black film on the china. She threw herself down on the bed and kicked off her shoes. Bill came to her and kissed her tenderly. Then he brushed her hair back from her forehead. There was something slightly possessive about the gesture which she resented. He smelt of garlic from the lunch.

'I want to run naked in the rain,' she whispered to him, testing. 'When it's dark I'm going to explore the garden.' She giggled.

But he looked serious and kissed her again. 'Silly Molly. You can't possibly do such a thing. When it gets dark we'll be here together.' His deep blue eyes were close to hers. They were pleading and unsure.

She turned her head away. 'It's not working, Bill, is it?' Her voice was so soft she wondered if she had spoken aloud at all.

'You haven't let yourself make the break, sweetheart, that's all.' He stood up and walked away from her, hiding his face. 'It's not too late to go back, Molly. If that's what you want.'

She felt a tear roll down her face and brushed at it in surprise. She had not realized she was crying.

'I think I do, Bill. I'm sorry.'

He was looking out of the window, the chintz curtain partly obscuring his shoulder and his face. He turned and looked at her, his expression carefully impassive.

'Think about it, Molly darling.' He blinked several times, quickly like a child trying not to cry and she felt a wrench of love and pity. 'If you want to get back before James finds your note we ought to leave pretty soon.' He glanced at his watch although she knew he couldn't see it. 'I'll be downstairs having a drink.'

She sat for a while after he had gone, gazing at the pink and orange floral pattern on the carpet. Then suddenly she stood up.

Bill was in the lounge looking at a paper. 'I've squared the hotel,' he said without looking up, his voice dull and subdued. 'We can leave now.'

'You knew, didn't you, Bill?' She stood before him. 'Is that why you booked in here; why we didn't go all the way?'

'I had a feeling I might be driving you back, sweetheart.' He threw down the paper and stood up. 'You're not the type to run out on your husband. I knew it before you did. I was resigned.' He dropped a gentle kiss on the top of her head.

'And you don't mind?'

'Hell! Of course I mind.' He kicked savagely at some ash on the carpet. 'If I could I would throw you over my shoulder and take you away and keep you locked up somewhere safe, just for me . . . But I can't do that, Molly. You know it and I know it. You belong to James, I thought perhaps you could break away; I hoped you could, but . . .' he broke off shrugging his shoulders and turned away.

She followed him out to the car and climbed silently in beside him. He started the engine and then turned to her suddenly, the familiar grin once more playing round his eyes. 'Cheer up, Molly love. I don't like drama scenes. We've had a lot of fun, you and I.' He took her hand and kissed it gently. 'We didn't know when to stop, that's all. No harm done.'

He drove back very fast, retracing the journey of the morning. The rain had stopped at last and the afternoon sun turned the road into a ribbon of glass as the wet tarmac stretched before them. Trees, telegraph wires and fence posts were strung with diamond droplets.

Molly was thinking of the house. Supposing it was too

late. Supposing James had come home and found the note. Supposing Mrs White had been in and seen it? She found her hands were shaking in her lap. Bill was gazing ahead. Glancing across at him she saw his jaw set in a hard line.

The house looked strangely empty when the car at last drew up by the gate. Bill didn't move, so she opened the car door and slipped out herself, reaching over for her case.

'Will I see you again?' Her voice sounded timid, uncertain. She saw him swallow. Then he turned and smiled.

'If you want to, Molly; I'll be there. See how it goes, darling.' He raised his hand and then he had gone.

She went into the house quickly. She knew in her heart she wouldn't meet him again. It was over.

She put down her case in the hall and ran up to the bedroom. The envelope still lay on the pillow where she had left it. Clasping it to her thankfully she tore it slowly into a hundred tiny pieces, letting each bit drift into the waste paper basket.

She was still in the bedroom when she heard James's key in the lock. Her heart gave a little extra bump and she glanced in the mirror anxiously, patting her hair, then she ran downstairs. He was standing in the hall, looking blankly at her case.

'Oh James,' she held out her hands to him. 'James, darling.'

'Hello Molly.' He opened his arms as she ran to him and gently he kissed her hair.

'Oh James, I nearly did a silly thing today.' She buried her face in the breast of his pin-striped suit.

He held her away from him and gazed into her eyes. Then he smiled and kissed her again. 'I'm so glad you didn't, Molly. So very glad.' He stopped and handed her her case. 'Unpack, Molly. Then come and have a drink with me. I'm going to open some champagne.'

'Unpack?' She looked at him shocked. 'You knew? And you didn't say anything?'

'I've known about Bill for a long time. You had to make the choice yourself.' He laughed, suddenly boyish. 'Oh God, Molly, I'm so glad you chose me.'

The Heart Will Understand

' U nless you give me the authority to attend to these
. . . matters, your father's business will undoubtedly
fail and you will be able to look no further than to yourself
for the blame . . . Sincerely, Philip Dane.'

Helen looked up from the letter on her desk and gazed
out of her office window at the London street below, where
the dank grey morning teemed with traffic and people.

It was already three months since her father had died,
three months since she had made her way to Leabrook and
stood with strangers in the snow and looked down into the
open grave. One of those strangers must have been Philip
Dane. She must have shaken his hand and murmured
something to him as, one by one, her father's former
employees made their way past her and stammered their
condolences. Each one must have been wondering about
her, wondering what she would do now that she owned
the nursery, wondering about their future, their livelihood,
their jobs. And she had said nothing. She had returned to
the city.

Philip Dane's first letter had reached her three weeks
later. She read it and put it aside. He could cope. He had
been her father's manager. He must have been running
things for those last months of her father's illness. He could
continue to look after the place for the time being.

Someone knocked on the door behind her. 'Your coffee,

443

Helen – and there was a telephone call for you while you were out.'

Helen looked back into the room, still thinking of the fragrance of the formal gardens in which she and her father used to sit sometimes as it grew dark, listening to the last bees bumbling their way through the clumps of melissa and she frowned. 'Thank you, Sally. Who was it?'

'Mr Spencer. He was wondering if you could meet for lunch.'

After all these months of knowing him the mention of Stephen Spencer's name still made her heart do a quick somersault beneath her ribs. She sighed. Then slowly she stood up. 'Tell him I can't will you, Sally? Tell him I've been called away unexpectedly to the country for a few days. I'll contact him when I get back.'

The bank of elder trees by the gate was full of half-opened sooty green buds. Below them the stream ran red and muddy after the rain, the gurgle of water providing an accompaniment to the pure whistling of the blackbird which sat on one of the top branches of the still leafless ash.

Helen stood for a moment and looked around her in the twilight. The air was clean and strong after the city. And it was quiet. In spite of the bird and the water, it was quiet.

She glanced towards the house. Smoke rose from the chimneys and she could see a figure bustling around in the lighted kitchen window. Someone must have gone in to light the fire after she had phoned, to try to provide some kind of a welcome in the cold empty house.

She glanced across at the glasshouses and the buildings beyond them. Behind the high box hedge lay the long terrace of herbs, sloping away towards the south. Her father's whole life was represented by those buildings and the plants they contained. It had been a quiet, peaceful rewarding life as far as she could see. One which she had almost envied and sometimes despised.

She took a step onto the bridge which spanned the stream and looked back at her car. Leaving it there in the car park under the trees, its windows tightly wound up against the damp, its lights off, its engine quietly ticking as it cooled, she was leaving her link with the city behind her. And the link with Stephen Spencer.

When he had rung back that afternoon she had made Sally take the call. There was no reason to speak to him herself. There was nothing left for them to say to each other now.

She began to walk slowly up the path towards the house. It was warm and welcoming; womblike; clinging. It was so easy to feel at home there. Later, in front of the open fire she slowly unzipped her boots and sighed. The place would stretch out its arms and clutch, octopus-like, around her neck given half a chance. But she wouldn't give it a chance. She would sell it and return to her job in London. Sell the sentiment and the memories. Sell the millstone. Sell the worries which had been her father's life and which had eventually chased him into his grave. Sell her father's pride and joy. Leabrook had no claim on her. None at all.

The knock on the door took her by surprise. She glanced at her watch. She must have been dozing, for it was getting on for midnight. She padded barefoot into the hall and peered through the glass of the front door.

'Who is it?'

'Philip Dane.'

Her hair was untidy, her skirt rumpled and her boots still lay flopped by the fire.

'It's very late, Mr Dane.'

445

'Not for you, surely.' His voice behind the door was deep, with just a hint of the soft inflection of the hills.

She could see through the glass that he was tall.

Angrily she pulled back the bolt and drew open the door. 'It is late for me, Mr Dane. I had a long drive down this evening.'

He stepped into the hall without hesitation. 'I hadn't thought of that. But I won't keep you.' No word of apology. 'I merely wanted to welcome you to Leabrook and find out if you would like to come on a tour of the place with me in the morning.'

She looked at him. He was tall, broad shouldered, not handsome but ruggedly attractive in a weatherbeaten way, with a mat of untidy, straw-coloured hair.

She met his gaze steadily. 'I know the place, Mr Dane. It was my home once.'

'But not for some time, I think. Had I known you were coming, I should have been here to greet you properly.' He leaned his shoulder against the wall. 'You've come to sell up, haven't you?' He had not moved his gaze from her face. It was not a question. It was as if he could read her mind. She stepped back a little resentfully.

'I haven't decided what to do yet. There has been too little time.'

'It has been nearly four months since the old man died. You've had time to make up your mind.'

She felt herself beginning to seethe beneath his stare. 'There are many things to consider, Mr Dane. But I hardly think this is the time or the place to discuss it, do you?'

She reached for the door again, pointedly, opening it a little further, wanting him to go. He did not move.

'He said you'd sell. He said you were too much of a town girl ever to come here to live. And he's right. You wouldn't fit in here.' He swung on his heel and went towards the door. 'I'll collect you at nine, if that's all right with you and we'll walk round the whole nursery together.'

At half past eight she was already in the shop watching the staff sorting through the books and seeds, tidying the sachets of dried herbs, stirring the scents till they filled the old wooden building, carrying out the boxes of mints which were to be stacked outside on the nearly empty wooden benches. It was a misty morning, which hinted of sun later. Helen had dressed in jeans and a thick sweater against the cold. The ladies who helped in the shop were in large floral pinafores.

She could see Philip Dane through the window, making his way to the front door of the house and she watched out of the corner of her eye as he knocked and waited at the front door. It gave her considerable satisfaction to see him shrug and walk away. No doubt he expected her to lie in bed until mid-morning.

His expression as he saw her confirmed her suspicions.

'Good morning, Mr Dane. Forgive me for not waiting in the house, but there was a great deal to do this morning. I couldn't wait until nine to begin.'

He inclined his head slightly. 'When you're ready, I'll take you round.'

The ladies were watching them. Helen suddenly wanted to giggle. 'I'm ready now, thank you.' Meekly she followed him out of the door and towards the propagation beds.

'I handed in my notice this morning, Stephen.' Helen looked up into his face and forced herself to smile. 'I'm going to live at Leabrook. It's all arranged.'

He stared at her, his lean features suddenly nakedly

447

miserable and she felt a lump come to her throat. 'We've had fun you and I, Stephen, I know, but it wasn't working, was it?' She looked away from him, studying the menu in her hands as though her life depended on it.

'And everything there has been between us? It has meant nothing to you?' He spoke stiffly, his voice lowered as though he were afraid someone would hear.

'Of course it meant something to me. It meant a great deal.' She swallowed hard. 'Stephen, you and I have had a lot of good times. I'm . . .' She hesitated. 'There is something missing between us. There always has been. You know it as well as I do. I don't know what it is, but I've always sensed it and I think you have too. This is the right moment to finish it. I'm going away. For good.'

Suddenly she had a vivid picture of the last time they had gone out together. They had been to the theatre and after it had eaten in a little restaurant in Covent Garden. Then they had gone back to Stephen's flat and, gently, he had taken her in his arms and kissed her and later they had lain together, their arms around one another, their heads side by side on the pillows and she had been happy. Almost.

They were too tense together; too conscious of themselves. She knew that he was holding back. It was almost as if he were acting a part and she had felt a little chill of misery creep over her, an uncertainty which should not be there and she had wondered if he sensed the same in her. She did not know how to reassure him.

The silence in the room had been broken that last time by the sound of a car drawing up in the echoing street below. She heard the doors being opened and banged, voices and then, slowly, the silence again. But it was too late. Their aloneness was broken. She had not found out what was wrong. And now she never would.

She looked at him again now and was relieved to see

that he was once more in complete control of himself. His handsome face was impassive above the stiff collar, the discreet silk tie, the dark city suit.

'You've obviously made the decision, Helen,' he said quietly. 'I can see that there would be no point in trying to dissuade you.'

She bit her lip. There would. Of course there would. If he were to shout and rant at her, or hit her and drag her out into the street, or hurl the wine bottle across the room so that it smashed against the plate glass mirror on the opposite wall and splattered the decor with the musky Lambrusco – that would dissuade her. All or any of that would dissuade her and she would know that he cared.

She forced herself to smile. 'No, Stephen. There is no point in trying to dissuade me,' she said.

She saw him only twice after that before she moved. Both times they were like business acquaintances rather than people who had once been lovers. There was no acrimony, no heat; no terrible sorrow. Just a strange, deep regret. As a parting gift he gave her a Hermès scarf and a tight, distant kiss on the cheek. 'Let me know how you get on, Helen,' he said. 'I'll always want to know.'

And that was that.

She piled the last of her things into the back of her car, posted her flat key through the letter box for the landlord, slammed the lower door and climbed into the car. Stephen's scarf still in its glossy wrapping was in the glove pocket in front of her. She did not put it on.

Philip Dane came over that evening, not long after the van which had brought her few pieces of furniture from town had pulled away up the lane. He was carrying a bottle of wine.

'I thought you might like to celebrate or drown your

sorrows. Now that it's all over and there is no turning back,' he said. 'Tomorrow perhaps we can go out to dinner. They do a good meal at the White Swan.'

She stared at him. Then she smiled. 'It's been one hell of a day,' she said.

'No regrets so far?'

She frowned. No regrets. Not for the job or the flat or the people. Just one aching memory. Stephen. He was watching her closely. Seeing the doubt on her face. But she shook her head. 'No regrets. None at all.'

At her invitation he sat on the sofa beside her, stretching out his legs towards the fire.

'You know, I thought you were going to give me the sack.' He squinted down at her. 'You were, weren't you?'

'It crossed my mind.'

'That's what you came down here for, wasn't it, originally? To sell up and collect the money and go.'

'I suppose it was.'

'And instead you're going to take over and make decisions above my head?'

'And you don't like that idea?'

'Not one bit.' He grinned. 'I've run this place too long to have some pint-sized town girl lording it over me.'

'Not so much of the pint sized!'

He chuckled. 'You're not such a bad businesswoman from what I've seen so far. You must have been pretty good at that job in London.'

'I was.' It was her turn to smile. 'And I'll be good at this one too. And I'll lord it over you if I have to.'

'I realized that weeks ago.'

'Philip, did my father really say I was too much of a town girl to fit in here?' She twisted herself round so that she could see his face.

He laughed. 'Of course not. He said you could never

resist a challenge. So I made sure I presented you with one. And you rose to the bait beautifully!'

She and Philip worked well together, his training and skill with the plants combining with her flair for business. They recognized one another's strengths and of necessity grew close in the lengthening hours of daylight as the spring matured into early summer and grew warm. In the evenings they would inspect the herb beds walking slowly back towards the buildings as the last of the daylight lingered. And as they walked together, sometimes their hands would touch and she would glance at him and feel the strength of his attraction reaching out towards her. When at last he kissed her by the dew-wet sundial in the formal gardens where she used to sit with her father, the action had a kind of inevitability she could not resist. She was not prepared, however, for the wistful longing which came with the kiss and the thoughts, not of Philip, his strong arms round her in the dusk, but of Stephen.

It was weeks before she brought herself to write to Stephen and longer before she posted the letter. It was brief and defiant and though she didn't realize it, it was a little wistful too, as she thought of Philip's kiss which she hoped would blot out all memory, in time, of the man to whom she wrote.

Stephen read it in the tube, wedged shoulder to shoulder in the morning rush hour, scanning her writing with the same care he usually gave the City prices. Inside, he felt sick.

From the page came a shutter-speed glimpse of the countryside emerging into summer; of lavender beds and pots of rosemary, of the worries of small but growing mail order sales and the drying sheds. And the picture of a woman who had already changed, relaxed and grown in confidence. And at the end the casual mention of her manager. 'Philip is marvellous. Dad was lucky to find him and so am I.' No more.

Stephen closed his eyes, his hand automatically reaching up for the jointed handhold above his head as the train jolted across the points. He wondered why that morning's investment meeting had seemed to be so important – and why he'd let her go.

At first Helen found Philip's possessiveness refreshing. It was exciting to have someone to escort her with such obvious pride. She relished his admiration, but always at the end of the day she hesitated and drew back.

'Let me stay, Helen,' he would murmur in her ear as they sat before the log fire, which they still lit for company in the cool of the darkness, and she would close her eyes and whisper, 'Not tonight, Phil. Not yet.'

It had been too easy. Too obvious. She did not trust herself. Her excitement when he came near was real, as was her intense longing for him to efface the memory of Stephen and take over her life and yet, at the same time, she began to resent him a little. He was too possessive. Twice now he had countermanded her orders in the nurseries in front of the men and had laughed at her when she tried to argue. A nice laugh, but nevertheless a laugh. The last time it happened she asked him back to the house for a coffee and they had a blazing row.

Two days later she was in the White Swan with a couple of the men at lunchtime and she saw Philip in there with someone else; a pretty dark girl whom she had never seen before. He had his arm around her.

She didn't say anything and very soon she was able to

leave. The misery and jealousy she felt surprised her. Could she really be in love with him after all? He was fun and attractive and there was no doubt she was very strongly drawn to him, but this was not what it had felt like before.

But had she been in love with Stephen?

For several days she scarcely spoke to Philip as they met in the sheds or in the office over the account books or as she walked slowly down the lines of staging in the greenhouses, watching the seedlings turning to sturdy plants beneath his care. Then she knew she had to say something.

He looked down at her gravely as she approached him in the sunny privacy of the box hedges. Then he smiled. 'When you first came here, Helen, you said you had no regrets. That wasn't quite true, was it?'

She stared down at the grass. 'It was true, Phil. It's just I need longer than I thought, that's all. There's been so much to adjust to – so much that is different. Don't hurry me, please. Give me a little space.'

He shrugged. 'I'll give you space, Helen. However much you need. But don't take too much time, if you can help it.' He touched her gently with his finger. Then he turned away.

She watched him go without moving. Suddenly she felt like crying.

The next day it rained, and the day after. The stream gurgled and creamed an angry red brown and the trees scattered their leaves into the rushing flood waters. With a shiver Helen turned her back on the scene and closed the door. She had just seen Philip drive away for a weekend she might have gone on too, the tyres of his car throwing muddy spray into the air. She felt bleak.

Summer though it might be, she lit the fire to cheer herself and knelt before it, feeding it wet, spluttering twigs

453

and she almost did not bother to go to the door when she heard the knock.

It was Stephen.

They stared at each other in silence, her initial incredulous joy at seeing him damped almost instantly by their mutual hesitation. His reserve, his tight, careful restraint as he kissed her forehead and followed her into the sitting room were unchanged from the last time she had seen him. He did not fit at Leabrook. He never would.

They talked. They even laughed. They ate together and drank the wine he had brought with him. But something still held them apart and at last she slipped onto her knees on the hearth rug to feed the fire with logs and stare miserably into the flames.

He watched the shadows leaping on her hair. It was softer, more natural than he had ever seen it; prettier. She looked good without make-up, dressed in her old jeans. She seemed relaxed. Happy.

They talked some more and she began to sense a change in him. Puzzled she watched his face, yearning to reach out and touch the taut lines which ran from nose to mouth. Outside the rain battered the windows and they heard a gust of wind in the chimney and for a moment she thought of Philip.

'I'll show you to your room, Stephen,' she said at last and he did not argue. On the landing he took her hands for a moment and held them in his. Then he turned from her and closed the door behind him.

She lay awake a long time, thinking about him in the dark.

It was dawn when she was wakened by the distant sound of shouting. She lay staring at the ceiling, listening to the endless rain still beating down outside, then alerted by a sudden unexplained tremor of fear she got up and ran to the window. In the faint light she could see the stream spilling over its banks into the garden and car park, glittering across the lower fields. In the distance she could see several men working in the mud, piling sandbags, trying desperately to hold the water back from the greenhouses and the terraces. Frozen with horror she stared. One man was directing the others and with a moment's anguish she thought it was her father, his boots, his tattered raincoat, even his old hat which had still hung downstairs in the hall. Then she realized that it was Stephen.

Throwing on her clothes she ran downstairs, grabbing her own boots, her own raincoat and running outside into the rain.

He had heard the urgent shouts of the men while she had slept, it seemed and had let himself out into the dawn, sizing up the situation and taking charge, in Philip's absence, of the rescue operations. The taut lines had vanished from his face. The restraint had gone. Suddenly she could see the man behind the image she had always known.

By mid-day the level of the water began to fall back. It had come to within an inch of the top of the bank near the greenhouses.

Philip returned at half past twelve, leaping from his Land-Rover and running across the bridge to the shop. Helen smiled at him wearily. 'It's going down, Phil. We seem to have escaped the worst of it.'

He gave a grim smile. 'If we have then we're the exception. There's been bad flooding down the valley. I came back as soon as I heard, but the road is impassable in places. I had to go round – ' He broke off suddenly, staring out of the window. 'Who's that?'

Helen did not have to look. 'Stephen Spencer. A friend of mine from London. He arrived at just the right moment.'

Philip gave her a sharp glance. Then he was striding out of the door. Helen stared at the ground. The sunlight had broken through the clouds suddenly and struck blinding reflections from the wet ground where he had been standing.

His coat over the back of the old chair, the sleeves of his guernsey rolled up to the elbow, Stephen was sketching a map of the property at the work bench among the trowels and dibbers and the old pots of twisted thyme when Helen brought in the tray of coffee and sandwiches. Philip, with a couple of the men, was peering over his shoulder.

'Raise the bank here, and here,' he was saying, the pencil stump clutched between the mud-caked fingers, 'and take a bit out of the corner here, to allow for a faster water flow and you'll be safe in future. See?' He glanced up at Philip, who nodded thoughtfully.

Helen slid the tray in front of them. 'Since when have you been an expert on water engineering?' she asked softly.

It was Philip who answered, glancing up at her with the wistfulness of a man who knows he has already lost. 'I'll bet he has talents you never even suspected,' he said.

Helen laughed. 'I'm beginning to think he has,' she agreed. She held his gaze for a moment and then she looked away, blushing. It was obvious he knew and, somehow, she thought he understood.

It was Stephen who walked with her that evening as the sun set in a blaze of stormy red.

He did not speak. For a while he watched with her the bats flitting out of the darkness, then he turned and took her in his arms. There was no hesitation this time; no reserve as he brought his face close to hers. For a long time they were silent, clinging to each other, in the dark. Then softly he spoke.

'I was a fool in London,' he said, 'and I almost didn't find out in time.'

Party Games

'I often think,' someone was saying in the strident tone of a person who wishes their opinions to be heard, 'that James is a perfect fool to continue having these parties. They are so deathly boring.'

With pre-judged malice the owner of the voice leaned across and tapped her – it had to be a her – cigarette on the arm of one of James's more beautiful bronze nudes. The ash fragmented into the crook of the curved elbow and lay dusty.

Had she not seen me, this malicious woman, or was she deliberately trying to provoke me into defending my brother? Perhaps she didn't care, or more likely, didn't know me. Why should she?

'Meet my beautiful sister, Laura,' James had said to the first few guests to arrive. They had looked, smiled, accepted their drinks – and turned away. Soon James had grown bored with introducing me. I was obviously no ace to palm before this glittering troupe. As they moved slowly round his studio, delicately touching this, ostensibly averting their eyes from that, James turned to watch them, anxious, frowning behind the eyes, although his outward manner too was arrogant.

'For God's sake put some fig leaves on some of those figures, James,' I had said at dinner, still confident then, still excited.

He laughed and ruffled my hair. 'This is London, sweetheart; you don't have to pretend men don't have balls here.'

I blushed. I was mortified, angry and embarrassed. Was I then so provincial?

The studio was hot and crowded now and smelt of perfume and, strangely from the so glitteringly arrayed, of sweat. Smoke and drink fumes mingled and spiralled towards the high skylight windows. The gentle murmur of conversation had grown to a steady roar as story competed with story, joke capped joke.

'Smile, Laura; who's going to want to talk to you if you look so miserable all the time?' I could hear my mother's words echoing down through the years. She had said that to me sometime at nearly every children's party I had attended. And she would have said it at every teenage party too had she not then been left at home.

Her advice made no difference. Other people seem to acquire some strange charisma at parties which I cannot find. Parties leave me cold, claustrophobic and embarrassed, both for myself and for those I see around me. I am too detached and with the best will in the world, even with a serious attempt to get drunk, cannot lose that detachment.

I dangled my glass, empty already, from nervous fingers and watched the owner of the malicious voice as she circulated out of earshot. She was very beautiful: hair, jewellery expensive and tasteful, her dress a masterly combination of chic and casual. I envied her. Almost. Why, though, I thought sadly, does she accept James's invitations if she despises him so much? I wondered if James knew how she really felt. Perhaps it was a game they played: he asked her, although he knew she didn't want to come, hoping she wouldn't; hoping she would: I didn't know which. And she came, afraid perhaps to miss out on a Social Occasion, or knowing that James didn't want her there; or knowing he did. I sat down, thoughtful.

There were several chairs in the studio and they were all empty but mine. No one dared to sit; if they did that they might miss something. Or they might see themselves as I saw them, dispassionately; packed, noisy and rather silly.

I decided to play a game. I would pinpoint the best-looking man in the room and follow him with my eyes until he turned and saw me. If I could entice him towards my chair I would buy myself a present tomorrow; if I couldn't I would offer to wash the glasses after the last guest had gone. It was a daring game for me; a London game.

I sat up and began to survey the room.

'Hey; would you just move your chair a bit, gorgeous? You're right in the way there.'

Instead of retaining my cool and telling him to go to hell I leaped to my feet guiltily. Gorgeous indeed! The tall, handsome noble lord had not even looked at my face. He and I had been introduced. I remembered the purple satin of his shirt. I watched as he moved away, conscious only of the décolletée blonde at his side. As far as he was concerned I was just another statue.

Start the game again.

I looked around carefully, determined not to be shifted or put off again. It was strange that there should be so unattractive a selection of men present. Or was I suffering from sour grapes because none of them were mine? I tried again, leaning a little to get a better view of the far side of the studio.

'It's Laura, isn't it?' Someone was standing over me again. At least this one knew my name. I peered up at his face.

He grinned. 'We met yesterday at Solti's preview, d'you remember?'

I did not. 'Really?' I borrowed my mother's most withering tone. One day I'll buy myself a lorgnette; that will, I am sure, keep the whole world at bay. The young man looked suitably crestfallen and I was immediately repentant. 'I am sorry,' I said. 'I'm hopeless at names.' I shrugged, hoping he would forgive the commonplace insult which we all hand out so often.

Amazingly he seemed to, as people do, anxious to give a second chance.

'I'm John Divers,' he commented modestly. I should have been immediately on my guard, but I was past caring. 'Good,' I said. 'Please could you get me another drink?' I handed him my long-empty glass.

I watched him push his way through the people, purposefully elbowing them aside with an enviable offhandedness. I saw Madame Malicious totter slightly to his thrust and felt myself grinning. I hoped he would come back.

'You look a bit happier at last,' James was momentarily above me, hovering, anxious. 'For God's sake circulate, Laura. A fine hostess you've turned out to be.'

Hostess! It was the first I'd heard of it. To have heard James curse when I arrived on Thursday with my suitcase you would have thought I was the last person on God's earth he would have allowed to act as his hostess.

'Where did you dig up all these dreary people from Jimmy?' I asked a little too loudly. I was beginning to sound like *her*.

He shushed me, looking, scandalized, over his shoulder. 'Someone'll hear. You've had too much to drink.'

'I haven't. I've only had one glass and now I've lost that.' It's true I was acting a little drunk and it wasn't entirely deliberate. Perhaps some strange defence mechanism had come into play to give me courage or comfort.

'Well, for God's sake keep your voice down,' James hissed and he had gone.

I was stung by the injustice of that, as I had scarcely spoken a word all evening, but I was still enough in awe of big brother James to feel chastened and subside, miserable again, onto my chair.

To my amazement John Divers reappeared with my glass. 'You don't happen to know who that ravishing dark girl over there is, do you?' He leaned down confidentially, close to my ear. So that was it. The inevitable bucket of cold water.

'I gather she's a handful,' I murmured sweetly, sipping my wine. 'A nympho; I shouldn't try your chances there unless you're pretty hot stuff.' It wasn't true of course; I had no idea who the poor girl was.

The room was becoming unbearably hot; the pale chiffon of my dress clung to me uncomfortably. I wanted to pick the skirts up round my thighs, rid myself of the horrible cloying tights and kick my shoes up towards the smoky glass skylights. High above them the summer sky was at last growing dark. For a wild moment I contemplated actually doing it. I would have to jump on a table of course; such dramatic gestures could not be practised in a dark corner, or discreetly behind a marble nude.

What were the chances of getting away with it? Tights are not a garment one can strip off gracefully. One is too liable to fall flat on one's face.

I should have taken James's advice. 'Don't bother with tights and don't wear a bra with that dress,' he had said coming in, to my acute embarrassment, as I was dressing. 'Don't be silly, Laura. I am your brother, so you needn't cover up your tits. Don't be such a prude. Nude women are my job.' And when reluctantly I took away my hands he had been quite approving. 'I must get you to sit for me while you're here.'

But in spite of his ridicule I had insisted on my bra and tights.

I compromised now by kicking off my sandals and closing my eyes for a minute, allowing the party to revolve around me.

'You know, he's really quite talented.' Strange how words sort themselves out and emerge from the general babble when your eyes are shut. 'I think James is a fool to allow all these people into his studio. They might damage his stuff.'

'And they're not really interested in him as a sculptor, you can tell.' Another voice.

So I had two sympathizers in the room. I opened my eyes and looked around but in the tide of coming and going the owners of the voices were lost. I picked up my sandals and walked slowly across the floor.

People were sitting on the spiral stair which led up to the small gallery bedroom, with its curtain wall. I thought of the quiet oasis I would find up there among the coats and climbed purposefully upwards.

I had drawn back the curtain and was inside the little room before I realized there were people on the bed. Two people. One of them was Sandra, my brother's lady. The other was not my brother. It was too late to withdraw; too late to pretend I hadn't seen; too late for them to hide. The three of us stared at one another in stark embarrassment for a moment and then Sandra began to pull the bedspread up around her shoulders. Her dress lay tangled on the floor at my feet.

'Don't tell James,' she said.

I backed away, drew the curtain again and went to sit with the others for a moment on the spiral stair, resting my head against the wrought iron newel post. Below me the party raged like a forest fire. Automatically my eyes sought out James. He was standing alone for a moment, watching. Perhaps he was watching for Sandra. I pulled myself wearily to my feet and made for the kitchen.

There too were people. Someone was bleeding profusely into the sink. 'Can I help?' I asked distantly, half of me still upstairs, an invisible, sick voyeur. Several pairs of eyes turned towards me.

'Do you think it's an artery?'

'He did it on a glass.'

'I hope James doesn't mind; there's blood all over the tea towel.'

They greeted me with relief, like children who, when the game has stopped being fun any more, turn for reassurance to the nearest adult. I knew at least where the plasters and antiseptic were because James had stuck a chisel into his thumb the night before.

'Apply pressure to the wound,' I directed, as he had done then, bringing out the first aid kit.

They obeyed.

'Sit down so I can fix it.'

He did.

It was really quite a bad cut. 'It might have to be stitched.' I recognized the purple shirt and felt foolishly even spitefully pleased. So his lordship had to recognize me in the end. 'You really ought to see a doctor, you know.' I glanced up and met his eye.

He grinned, his face a little pale. 'You're doing fine. Thanks awfully. Silly of me.' He laughed uncomfortably. 'Always get a bit nervous at do's like these.'

You too, I thought. I would never have guessed.

'Damion, darling, are you all right?' I was elbowed out of the way by a vision in frothy lace. But Damion was now concerned more with the spillage of his blood than with dalliance with his lady. 'Shut up, Sue. Let Laura get on with it. She's patching me up beautifully.' So he had even remembered my name.

The circle of admirers watching my every move with the antiseptic was still there, morbidly curious.

'Make some coffee, someone,' I directed without looking up. 'Damion could do with something hot.'

Amazingly I heard the kettle being filled. Then James was there, fussing and apologetic that one of his glasses should have perpetrated the damage. I left them to it.

Slowly the party thinned. I saw Sandra, dressed and hair immaculate, go to James and take his hand and stand on her toes to kiss his chin. For the first time that evening his face relaxed and he smiled. Then she looked across and saw me watching.

'I wondered if you'd come and have some dinner with me one day.'

I remembered his name this time: John.

'Thank you,' I said. 'It might be fun.'

My eyes still followed Sandra and James. He had his arm around her and was talking to her with pathetic eagerness. 'Yes, John, that would be nice.' I smiled at him, knowing I was second best, but still happy. I rather liked his face.

He grinned. 'You were right about the nympho lady,' he whispered confidentially. 'Much too hot for me to handle.'

'God, I do hate parties,' James said when the last guest had gone. He threw himself down on the studio couch and stretched his arms high above his head. Dawn was breaking and high above the skylights tiny puffs of pink-tinged cloud were floating in the blue-black of the sky. Cigarette smoke still drifted beneath the high ceiling; the smell of it clung everywhere.

'Why do you give them, then?'

He rubbed his eyes slowly and then looked hard at his knuckles. 'I often ask myself that.'

464

'Do you think anyone enjoys them much?'

He laughed. 'I sometimes wonder. I know I used to. But now . . .' He sighed.

'It's a sort of ritual, isn't it? Everyone comes, even when they don't want to; everyone pretends to enjoy themselves, even when they aren't; everyone talks to the people they'd rather never see again and miss the chance of meeting the people they want to see because no one remembers, or knows, to introduce them. Relationships are made or broken and next day no one can remember why.' I looked at him sadly.

'Perhaps I give lousy parties.' Wearily he bent to collect the glasses round his feet. 'Do I gather you didn't enjoy it?'

'It was another party.' I knelt to help him. 'Sandra didn't stay then?'

He shook his head. 'She often doesn't. She has to be at work early tomorrow, poor love. I'm surprised she stayed so long.'

'I expect she was enjoying herself.' I rose, my hands full of glasses and went through to the kitchen. The bloody tea towel still lay on the table; plasters, antiseptic, coffee cups heaped anyhow around it. In the sink the tap slowly dripped, etching more deeply the groove in the stained enamel.

'I'm glad you met Sandy tonight.' James came in behind me. 'Did you like her?'

'I hardly spoke to her.' I knew my voice sounded guarded but I couldn't help it.

'She's a super person, Laura; one of the best.'

'I shouldn't let yourself get too fond of her, Jimmy.' I spoke very quietly, gathering up the towel to rinse in the sink. 'I'm sure she's nice, but . . .'

'But what?' He flared up at once in her defence. 'You know your trouble, Laura. You're a cynic.' His hands shook

465

as he pushed a trayful of glasses onto the table. 'You always look for the worst side of people. You never take them at face value.'

I watched the red stain flowing out into the running water and gurgling away down the sink. 'I'm sorry, Jimmy,' I said. I thought of Sandra's surprised face and tousled hair as she sat up from the arms of another man in James's own bed. 'I'm sorry. I suppose it's just the way I'm made.' I went and gave him a quick kiss on the cheek. 'Take no notice of me. You're right. I am a cynic and I'm afraid I always will be.'

I went slowly back into the studio and looked around. After all, for all I knew James was well aware of what Sandra was like. Whether he did or not I had to let it rest there. I could say no more to James about it.

I wandered over to the beautiful bronze nude and gazed at her serene expression. It was Sandra, of course. I should have recognized her. Gently I blew the cloying ash from the angle of her elbow and went to turn out the lights.

A Stranger With No Name

Sally paused to pick up another piece of driftwood and throw it into the bag she had dropped on the frozen sand nearby. Her back ached and her eyes were sore with the icy glare from the sea and for a minute she straightened and gazed back along the beach. Far away near the dunes she could just make out the distant figure of a man.

Her heart leaped. Forgetting the bag she ran a few steps towards him, pushing her hair out of her eyes as the persistent stinging wind blinded her momentarily, hiding him from her. Then she stopped and waited.

His was the first figure she had seen on the beach in three days, the first in fact since she had watched him walk away. It had to be him. She had known he would come back . . .

They had been walking along the edge of the sea in the rain, watching the pock marks hammered by the shower into the heavy slate of the tide, picking among the seaweed for shells, slipping them, sandy and wet and cold into their pockets, staring out across towards the distant rocks where the smoothness of the sea humped itself into an uneasy swell. It was a lonely place, a place of solitary wheeling seabirds and infinite wind-torn skies, a place where one could dream and think; a place where one could feel free.

She had been happy and at peace, linking her arm through Oliver's, savouring the salty rain on her lips, the sting of the cold clean air on her cheeks and she had not guessed what he was thinking; there was no warning, no premonition, of the outburst which was suddenly upon her.

'I can't stand this any more, Sally! When are we going to stop coming to this dreadful place?' He had pulled away from her, his gesture angry and impatient. 'Don't you ever long for company and lights and sunshine?'

She stood for a moment unable to say a word, stunned into silence by her total surprise. Then reproachfully trying to refocus her thoughts, to understand what he was saying, she turned to him. 'I thought you loved it here.'

'I do.' He hurled a pebble at the water. 'It's just that sometimes I would rather go to other places; do other things. I feel trapped in this place . . .'

'I'm sorry. I didn't realize.'

She couldn't have said anything worse.

'No, that's your trouble. You don't realize. You think everyone else is the same as you. You don't bother to try and put yourself in their place. You adore it here, so everyone else must. You revel in introspection so you think it must be good for others too.'

'Oliver! That's not fair; you said you liked it here. You said you loved the quiet . . .'

'Well, I've changed my mind. So let's go! First thing tomorrow. Right?'

And then, as though at a signal, it started; the flying words, the recriminations which had led to the bitter analyses of their oh so short marriage, both of them saying things they didn't really mean, hurling the insults into the face of the rain.

At least Sally hadn't meant them . . .

When they regained the cottage at last Oliver had heaped the driftwood onto the fire till it blazed and ostentatiously made himself a bed on the sofa in front of it and Sally had crept into the cold bedroom alone.

The next morning she had been watching the cool early light slanting across the sands from the sea. She had leaned on her elbows and taken a deep breath of the salty air, watching the darting swooping flight of the terns as they skimmed the green water. They had not spoken since the night before.

Behind her Oliver was stirring the coffee in an old saucepan on the stove, filling the kitchen with the pungent bitter smell of it.

'Well, have you made up your mind? Are you coming?' His voice, coming out of the silence, had sounded politely casual. She could hear him picking the strainer off the draining board, carrying the saucepan to the table, pouring it into the two cups.

'I'm staying, Oliver.' She did not turn.

'OK. I'll leave you the car. I shall walk up the shore to the village and pick up a bus.'

'Fine.'

They might have been discussing their plans for any day of the holiday.

'Your coffee is on the table,' he said softly and she heard him pick up his own cup and walk away into the other room. Then, at the door he hesitated. 'I'm sorry, Sally.' His voice was slightly muffled. 'It's probably not your fault.' And the door closed behind him.

But she had not believed him. Her knuckles were white on the edge of the window and her eyes blurred with tears as she stared at the dancing terns and still she did not move or make any attempt to call him back. What had happened? What had gone wrong? Why should last night's row more than any other have led to this? Of course it was her fault. It had to be.

She had watched him later, striding up the beach until

he was a tiny speck in the distance. Then with a sick knot of misery tightening in her stomach she saw him turn up into the dunes and he was lost to sight.

She stayed on at the cottage on her own. At first she was sure he would come back and she waited for him, never going out of sight of the pretty white-washed building which had turned so swiftly for him from dream to prison, trailing disconsolately near the cold sea's edge, gathering driftwood for the fire, sketching the sunsets, the fingers which held her pencils numb with cold, uncertain what to do. She could not go home. Without him it would not be home – and her only certainty was that he would not have gone back there either.

They had chosen the Victorian cottage of their dreams the day he had asked her to marry him, walking down the street arm in arm, pointing at the terrace of little houses, deciding without argument that they would choose the one with the white front door. When days later they had seen the agent's board go up it had seemed like a special omen and Oliver had bought the cottage, selling without hesitation the flat he had owned for fifteen years. Half his furniture had had to be sold too and some of his books, to fit into so small a house, but they were happy and in love and he did not seem to care.

And when she told him of the sea where she had gone so often as a child he had agreed to come, loving her shy eagerness and he had said he liked the empty shore, liked it enough to come again when the November gales were lashing the coast and they had huddled together before a fire of wood which he had chopped all afternoon and they had laughed and planned. And one of their plans had been to come again. And now it had all gone wrong as if he had awakened from his dream and, looking round, had hated what he found.

And yet he had come back.

After a few minutes watching she began to run again, afraid he might stop and turn or, like a mirage on the sand, shimmer and dissolve as though he had never been.

There were only the two of them on the whole beach. It was too far from the village to encourage trippers, even in the summer and the fishermen kept away except for the occasional boy digging for worms. She ran a few steps more and then she stopped uncertainly trying to get her breath, her hands defenceless at her sides, her shoulders stooped with disappointment. It was not Oliver at all.

He came on at the same steady pace; tall – taller than Oliver and much younger, nearer her own age perhaps; his blond hair longish and windblown, his jeans bleached white by the sea, rolled to the knees.

'Hi,' he said when they were close enough to speak.

'I'm sorry.' In her confusion she was staring at him angrily. 'I thought you were my husband.'

'I'm sorry to disappoint you.' He bowed gravely, giving a strange old-world courtesy to the otherwise obvious reply.

'You didn't pass him, I suppose?' she was floundering now, trying to conceal her embarrassment. 'I was expecting him back any moment.' Why was she so uneasy in the face of his politely distant manner?

'I'm afraid the beach was deserted.' He resumed his walk slowly and she found herself turning to walk beside him. In the distance the tide was licking gently round her bag, nudging the pieces of driftwood, teasing them free of the canvas.

She gave an exclamation of annoyance as she noticed

and he saw too, following her gaze. 'I'll get it,' he called and before she could protest he had broken into a loping run, splashing carelessly into the ice cold water and scooping up the precious fuel.

He was laughing when she came up to him. 'Making a camp fire?'

She felt herself blush. 'No. It's for the cottage. There's a load of logs in the shed but I can't chop them so I'm stuck with driftwood.'

He looked at her gravely, the wet bag in his outstretched hand. 'Does your husband not chop wood?'

She bit her lip. 'He . . . he forgot to do it before he went. He had to go away for a couple of days, but he's due back anytime . . .' her voice trailed away.

He nodded, glancing at the white-washed cottage set back against the grassy dune. 'I'll come up and chop some for you if you like.'

'Oh but I couldn't let you.'

'For the price of a meal?' Again the easy grin.

And suddenly she found she didn't want to refuse. She was sick of her own company, sick of collecting firewood, sick of the smoky damp flame it gave in the lonely little room while she went over all the things that had gone wrong, the mistakes she must have made, the disappointments he must have known during the short time of their marriage; as she wondered what had happened to the wonderful closeness she and Oliver had shared in the first few carefree weeks. How could it so suddenly have turned to such bitterness? Whatever it was that had happened she did not want to think about it any more. Not for a while. For a while she would let herself forget if she could.

She found she was grinning back at the young man. 'OK. It's a deal.' And she turned up the beach and led the way.

Throwing down the bag on the doorstep he went

472

straight to the wood shed heaving out the heavy logs and reaching for the axe. She stood for a moment in the doorway watching as he lifted it high above his head and brought it down with a crash onto the first up-ended log, splitting it cleanly and evenly with one blow and then she went into the cottage.

She threw open the kitchen window and reached into the cupboard to see what she could find. She had not bothered to walk up to the village store for food; she had not been hungry. But she found eggs and suddenly she found she was looking forward to cooking again. She reached for the heavy iron skillet which hung on the wall above the cooker and began her preparations to the steady sound of chopping outside. By the time the food was ready he had laid her fire and filled the log basket and there was a neat stack of wood piled in the woodshed.

She could hear him whistling merrily as he washed in the little lean-to bathroom and then he was at the table, his tall frame dwarfing the room. The omelette was succulent and rich, full of herbs and she saw his look of appreciation as he took his first mouthful.

He raised his glass. 'To the cook. My compliments.'

She acknowledged the gesture with a grave nod. 'Thank you, sir.'

'Your husband is mad to go away, even for two days with food like this at home.'

He meant it gallantly, making conversation, but her mood was too fragile to cope with the pretence any longer. She stared hard at her plate.

'I don't think he's coming back,' she said quietly. 'He's left me.' It was the first time she had really admitted it even to herself.

He stared. 'Why?' he asked quietly.

She shrugged. 'So many reasons. So few. I don't understand. We were happy I thought . . .'

Glancing up he saw that she had laid down her fork and was biting her lip.

He frowned, staring at the top of her head, at the curtain of honey blonde hair and the golden slightly freckled complexion. Her knuckles were white beneath the taut skin of her hands clenched on the edge of the table top.

'How long have you been married?'

'Only a few months.' Her voice was a whisper. She glanced up. Her lips were smiling but her lashes were salty wet. 'Sorry. Ignore me. Women get so emotional.'

'So do men,' he said, very quietly. He put his hand lightly over hers. 'Tell me about him.'

'He's older than me, you see. A lot older. He's tall and fair, a bit like you, but his eyes are grey and he's older . . .' She was looking past him out of the window of the small low-ceilinged room. It was very quiet suddenly. He had not moved his hand. 'He had never married before. A lot of women wanted him, but he was so independent, so free . . . He didn't want to be tied down.'

'Until you came along.'

She looked directly at him for the first time. 'Until I came along. But why? Why me?'

'You're very beautiful.'

She seemed to be considering for a moment. The colour rose imperceptibly in her cheeks and she gave a faint smile. Almost reluctantly she slid her fingers out from beneath his.

'That would not matter to Oliver. I think he believed I was deeper than I was – someone else, some dream he had conceived of the ideal woman. Perhaps he thought he could mould me to be her. But he found he couldn't do it. And it's my fault.' She pushed back her chair and stood up abruptly. 'I'm sorry. Your omelette is getting cold.'

'It's fine.' Picking up his fork he grinned, his blue eyes

sympathetic and gentle. 'Can you make coffee as well as you cook?'

She grimaced ruefully gathering up her own plate, the food untouched. 'Oliver always made the coffee.'

'Then let me. I'm good at coffee. It's man's work.'

She watched him as he ate and stood aside unprotesting when he waved her away from the sink to rinse the plates and fill the kettle. He made the coffee in a jug and they carried their cups outside into the frosty sunshine and stood looking at the water as it lapped gently up the beach.

'I'm sure you're not right to blame yourself alone, you know,' he said tentatively after a long silence. 'If he really did want to change you he must have been mad, but I doubt if that was it. Not really. How long did he know you before you were married?'

'Two years.' She did not resent his interest. It was a relief to talk.

'Then he must have known you as you really are. I wonder . . .' he paused for a moment. 'I wonder if it was himself he was running from? People do you know. Sometimes. I did myself once.' He stared thoughtfully out towards the rocks.

'But why? Why should he want to run at all? I don't understand.' A little of her anguish escaped the tight grip of her self control. It deepened and matured her voice.

He turned and looked at her. She was totally self absorbed. She had not noticed the wistful longing in his voice as he remembered for an instant his own pain; the problems he had faced when he had lost the one person in the world whom he had loved. She was overwhelmed with her own desolation. He felt a quick rush of pity. Suddenly he wanted to touch her, to comfort her and reassure her and show her she was not to blame, but resolutely he kept his fingers linked around his cup. The steam from the coffee was white in the crisp air.

475

'You can only ever be yourself,' he said gently. 'Anything else would be a betrayal of him as well as yourself. Always remember that.'

'I know.' It was a whisper. 'He asked me to go with him and I refused. I couldn't do it. Not like that.'

'Then you did right.' He bent and picked up a fluted sandy shell, hurling it towards the rippling tide. They both stared at the place where it had disappeared. A streak of red weed hung and breathed back and forth below the curve of the beach. It could have been blood on the surface of the sea. She gave an involuntary little shiver.

'When did he go?' He was watching the tiny gold hairs on the back of her wrists stir and rise and he thought it was the icy wind which combed the grasses behind them in the dunes which made her shiver.

'Three days ago.'

'What would you do if he didn't come back?' he said gently.

He thought she hadn't heard and glanced sideways at her face. It was bleak.

'I'll wait for him.'

'You can't wait for ever. Won't you go home?'

She shrugged. 'For ever is a long time, I suppose. Perhaps when the storms come, then I'll go. I don't know.' She gave a wan smile. 'Perhaps he won't be that long.'

He found himself staring at her. The smile had transformed her face. Instead of a cold shuttered prettiness she had for a second betrayed a shadow of vibrant beauty. Then the sadness returned.

He had to bite his lip to force himself to keep from reaching out to take her in his arms to comfort her, to stop him from begging her to forget this treatment and lose herself instead in him. He swallowed hard, staring into the depths of the empty cup in his hand. After all, he was a stranger; she had not even told him her name. He had come here to forget his own unhappiness not become involved in that of another.

'It won't be long,' he said with resolution. 'Take my word. He'll be back.'

'Do you think so?' Her eyes were full of hope. She set her cup in the sand and stood up again, staring along the beach as though she expected to see Oliver that moment, striding towards her.

'I think so. After all, you are here for him to come back to.' He looked away from her sadly. When he had gone back his love had gone. She had not waited as this girl was waiting. She had left him without compunction, or so it seemed to him.

He followed Sally slowly to the sea's edge where the cold white dribbles of water nudged at the heaps of stranded weed; her narrow shoulders were taut beneath her heavy guernsey and there was pathos' in the angle of her neck.

Without knowing he did it he slowly shook his head. He had to leave her now. If he did not go now, then he would never go.

He held out his hand to her and unquestioning she took it. For a moment more they stood in silence. Then he let her fingers drop.

'Time's getting on.' He said it very gently.

She seemed to understand. 'Of course. Thank you for chopping the wood.'

'Thank you for cooking me the omelette.'

He turned away towards the village and took a few paces along the tide line. Then he stopped and looked back. She had not moved.

'You'll be all right?'

'Of course.'

'Is there anything else I can do?'

'Nothing. Thank you.'

'You're sure?'

There were tears on her cheeks as the cold wind blew her hair across her eyes. She did not look at him.

He stood for a moment undecided and then he was beside her again and his hands were on her shoulders. Gently he turned her to face him and he pulled her close. Her skin tasted of salt. He kissed her cheeks, her eyelids, her hair and then last of all her lips. They parted a little without protest and they were soft. But they were cold. For a moment he did not move, feeling the comfort of her presence within the circle of his protecting arms, knowing that somehow he was comforting her, then sadly he pushed her away. He began to walk without a word. And this time he did not look back.

She stood at the edge of the tide watching as slowly the leading ripples hesitated and lost their purpose and drew back, leaving the sand wet and clean and smooth. Only then did she turn and look into the distance. He had gone long since, just as Oliver had gone, along the beach towards the village out of sight. It was as though he had never been but there was deep inside her a small new warmth.

Slowly she wandered back to the cottage and hardly knowing that she did it she went round to the little lean-to woodshed and glanced in. The neatly stacked pile of split logs was real enough, as was the axe, newly-honed and in its place. Weakly she leaned against the wall and closed her eyes and thought about the stranger.

Much later as the moon was rising silver over the frosted dunes she lit the fire and watched the cheerful clear crackle of the logs in the hearth. She made some coffee as he had in a jug and then leaving it on the table she pushed open the door. The tide had gone out so far it was only a sliver of light on the shining moonlit sand and she ran down towards it feeling the cold bite of the wind in her face.

Strangely she was happy, her doubts and miseries resolved into a quiet confidence and resignation and the knowledge that Oliver would return and that when he did, however long it took, she would be there waiting for him.

She stood for a long time at the water's edge watching the trail of moonshine in the tide and then she glanced along the beach towards the village. For a moment she held her breath. She thought she could see a figure striding out of the dunes. She stared and then she started to run; then she stopped. It was too far away to see – perhaps it was just the shadow of a cloud thrown on the rippled sand. Her heart was beating fast as she waited, her shoes sinking into the softness of the wet silver at her feet. And then she saw the brightness of his hair and the tall, easy stride, and she began to smile. This time it was, it had to be, Oliver.

'You waited for me to come back?' he said as he came up to her and put his hands on her shoulder. His face was pale and strained in the moonlight.

'I waited.' She smiled up at him.

'I'm sorry I went away. I didn't mean to hurt you but I had to think. I had to be alone.'

'Is everything all right now?'

'Everything.' He kissed her lightly on the forehead. 'It wasn't your fault, you know.'

'I know,' she said quietly.

Hand in hand they walked back to the cottage and he sat down beside the fire and she brought him the coffee and watched him while he sipped it. She never mentioned the stranger who had chopped the wood and taken her so briefly in his arms. It did not seem important.

479

Just An Old-Fashioned Girl

It had happened the night before. She had worked late and was tired after the long walk back through the cold rain-washed streets. Neal had been home before her, letting himself in with his key, lighting the gas fire, straightening the room with, she was sure, a look of mild reproach.

Guiltily she had dropped her two heavy sodden shopping bags on the carpet and fumbled for the wet knot of her belt.

'I didn't expect you back so early tonight. I haven't had a chance to tidy up.'

He grinned. 'I've done most of it for you.' The room certainly looked very nice. There was a pot of nearly-hatched hyacinths on the table which hadn't been there that morning. Obscurely she felt irritated.

'Well, I've still got to get the meal and do something with my hair!'

But he shook his head. 'No need. I've booked us a table at the Captain's Bistro and your hair –' he took a step towards her and taking a lank wet strand of it in his hand gave it a gentle tug, 'will look fabulous once you've had a drink.'

And that was how it so often was. She, agitated, late, scatty; he always calm, organized – and punctual, soothing her ruffled feathers and her ruffled ego. And she had, she decided, always found it irritating. It made her want to stamp her foot like a spoilt child, instead of receiving his influence with the gracious calm a woman of her age should accord it.

And as always, he was right. Her hair piled on top of her head, swathed in a soft towel, an inelegant tumbler of sherry on the edge of the bath at her shoulder, she lay back in water liberally sprinkled with Boot's best and she could feel the tight spring inside her beginning to uncoil and the weight of her day at the library slipping from her shoulders.

She put on a simple dress that night and twisted her hair up into an exotic confection of clips and stars. By the time they had walked back down the cold High Street the wind had pulled most of it down, but the effect, even dishevelled was, she knew, attractive to Neal.

Just as some men were supposed to be bosom men and some bottom men, Neal was a hair man, making almost a fetish of it, burying his face in it, holding the weight of it in his hands, winding it gently round her throat till it formed a silken glowing collar.

The bistro was half empty as they forced their way in out of the gale, the night lights on the tables flickering and dipping in unison as the door closed behind them on the evening darkness.

Captain Ferguson was there to usher them in, to take their coats, to bring the menus and then at last they were alone, facing one another across the table, the small clear flame between them.

'Have you decided yet, Emma?' Neal's eyes were steady on her face, his voice low. Neither of them had opened their menu and she knew he wasn't talking about the food.

'Give me a little more time, Neal, please. There is so much to think about.

He scowled. 'There is nothing to think about. Either

481

we get married, or we go on as we are. Surely that's not such a difficult question!'

But it was. Surely he could see it was.

They had lived together on and off for five years, sometimes as now, sharing her flat; sometimes camping in his, sometimes apart for months on end when his job as an engineer took him away, but always returning in the end to one another.

Of course she had wanted marriage once. All young women dreamed of marriage didn't they, even in this age of emancipation? Surely the most hardened female libber had the occasional aberration and pictured herself in a swirl of white and orange blossom, but that had passed.

As she moved on into her late twenties life became real, and dreams were tempered with, not bitterness exactly, but resignation and, she supposed, maturity. Neal was part of that maturity.

They had met in the library where she worked now as head librarian. She had been an assistant then, when he had come in searching for some esoteric books on early music – his passion – and a friendship had developed.

Within three months there was more than that. They were living together and within six she knew Neal was thinking of marriage. Then it had been too soon to talk of it, but afterwards she realized there was more to her reluctance than that. She valued so much her independence; she valued her privacy.

Somehow she had evaded the issue for a long time, but lately Neal was becoming more persistent, hinting darkly that they would soon be too old to start a family . . .

Marriage or stay as they were was the choice he had offered, but there was always a third possibility. One he hadn't mentioned. That they part.

She swallowed, staring hard at the candle behind which his face had become a hazy blur. The thought of parting had sprung unbidden into her mind without warning; it was the last thing she wanted; the last thing in the world.

'Would you like to order now, sir?' The waiter's voice cut through her thoughts and she looked up. Neal was watching her across the candle. Visibly he pulled himself together, dragging his eyes from her face to that of the waiter.

'We'll both have steak.'

'No!' Rebellion flared again as the waiter raised his pad to write. 'No, I'll have the chicken.'

Neal shrugged. 'White wine then?' he queried, this time hesitant and, knowing that he preferred red, she nodded.

Neither of them spoke until the waiter had disappeared.

'All right, go on, say it. I'm a cow!' Guilt made her angrier.

He shrugged. 'If you say so.' Then suddenly he grinned. 'You're trying to be, anyway. Why Emma? What's wrong? I'm not the enemy, you know.'

'I know.' Crossly she reached for a piece of bread from the basket and began to break it up.

And then it had happened. Her hair, still precariously coiled had begun to slip and Neal, leaning forward, had hooked his finger into one of the long heavy tresses. Gently he pulled. 'You're going grey, Emma,' he said.

Later outside in the beating sleet she walked head up, her coat blowing open, alone. She followed the High Street winding down between the houses and turned across towards the quay. The light outside the harbourmaster's office burned solitarily through the streaks of wetness, reflecting in a shivery rippled line in the water at her feet. For a long time she looked down, then stiff and frozen she turned and slowly walked home.

When she got there all Neal's things had gone. He must have left the restaurant almost immediately after her and loaded his car without a second's thought. Head high, eyes blazing in her wind-pinked face, she stared at herself in the mirror. Then reluctantly she reached for her brush. At nine o'clock the next morning she was at the hair salon.

She met Chris four days later. He was in his forties, divorced, tall like Neal but very fair and broad shouldered and though he was outwardly quiet he had a tough rough streak in him that appealed to the Emma in her which had emerged as her hair fell to the salon floor. He took her tramping over the moors and, with feet and hands aching with cold, to watch rugger matches and once or twice to a point to point where she backed a horse and won herself five pounds.

Her flat without Neal was untidy now, defiantly untidy and she had put away one by one the things he had particularly loved. One especially, the patchwork quilt so lovingly worked by her great grandmother out of minute squares of coloured silk. Even Chris had admired it, but it did not suit her new image of herself: cool, sophisticated, modern and ageless.

Instead she bought a black satin bedspread by mail order and secretly, for sewing too was for the birds, she appliquéd on it a huge scarlet 'EM'. She almost wished when she had finished it that Neal could see it. She wanted to watch his reactions.

'Come on, Em. Let me stay.' Chris had his arm around her shoulders, his right hand firmly anchored over her right breast. She squirmed uncomfortably.

'Chris, I've told you. I'm not ready. Not yet.'

'And how long does it take for you to be ready?'

She smiled and edged a little further away from him

on the sofa. 'Not long, I promise. Come on, have some more coffee. Then you will have to go. I must get to the library early tomorrow.

He was frowning this time as he stood up and she knew that he would not take her excuses much longer. Either sleep with him or break up with him. Chris would not waste time on a relationship that was going nowhere.

She ran her fingers through her hair, exasperated, after he had gone. Why did men always want something more? Why when there was so much to a relationship besides sex did they reduce everything to that one denominator and threaten so much else that was good?

Of course she knew her reaction meant she did not love him. How could she love him when at night, alone, shivering beneath her black and scarlet satin, her thoughts always came back to Neal. Neal who was gentle. Neal who was strong and understanding and patient with her.

Next morning she rang Chris from her tiny private office behind the book stacks. 'Chris. Tonight. Come to my place for a meal. We won't go out anywhere, OK?'

'You mean it, Em?' From his voice she knew he understood.

'I mean it, Chris.' She stared down at the phone for several minutes without seeing it after she had hung up. Then, with a shrug she turned back to her desk.

Chris went to considerable trouble with his appearance that evening. And on his way to her he stopped off at the florist and bought, for a small fortune, one single hot house rose. Somehow it seemed right for Em.

For her part she had bought two bottles of red wine. Only one bottle, all to herself, would bring her to it and if Chris wasn't going to drive home that night he might as well have one too.

Rain was lashing the windows as she pulled the curtains closed and turned up the gas fire, listening for a moment to the reassuring purr as the flame licked across the cold elements. She laid two places at the low coffee table before it and set the two cushions in place. Then she searched out a record to match her mood.

The bedroom was perfect. Small, intimate, the huge scarlet letters writhing across the swell of the pillows. The room had none of the warmth and love which Neal had known but then, she swore at herself sharply, it wasn't Neal she was expecting.

She was in the kitchen when the bell rang, a wooden spoon in her hand, dabbing ineffectually at a creamy mushroom sauce which was sitting on the cold burner waiting only to be poured over the chicken and put into the oven. Her bottle of wine was already a third empty.

She stared at Chris, her stomach suddenly contorting into a cramp of apprehension as he stood in the doorway, his hands behind him. He looked different, strange; scrubbed and almost shy, like a schoolboy on his first date as reluctantly, even awkwardly, he produced the rose. 'Do you want to stick this thing in some water?'

She took it, more embarrassed than he was, ridiculously touched at the gesture and fumbled in a kitchen cupboard for a tall glass to hold it while he stood in the doorway behind her watching. Then, all at once, they were laughing. The strain had vanished. They were no longer circling teenagers, awkward because of the contrived situation. They were adults again. He poured himself a tumbler of the wine and hauling himself up onto the worktop he sat and watched as she anointed the chicken with her sauce and put the dish into the oven.

They ate, they talked, they sat lounging on the cushions before the gas fire listening to records which almost but not quite drowned the sound of hailstones lashing against the windows under the heavy curtains. Chris made no move to touch her, watching her from time to time from beneath his heavy brows as she talked and laughed, her face a little flushed from the fire.

She was, he thought, more beautiful and more vivacious than he had ever seen her but quite unlike herself. Surely she knew that he had guessed she was playing a part, wearing a pretty social mask. He had realized from the moment he set foot through the door that he would never sleep with her now.

The little clock on the mantelpiece ticked round to one o'clock and she was still talking hard into every silence when at last Chris leaned forward and put his hand on her wrist. She stopped, electrified by his touch.

'It's late, Emma,' he said gently. 'We've both got to work in the morning.'

She nodded and clutching the coffee table to steady herself she stood up.

'I'll make some more coffee, shall I, before . . . ?' Her voice trailed away.

'Before I go. Yes, please, Em. I've drunk a bit more than I should.' He smiled. In fact he was stone cold sober. It was Emma who was a little tipsy.

'Oh but you can't go, Chris. I don't want you to. I want you to stay. Truly.' She waved vaguely towards the bedroom door.

He put his hands on her shoulders and pulled her towards him, staring down at her. 'Thank you, Em. But no. I'm not blind. I can see how it is with you. I understand.'

After he had gone she sat down again in front of the fire and stared into the hot depths of the flames.

But how is it with me? she thought miserably. I just don't know.

*

She still saw Chris; they were too fond of one another to part, but their relationship had steadied into a warm friendship which contained no demands. She had never mentioned her past to him. He knew there must have been other men, but she was a creature of mystery, a strange old-fashioned type of person inspite of her efforts to be different and he respected her for it. He was even pleased with himself now for taking her the rose. It hadn't been such a silly gesture after all.

Neal saw her several hundred yards away, threading her way towards him up the crowded Saturday High Street, her duffle hood pulled forward around her face, her hands deep in her pockets, a basket hitched onto her elbow.

He stopped and stared at her for a moment, then he turned away towards the nearest shop to avoid her. In the doorway he stopped abruptly, his eye caught by his own reflection, by the acute misery he had surprised on his own face and he felt a surge of anger. Pride had kept him from her all these weeks, but now she was there a few hundred yards from him and he would stay away no longer. Swinging back into the thoroughfare he pushed his way through the crowds and caught her arm.

'We're going for a walk.'

Emma, dreaming, had not even seen him coming and she bit back a cry of surprise as she found herself being pulled round into the teeth of the wind, but after only a second's hesitation, she went.

Stormbound, the fishing fleet clustered into the shelter of the sea wall and down river the slate water blended with a slate sky heavy with unshed snow. Side by side they stood and stared down at the restless decks jostling against the quayside. Then slowly Emma raised her head and grinned at him.

'You know, I think I've missed you.'

'And I think I've missed you.' His eyes narrowed. Her hair whipped from beneath the hood and was flailing around her eyes. He raised his hands and pushed the hood back from her face.

She waited, defiant.

He shook his head. 'You cuckoo. Why?'

The gesture seemed so empty now. 'I wanted to change my image.'

He laughed. 'And have you?'

'Of course. Can't you tell?'

'Not yet. But then I haven't seen much of you. Come and have a coffee.'

Thankfully she followed him into the warmth of the coffee house near the church where they found a corner table and faced each other free of the blinding wind at last. He stared at her critically as she slipped back her duffle coat.

'You've lost weight, but so far you're the same Emma. Say something, then perhaps I can tell.'

She grinned. 'Pearls of wisdom fall from my lips these days. And I'm called Em.'

'Why not Fred, it's more feminine. To me you're Emma and always will be.' He sounded sterner than she had ever heard him, almost schoolmasterly, and she resisted the answering urge to stick her tongue out at him and chose instead a large Danish pastry from the trolley.

He watched amused. She was different. More confident perhaps; more mature; calmer and more ordered.

'I hear you've been going around with Chris Foster,' he said after a moment's silence.

She met his gaze squarely. 'For a couple of months or so now.'

'Serious?'

'Depends what you mean by serious.' She stared

beyond him towards the window where the snow was again feathering down; a sign, back to front on the glass read, *Order Your Valentine Cake Now* and there was a picture of a thick creamy chocolate heart. Suddenly her eyes were full of tears. She blinked them back angrily. Grown women do not cry in public at the sight of a piece of romantic tomfoolery aimed at teenage children.

She groped in her bag for a handkerchief and blew her nose hard, still not looking at him.

'Could he spare you one evening, do you think?' His voice sounded husky against the usual coffee house squawk of women.

Squaring her chin she looked at him at last. 'That's for me to say, not him.'

She chose a date a week away so as not to seem too eager and they met, impersonally, at a pub they had never visited together before.

But he had a present for her – a tiny silver pendant – very modern in design. Not once did he mention her hair.

She ached for him to touch her, but he was strangely distant and formal with her, meticulously polite. But for the pendant which grew slowly warm against her skin as she played with it nervously on its chain, they might have been strangers as they sat facing one another across the table, their hands a few inches apart. There was no candle between them, but she felt as though there might have been a hundred miles.

And then suddenly he pushed back his chair and relaxed and laughed. 'You know, Emma, you haven't changed one bit. You're still the same delightful old-fashioned girl at heart, for all the sculptured haircut and the space age dress! I'm glad. I wouldn't have you any different for anything.' And his hand reached out at last and covered hers.

She grinned, thinking suddenly of the black satin bed-spread. The day she had met him again she had put back her patchwork quilt. The effect had been devastating. She felt calm and reassured; back home; undeniably herself once more. But perhaps it was too late. Perhaps Neal no longer wanted her. Perhaps after all she no longer wanted him.

'How can you tell I'm the same?' she asked him, her fingers lying easily in his.

'The way you talk, the way you sit. Even the way you do your hair.'

'But –'

'But it does suit you, you're right,' he went on critically, his head a little to one side, 'although of course it makes you look older . . .'

She had spotted the glint in his eye. 'I could grow it again if you really thought I should,' she said. 'But it would probably take fifteen years.'

He looked thoughtful. 'As long as that?' Then he was smiling again. 'OK. I'm prepared to wait. I'll hang around until it does. If you want me that is?'

It was what she had been hoping he would say and yet now she hesitated. 'I'm more changed than you think, Neal. It might not work, us being together again. I want it to, but . . .'

The grip of his fingers tightened for a moment. Then he released her hand. 'I won't push you, Emma. But think about it, won't you?' He smiled and picked up the menu. 'This was where things went wrong before and I'm not going to make the same mistake again. You ordered chicken and white wine, remember?'

She grinned. 'I'll promise you this much, Neal. If I walk

out on you this time I'll wait around long enough to pay my half of the bill, does that seem fair?'

His eyes met hers and held them. 'Very fair,' he said.

All This Childish Nonsense

*R*ichard. *I've done something dreadful.* Pat looked in the mirror, screwed up her face and tried again. *Richard, darling, I've done something rather wonderful.* That didn't work either. Not at all. Better to say it straight out. *Richard, there's someone coming to stay. For two weeks.*

The mirror was steaming up. Her palms were growing sweaty. *Richard, I know I should have told you a long time ago, but I never plucked up the courage. Richard, I know you'll want to throw me out . . . but the child was alone and it is Christmas. Richard, please . . .*

'You've done what?' His voice was too quiet. Pat looked hard at the floor and explained again. This time it was easier. She just told him; straight.

'They'd have had to put her in care or something. Richard, she is a relation of mine, sort of. I couldn't say no, could I?' Could I? Just as when Sarah had said: 'I know you and your husband won't mind, just while I'm in hospital.' She hadn't dared say: 'He's not my husband.' She had looked hard at the wall, above the white radiator and the telephone receiver had hurt her ear it was so tightly pressed. 'He's not my husband, we're only living together. Something like this could ruin everything. He says I'm taking him for granted . . .'

'How old is this child anyway?' Richard's voice was still enigmatically cool.

493

'Six, I think.'

Richard stood up and threw down the paper. 'That's all I need; a child of six, in a flat this size! I don't want anyone else here upsetting things. We're fine as we are.'

He went to look out of the window. Pat could see his knuckles on the green and white print curtain. She winced, waiting for the rip. Those curtains had been her first bad mistake. Attractive, light, airy, hand-made. By her . . . 'I hope you're not going broody or something,' he'd muttered, instead of thank you. Then he had ignored them. And they did look so lovely once she'd tidied the room a bit.

Of course later, in bed, he had murmured in her ear, his voice so soft and dreamy she wondered if she had heard right: 'Those curtains make the room, Pat. It might be nice to have new ones in here, one day,' and she knew it was his way of saying sorry and thank you. His way; in the dark.

'She won't be any trouble, Richard. Her mother says she's a very quiet, obedient child. She's used to going to stay with people.'

'Good, so let her go and stay with them again.'

'It's difficult, Richard. It's Christmas.'

'All the more reason for them to have her.'

He went into the bedroom. She followed him, hovering. He went back into the living room. She followed again. She knew she was irritating him. She wanted to disappear. She felt sick.

'What shall I do?'

He had picked up his jacket. 'Do what you like, but don't expect me to entertain her if she comes here.' He was at the door and going; then for a moment he was back. 'And don't,' he said, his chin set in the way she knew so well, 'expect me to dress up as Father Christmas.'

In the morning Richard ate the breakfast she prepared

and went to work with a smile and a kiss. She liked that; like it must be with real married people. Neither of them mentioned the child. She wished suddenly she was going to work, too. It had seemed fun to finish a job the last week before Christmas, start another in the New Year; have those two or three weeks free.

Then Richard had said: 'I hope you're not going to waste money buying me presents, all that childish nonsense.'

'I like childish nonsense,' she had wanted to wail, but hadn't the courage. What if he despised her for it?

So the cards she sent had been secret, although she'd written, defiantly, 'from Pat and Richard' and the ones they received had been gloated over and loved and then reluctantly put in a drawer. She went cold suddenly. The child would expect a tree.

She gazed round the room. Nothing was ready. The spare bed was still folded behind the door.

When the time came to meet the train she was there at the barrier and her face was smiling, but inside she was terrified and resentful. Suppose Richard never came home again? Suppose he threw her out? Suppose the child was uncontrollable? Even delinquent?

She saw the child at the other end of the platform. With it was an adult, responsible for the length of the journey only, who exchanged names and addresses and vanished into the crowd, not seeing or guessing Pat's panic; leaving a suitcase and the little girl to Pat.

Pat licked her lips nervously and tried to smile. 'Hello, Annabel,' she said, experimenting.

The little girl had enormous blue story-book eyes and was solemn. 'Hello, Aunt Pat,' she said. 'My name is Bel.' She put her hand in Pat's and waited expectantly.

My God, thought Pat, what now?

Somehow they got home. The little girl was enchanted

to have a bed which wasn't ready and which folded up behind the door.

'It's like a horse,' she exclaimed and mounted it, pretending to ride. The floor began to shake and Pat bit her lip. She was thinking of Richard's reaction. *Please let him like her*, she prayed silently, *please*.

'I'm hungry,' said Bel and Pat looked at her watch. What do children eat for lunch? Not yoghurt, crispbread and cottage cheese, that was for sure. She had better ask.

'Chips,' came the reply. 'Chips and sausages and fish-fingers and chocolate pudding. Where's your Christmas tree, Aunt Pat?'

Richard looked for a long time at the small green fir, wedged with newspapers into his wastepaper basket. The whole flat was full of the scent of resin and pine needles. It was fragrant and beautiful.

'Uncle Richard, Uncle Richard, will you help us decorate it?' The child was already in her nightie with furry-bunny slippers.

Pat peered furtively through the kitchen door. She was hiding; she admitted it. But surely the pretty child could manage Richard better than she could? She breathed a quick prayer as Richard set down his papers and slowly began to unbutton his jacket.

'You fraud!' she whispered in the kitchen later. 'You utter fraud. All that silver tinsel in your briefcase; and baubles! How did you know I'd buy a tree? How did you guess?'

He grinned. 'I knew,' he said.

They had to bring the TV and the table lamp and their books into the bedroom so that the child could sleep. Pat saw Richard frown and she cursed silently. She hadn't thought of that, as she hadn't thought of the pools of water cascading from the bath onto the floor, the piercing giggles and screams, the enthusiastic assault on Richard's typewriter, or the scribbles in his books. ('It's not scribbles, it's my bestest writing.')

Bel found Pat's photographs in a box and scattered them, delighted, on the carpet, making patterns. 'Look, look,' she squeaked. 'You – on a pony. What's he called, Aunt Pat?'

Pat looked. She had been about fifteen. 'Black Beauty?' she hazarded hopefully.

'But he's not black, Aunt Pat.'

He wouldn't be!

'Oh, look! Here's Uncle Richard.' The child held out another picture, her head a little to one side. 'I like Uncle Richard.'

So do I, thought Pat. Lots. She reached for the photo. It was of them both. He had his arm round her shoulder and was smiling down into her eyes in that gentle, intense way of his which she loved so much. It had been taken the summer she had first met him, two years before. Was it really two years?

'Why are you smiling, Aunt Pat?'

She had met him at a friend's party. Both had gone alone, both planning to leave early. They had left early, but no longer alone. From the moment they started talking Pat had realized that she could never be alone again. Not as long as Richard was any part of her life.

It had taken a long, long time, though, for Richard to ask, half diffident, if she would move in with him. Scarcely believing it, she had arrived, suitcase and pot plant in hand, before he could change his mind and, laughing, he had found a saucer for the plant. 'You've brought your family, I see,' he'd said.

The pot plant was still there, on the windowsill.

'What are we going to give Uncle Richard?' Bel asked, confidingly, on Christmas Eve.

How could Pat say 'nothing'?

So they went shopping together and bought him some aftershave and some socks and a paperback. Then Bel had a brainwave.

'I'll pretend to be Father Christmas.' She gave a high-pitched giggle. 'Won't that be a surprise for Uncle Richard? We'll hang up the stocking for him and when he's asleep I'll tiptoe in and fill it with presents like the real Father Christmas does for children.'

The real Father Christmas?

Well, Pat had thought of it. She had managed to keep a few small things hidden besides the little girl's present from her mother which Pat had found tucked in the suitcase. But what would Richard say? Pat licked her lips nervously. *All this childish nonsense.* But there was a child.

Pat and Bel listened to carols on the radio while they made a Christmas cake. Not a rotten old cake, with currants and things in ('Yuk,' said Bel), but a chocolate sponge with thick squidgy icing. Pat hadn't made a cake before.

'My mummy doesn't need a book,' said Bel with peals of laughter. 'Books don't tell you how to make cakes.'

They'd better, thought Pat . . .

The amazing thing was, she found she was to have a stocking as well.

'Hang it up; hang it up,' the child shouted, dancing with excitement. Pat was embarrassed. There would be nothing in her stocking. She hadn't thought of it and of course Richard wasn't in on this conspiracy. She wildly wondered what she could put inside the woolly sock she was handed.

'Uncle Richard says people hang their stockings round the biggest radiator when they live in flats,' said Bel.

Doubtfully.

'Oh he did, did he?' said Pat. She felt warm inside as she realized Richard must be entering into the spirit of things, that he wanted to join in, to belong even.

She filled her own stocking, quietly, with a couple of unopened packets of tights and some perfume she had been given for her birthday. Then, lump in throat, she filled the other two and crept back to bed.

Richard seemed to be asleep. She had hoped he might help her wrap Bel's presents, but he hadn't offered. He had sat in the kitchen reading the paper. But she suspected he was taking an interest, his eyes glancing now and then at the lumpy packages.

Bel woke at half past five with shrieks of excitement. Sleepy and half apprehensive, with a wary look at Richard, Pat allowed herself to be dragged from the bed. She gasped. The stockings which she had left limply stuffed were bulging. Bel's had overflowed onto the carpet.

'I . . . er . . . think we must have duplicated.' Richard was sheepish as he peered around the bedroom door.

She looked at him. His hair was rumpled; his bathrobe torn. Looking down at the child, he was smiling, watching expectantly as her stocking was carried, bulging, to the sofa.

Bel stopped. 'Aren't you going to open yours?'

They smiled at each other, catching the little girl's excitement and reached, each a little embarrassed, for the grossly swollen socks which lay on the floor. Pat's heart began to beat a little faster.

The packets in hers were carefully wrapped in gold and black paper. 'Nothing very exciting,' Richard grinned. 'I'm afraid Father Christmas was a little rusty.'

Nothing very exciting! A silk scarf; a pendant; a tiny teddy bear.

'For me?'

'Look, Aunt Pat. I've got one, too!'

Pat went down on her knees to grope inside the stocking. A paperback. The sequel to the one she'd bought him! They held them up together and laughed.

'It proves we must be compatible after all,' he teased. 'We'll have to live together long enough to read each other's.'

She made mountains of toast and they ate it all sitting on the big bed getting butter and honey on the duvet and giggling. Then Richard lay back, contented and began to read aloud the story of *Thomas the Tank Engine*.

'Well, I liked it when I was six.'

'But, Richard, she's a girl.'

'I do like it, Aunt Pat; I *do!*'

The flat lay beneath a drift of coloured paper. She put on the chicken and wished she had risked a Christmas pudding. In the end they stuck five-pence pieces into the chocolate cake. ('You know, love, if you don't mind me saying so, it's really more like a pudding in the middle anyway.') But she knew he liked her attempts at cooking. It was one of the things on her side.

'My God,' said Richard in despair. 'Look at me. The picture of a happy family man.' He ran his fingers through his hair and groaned as Bel bounced onto his lap. 'This would put you off marriage for life, this would.'

He had meant it as a joke but the air was suddenly electric. He saw Pat, her eyes brimming, turn away to put the kettle on. Damn, he thought, damn, damn, damn!

Pat sniffed and shook her head as she filled the kettle. I knew it was all pretend, she thought, furious with herself. He's always told me he's not the marrying type. So why am I worrying? I never expected it. It's a lovely day and I'm not going to spoil it. She blew her nose angrily, then she plugged in the kettle.

But Richard was there behind her. His arm was round

her shoulder. 'Happy Christmas, lover,' he whispered and gently he kissed the back of her neck.

Bel was watching solemnly from the doorway. 'Have you given her your special present yet, Uncle Richard? I know where it is.' The child was clutching the doll ('Look, Uncle Richard, she wets her nappy!') which her mother had sent for her. 'Shall I fetch it?'

Pat turned. 'What special present?'

Richard shook his head in despair. 'Don't I have any secrets any more? Fetch it, then. Carefully.'

The present was wrapped in the same stripy paper. It was so tiny the sticky tape enveloped it. It was a very little box.

'I thought it might get lost if I put it in that great hairy stocking,' he muttered as he took it.

The kettle was clouding the room with steam but Pat took no notice. Shaking, she held out her hand and he gave her the box. A ring box.

'And besides,' he went on, 'I didn't want you to get the wrong idea. I expect Father Christmas is married already.' He grinned mischievously.

'I'm the one who wants a wife . . .'

A Love Story

'*Chérie, je t'aime.*'

I nestled into André's arms, his soft whisper so close to my ear that I couldn't tell if I felt the warmth of his breath or the brush of his lips on my hair.

'My Suzie, we must go.'

Reluctantly I allowed him to push me from his knees and I stood up, conscious of my crumpled skirt and unbuttoned blouse. I was a mess. I could never look glamorously dishevelled as I imagined his French girlfriends would have looked under similar circumstances. My make-up would certainly have run and my tights had snagged on the cushion zip as we sat down. I felt overwhelmingly depressed.

I had met André three months before at my niece's graduation party. He was twenty-three and I was nearly forty. At first I had been amused by his attentions, and flattered of course.

'But *chérie*,' he had said, gently teasing. 'The Frenchmen are always fascinated by older women. Surely you know that?' And I laughed and accepted first his compliments and then his invitation out to dinner.

But that one evening together had led to more and before I knew it I was falling in love with him. It was no use my telling myself every morning as I gazed in the bathroom mirror that I looked old enough to be his mother.

I didn't. I had a good skin and as yet the crows' feet were minimal, but even so I found I was spending far more time and money on my appearance than I had before I met André. I had the notion that Frenchmen expected their women to be chic and feminine and I intended to live up to André's every expectation. Even in bed. When he first made it clear that he wanted so sleep with me I had objected, in a real panic that once we had slept together there would be nothing left to attract him, but I did us both an injustice. When at last I gave way unable to hold out any longer against something I wanted so much, he proved a superb lover and his attentions became more marked and more loving every day.

As an assistant lecturer in French at the university he had a room in one of the men's hostels and acted as assistant warden there. At the weekends we would make toast in front of his electric fire and lie on his narrow bed together listening to tapes. But it was difficult there. We could never be sure that there wasn't going to be a knock on the door at any moment. The best times were when he came back to my flat and we knew we would be alone.

You may ask why I wasn't married. Most people did, in their usual tactless way. When I was twenty-two I had become engaged to a young man whom I worshipped. But our engagement grew longer and longer. Each time I tried to persuade him to fix a date he would find an excuse. At last after five years I had realized what my friends and family had probably known all along, that he was not the marrying kind. It broke my heart, but ours had not been the stable relationship which can last without marriage. After we parted I avoided any serious affairs, nursing my wounded pride beneath a stout campaign for the independence of women. Until I met André.

Now, in his cosy bed-sitter, in the dim light of the shaded lamp I looked up at him as he stood before the

503

mirror combing his hair and I knew I loved him as I had loved no one before and I was afraid.

He turned and smiled, holding out his arms. 'I wish you did not have to go, Suzie.'

I loved the way he pronounced my name. He made it sound exotic and a little wicked. Other people just called me Sue.

We kissed long and passionately and then reluctantly we went out into the dimly-lit hall, tiptoeing so as not to disturb any sleeping students. From behind some of the doors came the muted sounds of music, but most were quiet. The lines of light beneath the doors showed that few were asleep. It was only a week from the exams and I suspected that many a set of brains was being cudgelled that night to try and make up for lost evenings earlier in the term.

André and I sauntered down the moonlit road, breathing in the heady summer air. My flat was about two miles from the hostel through the peaceful sleepy suburb and on fine nights I loved the walk back there under the stars, with André holding my hand. I was entirely happy.

We reached the bridge across the river and leaned over the parapet, looking down into the dark water rushing far below. Only the occasional flash of white showed in the gloom as a wave hit the rocks.

André put his arm round my shoulder. 'Suzie, there is something I must tell you.' His tone was ominously serious. I turned to him and waited without a word.

After a moment he went on. 'I have been offered a job in France, Suzie. It is one I want very much.'

That was all he said.

I looked down at the water again, trying to bite back the tears. After all, I had known it could not last, but I had not expected this. I had thought he would grow tired of me and find another woman and that my own cynicism would be there to comfort me, but no. He had said the words as though his heart too would break.

I glanced sideways. He was looking down as though the river would hold his attention for ever and in the luminous night I could see his profile with its firm nose and chin, the high forehead, the irrepressible curly hair. Somehow I stifled a sob. He must not know that I was crying.

'Come on,' I said. 'It's late.'

He didn't come in for a coffee and as I shut the door I felt as though my whole world was shattered. He had gone off without another word.

In my living room which was really more of a studio – I was a painter as well as a teacher at the art college – my portrait of André stood on the easel, nearly finished. I gazed at it for a long time, pleading silently with those warm brown eyes as if he could really see me. I felt empty; dead. Then I blew a sad kiss towards the glistening oils and turned for my lonely bedroom.

The next two days were busy ones as a rule for both of us and we had agreed not to meet until the Friday. I don't know how I prevented myself from ringing him in the interval, but I did.

As the hour approached when André would be picking me up at my flat I grew more and more nervous. Tonight I would find out when he was to leave and whether I would ever see him again. I grew increasingly depressed as I dressed in one of my prettiest summer dresses, one which I knew he particularly liked, but to my surprise André himself looked anything but depressed when he had at last appeared at the door.

'Bring a coat and scarf, Suzie,' he commanded. 'I have borrowed a car.'

We were swiftly in the country and as we roared through the fragrant evening with the roof of the car folded down I lay back and closed my eyes. Wherever we were going I was not really looking forward to it. There was too much talking to be done over the meal.

When we at last drew up in the forecourt of an old pub my cheeks were burning from the rush of wind and my hair, in spite of a scarf, felt tangled.

'Wait, I have something for you.' André put his hand on my arm as I leaned forward to open the door. From the glove pocket in front of me he produced a single white rose, its petals creamy against the tissue paper in which it was wrapped. 'I hoped you would wear that dress,' he said quietly. 'It is for that dress that I chose the flower.' Gently he tucked it into my bodice.

Our table was in the corner by the windows which opened out onto a mossy lawn, bordered with sweet smelling heliotrope.

André ordered with his customary efficiency and as the waiter poured out our wine I sat bemused, unwilling to break the spell of silence. Then André spoke.

'I have given in my notice at the university; next year I commence my job at Toulouse.' He waited, looking at me hard, but I refused to meet his eye, too bleak and miserable to make any pretence of being glad for him.

'Suzie?' He took my hand. 'What is the matter?'

I shook my head, not trusting myself to speak.

'You are disappointed it is not Paris?' He closed my fingers around the stem on my wineglass. 'But that may follow after a year, or maybe two or three.' He looked at me hopefully.

At last I managed to say something. 'I am glad, André. Truly glad. I know it's what you wanted.' I took a sip of wine.

'You are not glad, Suzie.' He sounded hurt and reproachful.

'Yes I am.' I took some more wine. 'It's just that I shall miss you, that's all . . .' My voice cracked as I spoke the

506

words and I fought to hold back the tears. I would not spoil a beautiful evening by crying like a teenager. I clenched my fists.

'But, *chérie*,' André looked amazed, 'aren't you coming with me? I thought you had said so often you would love to live in France?'

It was my turn to look amazed. I hadn't thought; I hadn't understood.

We were silent as the waiter brought the vinaigrettes, but as soon as he had gone André pushed away his plate and took my hands in his. He looked so earnest, his brown eyes pleading.

'Suzie, I had not meant it to be like this. I had planned it to be so romantic, later. But I have decided. You will marry me. We will be married next month before we leave, then we have the rest of the summer to find a flat in Toulouse. See,' he fumbled in his breast pocket, 'I have brought you the ring.'

On his palm lay an exquisite little circle of sapphires and diamonds in a red gold Victorian setting.

I was speechless.

He smiled happily and took my hand. 'Let us see if it fits.'

He slipped it on and I gazed at it, enchanted. I was still looking at it when the waiter came to take our plates. He reappeared a few moments later with a half bottle of champagne and bowed in front of André.

'The compliments of the manager, monsieur. We could not help noticing the little ceremony just now and he hopes you will accept this with our congratulations.'

Amazed, we looked at each other and then round the room and to my intense embarrassment I found that everyone at the other tables was looking at us. They had been watching the whole thing. One man raised his glass in salute. 'To the happy couple,' he said smiling and one after another the other people followed suit.

It was I think the happiest evening of my life. It passed so quickly, in a haze of wine and food and good wishes. Then there was the scented moonlit drive back in the early hours of the morning.

It was an anti-climax to realize that I was to spend the next afternoon with my parents and my sister and her family at home. They had met André only a couple of times and knew nothing of my relationship with him.

Before I left to go to them reluctantly I took off my ring. I wanted to break it to them gently that I was going to live abroad and I wanted to be able to pick my moment.

I was still walking on air when my father opened the door to my knock. 'Come in, Susan darling,' he said cheerfully. 'Tea's all ready. Your mother is just bringing it through.'

I bent to fondle the little Jack Russell which had bounded out to greet me and then followed my father into the sitting room. My sister Gwen and her husband Phil were already there, curled up on a sofa by the fire.

'Hi,' Gwen said when she saw me. 'I hear you've got yourself a gigolo, Sue. I can't think how you managed to tear yourself away.'

'Gwen.' Father automatically stepped between us, but I saw at once from his amused face that it would only be minutes before he joined in with the teasing. With Gwen I could cope. We had been at each other's throats all our lives and I was used to her catty remarks. I put them down to jealousy – but Father – that was too hurtful.

My cheeks flamed. 'I can't think what you mean,' I said as repressively as I could and to forestall any further remarks I headed for the kitchen.

In the hall I stopped in front of the mirror. My face was flushed and my eyes suspiciously bright. How stupid not to be able to hide my feelings at my age. If only I hadn't known what Gwen meant. I wondered who had been gossiping.

Taking a grip on myself I went into the kitchen and kissed my mother fondly. One look at me told her something was wrong of course and before I knew it I had poured out the whole story. She listened quietly and then put her arm round my shoulders. 'Poor Susan. It must be dreadful for you to take such a decision.' She turned to the kettle. 'But I think you are right to turn him down. It might seem hard now but in ten years you'll be glad you did it.'

'But I didn't turn him down,' I sobbed, anguished. 'Mother, I love him. I want to marry him.'

'But dear, think.' She put the tea things down and looked at me hard. 'Think very carefully. There is not only the difference in your ages, as if that wasn't enough, but he's foreign. He wants you to leave this country and all your friends and go off with him heaven knows where. Oh Sue darling, you can't do it.'

In my heart I wondered if she was right but at the same time I was indignant and angry. How could she talk like that about André? He was mature well beyond his years. He was responsible. He would not ask me to do anything that would leave me unhappy.

Eventually I dried my eyes and gave her a watery smile. 'I'll think about it a bit longer,' I said as steadily as I could. 'Let's not talk about it any more now.'

Obviously Gwen and Phil and my father had reached the same conclusion because nothing more was said on the subject the whole afternoon. We just chatted about various things and I tried very hard indeed to ignore the deepening depression which was hanging over me.

My mother's words had reawakened my own terrible doubts about the difference in our ages. It was something I had tried to forget, but as I walked slowly home from my parents' house I remembered all the little things. André was still childishly optimistic and irrepressible and in some ways yes, he was a little irresponsible too, while I was cynical and inclined to be weighed down by cares. Possibly these were differences of character rather than age but to me they pointed to one thing only – my approaching senility, his carefree youth. I thought of his hard lean body; his cheeks and eyes, young and bright and I remembered the way I had to throw my shoulders back and pull in my stomach when I appeared before him naked. He told me that my body was beautiful, but I never quite lost my self-consciousness before him and dared not relax for one second.

We were not going to meet that evening so I let myself into the silent flat and went straight to bed, worn out with misery.

I knew I looked pale and haggard the next day when I met André for coffee after his last tutorial. I saw him give me a sharp look and then as we sat down he let out a sharp exclamation.

'Suzie, where is our ring? Why are you not wearing it?'

I jumped guiltily. That morning I had slipped it on, tried to recapture the joy of having it on my hand, had worn it all the time I was making my toast and coffee and then just before I left for work I had taken it off, kissed it longingly and placed it in the drawer.

'I didn't want to wear it to work, darling,' I lied hastily. 'I was giving pottery lessons and I didn't want to get it covered in clay, or take it off and have to leave it lying around.'

He accepted my explanation with a smile and a squeeze of the hand, but he still looked crestfallen. Like a disappointed schoolboy . . . I stopped myself abruptly. There I went again, harping on his youth. I forced myself to smile.

'Where are we going this evening, André?' I said, trying to change the subject. 'What about that French film you wanted to see?'

But he shook his head. 'Suzie, I know something is wrong. You must tell me.'

I glanced up at his anxious face and sighed. 'All right. But not here. Can we go back to my flat?'

'What is wrong with here?' His chin suddenly took on a stubborn set and he gestured round the dark café with its intimate little tables. The atmosphere was fragrant with coffee and cigarette smoke and there were only two other couples there.

'All right,' I said quietly. 'I'll tell you here. Darling, I love you more than I can ever say, but I don't think I should marry you.' To my surprise the words sounded very calm and reasonable.

André's expression did not change. He had obviously been expecting this. 'Can you tell me why, *chérie*? Is it that you don't want to live in France?'

His hand was trembling as it held his cup and I felt a lump come to my throat.

'No, no. Of course not. It's because I am so much older than you. Don't you see? I don't think it would work.'

He gave a pained sigh. 'But we have been over this so often, Suzie.' He sounded a little impatient. 'I told you that for me this is not a problem. It just does not matter.' He accentuated the words by striking the table with his fist. The cups rattled on their saucers and there was a moment of silence at the other tables. Then the muted murmur of conversation continued.

I looked down at my coffee, embarrassed. 'It doesn't matter now, but in ten, fifteen years' time, what then? When you are forty and I am nearly sixty; how will you feel about it then, André?' My voice cracked as I spoke and immediately his hand caught mine. It was reassuringly firm.

'In France a woman is considered to be at her most attractive in her fifties and sixties, *chérie*. That is when she has the experience to please her man. She is mature. She is no longer just pretty and frivolous; she is *beautiful!*'

He gazed deeply into my eyes and smiled suddenly. 'Look at Deneuve. She is fifty!' He shrugged his shoulders in the very Gallic way he had.

I had to laugh. 'But I do not have quite the same advantages as her.'

'No,' he snorted. 'But for me you are much better. Listen.' He captured my other hand and leaning across the table gazed at me earnestly. 'You are worrying about what will happen in twenty years' time. My love, if we have so much as twenty years happiness we shall have a great deal to thank God for. Do you not think that to ask for more is being greedy? You are saying, "I want a promise of half a century perhaps of perfection" – but who knows what will happen then? Let us take our happiness now, while we have it. We will leave the future until it comes, eh?'

He was silent for a minute and then abruptly he released my hands and began to drink his coffee.

I sat for a while unable to think of anything to say. I wanted so much to be convinced, but somewhere deep inside me there was still a niggle of doubt. His argument sounded so reasonable. I was facing problems which might, probably would, never occur.

'What would your parents think?' I said at last, cautiously.

André's face broke into a beaming smile. '*Enfin*,' he said triumphantly, 'she has seen how foolish she is. They will love you. I have already written to *maman* and she is longing to meet you.'

He stood up. 'Come on. Let's go to see that film.'

He was irrepressibly happy for the rest of the evening and eventually I cheered up too. We laughed and much later as we wandered back through the warm night towards my flat, we began to make plans. Once more he left me at the door. He had a few more essays to mark, he admitted with a grimace. He blew me a kiss from the corner of the street and was gone.

I opened the door of my flat and was amazed to find my father sitting there sipping coffee.

'Your mother lent me the spare key,' he explained lazily. 'Where's young André got to?'

'Young . . . ?' My heart missed a beat. 'he's gone back to the hostel. Why?'

'Just as well.' My father heaved himself to his feet. 'Your mother told me all about it, Sue. You know it just won't do, don't you?'

'Why not?' My hands were suddenly terribly cold. 'We have discussed it a great deal. I'm going into it with my eyes open.'

'Yes, but is he?' He put his arm round my shoulder. 'Listen, Sue. The last thing I want to do is hurt you; but think of him. He is young and in love. He sees you as some perfect English dream he's thought up for himself. But when he takes you home, what happens? His friends are married to girls fifteen years your junior. Are *they* going to be your friends? He is bound to make comparisons. He will be too loyal perhaps to hurt you if he can help it, but one day you can bet he will take a little mistress . . .'

'Father, how *can* you!' I was furious. 'How can you be so horrible and unkind? You make me feel ugly and old and *unloveable*.'

He held me close. 'Sue, Sue. I'm sorry. It's because I'm trying to save you from being hurt later.' Sadly he looked at me and then he smiled. 'But of course, it is for you to make the final decision, my love. Whatever you decide we'll stand by you.' He dropped a quick kiss on my forehead and then said, unbelievably, 'Have you ever thought of having an affair with this chap, Sue? Just to get it out of your system.' He looked embarrassed. And I felt suddenly horribly ashamed. I had been having 'an affair' as he meant it, with André for months now and here he was suggesting it! Putting aside all his principles and suggesting something which would shock him so profoundly. I wanted to cry and after he had gone I did. I cried myself to sleep.

Next morning I sat for a long time at my dressing table gazing at the mirror, my fingers gently trying to coax the lines of exhaustion from beneath my eyes.

I had considered André. I had considered my mother and father. I had even considered Gwen and Phil. Now at last wasn't it time to consider myself? Wasn't André right to say think of today? Who could tell what the future would bring? What did I want? Now.

Slowly, deliberately, I reached into the drawer, found my precious, beautiful ring and slipped it onto the fourth finger of my left hand. I stared at it for a long time then I stood up. Today I would wear it. Tomorrow could take care of itself.

A Window on the World

Mrs Benton was old and very frail and she seldom
went outside her house, relying instead on Mr
Folkestone, the 'paying guest' who lived upstairs to do her
shopping for her. But she didn't feel cut off from the world
for she had her front window. For hours at a time she
would sit in the rocking chair which had been her mother's
gazing out at the road, occasionally moving the net curtain
aside so that she could get a better look.

It was a lonely life, but Mrs Benton never complained
for she had one especial interest, and this was the young
man who lived in the house directly opposite. He had lived
there with his mother for about six months now and his
name was Jeremy. She had persuaded George, the post-
man, to tell her that much. Jeremy Hall. He was tall and
good looking with soft floppy chestnut hair and green eyes.
George thought he lectured at the technical college three
miles away, but he could not be sure. Certainly Jeremy
left nearly every morning at about twenty minutes to nine
on his blue scooter and more often than not he had a stack
of books with him which he strapped behind his seat. Some
days he came home early, at about three and others not
until after six.

Mrs Benton had made up a story about Jeremy. She
pretended to know all about him and his family and his
work and in her imagination he would come across and see

her and tell her his troubles and his plans. And she would listen and nod and stroke the cat which purred on her knee.

That cat was all the family Mrs Benton had now. Once she had a daughter and a son-in-law and a little grandson, but they had all gone to live in Australia. There had been letters at first and then just cards and then nine Christmases ago even they had stopped. Her grandson must be about twenty-eight now, she thought wistfully. Sometimes in her dreams Jeremy would call her 'Grandma'.

One afternoon it was raining particularly hard. Mrs Benton saw Jeremy come home, the rain streaming from his hair and coat, his books carefully wrapped in a polythene bag. She knew his mother was still out shopping for she had seen her go half an hour before. Jeremy dived into the house, beginning to take off his coat even before he shut the door. Mrs Benton nodded. Sensible boy. It would not do to catch cold. She wished she could afford to buy him a proper briefcase for those poor books.

She rocked back and forth a couple of times and then leaned forward again in astonishment, for someone was coming to her own door. Or to be exact an umbrella was coming. A pretty pink and red floral umbrella. Mrs Benton raised the corner of the curtain expectantly. Yes, it was definitely coming up her front steps.

Suddenly deciding that she must answer the door herself and not wait for Mr Folkestone to do it she heaved herself slowly to her feet and groped for her sticks, waiting impatiently for the ring on the doorbell. But it didn't come. Disappointed Mrs Benton hoped whoever it was would not go away before she got there and she shuffled as fast as she could in her floppy slippers out into the hall and groped for the door latch.

Standing on the doorstep was a girl, dressed in a tightly-belted blue mackintosh, the umbrella daintily twirling around her head. She had long fair hair, darkened into streaks by the rain, and enormous grey eyes.

'Hello,' she said, startled because Mrs Benton had opened the front door before she had plucked up the courage to ring. 'I am sorry to bother you, but I wonder if you,' she hesitated a moment looking at Mrs Benton's arthritic hands and then went on, blushing prettily, 'I wonder if there is anyone who can help me? It is silly really, but I can't get the top off this jar.' She held out an enormous bottle with a screw top lid. 'There isn't anyone else in the house I've moved into round the corner and I must have this open.'

Mrs Benton smiled. 'Of course, dear. Come in and I'll call Mr Folkestone. I am sure he can help you.'

Then she stopped suddenly. How silly. What did a lovely girl like this want with a couple of old fogies like herself and Mr Folkestone? No, she had a better idea.

'On second thoughts I don't think he's in.' She frowned and leaned a little more heavily on her sticks. 'But I know who can help you, my dear. You run across the road there and ask Jeremy. He's such a nice boy and I am sure he's very strong.'

She stood watching as the girl turned back down the steps and made her way across the wet pavement. Then she closed the door. She did not want them to see her watching. As fast as she could Mrs Benton shuffled back to her chair, lowered herself painfully into it and twitched back the curtain.

The beautiful girl was knocking on Jeremy's door and after a moment or two he opened it. He had put on a thick rust-coloured sweater, Mrs Benton could see, which went beautifully with his hair.

She watched the girl explain and hold out the jar and she saw Jeremy laughing as he took it. He opened it with one quick tug and handed it back to her. Then they stayed talking for several minutes before the girl turned and waving, set off home. Jeremy stood and watched her go out of sight round the corner before he shut the door.

With a sigh Mrs Benton let the curtain fall.

Soon after that Jeremy's schedule began to change. Often he came home much later than before and his scooter would turn into the road from the opposite end to the college, from Mrs Benton's end. She wondered whether he had changed his job and day-dreamed excitedly about the day when he would come and tell her all about the new people he was meeting and especially about the girl in the blue mackintosh.

Twice she saw her go back to Jeremy's house. Once she went in. It was teatime on a Saturday and his mother was there. And once she just collected him at the door and together they walked off up the road, talking excitedly and holding hands.

Mrs Benton's pleasure and happiness in seeing them together like that would only be bettered by one thing and that was the piece of excitement of her own which was coming. One of her rare expeditions outside the house. Mrs Carnaby who used to lodge with her before Mr Folkestone had written to say she had bought a car. She was coming to town for the day especially to take Mrs Benton to see the Christmas decorations in Hartleys and help her do her Christmas shopping.

Leaning heavily on her two sticks, but with her eyes sparkling with delight, Mrs Benton walked slowly and determinedly down the aisle between the scarf counter and the gloves. Mrs Carnaby tactfully leaving her on her own for a while knowing there were chairs for her to sit on here if she got tired. She paused now and then to look at the lovely squares of chiffon and silk, hanging her sticks on her arm as she gently touched the cool beauty of the fabrics.

Then she looked up to see which counter she would visit next and there, almost next to her, stood Jeremy and with him was a tall dark-haired girl wearing a scarlet coat. Mrs Benton had never seen her before. He had his arm round her. 'Choose, Angela,' he was saying quietly, in a deep pleasant voice, very much as she had imagined he would sound. 'Choose which you'd like, my dear. I think this one suits you.' He held up an emerald green silk scarf studded with tiny black stars. Mrs Benton glanced up at the maker's placard over that section of the counter and gasped. Had he any idea how much that scarf would cost?

Evidently Angela at least did have, for at once she said, 'No, Jerry darling, I can't let you. It's much too expensive.'

Then the most terrible thing happened. Mrs Benton, turning from the counter, saw *her* coming towards them across the shop. Still wearing her blue tightly-belted mac, her hair swinging beneath a black velvet head band. Her face was radiant and for the last few steps she almost ran. 'Jerry,' she called breathlessly. 'Jerry, love, I thought it was you.' Then she stopped dead. She hadn't seen Angela who had been hidden by Jeremy's broad shoulders and now suddenly she was face to face with her. Uncomfortably Jeremy let fall the green scarf. He unwound his arm from Angela's shoulders.

'Pam, I didn't know you'd be here.' His voice was uncertain and Mrs Benton, now unashamedly staring, saw an uncomfortable flush spreading to his cheeks.

'No, I can see that.' Pam's eyes blazed. 'Please, Jerry, don't stop your transaction on my account.' She leaned forward and plucked the scarf from the pile again. 'It suits the lady perfectly I should say!' She pushed the scarf into his hands creasing the silky folds. 'They do hold football matches in strange places nowadays, Jerry, don't they? I never dreamed you'd be playing here when I rang you yesterday. And with such a lovely opponent. No wonder you couldn't come to the cinema with me.' The girl's voice was taut with grief as she rushed on. 'I suppose fields get so muddy don't they and men are so boring to play with . . .' She turned and walked quickly away, her head held high, but not before Mrs Benton caught sight of the tears in her eyes.

Jeremy and Angela looked at each other, then Angela suddenly gave a nervous giggle. 'Jerry, what have you been doing? I didn't know you ran a harem, my darling. How intriguing.' Her smile was suddenly frosty. 'I didn't think simpering blondes were quite your style though. You've never shown any interest in them in college.'

Mrs Benton's blood was boiling. So that was it. A girl from the college. Pam wasn't a simpering blonde. She was beautiful and sweet and . . .

Placing her sticks firmly on the carpet she began to walk forward, intent on saying her piece, but already the two young people had turned away.

'There's no need to be vicious, Angela,' she heard Jeremy's voice, suddenly loud in the discreet hush of the shop. 'Pam is a lovely person. She's hardly a harem. She's a very dear friend and I won't have her hurt.'

'You mean you'd rather hurt me?' Angela's voice, though as low as his was loud, came surprisingly clearly across the thick carpeting.

'No, but you're better at taking care of yourself. You're tough, Angie and Pam is vulnerable and lonely. She knows no one here.'

'It sounds to me then as though you ought to rush after her to console her, Jerry dear.' Angela dropped the hushed voice and faced him suddenly beneath a shimmering Christmas mobile. 'And don't worry about me or that lovely Christmas present. As you so rightly imply I have others to turn to for comfort,' and she swept away, leaving him standing on the carpet.

He hesitated for a moment looking after her uncomfortably then he shrugged and, suddenly seeming to make up his mind, he turned and almost ran after Pam, disappearing into the crowds of afternoon shoppers.

Mrs Benton breathed a sigh of relief. He had made the right decision, of that she was sure.

The next few days Mrs Benton could hardly bear to leave her chair at the window in the evenings; but there was no sign of Pam. Jeremy came home at his usual time, went in and uncompromisingly slammed the front door. If he went out again it was not until after Mrs Benton had gone to bed.

Then one traumatic evening Angela turned up. Mrs Benton clenched her fists angrily, twitching the curtain in her anxiety. He let her in, but she stayed no more than ten minutes. When she left she paused for a moment on the doorstep to hurl abuse at the figure inside the door and then she ran down the road.

'Good, that's finished.' Mrs Benton sat back satisfied. Then she stiffened. Jeremy had come out on his freezing doorstep to look after Angela. He gazed for a moment then as he was about to turn away he looked straight at Mrs Benton's window. It was too late to let the curtain fall and pretend she wasn't watching. She felt herself blush, but to her surprise he didn't seem to be cross at being spied on. He gave her a friendly grin and a wave. Then as if suddenly realizing that she must have seen everything he jerked his thumb in the direction of Angela's retreating back and with a heavenwards glance of exasperation gave a dramatic shrug of his shoulders. Then with another wave he had gone.

Mrs Benton let the curtain fall gently. He had let her in on his secret. She was an accomplice and he knew she was there. She was so happy that evening she didn't know what to do. In the end she treated herself to half a glass of sherry in celebration.

Three days later she was watching some damp wintry flakes of snow nose down past her window at lunchtime when Jeremy came home unexpectedly early. He had no books on his scooter. She watched him undo the strap on his crash helmet and, leaving the helmet on the seat of the bike, he ran indoors. He had not even glanced in her direction. She could not suppress a tiny feeling of disappointment, but this was soon forgotten as she saw Pam. The girl walked slowly hesitatingly down past Mrs Benton's house, and then almost reluctantly crossed the road. She hesitated so long on Jeremy's doorstep Mrs Benton almost got to her feet in anxiety and then miraculously, before she rang, the door opened. She stood for a minute on the doorstep before she disappeared inside. Mrs Benton's fingers were not so arthritic that she could not still just cross them in an emergency.

She was so intrigued about what would happen she forgot to go and make her own lunch. Instead she sat and rocked and watched.

Forty-six minutes later, by her watch, the door opened and Jeremy and Pam both appeared on the doorstep. He slammed the door behind them and together they stood for a moment by his bike. Then at last, gently, he gave her a long, lingering kiss. He watched as she turned away and walked quickly round the corner. Then he reached for his helmet and strapped it on. As he was about to mount his machine he seemed to remember something. He paused and glanced across the street towards Mrs Benton's window. She hadn't moved the curtain today, so he couldn't possibly see her, but even so he gave that cheery grin and waved and then this time, just for her, he gave the thumbs up sign.

She never saw Angela again.

Christmas was getting close now and the evenings grew dark so very early but from the lights of the street lamps she could see Jeremy and Pam come and go. And now they both waved, and once Pam, her face radiant as her hair blew free of the blue crash helmet she wore as she went pillion on the scooter, looked up and blew her a kiss.

Then one Saturday morning came the awful news. Mrs Benton had opened the door for George who had brought a large exciting parcel. It was for Mr Folkestone.

'I see your young Mr Hall is leaving us then,' he said cheerfully. 'Got himself a new job, I hear and leaving home.'

Mrs Benton felt the tears rush to her eyes. He couldn't. He couldn't go and leave her. Not now. She clutched at the door, swaying suddenly.

'Hey, ma, are you all right?' Dimly she heard George's voice, and felt his strong hand under her arm. 'Here, let's go and sit down. Where's your chair, ma?' He helped her back into the front room. 'Hadn't he told you then? I'm sorry; I shouldn't have said anything.'

Mrs Benton sniffed loudly and groped for her handkerchief. 'No,' she gulped. 'He hadn't told me; I didn't really expect him to.'

She sat for a long time after George had gone not even bothering to look out of the window. No more Jeremy; nothing to look forward to in the afternoons when he was due to come home. No more of the cheerful puttering of his scooter engine and waves from him and Pam.

She dabbed at the tears which insisted on running down her cheeks and did not even hear the doorbell. Mr Folkestone must have opened it for the next thing she knew there was a tap on her own door. She looked round to see it being pushed quietly open.

'Excuse me; can we come in for a moment?' The girl, still dressed in her blue mackintosh, was peeping round it.

Mrs Benton hastily blew her nose and smiled, her heart

giving little irregular bumps of hope and excitement. 'Come in, my dear, of course.'

Pam came in and she was closely followed by Jeremy. Hand-in-hand they crossed over to the rocking chair. The girl knelt down suddenly and in a spontaneously happy gesture took Mrs Benton's wrinkled hand in her own. 'I wanted you to know that Jerry and I are getting married. You really introduced us, you know. We have you to thank for everything.'

'And we would like you to come to the wedding,' Jeremy added. 'Please, will you? And here:' he thrust a small parcel into her hand, 'a small Christmas present to say thank you.'

Mrs Benton could not answer him. She was crying again. But this time with happiness.

It was not until a little while later when Pam had made them all some tea that Mrs Benton felt better.

Then she could not stop smiling. She made Jeremy sit next to her on the old sofa which she found so hard to get out of with her legs and listened as they told her of their plans.

They had found a small house on the northern edge of the town and they asked her to come and see them as soon as they were settled. Jeremy was anyway planning to sell his scooter and buy a second-hand car, so he would be able to come and fetch her.

By the time they had left Mrs Benton would have called herself the happiest person in the world. Slowly, after they had gone, she opened the small present. It contained a bottle of cologne and two exquisite lace handkerchiefs. She went back to her chair, holding them tight and sat down slowly gazing out into the sunny frosty street. Pam had brought two lengths of yellow ribbon with her and with them Jeremy had tied back her old net curtains.

'We like to see you sitting here, Grandma,' he said

gently before they left. 'Not only us, but the whole street love you, you know. They'd miss you dreadfully if you ever skipped a day.' He dropped a quick kiss on top of her head and with that cheery wave of his hand she had come to love so much, he had gone.

A Promise of Love

There was misty sunshine in the distance now, sending shafts of pale light over the sea. Louise stood motionless, her hands gripping the cold rail on the promenade, watching each wave crash up the steep beach and ebb again, sucking hungrily at the pebbles below the barnacle-encrusted concrete. Her hands were blue with cold, covered in little salty droplets of spray. She had forgotten to bring any gloves.

A heavy shower swept across the empty roadway behind her, soaking her hair, her coat, her shoes. But she ignored it. Her eyes were fixed desperately on a sea suddenly slate-black beneath the rain, save for far out where the light remained. On her cheeks the raindrops mingled unnoticed with her tears. Why, oh why had she come back? What was she seeking from this same cold, cruel water?

The top of the tide had left piles of seaweed, dead and ugly, heaped on the road. It didn't matter though. There were no cars; no people. The town in February was dead. It didn't seem possible that she was looking at the same element as the sleek blue summer sea when the world had been happy and perfect and she had quite wilfully ruined everything.

They had been going to stay in a cottage at the end of the town, where the old fishing village was, where the pebbly beach and the harbour gave way to sand dunes which stretched for miles, shifting and changing shape in the wind, so that they, like the sea, were never the same.

John had seen the advertisement in the paper; end of season let. And on the spur of the moment they had decided as the days were still warm, to go.

'Are you pretending we're married?' she had asked as he sealed the letter and he had laughed. 'Whatever for?' he said and he kissed her fiercely.

Whatever for indeed, after all this time? She had gone to the long narrow kitchen of the flat they shared and beaten the eggs for the omelette until they frothed angrily, spluttering in the iron pan.

'It'll do you good to go away, Lou,' her boss had said. 'If you don't mind my saying so you have been looking a bit run down. Going with your nice friend from the flat are you?'

She forgot to fold in the carbon as she scrunched it in her fist and her hands became all black. 'Yes, Mr Fielding. My nice friend from the flat. That's right.'

They packed and threw their cases in the car and left early to avoid the Friday rush. At the first traffic lights John turned and looked at her with a little smile. He drew his hand, electric, along her thigh. Then the lights changed and he reached for the gear lever, leaving her heart bumping a little at the message she had seen in his eyes. Resolutely she gazed through the windscreen; she hated herself sometimes for loving him still so much; for knowing herself to be so dependent on him while he remained so free.

The cottage was built of stone, sparsely furnished beneath its roof of slate at the edge of the sea. The only colour in the white-painted bedroom under the eaves came from the exquisite patchwork quilt on the bed. Dropping the cases John turned to Louise.

'At last,' he said, and held out his arms.

Outside they could hear the whistle and crackle of gossiping starlings somewhere in the heavy-laden apple tree on the lawn at the back.

'Stop!' she laughed. She struggled in his arms, pushing him away.

But already his lips were pressed urgently against hers; she felt the edge of the bed behind her and they fell, clinging together on the gaily coloured patchwork.

Then at last he allowed her to push him away. 'What's wrong?' he asked.

She sat up slowly, watching the dust dancing in the shaft of sun which shone through the window. If only she knew how to tell him what was wrong; tell of her fear and her insecurity; of the longing in her heart to hear that he needed her as much as she needed him.

As he got up and wandered over to the window she glanced down at the brilliant colours in the quilt she was sitting on. Some woman had spent hours, months even, of her life stitching the tiny fragments of cloth into this beautiful pattern. Surely the pattern of a relationship between two people who love one another and are prepared to declare their love to the world should be a little like that? Thousands of intricate multi-shaped pieces formed with time and caring into an enduring whole. Gently, wistfully, she stroked the patchwork.

'Louise?' He had been calling her name.

She looked up. She saw his hands and rose and went to him, as she knew she always would.

They wandered along the beach beyond the dunes, over the strip of flat wet sand collecting the fluted razor shells which lay nestling in among the scattered weed. The hazy September sun had been warm on Louise's shoulders as she glanced round the deserted beach. Then her depression vanishing as suddenly as it had come, she began to run, feeling the sand between her toes, the spurts of sun-warmed water beneath her instep. And she laughed as he began to chase her.

They walked for miles, not talking, as the sun sank lower in the sky, watching the tiny high, flecked, white clouds turn pink and gold. Imperceptibly the tide turned and the mother of pearl water crept once more slowly over the evening sand.

Near the point the beach grew steeper and the dry shifting dunes drew near the water. There were no other people in the world. At the water's edge an oystercatcher ran jerkily through the dribbling tide, thrusting its red beak ramrod straight into the sand. Then it flew arrowlike out towards the distant mistiness of the sun and they heard the eerie sad whistle of its cry.

The sound made Louise shiver suddenly. John looked at her, then he drew her to him, his arms strong. As he said her name there was no mistaking the tone of his voice.

High above them a plane flew straight and sure across the indigo arch of the sky, too high for them to hear it, its vapour trail a ruled line of silent gold. Slowly, his hands on her shoulders, he turned her to face him and kissed her. She closed her eyes and he kissed each eye-lid, his kisses growing more fierce and demanding, tracing the line of her lips with his finger. This time she didn't push him away. Her desire rose at his touch, a new warmth of love flooding through her as she felt the urgency of his love, unconscious of the warm wind which stirred the wiry marram grasses near her head or the thin mist of sand which had blown across her discarded crumpled dress.

They were roused at last by the gentle lapping of the water on the beach. John sat up and looked round him. Then smiling to himself he leaned forward, grasping a shell which lay near his hand and began to draw, watching the crisp curl of sand beneath his sharp strokes. With a sardonic lift of the eyebrow he drew an enormous heart.

Louise, pulling herself dreamily to her knees ran her finger through the crisp tangle of her curls. Then she reached for her dress. She laughed when she saw what he had done. 'You old Romeo,' she teased; 'who'd have thought you were a romantic!' Snatching the shell from his fingers she added a cupid's dart and put their initials, LM and JG. 'There you are. A Valentine heart!'

He grinned wryly. 'What else?' A deep haze was drawing in from the sea. The gold of the sunset was distant now, shrugging out of sight beyond the cloud. 'Come on, it's time to go,' he said abruptly. 'You've got to find the food and get us a meal, remember?'

Already the water was nibbling the edge of the heart.

'You know something?' she said casually, brushing the sand from her breasts as she buttoned her dress, 'I had always hoped, a little, that our first holiday would be our honeymoon.'

Seeing him frown she bit her lip. 'It would be nice, wouldn't it, John? To be married?' she persisted gently.

He hesitated, straining the sand through his fingers. 'For some perhaps. But not us . . .' He gazed out to sea, not looking at her.

A thin trickle of water was flowing round the heart in the sand, blurring the edges, gently smoothing away the J. She didn't notice. 'There isn't any reason we shouldn't get married is there? We love each other so much . . .' Her voice trailed away.

'No reason, except that I don't want to. We're happy as we are. Marriage would spoil it. I don't want to be labelled and slotted into the system . . .' He turned to her, narrowing his eyes and took her hands in his. 'I thought you felt the same. We don't need marriage. Haven't we proved it after all this time?'

The lapping water had washed the sand again. Both John's initials had gone. It was growing cold.

Louise leaned towards him, frowning a little; intense. 'John you did say a long time ago that we would get married. One day.'

He looked away, a little guiltily. 'Did I? Well one day perhaps we will. But not yet.'

But she couldn't leave it alone. Some demon had made her go on.

'John. I want to get married. Now.' She rose to her feet, her toes sinking a little into the soft sand.

'No.' He cut her short. 'No, Louise. I'm sorry.' He glanced down angrily.

The drawing had gone. The transparent tide rippled gently over the place where the pierced heart had been, a strand of sea-weed fluttering gently in the bubbles in the half-light.

John said nothing. Then slowly he turned to her. She was crying suddenly, blindly gazing down. 'It went so fast,' she sobbed. 'And you think our love is like that. You think it will disappear like a drawing in the sand . . .'

'No, of course I don't.' He was impatient. 'Come on, Louise, nothing stays the same for ever, you know that. What if the sea does take away the heart? We'll draw another. We'll come back on Valentine's Day itself, if you like. Come on; stop crying. You can't trap things. You can't freeze them and preserve them. Relationships change; love develops. It needs to be free, don't you see?'

She shook her head wordlessly as the evening breeze teased the blues and greens of her skirt in the dusk, thinking suddenly again of the patterned patchwork in the bedroom of the cottage. 'The sea knew. The sea knew it couldn't last. *Your love* couldn't last.'

'Louise, that's rubbish. Stop making a scene.'

'I'm not. How long have we lived together? *Years*, John. If you're not sure now, you never will be.'

He shrugged bitterly. 'Then you must look for someone else. If the security of my love isn't enough, you must look for someone who can give you more.' He turned away from her suddenly, his voice grating, and stood, his hands in his pockets, staring hard out to sea.

She took a step towards him, frightened by the bleakness of his voice, but the uncompromising line of his jaw stopped her. Her eyes were full of tears.

'All right then, I will.' Her voice broke on the words. She hesitated, but he didn't move and suddenly overcome with misery and hurt she turned and stumbled away from him up over the shifting sand of the dunes and half ran, half staggered back towards the lights of the town. She didn't look back. In any case he was soon lost to view behind the dunes. She didn't turn, didn't see the look in his eyes as he gazed after her.

The cottage was in darkness. She lifted the latch with shaking fingers and stepped in, her heart thumping. Then she picked her way slowly up the stairs, dashing away her tears and clicked on the light in the bedroom. Their two cases still stood side by side on the carpet where John had dropped them. She had never even unpacked. Listening for his step in the garden she ran to the window and leaned out, but the dunes beyond the hedge of osiers at the edge of the lane were silent and empty.

'I must go. Now. I must,' she had murmured.

She bent to pick up her case. If he came she knew she would weaken; if he took her in his arms and kissed her she would be lost.

She hesitated, praying he would come, knowing she must go.

Then at last, when she knew he wasn't coming she

carried the case down the stairs and walked out into the misty night towards the station.

John did not return home to the flat the next day, or the next, so she packed her belongings slowly and miserably and took a taxi to her sister's flat. There she waited, desolate, for him to ring her. A hundred times she picked up the phone herself and began to dial his number – the number which had been hers as well. But something stopped her. Pride? She supposed so. Rather desperately she began to go out with other men, but each date was a hollow meaningless pretence and not repeated. She grew thin and permanently sad. And almost every night she would lie awake thinking of that evening on the beach. If only John had turned and called her back. If only he had smiled. If only . . .

Christmas came and went without a word. Not even a card. And now it was February. Drawn irresistibly by the memory of the heart in the sand, masochistic, longing, she had come back. It was the fourteenth. Later, when the tide had gone down a little, she would walk back alone down the beach and look for the place where the heart had been and they had made love for the last time.

'Louise!' The voice sounded close to, but she dismissed it from her mind as she always did. Her hands had grown numb from gripping the ice cold railing so long. Shakily she raised one of them to brush away the tears which were hot on her cold face. The tide had withdrawn a little now, leaving a strip of shiny glossy pebbles. The sunlight in the distance had come closer too.

'Louise!' Again she heard the voice and again, 'Louise . . .' She could hear feet on the road behind her. Incredulously she turned. It wasn't a dream. It was John.

'Hello,' he said. He was looking down at her, his face

very close to hers, his dark eyes anxious, but warm and loving. 'It's Valentine's Day. I didn't dare hope you would remember.' Hesitating a little he held out his hands.

She smiled, biting her lip to stop it trembling. What did it mean, his being here like this? Suddenly she realized how much courage it had cost him to come at all.

She heard his voice again, as if from a distance. 'I was determined not to contact you. I knew you must have the chance to find out what you wanted.' He looked down at her with a wry smile. 'If you knew how many times I've picked up the phone.' Suddenly she felt his lips on her hair. His arms went round her, hard; hurting. Then he released her. 'Come on,' he said, taking her hand. 'Let's go to the beach . . .'

Excavations

The bulldozers and JCBs were already there, lined up by the high chain-linked fence. The excavation was a sea of mud. Frances felt her eyes fill with tears. Only a few more hours and the machinery would begin its destruction; two thousand years of history would be shovelled aside to accommodate an underground car park beneath a store.

People were picking their way across the duckboards over the mud, staring at the markers being pointed out by the rescue diggers.

'Don't call us archaeologists,' one woman had said bitterly to Frances. 'This isn't archaeology. All we can do now is throw things into boxes and run.'

She heard a child shriek with fright and excitement as it slipped off the walkway into a trench in the rain and her heart gave a lurch. It had sounded so like that other child. The child in her dream. She watched as a group of people gathered, retrieved it, wiped it down and moved on. Behind them the bottom of the trench filled slowly with water, the neatly cut layers of soil blending and turning a uniform mud colour, even the scorched red clay which showed the year the city had burned nearly two thousand years before obliterated now for ever.

She hadn't meant to come again. She had seen the temporary exhibition a dozen times, talked to the men and women working there, read up the accounts of the ancient city which was losing yet another piece of its history for ever and wept for a past she couldn't regain. She had tried to stop. Tried to beat the obsession, tried to control the need to return, but still she found herself walking through the gate and staring down at the neat square where two weeks earlier they had found the mosaic floor. It had gone now, rolled up like a carpet to be cleaned, relaid and set behind glass, never to be walked on or played on again.

'Hello.' The voice behind her startled her out of her reverie. 'Good to see you again. I'm afraid it's the last time, though, before the new precinct is finished.'

Frances turned. The tall, bearded man had been in the exhibition trailer last time she saw him, wearing boots and a waterproof coat, with his hands covered in mud.

She smiled. 'No more mud for you, I see.' He was wearing the same jacket but this time with clean cords and shoes.

'No more mud. Not here.'

'Even Boudicca's effort must have looked feeble compared with this devastation.' She tried to make her voice sound light and disinterested.

'I doubt if she was as systematic as this in her destruction,' he agreed. 'She burned the place but she didn't then bury it under a hundred million tons of concrete. On the other hand, I suppose we should be glad they're not putting the population to the sword.'

Frances flinched, but she managed a wry smile. 'You try standing in front of one of those diggers tomorrow,' she countered. 'You might find them just as bloodthirsty.'

He laughed. 'I don't intend putting it to the test. I couldn't bear to see it happen. Do you want to come and have a cup of tea? The kettle is on in the trailer.'

He had noticed how often she came to the site. He was not normally attracted to redheads, but this slightly built,

536

beautiful creature had a strange grace about her which fascinated him. And her interest had been so intense, so painful as she watched the men and women in the trenches that he had stopped and watched her and then spoken to her, caught by the poignant droop of her shoulders. It was the second time he saw her that he recognized her. Then he had understood. Then he had known that he must get to know her; must find out if the stories were true . . .

She had a friendly smile, but the sadness was always there in her eyes. 'That would be nice,' she said at last. 'I should love a cup of tea.'

She followed him across the site to the exhibition van. It was closed today, exhibits already packed away. He unlocked the door and gestured her inside. 'We have to clear the site by five. Then they're putting in the security guards.'

'Then only the ghosts will be left.'

'That's right.' He glanced up as he put the kettle on the small Calor gas stove and lit the flame. 'I'm Charles Wentworth, by the way.'

She smiled. 'I'm Frances.' No surname. No catch.

She sat down on the stool by the table. Boxes of shards still lay there, hastily labelled. The dust of the site lay over everything. It had a strange sharp smell which caught at the back of the throat.

'Do you believe in them?' she said suddenly.

'Ghosts?' He reached down a tin of tea-bags from a locker. 'Sometimes.'

'Sometimes?'

'When a site is taken over by the developers like this, I'd like to think they'll be chased screaming from the excavations.' He kept his tone humorous.

'Has it ever happened?'

'Yes. But sadly never for long. Incentive payments usually overcome superstition.'

'What a pity.' She picked up a small square tile from a pile, stroking it with her fingertip to remove the dust.

'Those are Roman tesserae. Probably from the Boudiccan period. You can have them if you want.'

'Really?' She stared at him. 'Aren't they important?'

'Possibly. It's too late. The markers are about to be ploughed in, remember? All this lot is more or less rubbish now.' He sighed. 'There was so much left to do, but we ran out of time. I suppose we were lucky to get so much, given modern day priorities.'

She glanced up at him, sympathizing with his helpless bitterness.

'It is sad they couldn't have incorporated all these remains into the development and used them to bring in tourists,' she said cautiously. 'Every town in England has a shopping precinct. Very few have a Roman city.'

'They'll think of it. When it's too late,' he agreed. 'They'll say, "let's develop the town for tourists. Now what shall we show them." '

They both laughed wryly. He watched her closely as she took two of the small tiles in her hand and closed her eyes.

'I wonder who walked on these,' she said dreamily.

'Men, women, children. Much like us.' His voice was very quiet. He held his breath.

'I see a woman with a long blue gown, her hair bound up with ribbons,' Frances said slowly. She frowned, frightened by the force of the picture which had come into her head. Please God, don't let it happen here, not in front of a stranger. She gripped the tile till her knuckles whitened, trying to push away the images as they crowded in. But they came, as they always came, whirling out of nowhere, filling her mind.

He was watching her closely. He bit his lip, trying to

538

conceal his excitement. 'What else can you see?' he prompted quietly, hardly daring to breathe.

Frances sat for a moment, holding the tile. 'She's afraid.' It was too late to stop. She had to go on. Her voice strengthened and she began to breathe more heavily. 'She's lost Claudia! She's lost her child!'

'Claudia! Claudia!' The woman's voice rose to a scream. 'Where are you?'

She stared round frantically. The streets were teeming with panic-stricken people. Near her a cart overturned and she heard a horse shriek with fear. From the distant suburbs the sound of the watchman's horn echoed across the city again and again.

The child had been at her side only moments before, happily skipping down the gravel road between the shops, her new long red dress a small flame in the dullness of the misty morning.

Boxes of fruit fell from a stall near her as it overturned and the two men behind it vaulted over the planks which moments earlier had been their display area and ran. From the pouch of one fell a scattering of coins. He did not bother to stop and gather them.

'She's coming! The Queen of the Iceni is coming!' a man near Julia shouted. 'Save yourselves. Run!'

Run! How could she run without the child? Her daughter. Her little Claudia. Julia whirled round, confused and terrified.

Her husband, Claudius, had told them not to pull down the town walls. He had told them it was crazy. He had told them again and again. But no, it was the policy. This was a peaceful country now. This was a land of rich villas, wealthy retired men and their families. There was no danger, they said. No danger at all. That was before they had flogged the British queen.

At her side for a moment she recognized one of the servants from the villa. He was a tribesman, long Romanized. 'Save yourself, Lady. They will spare no one,' he shouted, momentarily sorry for the woman who had been kind to him. 'This is the day we throw the Romans out of our island. Your only hope is to get away!'

'I can't go without Claudia.' She was sobbing now.

'Then you will die. They will spare no one!' Already he had gone, running through the crowds towards the temple. In moments he was out of sight.

'*Claudia!*' She spun round desperately, trying to swallow the nausea which had risen in her throat. 'Claudia! Claudia!'

'Run!' The shouts and screams echoed down the narrow street. 'Run!' And now she could smell the smoke, acrid and thick; the smoke which drifted across the city from the villas which had been fired in the wealthy western suburbs of the town, the area where she and Claudius lived.

Tears in her eyes she flung down her basket. 'Claudia! Claudia, where are you? *Claudia!*'

The sound of racing hooves was coming closer. The echo of chariot wheels on the distant road.

'Claudia . . .' Her throat was dry, her stomach knotted with terror. She must run. But where? The crowds were panicking, screaming, milling in all directions. She tried to keep her balance as a man bumped into her, failed and fell on her knees on the tiled forecourt of a shop as he leaped across her and hurtled away up the road.

'Mama?'

She was there! Suddenly the child was there, her little hands outstretched, her eyes huge with fright. 'Mama! What's happening?'

Julia threw herself at the little girl and hugged her,

then frantically she set off, dragging her after her. In a second she and the child had disappeared into the crowded, panic-stricken streets.

Moments later the first of the wooden Iceni chariots hurtled around the corner, the driver carrying a burning torch which streamed flame and smoke in its wake . . .

Only the sound of sobbing broke the silence.

'Here. Drink this.' Charles folded her hands gently around a mug. 'Are you all right?'

Frances sipped the scalding liquid and spluttered.

'I put some brandy in it. We had some in the first aid cupboard.' He sat down opposite her and smiled reassuringly. His heart was thumping with excitement.

Frances put down the mug and groped in her pocket with shaking hands for a handkerchief. The sobs she had heard were her own. She blew her nose shakily. In front of her, on the table, lay a heap of dusty tiles.

'What did I say?' she asked at last.

'You described the sack of Camulodunum. It was as if you saw it all.' He tried to hide his excitement.

She bit her lip. 'You must think me such a fool.' She drank some more of the tea, grateful for its biting warmth. She was still shivering violently.

'No. I don't think you're a fool. I think you are a clairvoyant of some sort.' Charles leaned across and picked up one of the little tiles, holding it experimentally in the palm of his hand.

'No. Don't be silly. I have an overactive imagination, that's all . . .' That was what the judge had said. That was what she clung on to. It sounded normal. Explainable.

'Are you sure that's all it was?' He glanced up at her. 'I've met someone who did something like this before. She came to the centre. We gave her various things to hold and she told us about them – their history. Who they had belonged to. Things like that. It was uncanny. But she stayed quite detached. Purely an observer.'

'It was my imagination,' Frances repeated stubbornly. To her chagrin she found her legs were shaking so much she couldn't stand up. 'I ought to go.'

Charles glanced at his watch. 'We've half an hour before Tom comes for the trailer. There's no hurry.'

She smiled wanly and sat back, still fighting the panic, remembering the fire, the screams, the flailing swords.

'Did they get away?'

'Who?' She dragged herself back to the present with difficulty.

'Julia and her little girl.'

'I . . . I don't know.' She stared down at the tiles. 'I can't remember.' Suddenly her eyes filled with tears. 'I've never felt fear like that before – never in my whole life. Not even when – ' She broke off abruptly.

'Not even when?' he prompted gently after a few moments.

No, she mustn't tell him. She had told her husband and look what had happened. She touched the small tile with her fingertip gingerly, then abruptly she pushed it away. She stood up. 'I have to go.'

'Are you sure you feel well enough?' He didn't want her to go. She was a link, a channel to the past which was his whole life.

She tried to smile. 'I'm sorry. Have I shocked you?'

'No. I'm not shocked. I'm interested. Do you want to take the tiles?'

She shook her head vehemently. 'Put them in your museum.'

'OK.' He sat watching her for another few seconds. 'I think they made it, don't you? Julia and little Claudia.' He picked up the tesserae and tipped them into a cardboard box. 'I'm sure they hid somewhere until it was all over.'

She shook her head, biting back her misery. 'Claudia's father was killed, and her brother . . ,' She stopped. She had spoken without thinking. 'He was only fourteen. Oh God!' She sat down again and put her head in her hands. 'And Julia . . . Julia was raped . . .' She was sobbing again.

'The link is still there, Frances.' Charles reached out and touched her hand. 'It's all right. It will break. That is what the psychometrist who came to see us said. She said sometimes it stretches and stays, like a spider's thread, then it breaks. It always breaks. Then you will be free. Let me lock up and I'll walk with you. Have you got a car?'

She shook her head.

'Where do you live?'

She didn't want to be alone. Not any more. When she was alone the memories flooded back; the memories of another woman, another time. 'I live in Lexden. Not far.'

He nodded slowly. 'Lexden burned first of course. I'll walk you home if you'll let me.'

She smiled. 'Thank you. I'd like that.'

Her eye was outraged and confused by the muddy site outside the van. She could still see the neat row of thatched shops, the entrance to the villa, the gravelled road – and the smoke; the smoke that had rolled over the city and obliterated it.

Slowly they began to walk. They left the site, glancing sadly at the huge machines of destruction waiting in the wings and began to walk through the streets.

Glancing at her he smiled. 'Each time you go up one of the escalators in the new store they'll build there you'll remember today.'

She smiled and shook her head. 'No, I'll remember that day nearly two thousand years ago.' She took a deep breath. 'I've seen her before, you know.'

'Julia? I thought perhaps you had.'

'She haunts me. I think she must have lived where our house now stands.'

'It's possible.'

'You don't think I'm mad?'

'No.'

'My husband did.'

The divorce had been in the papers the week before, with all the gory details of her unreasonable behaviour; her year-long obsession with a ghost. It had made the national headlines.

Charles smiled sympathetically. 'I confess I did recognize you from the photos. But all that proves is that your husband is a racist.'

'A racist?' She stopped and looked at him, astonished.

'He obviously doesn't like Romans.' He smiled. 'Does all this make you believe in immortality?'

'No.' It came out more harshly than she meant.

'You should.'

'I would have thought archaeologists would believe in the utter finality of death.'

'On the contrary. We're professional resurrectors.' He could sense her pain; real pain beneath the shock and fear. She had walled off the vulnerable wounded part of herself; the part which encompassed the mortal echo which was all that remained of Julia and her child. He should help her to try to forget it. He wrestled with his conscience and lost. 'Don't you want to know what happened to them?' he asked after a long pause.

She shook her head.

'If you knew the truth they might rest in peace,' he persisted hopefully.

God! How he wanted to know the truth. What he would give to listen to her describe the scene again; an eyewitness account of the sack of Colchester. It was unbelievable! He could imagine the paper he would present; the articles he would write; the books . . .

She stopped in the middle of the pavement for a moment, looking at him. 'Why me? Why do they pick on me?' Her question had the ring of desperation. Slowly she began to walk on.

He pulled himself together with an effort and followed her. The woman was suffering. It was unfair to encourage her – to encourage Julia – and prolong her agony. 'As you said, perhaps you live on the site of their home.'

She gave a tight half laugh. 'We used to dig up things in the garden. Bits of pottery. A coin. A little statue which we gave to the museum. Things like that. We were so excited.' She tried to bite back her tears.

Her house was large and grey, set back a little way from the road. The garden was full of blossom, the flower beds beautifully tended, the lawns neatly cut. Even in the rain it was lovely.

There was a house agent's board nailed to the front gate. Charles noted it and frowned. Part of the tragedy of divorce.

As they walked up the drive – the high privet hedges cutting them off from the roar of the traffic in the road outside – he stared round, trying to get the feel of the past which here was so close beneath the surface, trying to reach out as she must reach out to touch the minds of the dead. If only he could do it too. Why was it that she, with no particular interest in history could see it, touch it, feel it, while he . . he must be content with books and shards and bones?

He put his hand in his pocket. The small tile lay there, abstracted from its fellows as he tidied up the van. Did it hold the key? Gently he closed his fingers around it. He closed his eyes.

They both turned in surprise at the sound of wheels on

the gravel. The gates behind them had been closed. For a moment he didn't understand; he didn't seem to be able to focus properly; the air was full of smoke.

Her scream turned his blood to ice. All he saw was the flash of the upraised sword, a glimpse of the eyes of the man who drove the chariot, then everything went black.

House of Echoes

Barbara Erskine

The past isn't always dead . . . and buried

When Joss Grant, adopted at birth, inherits Belheddon
Hall – a beautiful old house on the East Anglian coast – it
is like a dream come true. Eager to begin a new life there
with Luke, her husband, and Tom, her small son, she is
also impatient to find out about her newly discovered
family who lived there for generations.

But not long after they move in, Tom wakes screaming at
night. Joss hears echoing voices and senses an invisible
presence, watching her from the shadows. Are they spirits
from the past? Or is she imagining them? As she learns,
with mounting horror, of Belheddon's tragic and dramatic
history, her fear is very real as she realises that both her
family and her own sanity are at the mercy of a violent and
powerful energy which no one, it seems, can control . . .

0 00 647927 8

Barbara Erskine

Midnight is a Lonely Place

**A chilling story of passion, betrayal and revenge
by the bestselling author of *Lady of Hay***

'Vivid, romantic and deliciously scary . . . Erskine at her
storytelling best'   *Living*

After a broken love affair, Kate Kennedy, a successful
biographer, retires to a remote cottage on the wild Essex
coast to work on her new book. When Alison, her landlord's
daughter, uncovers a Roman site nearby, long-buried
passions are unleashed . . .

In her lonely cottage, Kate is terrorized by mysterious
forces. What do these ghosts want? That the truth about
the violent events of long ago be exposed or remain
concealed? Kate, Alison and her elder brother Greg must
struggle for their lives against earthbound spirits and
ancient curses as hate, jealousy, revenge and passionate
love do battle across the centuries . . .

0 00 647626 0

£4.99

Child of the Phoenix

Barbara Erskine

An epic novel by the bestselling author of *Lady of Hay* and *Midnight is a Lonely Place*.

Born in the flames of a burning castle in 1218, Princess Eleyne is brought up by her fiercely Welsh nurse to support the Celtic cause against the English aggressor. She is taught to worship the old gods and to look into the future and sometimes the past. But her second sight is marred by her inability to identify time and place in her visions so she is powerless to avert forthcoming tragedy.

Extraordinary events will follow Eleyne all her days as, despite passionate resistance, her life is shaped by the powerful men in her world. Time and again, like the phoenix that is her symbol, she must rise from the ashes of her past life to begin anew. But her mystical gifts, her clear intelligence and unquenchable spirit will involve her in the destinies of England, Scotland and Wales.

0 00 647264 8

Lady of Hay

Barbara Erskine

'Barbara Erskine can make us feel the cold, smell the filth, and experience some of the fear of the power of evil men…The author's story telling talent is undeniable' *The Times*

Jo Clifford, successful journalist, is all set to debunk the idea of past-life regression in her next magazine series. But when she herself submits to a simple hypnotic session, she suddenly finds herself reliving the experiences of Matilda, Lady of Hay, the wife of a baron at the time of King John.

As she learns of Matilda's unhappy marriage, her love for the handsome Richard de Clare and the brutal threats of death at the hands of King John, it becomes clear that Jo's past and present are hopelessly entwined and that, eight hundred years on, a story of secret passion and unspeakable treachery is about to begin again…

'Fascinating, absorbing, original - and hypnotic'
She

0 00 649780 2

Encounters

Barbara Erskine is the author of the internationally best-selling novel *Lady of Hay*, which was translated into seventeen languages and has sold over a million copies worldwide. This was followed by another bestseller, *Kingdom of Shadows*. Her third novel, *Child of the Phoenix*, was based on the story of one of her own ancestors, and provides a link between some of the characters from *Lady of Hay* and *Kingdom of Shadows*, again encapsulating the author's dual themes of the supernatural and of history. *Midnight is a Lonely Place* enjoyed the same international bestselling success of *Lady of Hay* and was shortlisted for the WH Smith Thumping Good Read Award of 1995, and was followed by her most recent bestselling novel, *House of Echoes*, which was shortlisted for the WH Smith Thumping Good Read Award of 1996. She has also published a second volume of short stories, *Distant Voices*.

Barbara Erskine has a degree in mediaeval Scottish history from Edinburgh University. She and her family divide their time between the Welsh borders and their ancient, crumbling manor house, near the unspoiled coast of North Essex.

Acclaim for *Encounters*:

'A marvellous mixture of emotional tales with the emphasis on love.'
                                                    Woman's World

'Short stories with the "unputdownable" quality of a good novel . . . convincing . . . an easy, compelling read.'
                                                    Eastern Daily Press